MY NAME WAS FIVE

A Novel of the Second World War

To Gregory Call
with warm regards,
Heinz Kohler

HEINZ KOHLER

Mill City Press, Inc.
212 3rd Avenue North, Suite 290
Minneapolis, MN 55401
612.455.2294
www.millcitypublishing.com

www.mynamewasfive.com

ISBN - 978-1-936107-37-7
ISBN - 1-936107-37-6
LCCN - 2009941272

Cover Design and Typeset by Melanie Shellito

Printed in the United States of America

To the memory of my parents,

who gave me so much,

and to my wife Linda,

who inspired me to tell the story.

CONTENTS

FOREWORD

In the spring of 1991, a private plane crashed in shallow waters near Key West, Florida. There were no fatalities. About a year later, the National Transportation Safety Board issued a report on the incident, but questions remained. As one witness had noted, the surviving pilot, when first interviewed, had made the strangest of remarks: "It was World War II," he had said. But look at the conclusion of the NTSB account that is reproduced here; it makes no mention of the pilot's initial reaction.

THE NATIONAL TRANSPORTATION SAFETY BOARD DETERMINES THE PROBABLE CAUSE(S) OF THIS ACCIDENT AS FOLLOWS:

An inadvertent in-flight collision with birds while on final approach, resulting in the loss of aileron and elevator control as well as engine power. It was confirmed that sea gulls and other birds feed actively at dusk, flying in flocks low over water, between sea level and 500 feet. Dr. Carla Dunn of the Smithsonian National Museum of Natural History in Washington, DC, identified one bird retrieved from the cockpit as a Black Vulture (Coryagyps atratus), which weighed 75 ounces.

Other factors contributing to the accident include

- unsuitable terrain encountered during the forced landing
- the pilot being blinded by the setting sun
- pilot fatigue after a long flight from New England, with a fuel stop at Norfolk, VA

Note: A review of the pilot's medical history reveals psychiatric treatment several decades ago.

And there the matter might have rested forever. But when I happened to come across this story, I was too intrigued by the pilot's initial comment to let it go. As executive editor of *Modern Aviation* magazine I had read hundreds of such NTSB reports and had developed a certain mistrust of them. To be sure, the board's investigations tended to be thorough, and admirably so, with respect to the *technical* intricacies of aviation accidents, but I had long considered them to be lacking in *psychological* sophistication. Indeed, my own experience as a pilot had given rise to a regular column in our magazine that examined the psychological causes of airplane crashes. At the time of the Key West accident, for example, the column in question carried an article, entitled *Get-There-Itis*, which noted that many pilots were dying unnecessarily (along with their passengers) due to the foolish but common belief that they *had to get there* at a predetermined time. To be sure, the belief in question was often nourished by pilots' fear of losing income or even their jobs, but such explanations didn't make their actions any more acceptable. The urge to go-no-matter-what blinded some pilots to the fact that their training or equipment could be unsuitable for certain flight conditions. Indeed, all of the past victims of this inner compulsion could have lived if they had just waited a day, or even a few more hours at times, till ice-laden clouds or violent winds and thunderstorms had moved past their route or till night had turned back into day! So you will understand why I pursued the Key West story.

After locating the pilot back in New England and, I might add, after many frustrated attempts, I finally persuaded him to explore the strange thought about World War II that he had once expressed and to let me capture the result on paper. That project, it turned out, took nearly two decades to complete and gave rise to the forty-seven chapters of this book. Each one of them is based on a separate taped interview and, with a minimum of editing, has been transcribed in the pilot's own voice, just as it was told to me. Many of these chapters are now also illustrated with historical material that the pilot kindly provided. As you will see, the story begins well over half a century *before* the Key West crash and takes us to a place far removed from where the mishap occurred. In the end, I dare say, this book as a whole makes a far better accident report than the one that is fully reproduced in the Appendix to this book. But you must judge for yourself. So come with me to Germany and visit 1937 Berlin.

Michael P. Scott
Executive Editor
Modern Aviation

1. THE ARREST

[February 1937]

Where shall I begin? With one of my earliest memories, perhaps… I must have been about four and a half years old and I still haven't managed to banish that scary night from my mind, almost sixty years later.

I was lying in bed, in my room. The steel braces on my legs hurt too much and I couldn't sleep. So I did what I always did and turned to my teddy bear. Together we listened to the pendulum on the wall clock. In the dim light, we watched the door at the top and waited for the cuckoo to appear. Three minutes to midnight; I was old enough to tell the time.

But I never saw my singing friend that night. The bell rang and I heard pounding on the apartment door, voices of strange men yelling and the shuffling of feet. Something crashed on the floor in the next room and I heard my mother cry out. I wanted to get up and look, but I was trapped. The braces had been locked for the night. Someone pointed a bright light at my face. Then the front door slammed shut and I heard an army of heavy boots make its way down the stairs to the third floor, somewhat more quietly down to the second, and then I lost count. My heart was pounding, but my mother was there. She was weeping.

"Where is Vati?" I asked.

"Had to go out," she said.

She pulled down my featherbed and unlocked my braces. Teddy and I could sleep with her in the next room, she said.

******

The next morning, my mother threw open all the windows, as she always did. Then she plumped up the pillows and the giant featherbed quilts. Together, we found a comfortable spot for Teddy, but not until I had dressed him for the day with his velvet jacket and pants and his shiny black shoes. As always, too, my mother gave me my medicine: one spoonful of white cod liver oil and a second one of orange *Sanastol*. Unlike Dieter downstairs, who balked at the cod liver oil, I liked my medicine. My father had said it would make me big and strong.

Later that morning, we walked to the hospital to get my therapy. Down four flights of stairs we went, past the front door of Harzer Strasse 82, so noted in black letters on a white enamel sign, then right along the cobblestone path to the poster column at the corner of the street, left to the footbridge over the canal, and right again on the other side to the whitewashed building with the Red Cross at the door. I could have made the trip in my sleep, my knock knees notwithstanding. In fact, I didn't know what the fuss was all about; I could walk as well as the next guy.

"Hello Hansel," the nurse said, "how are those bad X-legs of yours?"

"I am just fine," I said defiantly.

They put me on the stretcher, made me lie on my back, and attached heavy bags of sand at strategic places along my legs. Nothing new there. My mother sat in a chair nearby. She kept drying her eyes with a handkerchief, sobbing ever so quietly, and I just knew it had something to do with my father having had to go out in the middle of the night.

Once more, I watched a clock on the wall, but I distinctly remember not liking this one at all. Unlike the cuckoo clock at home that featured a castle set in a pine forest, the hospital clock looked like an empty plate, round and white. It had regular numbers, but I preferred the Roman numerals at home. My father had explained them to me. And this one had three black hands; one of them never moved at all, a second one jumped every once in a while, and a third one kept racing around with not a moment's rest. But this ugly clock would do. I could tell when thirty minutes were up and it was time to go to the next room.

There I learned to pick up objects from the floor with my bare toes—anything ranging from marbles to postage stamps—and the nurse was really happy if I could touch my lips with my big toe. Finally, I had to climb on the ball that was almost as tall as I, stand up on it, and try to make it roll on the shiny wooden floor from one end of the room to the other. When I failed and fell off, the nurse was angry.

"What is the matter with you?" she asked. "Don't you want to straighten out those legs?"

When I succeeded, she was jubilant.

"We'll make you into a fine Prussian soldier yet!" she exclaimed.

"The hell we will," my mother said under her breath.

******

We took the long way home, past Wildenbruch Park, where I fed the goldfish in the pond underneath the waterfall, while my mother sat on a nearby bench. She took out her *Nivea* jar and rubbed the cream on her arms, starting with her elbows and going down to her wrists and hands. She was always doing that, it seemed, and I liked watching her. When Mrs. Meyer walked up with Dieter, I was overjoyed. We found two snails by the edge of the pond and arranged for a snail race. Dieter had a golden coin with a red ladybug on it.

"Ladybugs bring good luck," he said. "Mama says so."

It seemed to be true; his snail won. But I didn't care. I kept looking at my mother who was sobbing and talking with Mrs. Meyer. I felt scared, but Dieter let me borrow the coin and I took it to Mutti.

"This brings good luck," I said. "Don't cry; when I'm grown up, I'll marry you."

My mother smiled and squirted me with a bit of *4711*, her favorite perfume. I liked the fragrance. Then we walked home together, downhill from the park and past the tram station where yellow streetcars kept turning into Harzer Strasse, wheels squealing underneath and electric wires sparking overhead, only to leave again, rumbling towards places in faraway corners of Berlin that I had never seen. I also remember Mrs. Meyer's red scarf and red shoes, red just like the ladybug. And that she wore a brooch shaped like a parrot. That one was red, too. I didn't know at the time that she did all that on purpose; she liked the Communists.

"Where is Vati?" I asked.

My mother told me not to worry. Mrs. Meyer and Dieter would come up to our apartment and we would all cook together. Also, Dieter and I could look at our favorite books. That afternoon, my mother baked a poppy seed cake and let me lick out the bowl. Mrs. Meyer made *Rote Grütze*, a delicious red pudding that tasted like raspberries and was served with sweet yellow vanilla sauce. Dieter licked out that bowl. My mother kept sobbing and talking about things I couldn't understand.

"But four years ago," she said, "after they banned the SPD, they just *killed* those Social Democrats in Köpenick. Martel told us all about it! They tortured them to death; later someone found them floating in the Havel River, sewn neatly into sacks."

"This is different," Mrs. Meyer said reassuringly. "Arthur is not a trade union man."

"What are Social Democrats?" I asked.

"Hush," my mother said, "don't worry about it. Go show Dieter your picture book."

We went into my room where I had stashed my grandmother's book under the bed. It was large and heavy, bound in red leather, and almost a hundred years old. My father had taught me to count and I knew that there were precisely 336 pictures in the book, not counting the one on the cover, which showed a massive chain of gray mountains in the back, a lush green valley in the front, and a castle on a hill in-between. The castle was surrounded by dozens of houses with red tile roofs and a light blue river flowing to the sea. The cover also had beautiful purple flowers, turtle doves, and a cherub on a bike. My mother's own grandmother, my father had told me, had put together these pictures way back in 1858 after buying many cans of *Justus von Liebig's Meat Extract*, produced, as the back of each picture testified, in Fray-Bentos, South America. Although I couldn't read it at the time, Mr. Liebig assured his customers that "*Liebig's Meat Extract* transforms the most watery soups and the most tasteless vegetables into lip-smacking meals. It's indispensable in any good kitchen. But beware of cheap imitations! Look for the blue signature on the label." I also couldn't read the recipes found on the back of each picture, but my father had taught me to read the inscriptions on the front. That day, I showed Dieter the colorful pictures about the rain and the sun, about lightning and hail, windstorm and snow. In infinite detail, each picture showed elegantly dressed people in the streets surprised by armies of little cherubs working in the sky: pouring out buckets of water to make rain, shoveling coal into the furnace of the sun, and so much more.

Our mothers kept whispering in the kitchen. We tried to join them, but they wouldn't let us. So Dieter showed me his *Struwwelpeter* book. Unlike mine, it was a new and modern book, filled with brilliant colors. We couldn't read the stories, but Dieter had memorized the words. In addition, the pictures were clear enough. One was the story of little Pauline whose parents had left her alone at home with two sweet cats. When Pauline discovered a box of matches, the cats lifted their paws and implored her not to light them.

"Father has forbidden it," Dieter intoned, "meow meoh, meow meoh."

But to no avail. The dress caught on fire, then the apron, then a hand, the hair, the entire child! In the end, only a pile of ashes remained, along with a pair of red shoes.

"Two cats," Dieter continued, "shed streams of bitter tears. Mother has forbidden it."

I was scared.

"I like my book better," I said and ran into the kitchen.

******

"Can people really burn up?" I asked my mother that night.

"Of course not," she said, "we just must be very careful with matches."

I didn't feel reassured because my mother kept crying. I watched her putting on more *Nivea* cream and then combing her long, beautiful hair. It had the same color as the chestnuts I had gathered in the park and put away in a little box under my bed.

"Can people bleed to death?" I asked.

"Hansel," my mother said, "why would you think such a terrible thing? You'll be fine. Come and sleep in my bed. We can forget about the braces tonight."

But still I didn't sleep well. I kept dreaming about that other *Struwwelpeter* story I had seen, about little Konrad who had been left home alone, warned not to suck his thumb. But when he did, there was pounding at the door and the tailor burst in with giant scissors and then he sharpened them and quickly cut off the boy's thumbs! Konrad screamed and screamed and there was blood all over the floor. And, as the pictures showed, when his mother returned, Konrad stood in a pool of blood and both of his thumbs were gone....

******

My mother never knew about my dream. As for me, it took ten years before I fully understood the significance of that day. In 1947, on the day I graduated from middle school, I came across a small pile of documents, carefully preserved in a chest of drawers, with a blue ribbon around them. One of them was addressed to my father:

> **BASED ON ARTICLE 1 OF THE DECREE OF THE REICH PRESIDENT FOR THE PROTECTION OF PEOPLE AND STATE OF FEBRUARY 28, 1933, YOU ARE TAKEN INTO PROTECTIVE CUSTODY IN THE INTEREST OF PUBLIC SECURITY AND ORDER.**
>
> **Reason: Suspicion of activities inimical to the state.**

The remaining papers were letters addressed to my mother and written by my father. Most envelopes had a 12 Pfennig Adolf Hitler stamp on them, but some had two sixes. Each envelope had two rubber stamps, too. One simply said *Oranienburg* and gave a date; the earliest one was 28 Feb.1937, the last one said 30 Jan. 1940. The other rubber stamp read *Postal Censorship Office. K.Z. Sachsenhausen.* On the back, each envelope gave my father's name, his birth date, and *Prisoner Nr. 20412, Block 25.* Each page of the letters had a printed section, such as this:

> **CONCENTRATION CAMP SACHSENHAUSEN, ORANIENBURG NEAR BERLIN**
>
> Excerpt from Camp Rules:
>
> Each prisoner may receive and send 2 letters or 2 postcards per month. Incoming letters may not contain more than 4 pages with 15 lines each and must be easy to survey and read. Packages with whatever content are forbidden. Money transfers are allowed only via postal money orders, which must indicate nothing more than first name, last name, birthday, and prisoner number and may contain absolutely no messages. Money, photos, and picture inserts in letters are forbidden. Postal items that do not meet the aforementioned requirements will not be accepted. Unclear and hard-to-read letters will be destroyed. Everything can be bought inside the camp. National Socialist newspapers are allowed, but must be subscribed to inside the camp by the prisoner himself.
>
> The Camp Commandant

In addition, there were 15 preprinted lines on each page, along with two notations:

"Only write *on* the lines!" and "The day of discharge has not yet been determined. Visits at the camp are forbidden. Inquiries are useless."

von
Dr. Heinr. Hoffmann

Sieh einmal, hier steht er.
Pfui! Der Struwwelpeter!
An den Händen beiden
Ließ er sich nicht schneiden
Seine Nägel fast ein Jahr;
Kämmen ließ er nicht sein
Haar.
Pfui! Ruft da ein jeder:
Garst'ger Struwwelpeter!

Otto Moravec, Vienna, Austria

The cover of the *Struwwelpeter* children's book, a collection of short stories written to frighten children into good behavior. First published in 1845, the book was still popular during the Nazi era (1933-45) and beyond. Dr. Heinrich Hoffmann presents *Struwwelpeter* (the *Slovenly Peter*) as a disgusting and disobedient brat of a child who hasn't cut his hair or fingernails in a year. The stories show how bad things happen to such children, whether they play with matches, suck their thumbs, won't eat their meals, wriggle at the table, or walk in the street with their eyes on the sky. The inscription, which rhymes in the original, says:

Take a look, here he stands.
Fie! The Struwwelpeter!
For nearly a year,
He allowed no one
To cut his nails
On either hand;
He permitted no one
To comb his hair.
Fie! Says everyone;
Ugly Struwwelpeter!

2. SHARDS AND WHISPERS

[February 1938]

I told you about my father's arrest. I remember another event just as vividly. It must have been a year later. Once more, I see myself lying in my bed. The steel braces were gone by then; presumably my X-legs had been cured. But I was still struggling with something: The lace curtains in my bedroom had rows of evil faces leering at me!

My mother kept saying that I only imagined them, but I knew better. I was always glad when darkness came and chased them away. That particular night was especially bad. I closed my eyes and tried counting sheep, but I just knew those faces were still there. And in the midst of them I kept seeing my mother and Mrs. Meyer, forever whispering, just as they had a year ago after the men had come and taken my father away at midnight.

Dishes broke in the hallway outside, followed by voices and laughter, and more noise still. I knew this was not a dream, and I jumped out of bed. Just then, my mother appeared in my bedroom door.

"Don't worry," she said. "Lotte Wagner is getting married tomorrow. They are just celebrating. Come and see."

We walked to the outer door, and while my mother looked through the peephole, I spied through the mail slot below. A new group of guests arrived. They crashed old pottery and plates into the apartment door across from us. I remembered the custom. "Shards Bring Good Luck," the proverb said. People were always making sure.

When my mother left, I got off my knees and stood up. That's when I spotted Mrs. Nussbaum in the kitchen. She lived in an apartment two stories below us and was my mother's friend. She also ran a grocery store a few houses down the street on our block, where we always got our milk. Mrs. Nussbaum was holding a handkerchief to her eyes and my mother told me to get back into bed and tell no one that Mrs. Nussbaum had been there. She would leave the bedroom door open a crack, she said, but that only made things worse. The light from the corridor brought back those faces grinning at me from the curtains and I saw a big dark figure standing between the tile stove and the far wall.

There was no way I could sleep then. In addition, the Wagners made noise on the other side of the wall, Fritz's trumpet played along with the record player, and my mother and Mrs. Nussbaum kept whispering in the kitchen. I went to get my mother and told her I was scared, but she was annoyed. Firmly, she put me back to bed and pulled aside the curtains. My window turned into a black square, sprayed with stars.

"Count the stars," she said, "Look how pretty they are."

After she left, I got out of bed, tiptoed to the bedroom door, and quietly crawled down the corridor to a spot near the kitchen door. My mother and Mrs. Nussbaum were eating soup. I saw the moon though the window behind them; it was being swallowed by a cloud.

"So now I am to walk around with a giant J on my ID card!" Mrs. Nussbaum was saying. "Did you know we aren't allowed to buy soap anymore?"

"And David, he was told that Jews can't have pets!" Mrs. Nussbaum continued. "What's he supposed to do with his dog? He *loves* that creature! Where will it all end?"

"I don't know," my mother sighed. "But I remember the day it all *started*, back in '33. It was in early April, right on my birthday. I took Hansel to Dr. Weitzman's for the one-year checkup. And, just as Arthur had predicted, there were SA men out in front of his clinic, shouting 'Aryans Don't Use Jewish Doctors!' One of them spit on me when we went in anyway."

Then they whispered a lot and I couldn't hear what they said, but I saw the moon reappear from the cloud.

"That must have been the day Streicher let loose the SA. With his 'Aryans Don't Buy From Jews!' thing," Mrs. Nussbaum said. "How time flies. Almost five years already! I remember Wagner planting his fat self in front of my store, dressed up in his SA uniform, his booted legs spread apart, yelling 'Judah Perish!' He smeared it on my store window as well and the police just laughed."

"I know," my mother said softly. "He scrawled a slogan on our apartment door, too, because we were seeing Dr. Weitzman. I can see it now: 'Every Mark in a Jewish hand, is one less for the German fatherland!' And now he's marrying off his daughter to a bastard just like himself. What kind of a life will she have?"

"Better than ours," Mrs. Nussbaum said. "You know, David's in trouble, too. He's lost half his clients. 'Aryans don't use Jewish lawyers,' they say. But even Jewish clients are thinning out. Just the other day, he had a meeting with the managers at Tietz's. Can you believe it, they are supposed to *fire* their Jewish employees! In fact, they are supposed to give up their own jobs in favor of 'Aryan' managers. Looks like they are going to lose the store. It's supposed to become Hertie's, a 'purely Aryan department store,' they call it."

My mind wandered; I didn't comprehend most of what they were saying even if I could hear their words. I tried to count the dried mushrooms that hung on a string above the kitchen stove, but I didn't succeed. My mother's white apron blocked half my view.

"Martel tells me the same thing is going on at the Wertheim brothers' store," my mother said. "Some of their workers had joined the boycott; yet Fritz and Guenther were supposed to pay them full wages for the time they had refused to work! It's insane."

Just then I coughed. Mrs. Nussbaum's gaze jolted up from her dish to meet my mother's eyes. For a moment, there was total silence. Then my mother jumped up and I saw her eyes, glassy with tears. She put me to bed once again and made sure I stayed there. But later, I remember, she brought me a bowl of soup and I ate it eagerly to find the pretty flowers underneath.

"Don't ever say a word about any of this to anyone," my mother said. "Not ever."

She sat at my bed and she smelled so good. It was the new perfume, called *Toska*. Of course, she needn't have worried about my telling anyone. I was just a child after all; it took years before I fully understood what their conversation had been about. In addition, it had been a year since my father had disappeared and I had heard my mother's warnings every day: "There are bad people out there. Never tell anyone anything!" That night, I ended up sleeping in the big bed. We talked of my father and my mother wept. She always did, even though she tried not to show it. I swore to myself I would protect her from the bad people the moment I was a bigger boy.

The next morning, when we went to get our hot buns from the baker, we ran into Mr. Wagner. He was carrying a large box of shards down to the garbage bins.

"Shards Bring Good Luck," he said. He was laughing.

The names of Jewish-owned department stores above a skeleton hand (presumably Jewish) grasping Fritz Schulze's grocery store (presumably non-Jewish). The caption, in line with the Nazi habit of treating Jews as non-German:
Therefore:
Germans! Shop Only in German Stores!

Langewiesche-Brandt, Ebenhausen near München, Germany

3. ARYANS ALL
[February 1938]

My Aunt Martel came to visit us the day after the Wagners' pre-wedding celebration. True enough, I didn't keep a diary of events in those days, as I did in later years, but I figure the timing must be correct, because weddings were always scheduled for the day after the pottery smashing and Aunt Martel had seen the bride on her way in. She had arrived, she told us, just as Lotte Wagner, dressed in a fancy white wedding gown, followed her family down the long set of stairs to the level of the street where a white carriage, with two white horses in front, was waiting for her. Aunt Martel had let the entourage pass, had watched them leave towards the Neukölln town hall, and then had made her way up, slowly and out of breath, to the fourth floor. I opened the door and jumped into the arms of my favorite aunt.

As usual, she brought me a package of *Leibniz* cookies. As usual, too, she wore a fur muff, held around her neck by a cord. She also had fleece-lined boots and a matching fur coat. I confiscated the muff and the boots. They were perfect toys.

Aunt Martel was my mother's oldest sister. She had come, my mother explained, to help with an important family project. In preparation, my mother had pushed aside her new *Pfaff* sewing machine that had recently replaced the old *Singer* and opened up the bookcase behind it. The top three shelves held my mother's favorite books; the drawers underneath were crammed with old letters, hundreds of photographs, and all sorts of documents.

"The story of my life," my mother said with a sigh. She pulled out the top drawer and placed it on the living room table.

"I can't believe we are doing this," my mother said to Aunt Martel. "Those bastards! But unless we comply, Hansel won't be able to go to school next year. I hate this, I hate this, I so hate this!"

She inspected one item at a time, while Aunt Martel took notes on a pad of paper, which gave me time to explore my mother's books. While I couldn't yet read any lengthy text, my mother had taught me the alphabet and I could decipher the names of most of the authors. On the top shelf, there was Walther von der Vogelweide, followed by Hans Sachs, Gotthold Ephraim Lessing, and Johann Gottfried Herder. Several volumes, all bound in red, said Wolfgang von Goethe; several others, all in blue, featured Friedrich von Schiller.

I took the books out of the next shelf, where I found Friedrich Hölderlin, Heinrich von Kleist, someone simply called Novalis, and Annette von Droste-Hülshoff. They sat right next to Hermann Hesse,

Arnold Zweig, Bertolt Brecht, Erich Maria Remarque, Gottfried Keller, and Gerhart Hauptmann.

Aunt Martel took another sip of *Himbeergeist*, her favorite raspberry liqueur, and then she helped me read the names on the last shelf: Sigmund Freud, Heinrich Heine, Thomas Mann, Karl Marx, Jakob Wassermann, and William Shakespeare. I had trouble reading the last one and pronounced it with five syllables, like Sha-ke-spe-a-re. Aunt Martel didn't notice; she was suddenly preoccupied.

"Trudchen," she said to my mother, holding up Erich Kästner and Kurt Tucholsky, "some of these books can get you in big trouble, you know. They have been banned from bookshops and libraries and have been burning in the streets. You've got to be more careful!"

"I still get upset when I remember the bonfires I ran into at the Opernplatz," Aunt Martel continued. "There they were, a horde of thugs, really, standing right next to the statue of Alexander von Humboldt, 'Germany's shining exemplar of the Enlightenment,' it said on the pedestal. But nobody noticed that. Nobody thought of Humboldt University just a short distance away. Everybody was much too busy throwing *Nathan the Wise* into the flames, all the while making fun of Lessing's pleas for racial and religious tolerance. A scary bunch they were; you don't want to fight with them. Think of Arthur, always think of Arthur. You want to maximize the chances to get him out of there."

"Yes, indeed," my mother replied with an air of sarcasm, "that's why we are here, aren't we? To obey the Nuremberg Laws of 1935, to protect German blood and honor, to trace the family tree all the way back to January 1, 1800, to show there was no Jewish blood, to show that we are worthy of being called 'citizens of the Reich.' It makes me sick!"

For the longest time, Aunt Martel said nothing, leafing through *The Collected Works of Heinrich Heine* and sipping her liqueur.

"Here it is," she said finally, "A quote from Heinrich Heine: 'Where books are burned, in the end people will be burned too.' He said that in 1823. Over a hundred years later, nobody has learned a thing!"

Then she opened the cast-iron door of our dark green stove, added a couple of brown-coal briquettes to the glowing embers, and went back to drawing the family tree. Silently, too, my mother kept handing her pieces of paper from the drawer on the table. I stood with my back against the hot glazed tiles, warming up Aunt Martel's boots and muff. I tried my best not to think of Pauline burning up in Dieter's *Struwwelpeter* book.

******

Decades later, I discovered the Ancestor Passport that had been issued in my name way back in 1938, presumably the result of all the research put into motion on that night. Relevant laws were reproduced and commented upon on pages 2-8. Instructions on finding valid documents followed on pages 9–13. My name, birth date and place, the names of my parents, and my baptism in a Christian church were listed and certified on page 14, complete with signature and swastika rubber stamp. Similarly, certified entries for each of my parents, going back to 1906 and 1907, respectively, appeared on pages 16–17. My father's parents, born in 1865 and 1870, followed on pages 18–19, those of my mother, born in 1872 and 1871, on pages 20–21. Later pages, and similarly impressive rubber stamps, certified the Aryan blood of eight great-grandparents (variously born between 1816 and 1847), of sixteen great-great grandparents (born between 1732 and 1822), of thirty-two great-great-great grandparents (born between 1759 and 1790), and even of sixty-four great-great-great-great grandparents (with only death certificates available). According to certificates of birth, baptism, confirmation, marriage, and death, there was a blacksmith, a bricklayer, a carpenter, a farmer, a gardener, a laborer, a leather worker, a Methodist preacher, a miller, a policeman, a royal guard, a tailor, a salesman, a shoemaker, and a weaver, but—lucky me—not one Jew.

My mother had several Jewish friends besides Mrs. Nussbaum. In retrospect, it is easy to see why she was so upset on the day she had to trace the family tree. She was even more upset the next morning when the bell rang in the street and the man in the pickup truck called upon all to exchange "kindling wood for potato peels." I fetched the pail full of potato peels and we went down together to make the exchange, only to run into Mr. Wagner who was beside himself.

"Look at this, look at this," he said to all who would listen, "the marriage officer gave Lotte a copy of *Mein Kampf*! Personally signed by the Führer."

My mother turned away.

The Ancestor Passport

A multi-page document required by the Nazis as proof of a citizen's Aryan ancestry. According to the document, "any person is of Aryan ancestry (= German-blooded) if he is free, from the point of view of the German people, of the blood of a foreign race. In this connection, foreign is defined above all as the blood of European Jews and Gypsies, of the Asian and African races, and of the aborigines of Australia and America (Red Indians). On the other hand, an Englishman or Swede, a Frenchman or Czech, a Pole or Italian must be treated as Aryan, as long as he is free from the above-noted foreign blood, regardless of whether he is living in his own country, in East Asia or in America, regardless of whether he is a citizen of the USA or some South American free state. It goes, of course, without saying that for purposes of marriage a German citizen, a girl of pure German ancestry, is closer to us than some other Aryan...."

"Naturally, adoptive parents, as well as stepfathers and stepmothers, do *not* belong in the ancestor passport. With respect to blood and race, they have no influence on the genetic make-up of the person in question. It is important to remember this fact when dealing with foundlings or persons born out of wedlock. In all such cases, it is crucial to determine the real birth parents and to enter *their* ancestors into the document. There is no room here for false shame. No reasonable person nowadays will consider a citizen less worthy if he or one of his ancestors was born out of wedlock...."

4. THE ACACIA TREE
[July 1938]

As I told you earlier, in those terrible days preceding the Second World War, getting a "clean" Ancestor Passport was a precondition for entering first grade in Berlin. For me at least, that time was fast approaching, but I looked upon my first day of school with mixed emotions. In my case, the dreaded date was to be January 1, 1939, and not, as you might imagine, the day after that! But that bit of Prussian compulsiveness was not what was bothering me. The truth is, I was afraid to leave my mother for any length of time and you will understand the reason once I tell you about my last spring and summer before school when I slowly emerged from the safe cocoon of our apartment and became acquainted with the world outside.

When I think about that time, strange as it may sound, I keep picturing an acacia tree. It stood in front of our house and was huge, reaching all the way up to the fifth floor. On the typical spring day, the sweet smell of its flowers drifted through the open glass doors of our balcony. On hot summer afternoons, thousands of its tiny leaves cast trembling shadows on the white-washed inner walls of my balcony playroom. Sometimes I crouched in its far corner and let my imagination run free, watching the shadows of tigers and lions, of kangaroos, gazelles, of Indians and trappers, Snow White and her dwarfs.

When my mother wasn't looking, I climbed on the balcony bench and, through the boxes of flowers, looked at the world below. I tossed bread crumbs to the sparrows on the sidewalk, four stories down; and when I was lucky, their fighting attracted seagulls from the canal. They circled above the geraniums and caught every piece of food I tossed into the air.

But everyone said hiding on our balcony and feeding gulls was for little kids. I had become a big boy, they said, ready to go to school in half a year. I should get out more, they said. I suppose even my mother agreed with the neighbors and various aunts and uncles. Presumably, that's why she urged me to go down to the street and play marbles with Dieter. Marbles—what a beautiful collection I had! There were the ordinary ones, made of clay; painted brown, red, or purple. But I also had others made of glass, some as small as a pea, but one or two as large as a plum. All of these had swirls of colors reaching to their center: yellows, pinks, and greens.

We met at the foot of the acacia tree, and there was a playground there as well: some twenty square meters of real soil. We had to share it with the soot-blackened trunk of the giant tree, and had to fight off an occasional dog, but pretty soon we looked upon the spot as our home away from home. There we could dig shallow holes to play marbles the right way; and that beat the concrete floors of balconies or the ribbons of cobblestones everywhere else.

One day, though, everything changed. We were playing the second round of our tournament when they came. They just stood there, looking down at us. All six of them wore identical shoes, made for hiking. All six wore black corduroy shorts, black leather belts with big knives attached, the same brown shirts, the same black ties, and red-and-white swastika armbands. I was crouched to the earth, and it seemed that the giant tree had sprouted a dozen little trunks, planted firmly, and also reaching to the sky. A boot lifted off the ground, returned to my mound of marble-wealth, turning, crushing.

"This place belongs to us," someone said, "it looks like we have to teach you a lesson."

They dragged us through the portals of our house, down the hallway, out the back door, into the yard. The yard was laid out in the form of a square, with five-story buildings on three sides, known to the postman as the front house, the side house, and the rear house. Half a kilometer of open space stretched to the east where hundreds of weekend gardeners tended their weedless tiny plots of land, each crammed full of lilac trees and trees of many fruits, bushes of gooseberries and red currants, rows of carrots, kohlrabi, and parsley. Using my father's binoculars, I had seen all this many times from our front-house balcony, but I could see none of it from the backyard. A two-meter wall of concrete stood between the yard and the gardens, and hundreds of sharp pieces of glass, from broken beer bottles, had been placed along the top of the wall while it was being built and the cement was still wet. Although I didn't know it then, these types of walls were standing all over Berlin in those days, designed to keep undesirables out. Just as did the builders of the Berlin Wall some twenty-three years later, Dieter and I quickly noticed, of course, that such walls were just as useful for keeping people in. We watched the sun play, almost mockingly, with the shards of green and brown and knew there was no escape across that backyard wall.

The yard itself was filled with garbage bins, a few goldenchain trees, an old oak, and a lot of dust. Our captors had a rope, and they tied me to the oak, arms and legs spread out and bound together on the far side of the tree. Three of them emptied the marbles from Dieter's pail, took Dieter by the neck, and passed out of sight. The others pulled out pocket knives and, standing two or three meters away, hurled them at the tree as close to my body as they could. To the right of my head, under my arm pit, between my legs, the knives came—and missed.

******

When Dieter returned, I was sitting on the ground between two garbage cans rubbing my wrists and trembling like the acacia leaves way up in front. Dieter carried his pail, but there were no marbles in it. He had been forced to gather horse apples near the pub down the street where teams of horses every day delivered barrelsful of *Berliner Kindl* brew. Then he had been asked to eat a horse apple and, with three knives next to his head, he had eaten it and chosen to keep his ears.

They told us not to breathe a word to our mothers, and we never did.

"Remember," one of them said, "pretty soon you will walk to school with us, and it's a long way along the canal. People drown in it all the time."

"But you may play under the acacia tree," another one said, "as long as you pay for it."

Over the coming months, all of my favorite toys passed hands: my suitcase full of racing cars, my submarine that dived under water and surfaced again, my World War I soldiers in their colorful uniforms, and even the tank car that sprayed water on dusty city streets.

"Obey and you'll be safe!" they said. "Heil Hitler!"

They were right. We played a lot of marbles that summer. And we watched the big boys who soon owned the rubber tires and the batteries for my erector set, Dieter's wind-up white convertible with remote control, and, finally, my roller skates.

******

I remember something else. Shortly after we had moved our playground from our fourth-floor balcony to the sidewalk in front of our house and had made our deal with the Hitler Youth, Dieter and I began to explore the neighborhood. At the corner, near the pub, we ran into the organ grinder who was collecting coins for the concerts he gave. He had a monkey with sad eyes who was tied to the organ with a chain. Dieter and I figured he wanted to be free, but there was nothing we could do. In the other direction, among the garden plots, we met the man with the small pickup truck who was forever exchanging "kindling wood for potato peels." He had a shed where he kept two pigs and a cow. He let us watch when he fed the potato peels to the pigs and gave hay to the cow. He also told us to stay out of the other gardens and never to climb the little fences that surrounded each and every one of them. "Read the signs!" he said.

Dieter and I couldn't read much, but we made a copy on my writing pad and Mrs. Meyer explained one of the signs to us.

"Trespassers Beware!" it said. "Automatic Bullets!"

"They have trip wires in the gardens," Mrs. Meyer explained. "If someone climbs a fence to steal the cherries off a tree or pull a carrot from the ground, such a person can be killed by a bullet that is *automatically* released."

When my mother heard this, she became very upset. She told us never to go near the gardens again. She suggested a different adventure instead. We could stand outside the tobacco store and ask customers to give us the coupons hidden in their newly purchased boxes of cigarettes and cigars.

"Remember," she asked, "how *my* Grandma, a hundred years ago, made your pretty picture book after collecting coupons from cans of *Liebig's Meat Extract*? Tobacco coupons allow you to do the same thing."

Before long, Dieter and I were engaged in new projects. I was determined to create a beautiful book of *German Fairy Tales* by trading coupons for colorful photographs and filling in all the blank spots in the book that my mother got for me. It had 120 pages full of printed stories and precisely 100 gaping picture holes. The cover showed a magical scene of a dwarf playing the flute under a large fir tree. He had an attentive audience, including an owl, a squirrel, a rabbit, a hedgehog, a frog, a mole, a spider, a butterfly, and a pretty yellow bird with a blue head. There were 51 stories inside and my mother said she would teach me to read them all. I knew some of them already: Snow White, Hansel and Gretel, Rapunzel, Red Riding Hood, Sleeping Beauty, and The Emperor's New Clothes. There were just as many others that I had never met before: Doctor Know-It-All, The Fisherman and His Wife, The Princess on the Pea, The Courageous Little Tailor, The Flying Suitcase, and The Wild Swans.

Mrs. Meyer got a different book for Dieter, entitled *Of Forest and Field*. That's why he was looking for different kinds of photographs. On the title page of his book, we counted 20 different animals, and there were 128 pages inside. Exactly 122 pictures were missing and were needed to complete the stories. Before long, Dieter exchanged his first coupon for the picture of a huge elk, standing in a pond by the edge of a forest. Soon thereafter, he got the Alpine ram, and I gave him the wild boar and the fox with the rabbit in his mouth in exchange for pictures of the flying suitcase and rat king Birlibi.

******

One evening during our coupon campaign, Dieter and I invented a new game. Upon entering the main door of the front house, we found the stairwell to be pitch-black. But we also discovered the little phosphorous button next to the door that would turn on the lights on all the floors—temporarily. By the count of ten, we noted, everything would be dark again and we challenged each other to race up the stairs to push the button on the next landing before everything got dark. We were quite out of breath when we got to my place where my mother and Mrs. Meyer were waiting for us.

The radio was giving the news. Adolf Hitler had given a speech at the Sports Palace, to 15,000 people, about Eduard Benes and Czechoslovakia, "a state conceived as a lie and conducted as a swindle for twenty years." A four-power conference would occur in Munich in three days, it said. Adolf Hitler, Benito Mussolini, Neville Chamberlain, and Edouard Daladier would deal with the Sudetenland crisis…

None of this made sense to me. At the time, of course, I was too young to have noticed that Germany had annexed Austria a few months earlier; nor could anyone know that the German army would soon march into the Sudetenland, the Czech region coveted by Hitler, and would even occupy Prague a few months after that. But the grown-ups must have sensed what was coming.

"Arthur always knew," my mother said, "Hitler means war."

As if to answer her, Zarah Leander was singing on the radio, *Yes, Sir*!

"Talking about war," Mrs. Meyer said, "did you hear what your upstairs neighbor did?"

"Captain Rosenzweig?" my mother asked.

"The very one," said Mrs. Meyer, "changed his name to Schiller yesterday. Thought a 'Jewish' name would ruin his navy career!"

My mother just sighed. She was looking at Dieter's *Of Forest and Field* book.

"Did you read this Preface?" she asked Mrs. Meyer.

"Just listen to this," my mother continued, not waiting for a reply. "Our love and respect for all creatures is a valuable inheritance from our ancestors, it says. History shows the Aryan race to have been close to the world of nature always, right back to prehistoric times. This animal-friendly attitude is in our blood, in German genes. We are born into it, it's deeply rooted. What we love, we want to preserve and protect. National Socialists realize that precious treasures of nature are part of blood and soil to be protected. No people on earth has better laws for this… To protect each and every creature from want and pain, man must listen to the cry of creatures and improve their lot. Their fate is our fate… What we do for the animals ennobles us."

"Right back to prehistoric times, eh?" Mrs. Meyer said. "How would they know?"

"If the Sudetenland is ceded, Germany will have no more territorial demands in Europe," the radio announced.

As I said before, Dieter and I understood none of this. Nor did it occur to us at the time that Mrs. Wagner's silver fox coat was surely responsible for the deaths of countless little animals.

Langewiesche-Brandt, Ebenhausen near München, Germany

Hitler's SA

Hitler youths saluting SA "brown-shirt," while "money-grabbing Jews," as the Nazis put it, wring their hands in despair over the new order. SA = Sturmabteilung (Storm Troopers).

5. CRYSTAL NIGHT

[November 1938]

The events of some days are etched into my memory so indelibly that they seem no farther away than those of yesterday. Such is the case with November 9, 1938, which began innocently enough.

It was our wash day and my mother had reserved the attic for us. Early in the morning, we carried kindling wood and brown-coal briquettes to the washroom two flights above. My mother filled the giant copper tub with cold water, right up to the halfway mark, and made a big fire under it. Then we carried our dirty clothes up, one wicker basket at a time, and took a break while the water heated up.

I ran down to the baker to fetch a dozen crisp little buns, still hot to the touch. By the time I returned, I could smell the coffee my mother had brewed. I didn't care for the coffee; much more to my liking were the eggs she had boiled. They sat on the table in their separate receptacles, each properly covered with one of the knitted caps my grandmother had made. Her tablecloth was there, too, the one she had decorated with the pretty flowers in the four corners and the mushrooms and butterflies in the center right next to a baby deer. As my father had taught me, I stood by the table until my mother sat down and even then I didn't reach for the butter and my favorite plum jelly until she made the first move.

"You must always show respect to your Mutti," my father had said, "she is the most precious being on earth."

After breakfast, we returned to the attic, where my mother poured the clothes into the tub and I added just the right amount of detergent. "*Persil*, White as the Snow," it said on the label. My mother also let me help her stir the clothes with the giant wooden ladle, while she worked the scrub board, but I had to be careful not to fall into the tub when the water got to the boiling point. My mother also made sure I didn't touch the cast iron doors which slowly turned from black to gray and then to red as we fed the fire underneath.

When the clothes were done, my mother wrung them out as best as she could over a nearby sink. I hung up all the small pieces on the clotheslines that were strung throughout the rest of the attic. Later, we took all the big pieces—bed sheets, tablecloths, and the like—down the stairs to the ground floor and then to the soap store diagonally across the street. My mother had reserved the big steam press in the back room and, while she made everything look like new, I explored the new devices being sold in the front room.

They were called washing *machines*, and I had never seen anything like it. There was a large wooden tub with an agitator in the middle, also made of wood. One was supposed to boil one's clothes in a copper kettle, as usual, then throw them into the machine, which would do the work previously done by knuckles and scrub board. After that, one could guide each piece of clothing through a pair of wooden rollers sitting on top of the machine and obeying a hand-held crank. How neat! What would those Miele people think of next? They even had an advertising jingle attached to the front of the machine. It rhymed, of course, this was Germany after all; and I sang it for my mother when we were ready to leave the store:

"Nur Miele, Miele, sagte Tante,
die *alle* Waschmaschinen kannte."
["Only Miele, Miele, said the aunt, who knew *all* the washing machines."]

******

When we came out of the store that early afternoon, the world had changed. It seemed there were a million people in the street and the noise was deafening. At the corner, the street cars had come to a standstill, while hundreds of SA brown shirts marched along the tracks in the center of the street, playing trumpets and singing their special song. There were companies of Hitler Youths as well and even two groups of BDM girls. I knew who they were; Dieter had told me. If you were old enough and a girl, you couldn't be a Hitler Youth, but you could join the *Bund Deutscher Mädel* [League of German Girls] and do handicrafts and sports.

On the sidewalks, people were gawking at the endless procession, raising their right arms in salute to the passing flags and yelling "Heil! Heil! Heil!" My mother asked me to hurry to get back to our house, but there was no way we could cross the road. We stopped in front of the Geyer Works, the big factory facing our house, and my mother made me stand in front of her so she could rest her pile of sheets on my back. I got scared when a man yelled at her for not joining in the festivities, but before she could answer, a trumpet sounded and a disembodied loudspeaker voice drowned out all else.

"The National Socialist citizens of Berlin," the voice said, "are demonstrating against world Jewry and their black Monarchist and red Bolshevik allies. They are demonstrating for the freedom and security of the nation and all Germans throughout the world. Tonight, in response to the killing of Ernst von Rath, come and hear Adolf Wagner and twenty other Party speakers! Come and express your outrage over another heinous murder by a cowardly Jew!"

The marching had stopped and my mother took the opportunity to get us to the other side of the street. We raced up the stairs to seek our haven on the fourth floor, but a haven it was not. The

Street Warden stood at the apartment door! As we climbed the last thirteen steps, our eyes met his black boots, his brand new brown suit, and then the swastika armband.

"Inspection," he said, "let me see your radio, please. Just want to make sure you haven't been listening to foreigners."

He walked right into the living room, checked the setting of the dials and, being satisfied, attached a red warning label.

"Punishable by death ..." it said.

"Listen," he added almost amiably upon leaving, "I strongly urge you to buy the new People's Receiver. It has much better reception and it can't get you into trouble."

"The hell I will," my mother said after he was gone.

******

"So he wants you to get the Goebbels Snout," Mrs. Meyer said later when my mother told her the story at suppertime. "You know why, don't you? The new People's Receiver can only receive Nazi stations. You won't get the BBC no matter how much you twist that dial!"

My mother gave her one of those looks and asked me and Dieter to go and play in the next room.

"What's a Goebbels Snout?" I asked.

"Never mind," my mother said rather impatiently, "why don't you go and show Dieter your new zither."

I was glad to oblige because I had been eager for days to show off my latest gift from Aunt Martel. My zither was a beautiful instrument, made of lacquered red wood and silver strings. I had a silver thumb pick as well and I could play all sorts of songs already. My zither, you see, came with dozens of cardboard templates that could be inserted underneath the strings. Then all I had to do was to pluck the strings at the spots and in the order so noted on the cardboard. In no time, Dieter learned to be an expert player as well. *Golden evening sun, oh how beautiful you shine* was our favorite song.

******

Later, after Dieter and his mother had left to return to their apartment in the rear house, my mother told me never ever to talk about the Goebbels Snout again.

"Goebbels is a bad man, one of those who took Vati away," she said. "He talks on the radio a lot and some people look at the radio as his snout. But you must never say so out loud to anyone."

Then she put me to bed, but I was too scared to sleep. I thought of my father and of the man who had yelled at my mother in the street. I kept seeing creepy faces grinning at me from amongst the lace curtains. I saw a ghost lurking behind the tile oven that stood in the corner of the room. I put the light on, but my mother told me to put it out and not to touch the switch. And then I heard tinny music in the street.

Quickly, I got up and parted the curtains in front of the balcony door. Flames mirrored in the big factory windows across the street. I opened the doors, climbed onto the bench, and looked down. A stream of dark figures flowed along the center of the street, with hundreds of torches held high and an eerie sound of drums. I went to get my mother, but she was angry. She put me back to bed—she always seemed to do that in those days—locked the balcony door, closed the curtains, and told me to keep things that way no matter what. The grinning faces came back. This time, they had red, fiery eyes.

The next morning, when the bell rang at the corner, my mother took me with her to get a new block of ice for our freezer. We couldn't believe what we saw when we came out of our house. Mrs. Nussbaum's grocery store had been smashed to bits! The door was dangling from broken hinges. The giant store window lay in a thousand pieces on the sidewalk. Some shelves were lying in the street, too, along with hundreds of cans and boxes and blue paper sacks.

Mrs. Nussbaum was sweeping up her store window. She was sobbing. We stepped over huge slivers of glass, each one like a sword, past broken chairs, half a bed. Pots and pans floated in a huge puddle of milk on the sidewalk.

"We have to leave the apartment," Mrs. Nussbaum whispered to my mother. "They promised it to Lotte Wagner right after the wedding."

My mother cried and gave her a hug. She also whispered a lot, but I couldn't understand what she said. Just then I spotted Uncle Herbert at the door of the pub. He was pasting a big yellow poster to the door. I saw an eagle on it and a swastika. I tried to run to him to see what he was doing and also to get the postage stamps I'd asked him to save for me. But my mother held me back, and he looked right past me anyway.

"I saw you talking to that woman," Uncle Herbert said to my mother. "Do it again, and I'll have to turn you in. Aryans and Jews don't mix."

"Nor do we," my mother said icily. She looked him right in the eyes.

******

"That'll be 20 pfennigs," the iceman said loudly. But I also heard him whisper to my mother. "They've just picked up Mrs. Meyer," he said under his breath. "Called her a Bolshevik. That damned red scarf of hers."

As we turned back, my mother read Uncle Herbert's big yellow poster on the door. About all the great deeds Adolf Hitler had done:

BIT BY BIT

Adolf Hitler tore up the dictates of Versailles!

1933	Germany withdraws from the League of Nations
1934	The reconstruction of Army, Navy, and Air Force is begun!
1935	The Saar is brought home
	The military sovereignty of the Reich is recaptured!
1936	The Rhineland is fully freed!
1937	The war guilt lie is solemnly extinguished!
1938	Austria is annexed to the Reich!
	Greater Germany becomes a reality

Therefore all of Germany acknowledges its liberator Adolf Hitler

All say: Yes!

"Poor Liesel," my mother said to the iceman. "Imagine my sister being married to that monster! And thanks for the information. I'll check on Dieter."

When we got home, my mother turned on the radio, just in time for a special report from Munich. "We, too, in Munich," the announcer said, "have given world Jewry the kind of reply it deserves. The synagogue has been burnt to the ground! Jewish stores are closed! The most impudent Jews have been arrested!"

"Those bastards," my mother said. It had become her favorite word.

"Here in Berlin, too," the radio continued, "the murderous deed of that 17-year old Polish *maggot*, Herschel Grynszpan, has not gone unanswered: the Fasanenstrasse Synagogue has been destroyed; so have been the stores and homes of many others of those *bloodsucking Jewish spiders* who live among us, yet fail to respect the new order in our land. Let there be no doubt…"

My mother turned off the radio. She told me to play on the balcony that day; she would get Dieter to stay with us until his mother returned. But I wanted to go along to get him, and she took me.

Mrs. Richter was sweeping the stairway, as always.

"Heard they are going to pick up the old people next," she whispered. "You know what they say: They who do not work, neither shall they eat."

I thought of my grandmother. And in my bedroom that night, six rows of fiery eyes pierced my chest….

But I was lucky, in a way. I was too young. I didn't know at the time about the mental agony that my mother and her Jewish friend must surely have endured in the days after Crystal Night, after thousands of Jewish stores had been destroyed, nearly two hundred synagogues torched, and tens of thousands had to make a terrifying choice: Hand over all possessions to the state and emigrate *or* live a life wherein art exhibits, cinemas, concerts, and theaters were forbidden, where licenses to drive, practice medicine or law were revoked, and where nobody knew what other kinds of evil would strike next.

Directive!

Reich Minister Dr. Goebbels announces:

"Last night, the justified and understandable outrage of the German people about the sneaky murder of a German diplomat in Paris by a cowardly Jew was vented in wide-ranging ways. Actions of revenge against Jewish buildings and stores were carried out in numerous cities and towns throughout the Reich.

Now, however, I issue a strict directive to the entire population to cease and desist at once all further demonstrations and actions, of whatever kind, against Jews. The ultimate reply to the Jewish assassination in Paris will be given to the Jews by way of legislation or, possibly, executive order."

Langewiesche-Brandt, Ebenhausen near München, Germany

6. THE YELLOW UNCLE

[January 1939]

Although I didn't know it at the time, the rather hypocritical directive issued by Dr. Goebbels was quickly followed by all sorts of new restrictions for the Jews of Berlin. They were forbidden to enter the government district and the fancy western suburbs; they were banned from concert halls, movie houses, and theaters; and their presence in such public places as the broadcasting tower and various sports arenas was made illegal. Indeed, as I later learned, even half-Jews, quarter-Jews, Jews married to Gentiles, and "war-decorated" Jews lost their previously special status. But, as you can well imagine, none of this affected me; I had an Aryan passport.

And so I entered school on January 1, 1939, a date that may strike you as odd. The selection of that particular date, a holiday in the rest of the world, was in itself something of an omen. It was a portent of the Teutonic compulsion for "perfection" that we first graders were about to meet and that was to pervade our education in the years to come. Starting off our schooling on the *second* day of the year was just not an option. That would have indicated a lack of seriousness, insufficient rigor, and a quite unacceptable degree of slovenliness, worthy of Struwwelpeter himself!

I remember it being a cold and sunny day. There was no snow on the ground. When I surveyed the world from our balcony, as I did every morning, I noted the beauty of the morning sky. The sun was just rising in the east; the western sky was covered with parallel bands of wispy clouds turning pink. In later years, while studying to be a pilot, I would learn that such clouds consisted of windblown ice crystals and were known as *cirrus radiatus*. On that day, however, I didn't know that, nor did I have time to consult the *Book of Clouds* that Aunt Martel had given me for Christmas. Before I could even open my storage box and reach for it, my mother pulled me from the balcony to get dressed. She helped me put on the garter belt and the long woolen stockings that all boys wore in those days and then a sweater and above that the brand-new sailor's suit that I had been eyeing in the closet all week. I adjusted the cap with all the colored ribbons. It had the name of a famous ship on it, *Bismarck*. I admired myself in the mirror and strapped the big leather satchel to my back. It was stuffed with abacus and spelling book; sponge and drying cloth; pencil and tablet of slate. I slung the smaller satchel over my left shoulder, though not before checking that the right kind of sandwich was inside. Nothing but liverwurst would do.

Dieter and his mother were waiting in the hallway downstairs. Yes, she was back, not a Bolshevik after all! Dieter wore a new outfit, too: Bavarian leather pants and a heavy white shirt to fight off the cold. He had a large *Edelweiss* flower in the middle of his chest. He looked just like the little man in the weather house standing in our living room. This small replica of a typical Bavarian house featured two open doors and was actually a barometer. A tiny man would come out of one door to forecast rain, but a tiny woman in a pretty red dress would come out of the other door to predict sun. Come to think of it, she looked just like Dieter's mother on that sunny morning, red scarf included! Mrs. Meyer adjusted the scarf she always wore, and off we went.

We already knew the route: Five houses to the right; turn left; straight to the footbridge and across the canal; left along its southern edge; turn right at the second bridge. And there we were. "Stuttgarter Strasse 35-38," the sign said. Two four-story buildings dominated the lot, each made of red brick and each surrounded by an 8-foot cast-iron fence, painted black. There were giant iron gates, too; each had another sign, "People's School #19, Berlin-Neukölln."

We passed the first structure. It was for girls and had only women teachers. As instructed, we left our mothers behind at the second gate. Then we went into the second building which was for boys and where only men could teach. The front door was about ten times taller than a normal door, which was thrilling and also intimidating. Instantly, two big boys appeared. They wore familiar brown shirts and swastika armbands, and they marched us across acres of polished floors to the third-floor room of Mr. Eisler. They said he would be our teacher for the next three years.

Mr. Eisler sat behind a desk on a platform. He checked off names and assigned seats as we came in. In front of him stretched ten rows of church-like pews. They were made of heavy oak and rose towards the rear of the room. This reminded me of the movie theater at the Treptow observatory to which my father had always taken me. Here the seats were numbered as well. "One" was in the farthest row and "Sixty" in the nearest, diagonally across the room. A large portrait of Frederick the Great looked down upon us. It hung across from the row of cathedral-sized windows. Each window had its own set of iron bars.

A bell rang, three times, slowly, as if it was about to fail. Mr. Eisler stood up. He was very tall and looked like the picture on the wall, except that the medals were missing. He opened a closet behind his desk and took from it a yellow bamboo cane. He slapped the top of his desk twice and made an ominous swish through the air.

"This," he said decisively, "is the Yellow Uncle. If need be, he will teach you everything a first grader should know. Here is lesson Number One: You are to be quiet unless spoken to by me, quiet as a mouse. Is that understood?"

No one said a word, but one could hear the clanking of the radiators.

"Lesson Number Two: You are to stand at attention when spoken to and whenever I enter the room. Is that understood?"

"Atten–tion!"

We jumped to our feet, fast learners all.

"Good, you got the point," Mr. Eisler said.

For the rest of that morning we stormed through the picture pages of the spelling book: From the cow that said "moo" to the cat that said "meow"; from the duck that said "quack-quack" to the dog that said "bow-wow." We raced through half the animal world, from neighing horses to roaring lions, from squeaking mice to croaking toads …

All that was easy for me; my mother had already taught me to read. Dieter was not so lucky; he got stuck a lot. The school bell rang in the middle of the farmer's yard.

"Atten–tion!" yelled Mr. Eisler; and, two abreast, we were marched down the granite stairs to the yard behind the school. The boys in uniform showed us how to merge with the boys from the other grades. We formed a single circle and slowly moved around the walled outer edges of the yard. I thought of the second-hand of the grandfather clock at home, and its fluorescent tip going around at night. And clockwise our endless circle moved, two abreast, silently. I thought of the horses and zebras in the circus. They had moved with similar precision. Presently, our trainer appeared.

A teacher entered the center of the moving circle and, with a bullhorn, gave permission to eat. A thousand hands opened five hundred leather satchels, but a thousand feet hardly missed a step. The bullhorn teacher helped us walk the proper way.

"Left, Two, Three, Four---Left, Two, Three, Four---Left," the bullhorn blared.

Once we got it right and knew how to march, we were also told how to eat.

"Just like the Führer, you should eat lots of flour soup and always, always eat 12-Grain Bread," the bullhorn roared. "It'll keep you healthy and give you rosy cheeks. Tell your mothers when you get home!"

******

When we returned to class, Mr. Eisler stood at the door with his yellow cane. A couple of well-aimed slaps hit the calves of the last two boys marching in.

"A lesson from Frederick the Great," Mr. Eisler said. "Never be last!"

There followed a whirlwind of activity. Mr. Eisler had a question for each of the sixty of us, allowing about two seconds apiece for an answer. If the answer was correct, we were assigned another seat with a lower number; if the answer was wrong, we got a higher-numbered place to sit. Our names were not involved.

"Thirty-one," Mr. Eisler said, pointing the cane toward the boy in that seat, "read page five."

And Thirty-one jumped to his feet, grabbed the spelling book and read something like: "Croak-croak, quack-quack, meow."

"Good," Mr. Eisler said, "you are Twenty-two."

And fifteen seconds after it all started, nine boys, named Twenty-two to Thirty, moved over one seat, making room at one end, while filling a gap at the other. But not everyone was as lucky as Thirty-one.

"Seven," Mr. Eisler said, pointing the cane at him and dangling a stop-watch from a silver chain, "repeat after me: Fisher's Fritz fetched fresh fish fast; fresh fish Fisher's Fritz fetched fast. Go!"

But poor Seven mumbled: "What?" and Mr. Eisler announced triumphantly: "I knew it: You *look* stupid. You are Fifty-nine. And tape back those ears of yours: They stick out."

Boys with runny noses, pimples, and bowed legs were moved toward the front as well, along with others who could not spell "bow-wow" or who drowned themselves in "Four Vienna washer women washing white vests."

I was so glad my X-legs had been fixed.

When everyone was seated "scientifically," as Mr. Eisler put it, he called upon the entire front row of "proven misfits":

"Fifty-five, six, seven, eight, nine, Sixty, Atten–tion!" he yelled. "Step out! About-face! Down with your pants; underpants, too. Bend over your desks!"

Each of them got to know the Yellow Uncle a carefully measured three times on the naked bottom. Except for Fifty-six. He had wriggled and kicked. Mr. Eisler held him by the hair and told him to show his hands. He slapped him a few extra times on the palm of his right hand, on the fatty part, just below the thumb. Saying "hello" to the Yellow Uncle, he called it.

Then Mr. Eisler handed each of us a note for our parents. It told them that we would be graded on ten subjects in half a year: Behavior, Attention, Industry, Religion, German, Geography, Handwriting, Arithmetic, Music, and Punctuality.

Finally, it was time to go home.

"Let us pray," Mr. Eisler said. "We thank thee, Heavenly Father, for teaching us the meaning of order and discipline, of perfection and cleanliness. Preserve us as we now are, One People, One Nation, One Führer. Amen."

Mr. Eisler smiled at me as I left. He sat again at his desk, and this time he was rubbing the Yellow Uncle with an onion.

"Adds elasticity and makes for a longer life," he explained with a grin.

I felt safe enough. My name was Five.

The Nazi view
of schoolchildren:
**You, too, belong
to the Leader.**

Langewiesche-Brandt, Ebenhausen near München, Germany

7. HAIL TO THE VICTORS!

[February – December 1939]

When I look back at my first year of school in Berlin, from the vantage point of someone who has by now spent several decades on the other side of the Atlantic, one thing strikes me as amazing: The speed with which we learned things in those days. It exceeded greatly the academic progress made by the typical first grader in America today. Learning, in contrast to playing, was a serious business then, and we spent many hours at it every day, even Saturdays.

Mr. Eisler lost no time initiating us into the subjects he had promised to teach, but he had a special way of doing so, which surprised our mothers greatly. When *they* went to school, way back in the midst of World War I, different subjects were taught by different teachers during different hours of the day. Not so in our school. Mr. Eisler was our *only* teacher that year and he merged all the subjects into one. Dieter and I liked it a lot. In fact, we were fascinated.

Within a month of our arrival, Mr. Eisler put up a huge map that covered an entire wall. It was a map of Germany in 1918, he said. We all had to make our own copies of it, first learning about different provinces and then about the oceans to the north, the mountains to the south, and all sorts of rivers and towns in-between. In the process, we learned *geography*, but we also learned how to *read* and *spell* and *write* such fancy words as Bavaria, Rhineland-Palatinate, Saxony, and Silesia. Before long, I could spell *North Sea* and *Baltic Sea* and *Elbe* and *Oder* and even *Harz Mountains* and *Tyrolean Alps*. Moreover, I could find all of them on the map. And my own little map got filled with the names of cities, such as Berlin and Brandenburg, Dresden and Hamburg, Munich and Nuremberg.

Arithmetic came into the picture as well. Thus, we learned about the height of mountains, the length of rivers, and the numbers of inhabitants in cities. The Matterhorn was 4,505 meters high, Mr. Eisler told us, the Grossglockner peaked at 3,798 m, and the Zugspitze came to only 2,963 m. Just for fun, Mr. Eisler made us add or subtract some of the numbers, such as those found in the Matterhorn measurement:

$$4 + 5 + 0 + 5 \text{ came to } 14, \text{ while } 4 + 5 + 0 - 5 \text{ came to only } 4.$$

We played similar games with rivers, noting that the length of the Danube was 2,850 kilometers, the Rhine came to 1,320 km, the Elbe to 1,144 km, the Vistula to 1,059 km, and the Oder to only 898 km.

"How much longer than the Oder is the Elbe?" Mr. Eisler asked.

I knew:

$$1,144 - 898 = 246$$

Cities were fair game as well. Berlin, I found out, had 3.33 million people in it, Vienna had 1.76 million, and Hamburg 1.61 million. And thus we learned about decimal points and numbers being divided into 100 equal parts.

There was more! By adding ever more colors to his map, Mr. Eisler showed us how the Führer had made Germany grow. Thus, the Führer added the Saar in 1935, Austria in 1938, and the Sudetenland in 1939, just a few months ago. Now, Mr. Eisler told us one summer day, Adolf Hitler wants Danzig to join the Reich and he has asked the Poles for a corridor road to link up East Prussia with Pomerania and the rest of us.

"And he has asked nicely!" Mr. Eisler exclaimed. "But are the Poles listening?"

Dieter and I didn't know the answer to that; in addition, our thoughts got sidetracked on the way home from school. The streets were suddenly filled with hundreds of red flags, hanging from poles at the corners of every street and also from almost every balcony, but not all of them had the white circle with the black swastika on them. Many flags pictured a five-pointed star with a hammer and sickle inside. For Dieter and me that was big news! What was happening to the world?

When we got home, my mother and Mrs. Meyer explained.

"The hammer-and-sickle flag is the flag of Russia," my mother said. "An important man of theirs is visiting Berlin today."

Mrs. Meyer, as usual, was fiddling with the radio. When the squealing stopped, we could hear an excited announcer tell the story:

"At this very moment, Vyacheslav Molotov, the Soviet Foreign Minister, who has recently replaced the Jew Maxim Litvinov in this post, is departing Tempelhof airport in his black limousine—on his way, we believe, to the Soviet Embassy. Earlier, he was cordially greeted by Foreign Minister Joachim von Ribbentrop who told us that a 10-year non-aggression pact has been signed in Moscow and important follow-up talks were about to begin. For additional news, we now switch to the Hotel Adlon where…."

The voice disappeared, as Mrs. Meyer had turned off the radio.

"And thus the Bolsheviks have conquered Berlin!" she said with a big grin. "Well, let's hope Arthur and his SPD pals were wrong with their 'Hitler means war' talk."

By then she was talking, of course, about my father.

******

Back in school, Mr. Eisler expressed a similar sentiment. He praised the Führer for his ceaseless efforts to make Europe a place of peace. And he showed us the outlines of our new friend Russia on his giant map. Before long, we added the Volga (3,688 km) and the Dnyepr (2,285 km) to our own maps.

We also learned that Moscow had 5.60 million inhabitants, while Leningrad had only 3.00 million.

"How much shorter than the Volga is the Dnyepr?" Mr. Eisler asked.

I knew how to do it and volunteered:

$$2,285 - 3,688 = -1,403$$

"One thousand four hundred three kilometers," I said eagerly.

My mother had already taught me about negative numbers. Mr. Eisler smiled at me and then called on Twenty-Nine to work a similar problem.

"How much smaller than Moscow is Leningrad?" he asked.

Twenty-Nine didn't know what to do and was made to say hello to the Yellow Uncle.

"Pay attention!" Mr. Eisler said as Twenty-Nine pulled up his pants.

Then Mr. Eisler made him go to the blackboard and add up all the numbers from 1 to 100. As he was working, ever so slowly, I remembered the trick my mother had taught me.

"In your mind, picture all the numbers between 1 and 100 in a row: 1, 2, 3…97, 98, 99, and 100," she had said. "Then note that $1 + 99 = 100$. That $2 + 98 = 100$ as well. That $3 + 97 = 100$, too. In this way, by the time you reach $49 + 51 = 100$, you have found a sum of 100 forty-nine times! And by then you have used all the numbers in your initial row, except the 50 and the 100. Therefore, the grand sum you seek equals

49 times $100 = 4,900$ plus the remaining $50 + 100$, or 5,050."

While Twenty-Nine was still struggling with the first ten numbers, I gave Mr. Eisler the answer. He said I was a talented and gifted child. He may well recommend a TAG child such as me for the special Adolf Hitler School in Munich. Being the conceited little creature that I was rapidly becoming, I felt very proud of myself.

"Elementary, really," I thought.

******

Mr. Eisler gave Twenty-Nine another task, counting backwards from 100 in steps of seven. As Twenty-Nine struggled with the list—100, 93, 86—Mr. Eisler returned to the main issue of the day. He was uncertain, he said, about the prospects for peace with other countries.

"Although the Führer has secured peace with Russia," he said, "unfortunately, one cannot trust the Poles."

"Four years ago," he continued, pointing to his map with a long stick, "the Poles had a map that showed Poland's western frontier reaching all the way to the Elbe River, right here. On their map, all the German towns you have learned about had Polish names. Apparently, their map was part of a secret invasion plan, but our Secret Service exposed it. That's why we must be ever watchful. We can't trust the Poles; they are not only defiant, but also deceptive."

Mr. Eisler then took the occasion to give us a spelling lesson and also teach us about rhyme. He told us about scary leaflets the Poles had recently dropped along the Oder River. And he copied one of them to the blackboard:

Betet noch ein Vaterunser, morgen seit Ihr unser!

[Quickly say another Lord's Prayer, for tomorrow you belong to us!]

Then time was up. Mr. Eisler told us, in turn, quickly to copy the message off the blackboard and take it home.

My mother said it was a Nazi fake and Mrs. Meyer agreed, which provided the occasion for their explaining to me and Dieter the meaning of *fake*, but that was not the end of the story. Just a week later, on September 1, 1939, the "Polish problem," as Mr. Eisler had called it, returned with a vengeance. At breakfast time, even before we left for school, the radio was filled with martial music and then Dr. Goebbels made another speech.

"Our proposals for a peaceful solution to the problem of Danzig and the Polish corridor have been rejected by Poland," he said. "Now, as if to add insult to injury, the Poles have visited atrocities on German citizens, especially women and children, killing many of them. Our patience is at an end. Accordingly, as the Führer has just put it, 'bomb will be met by bomb.' At this moment, under the command of General Walther von Brauchitsch, 33 German army divisions, supported by 1,600 aircraft, are doing what is necessary to defend our fatherland. And as of today, Danzig enters the Reich as a German city."

******

By the time we got to school, Mr. Eisler had already updated his teaching devices. A new map of Europe hung on the big wall, with Greater Germany highlighted in a pretty green. Judging by the color, Danzig had clearly entered the Reich, just as Dr. Goebbels had said. For the time being, all of Poland had been painted yellow by Mr. Eisler so we could better appreciate its place in the world. And, just to the left of the new map, Mr. Eisler had made other arrangements as well. I saw two photographs and a brand-new bulletin board.

One of the photographs showed Paul von Hindenburg, the World War I Field Marshal, who later became President and, just before his death, appointed Hitler as chancellor. The same photograph showed the Führer as well and a giant caption read "The Marshal and the Corporal—Fighting With Us for Peace and Equal Rights."

The second photograph showed the Führer shaking hands with the papal ambassador, Basallo di Torregrossa, who was quoted in the caption: "For a long time, I did not understand you. But equally long I have tried to. Today I understand you."

Actually, I didn't read this till the midday break. Before then, Mr. Eisler had focused on the bulletin board, onto which, he said, we would henceforth write the news. That in itself turned out to be a complicated process.

During the coming weeks, Mr. Eisler told us the latest news each morning. Then one of us had to write a summary sentence or two on the blackboard and possibly had to write it again and again until perfection was achieved. Finally, the rest of us had to copy the perfect product to our tablets of slate, while Mr. Eisler himself made the same entry on the bulletin board. Needless to say, the Yellow Uncle had to help some of us, but I was lucky. I never had to shake his hand.

This is what the bulletin board looked like as we left for our first winter vacation:

1939

September 1	German army enters Poland to defend the Reich
September 3	Britain and France declare war on Germany; Australia, India, and New Zealand follow suit
September 4	British liner *Athenia*, carrying 1,400 passengers, torpedoed and sunk
September 6	South Africa declares war on Germany
September 8	Troops of General Walter von Reichenau reach Warsaw suburbs
September 10	Canada declares war on Germany
September 17	Soviet troops march into eastern Poland
	German U-Boat sinks British aircraft carrier *Courageous*
September 27	After massive air raid, Warsaw surrenders to German troops
September 30	The war in Poland is over! Germany has won!
	Soviet troops invade Finland, bomb Helsinki airport
	Marshal Karl von Mannerheim leads defenses with success
October 14	German U-Boat passes through Scapa Flow submarine defenses in Orkney Islands, then sinks British battleship *Royal Oak*
December 14	German battleship *Admiral Graf Spee* battles British cruisers *Achilles*, *Ajax*, and *Exeter*, then seeks safety in Montevideo harbor. Denied refuge and shelled with mustard gas, German crew sinks own ship in the Rio de la Plata.

The bulletin board, however, gave only the barest outline of what we learned that fall. Each entry not only taught us to read and write better, it also gave occasion to all sorts of additional lessons from Mr. Eisler. Thus, the *Graf Spee* incident became the subject of our art class, in which we were asked to draw a copy of the vessel's tailpiece, a 3-meter tall bronze eagle resting on top of a swastika. The Scapa Flow story, in turn, led to our drawing of a detailed map of the 70 islands making up the Orkneys. And we learned that they had been settled by the Picts, only to be conquered by Norsemen in 875. They became part of Scotland in 1472. And yes, adding the numbers in the latter year came to $1 + 4 + 7 + 2 = 14$.

Similarly, the final victory over Poland excited Mr. Eisler greatly and caused him to devote a whole day to General Heinz Guderian's 1933 book, *Achtung! Panzer!* [Attention! Tanks!].

"That book," Mr. Eisler told us, "first proposed the recently so successful *Blitzkrieg* strategy. Such a lightning-fast war," Mr. Eisler continued, "avoids the lengthy and indecisive trench warfare of former times. Based on mobile forces, such as artillery, tanks, and aircraft, all of which are equipped with enormous firepower and are moving at rapid speed, such strategy defeats the enemy in a *single* offensive."

"Just as in Poland," Mr. Eisler concluded.

True enough, many of us had trouble with Mr. Eisler's approach. At first, his long sentences and all the fancy words he used just went above our heads. But he kept it up and never let a subject go until we had mastered it. In a matter of a single year, we moved from the duck that said quack-quack and the cat that said meow to reading, writing, and using such complicated words as *Blitzkrieg* and *aircraft carrier* and *military strategy*. Before long, our minds could move from Montevideo harbor to the Mannerheim line and back to the Tyrolean Alps just as easily as our feet moved us from home to school and back again.

My mother and Mrs. Meyer, however, didn't believe the Montevideo story, especially the part about the mustard gas. They always whispered about Mr. Eisler, particularly after the Street Warden had paid Dieter and Mr. and Mrs. Meyer a visit. In some miraculous fashion, the Warden had gotten hold of a little essay that Dieter had handed in to Mr. Eisler.

"What I had for Sunday Dinner," said the title. Dieter had written about pork roast and mashed potatoes with gravy, sauerkraut and applesauce and, of course, *Rote Grütze.* That was a problem.

"Apparently," said the Warden to Mrs. Meyer, "you are not paying attention to the Führer's edict about waste in time of war. You are to be less lavish, more economical, make *Eintopf* meals, saving food for our brave men at the front."

About two minutes after the Warden had left, Mrs. Meyer rang our door bell.

"Can you believe this?" she said to my mother, "I always knew that Eisler was a snake! Now he uses our children to rat us out! This time it's only about single-pot meals; what's it going to be tomorrow? And are we to live on nothing but Adolf's flour soup?"

"We have to watch more closely what the boys are doing at school," my mother replied. "Did I tell you the Warden came here, too? He wanted to know why I was never hanging out the flag from the balcony, can you believe it? I told him I couldn't afford one now that Arthur is gone."

"And you know what he said?" my mother continued. "Now that there is a war, things could change, he said. Maybe you could help bring Arthur home if you would just join the *Frauenschaft,* he said. Picture me joining the women's auxiliary of the National Socialist German Workers' Party!"

"But then," she continued, "maybe he has a point. I did say I would lend a hand with the Winter Help Campaign. Collecting money at the street corner for two days won't kill me. Who knows what they do with it, but maybe it helps the right people somewhere."

And my mother did volunteer for that campaign. The Warden was so pleased. He brought her a big red box and a bell and he said I could go along, hold the sign, hand out the little books, and even ring the bell. My mother said it was all right.

Before we left, I read the sign. "It is the highest duty of every German," it said, "to help those in need. This year's campaign is the first one in times of war. The Führer demands that you not just give, but that you *sacrifice*!"

I also read the instructions. Those who gave more than 5 Reichsmark were to be rewarded with the little booklet. "The Führer Makes History," the title said.

At the time, of course, except for what we learned in school and or heard on the radio, I knew relatively little about the kind of history he was making. My mother knew plenty more, given that her sister Martel worked at Gestapo headquarters and kept her abreast of secret things. Thus, as I later learned, she knew even then that Hitler had approved euthanasia centers, code-named T-4 hospitals, where "unworthy life" was to be destroyed, and had done so on the very first day of the war. People with mental diseases were to be sent there, along with elderly "useless eaters" and others exhibiting antisocial tendencies—being divorced too often, changing jobs too often, drinking to excess. They were herded naked into small rooms there, pumped full of carbon monoxide, and cremated.

But there I was, ringing that bell and loving it! And I loved wearing my grandfather's *Pickelhaube,* too, a pointed military helmet from World War I that I had brought along for the occasion. It had an eagle on it, clutching a scepter and a globe with a cross. There was an inscription, too. "With God For King and Fatherland," it said. Many people admired it.

"You'll make a fine Prussian soldier one day," Mr. Wagner said when he came by to make his sacrifice. My mother said nothing.

Langewiesche-Brandt, Ebenhausen near München, Germany

An early World War II poster:
With Our Flags is Victory!

8. THE INCORRIGIBLE ONE

[February 1940]

After my mother and I had collected all that money for him, the Street Warden may well have put in a good word on behalf of my father. I don't know, but I do remember the day my father returned. I was in the second grade by then and should have been getting ready for school, but my mother told me to sleep in that day. When I heard the singsong of the chimney sweep, I was up in an instant. I loved to watch him from our pantry window in the back of the house. He would appear on the roof of the side-house first, all dressed up in black, top hat included. In his right hand, he carried a black ball covered with bristles, and a long wire was coiled around his left shoulder. He walked as easily as the men on the tightrope at the circus. By the time he got to the tall chimney, I was half hanging out the window, waving my flag at him. As always, he took off his hat and made a deep bow in my direction. His left hand seemed to have melted into his hat, both were equally black, but I could see the white teeth in his sooty face when he smiled at me. He always smiled; chimney sweeps brought good luck. I wanted to be one, too.

"Oh, no!" my mother said. She yanked the flag from my hands. "Where on earth did you find this one?"

"Right here, behind the canned cherries and beans," I said.

"And that's where it's going again," she replied.

I felt tears coming to my eyes and when she had finished rolling up the black, red, and gold, she looked at me and pulled me tightly to her chest.

"Oh, I'm sorry," she said, "I guess we'll have to have another talk. Come, have a drink of this wonderful cherry juice."

She poured me a glassful and I took it eagerly. Just then the rumbling began behind the wall, and my mother dashed off to finish taping the kitchen stove to keep out the clouds of soot.

"This *is* a lucky day, Hansel," she said when she had finished. "This afternoon, Vati will be back! Mr. Meyer has promised to take us to the station. And that's why I wanted to talk to you anyway. Come here; sit with me on the couch."

Her arms felt warm around me, just like the featherbed before falling asleep. But I was wide awake then.

"Remember the time we talked about the tyrants?" she asked softly. "Remember when we talked about the bad men who took Vati away? They are just like the Wanselow kids downstairs who are mean to you and Dieter. They like to bully the whole world, the Nussbaums, the Meyers, and everyone else who doesn't agree with them. They like to tell everybody where they can play and how they should live. They like to take everybody's toys away…"

She saw the surprise on my face.

"Yes, I know about it," she said and held me tightly. "Well, Vati had a different idea. He thought people should be kind to each other, listen to each other and decide things together, and not allow any tyrants to rule. There was a time, before you were born, when this almost happened. That's when Germany had the black, red, and gold flag. Right now, though, the tyrants are in charge, and we mustn't wave that flag. If they see it, they will come and hurt us. But this is supposed to be our lucky day when Vati comes home!"

My mother hugged me and gave me another glassful of cherry juice.

"Shall we open a box of *Leibniz* cookies?" she asked.

******

That afternoon, while Dieter was still in school, we met Mr. Meyer outside his fruits-and-vegetables store, just around the corner from our house. He was sitting in his green delivery van, the funny one with only one wheel in the front. There were only three seats, all in front as well, and I made sure to get the right-hand one. That way I could put out the red arrow whenever we turned right.

Before we took off, however, my mother had a surprise for me. She had made a copy of my father's driver's license, but had changed the name, birth date, and place of birth to mine and had even put my picture in it.

"Having passed the practical driving test and having paid a fee of 4 Reichsmark," the document said, "Hansel is hereby given permission to operate a gasoline-powered vehicle of class #3. Signed at Berlin, February 14, 1940, by J.A. Hoffmann, Chief of Police. List Nr. 18730/40. Fee Register Nr. 282/I/40."

All that was left to do was sign underneath my picture and we were ready to go. I had so much fun putting out the red arrow whenever Mr. Meyer told me to that I was almost sorry when we pulled up in front of the railroad station. I had never seen it before and it certainly looked as if Silesia Station had been made for giants. The crowds of people in front of the main entrance reminded me of dwarfs. A huge eagle clutching a swastika was perched above them way up near the roof and I wondered what kept it from falling down. I read the signs.

"Frankfurt-on-the-Oder," and "Breslau, Dresden, Halle, Erfurt." I knew the places; all of them were on my map at school. There were other signs, too.

"Wheels Roll For Victory!" said one. "Keep Germany Clean!" said another, and I noticed an old woman with a broom sweeping up cigarette butts and used-up tickets and such. There was even an ad for my mother's favorite scouring powder, "VIM Polishes Everything."

My mother put a 10 Pfennig coin into a metal box and got me a roll of mints. Then we bought tickets for the platform, and the railroad lady was kind. She gave me a book of stubs for our games at home. Platform 3 was empty when we got to it, but there was a lot of hustle and bustle on platform 6 across the hall. I decided to sketch the inside layout of the station on my notepad that my mother had brought along. Way on the left was Platform 1, right next to the side wall that seemed to have dozens of tall entrances, three meters tall I figured, with curved arches made from red brick. Above each of these arches was a large window, equally tall and equally arched at the top. And above that rose the roof that itself arched to the center of the giant cavern in which we stood, only to descend again on the other side to another side wall that was a mirror image of the first.

On the ground, two railroad tracks ran parallel to Platform 1, they were followed by Platforms 2 and 3, two more tracks, Platforms 4 and 5, two more tracks still, and, finally, Platform 6 next to the far wall on the right. I tried to count the brick columns between the arches along our side of the building, but I gave up when I got to fifty-six. They got in each other's way at the far end near the three big openings through which the three sets of double tracks came into the station. Counting the glass panels in the roof wasn't any easier; they were so black with soot that I couldn't keep them apart. I kept thinking of the chimney sweep.

******

My mother held my hand tightly when the big locomotive entered at the far end.

"We must be careful not to fall onto the tracks," she had warned.

The locomotive filled the station with the loud sound of its horn, crawled past us inside a cloud of hissing steam, and stopped a few centimeters short of the barricade near the doors through which we had come. I wondered why the locomotive didn't have red wheels. The one in my picture book did.

My father didn't look like his picture either. His hair was very short, and he didn't wear his favorite tie with the sailboats. My mother ran into his arms, but I didn't know how to act toward him. He seemed like a stranger; so I put my arms around my mother. I noticed that she was crying, which I didn't understand. I thought this was to be a happy occasion. Perhaps, I thought, she didn't like his short hair.

Mr. Meyer gave my father a slap on the back, as he always did when he met other men.

"So they take you from Oranienburg to Berlin by way of Frankfurt-on-the Oder," Mr. Meyer said with obvious sarcasm. "Why *not* take the long way? Makes a lot of sense to me now that we are supposed to conserve fuel."

"Had to have a week of re-education first," my father said and my mother said "Hush, you two, let's get out of here."

My father took me by the hand till we found Mr. Meyer's delivery van. My parents went into the covered section in the back, right above the two back wheels; I resumed my position in the front, next to the right turn signal.

"Ready, Captain?" Mr. Meyer said.

I could see my parents through a little window behind my seat. My mother opened it and I asked my father about the tyrants, but my mother said that my father was tired from the long trip and I shouldn't bother him.

"We'll talk soon," my mother said. "We'll go to the Baltic, and Oma will come, too. Today we celebrate."

In fact, Mr. Meyer didn't take us home right away. He dropped us off at Glogauer Strasse 33, where my grandmother and Aunt Martel lived. I knew the place well because my mother and I had visited there often. It was an old building, much older than ours. My grandparents had moved into it way back in 1895 when they came to Berlin from Silesia, looking for a better life. That was also the year Aunt Martel was born, the first of six children, which is why they always called her "the old one." Uncle Walter was born next; then came Lotte, Liesel, Gertrud, and Fritz. But Fritz died in the very year I was born. And my father never called my mother "Gertrud." He called her "Trudchen."

"Who's here to celebrate?" I asked as we entered the dark hallway. I pressed the phosphorescent button to activate the lights in the stairwell and my mother said "Just Oma and Aunt Martel today." I ran ahead, pressing the buttons on each level as we slowly made our way to the fifth floor. When my parents weren't watching, I also stuck my tongue out at all the peepholes I passed, just in case someone was looking.

"It's not getting any easier," my mother said, quite out of breath and with a weak smile. My father was still holding her hand when the laborious climb had finally ended and he rang my grandmother's apartment door.

Aunt Martel opened it and let out a shriek, but I didn't have time to watch what happened next. I had to race to the bathroom and I knew my grandmother didn't have one. No one in the building had a private toilet, much less a bathtub or hot water, but there were common toilets on each landing between the main floors. I ran to the nearest one and found it unoccupied. Unlike ours at home, my grandmother's toilet had a water tank near the ceiling with a long chain hanging from it and a porcelain handle at the end. I liked to pull the handle and watch the water swirl in the basin below. I noticed the sign on the inside of the door. It was a war decree from the Mayor of Berlin, dated January 15, 1940, asking his fellow citizens to conserve coal by taking baths only once a week, on Saturdays or Sundays. That didn't make sense to me because in my grandmother's house there were no bathtubs, nor were there coal-fired water heaters such as the one we had at home.

By the time I finally got to my grandmother's apartment, the festivities were already underway. Although the heavy brocade curtains were drawn, the usually dark living room was brightly lit by the chandelier hanging above the large table in the center of the room. A perfectly ironed white table cloth made a stark contrast to the red oriental carpet underneath. And the table was set with my grandmother's finest china and silverware and there were pretty white napkins next to each plate. Most importantly, the table was laden with all sorts of goodies to eat. I spied a bowl of crisp hot buns and a butter dish and a large platter filled with favorites of mine: blood sausage with white chunks of lard in it, raw hamburger with diced onions mixed in, and, of course, liverwurst. A real Berlin treat!

Just then my grandmother appeared with a steaming pot of "peel potatoes," fresh off her cast-iron stove. I knew the drill. Whenever potatoes had been boiled with their skins, rather than peeled when raw, guests were expected to peel off the skins at the table—after all, potato peels were only for pigs! I also knew what would come next. On another plate, my grandmother brought in the inevitable eel and she also had red herrings that had been smoked to look golden like the ring on my mother's hand.

My mother brought me a bottle of the green woodruff soda that she knew I couldn't live without, while my father placed bottles of black malted beer next to the other plates. Meanwhile, Aunt Martel was busy concocting a special welcoming drink, a genuine *Berliner Weisse,* produced by a carefully measured mixture of light beer, white wine, and a bit of raspberry syrup! I knew the recipe, although other people preferred to leave out the white wine and add woodruff instead of raspberry syrup.

"Eat, eat," my grandmother said, and we did, but not before my father had said a prayer and we all held hands in a circle and said "Amen."

Not much was said during the meal and I occupied myself studying the four angels sitting on Plaster of Paris clouds way up near the ceiling at the corners of the room. I decided that their faces looked exactly alike, but two were playing the trumpet, while the others each held a lyre between their legs. By the time I had studied the rest of the stucco decorations on the ceiling, it was time to take the dishes to the kitchen, but my mother said I needn't help with the washing and drying today. I could go into Aunt Martel's room and look at her jewelry box.

I went reluctantly because I was eager to hear what the adults were going to talk about. So I skipped the jewelry box and briefly took a look at a few more interesting things. For one thing, the ceiling decorations in Aunt Martel's room were different, consisting of many kinds of flowers and birds. Because they were all white, I had a hard time identifying them, despite the fact that I had studied my mother's *Flora and Fauna* book at home.

I also studied my grandfather's picture on the wall. He had been a big man with a big head and a handlebar mustache, but he had died before I was born. My mother had told me that he had worked as a leather worker when he first came here from Silesia, tanning hides and dyeing leather for a shoe factory. Later he had been a policeman on foot patrol on Berlin city streets, and later still, he had become one of the Emperor's Guards. My mother said he had worshipped the Kaiser, but had changed his mind after he met him in person. In the Kaiser's palace, there were spittoons in the corners of all the rooms and the Kaiser had made it a habit to spit into one whenever he was pacing back and forth thinking about important things. One day, he had entered a room in which my grandfather was standing at attention and the Kaiser had angrily yelled at him.

"Wherever I want to spit, there stands another cop! I'd rather be guarded by a cuspidor!" the Kaiser had said.

From then on, my grandfather hadn't liked the Kaiser anymore.

As I looked at my grandfather's picture in the Imperial Guard uniform, complete with spiked helmet, high polished boots, and sword at his side, I wondered whether he had died from a broken heart. I also noticed that my grandfather looked just like President Hindenburg, whose picture was hanging in the corridor at my school.

Apart from my grandfather's picture, Aunt Martel's room was rather bare, containing only a bed, an armoire, and an interesting little cubicle with a big curtain in front. Of course, I investigated and found only three items behind the curtain. There was a pail that I knew Aunt Martel used for going to the toilet at night. That way she didn't have to go down the creepy stairway to the common toilet below. There also was a wicker rug beater that everyone always used in the back yard to beat the dust out of rugs, although I knew that bad children often made their acquaintance as well. I guess the rug beater was a relative of the Yellow Uncle at school. And then I found something really fascinating: a brand new black, white, and red flag! In a second, I took it to the kitchen where everyone was still doing the dishes, but nobody was happy with my find.

"My God," my father said to my grandmother, "you still have that flag! You know what kind of trouble you can get into? Get rid of it fast!"

"Over my dead body will we get rid of that flag," my grandmother said excitedly. "It's one of the few things of Paul's that I still have. No one is going to disrespect the Kaiser's flag in this house!"

With her gnarly hands, she grasped the flag, took it to her bedroom, and leaned it against the wall, right next to the crucifix. And that was that!

"Why isn't the flag black, red, and gold, like ours at home?" I asked.

My parents gave each other that strange look.

"Ours is the flag of the republic that came after the Kaiser left," my father said. "I'll explain it later."

"Don't worry about flags right now," Aunt Martel added. "Go and finish polishing my jewelry. You always do such a splendid job. I would be really grateful."

I pretended to comply, but I left the doors open a crack and was all ears.

"You really should get rid of that flag," my mother said to Aunt Martel. "Did I tell you that Fritz Wagner turned in his own brother last month? Just because he had raised his glass to the Kaiser at Lotte's wedding! What this world has come to…"

"We should bring Arthur up-to-date when he is done shaving," Aunt Martel whispered, but I heard every word. I also saw my father hunched over a mirror in the kitchen, his suspenders looping off his sides, lathering up his face with a brush. While his face slowly disappeared under the soap, he sharpened a straight-edge razor on a leather strap. And while he slowly made his face reappear, my mother gave him the update.

"You got to be really careful about Fritz Wagner. Always walks around with that swastika pin on his chest, a real loyal Party man. Herbert, sorry to say, is the same he always was. Loves to strut around in his brown-shirt uniform. And watch out with Walter, too. He's still with the Postal Service, but he's a big fish now. In charge of Germany's official clock, super-important for the radio and also the Armed Forces. Have never seen him wear the Party pin, but Martel saw a brand-new SS uniform hanging in his closet, complete with fancy hat, skull and crossbones and all."

"How are the Nussbaums doing?" my father asked.

"Have totally disappeared, we have no idea what happened to them," my mother said. "Perhaps Martel can find something out."

"How come? How would *she* know?" my father asked.

"Oh," my mother said, "you couldn't know. She's still at the Customs Service, a confidential stenographer now, but the Gestapo took over her division. They've focused almost entirely on Jews leaving the country or trying to leave and they use every possible excuse to take away everything they own. Their apartments, their houses, their furniture, their businesses. Often they get them for 'foreign currency crimes,' but nowadays they can use dozens of other excuses. Jews can be 'criminals' for visiting the movies or the theater—forbidden now—for having pets, for owning radios or cameras, the list goes on."

"And if that doesn't work, they have other means," Aunt Martel interrupted. "They can tear your fingernails out. Or torture you to death with steel whips and electric drills. Or pump up your belly with a water hose. Oh God, I took the oath of allegiance; I cannot talk!"

"Well, none of that is news to me, given where I have been." my father said. "One can also die after being force-fed gallons of castor oil or get shot 'trying to escape' or 'commit suicide by jumping out of a 4th-floor window while the guards were distracted.' I have seen it all."

"Actually," my father continued, "Jews are only one of several types of prisoners they have at Oranienburg. They also have Freemasons and Jehovah's Witnesses, homosexuals and real criminals, political prisoners and, most recently, a lot of Poles. Members of each group wear different insignia on their prison garb. Mine was a red triangle for 'incorrigibles,' which meant 'political prisoners' of one sort or another. But now, they think, some of us can be of use outside. So they have a job waiting for me at Osram's. Not making light bulbs and such, just working at the payroll office, because I am so good at math, they say. Well, I tell you, no more politics for me."

"Thank God," my mother said.

******

Still, when I said that my grandfather, with the upturned waxed moustache and all, looked just like Hindenburg, my father did have a political story to tell. He'd heard it from someone at the camp, he said, someone who had been on Hindenburg's staff, and it concerned the puzzling question of *why* Paul von Hindenburg, the Kaiser's Field Marshal and hero of the Battle of Tannenberg, in his later role as President of the Weimar Republic, had appointed Hitler as Chancellor. That act had always been an enigma to him, my father said, given the monarchists' utter disdain for the Nazi brownshirts.

"But," my father said, "there may be a simple answer: By 1933, Hindenburg may well have had some form of dementia and, contrary to his public image of strength and wisdom, he may have been weak, senile, and fatally susceptible to the manipulations of those around him, including his son Oskar and Otto Meissner, his chief of staff."

"Here's but one case in point," my father continued. "Remember that big torchlight parade on January 30, 1933, the day of Hitler's appointment? Groups of SA brownshirts, Steel Helmets, and SS men marched in a giant circle through the Tiergarten, the Brandenburg Gate, briefly Unter den Linden, right along Wilhelmstrasse, and then past the Presidential Palace and later the Chancellery. By circling the area again and again, the marchers gave the impression of an endless procession, which did not fail to amaze Hindenburg who watched it all from a balcony. Before long, he raised his cane and kept time with the music in the street. Then he turned to a bystander, saying: 'Ludendorff, how well your men are marching! And what a lot of Russian prisoners we've taken!' Needless to say, Ludendorff, the World War I Army Chief of Staff, wasn't there, and the Battle of Tannenberg had been fought and won almost 20 years earlier, in the summer of 1914!"

"Fine, so the old man was befuddled," my mother said impatiently. "Now let it go!"

******

That night, after we got home, my father showed us the Social Democratic election posters he had hidden underneath a floorboard in our pantry. We all looked at each of them. Then we burned them in the kitchen stove.

One of the posters showed a workman with a broken back tied to a huge swastika, sort of like Jesus on the cross. "The Worker in the Reich of the Swastika," the caption said. "Therefore vote List 1. Social Democrats!"

Another poster foreshadowed the German-Soviet non-aggression pact of 1939 by a full decade. It showed a Soviet soldier with a red star and hammer-and-sickle hat. And a dark figure with a swastika on his head and a dagger in his hand. And the caption said: "These Are the Enemies of Democracy! Do Away With Them! Therefore vote List 1. Social Democrats!"

A final poster was prophetic as well. It showed a frightened mother looking at her five children, grown up and in military uniform. But their bodies had turned into skeletons. The caption said: "Mothers, Is That Why You Gave Birth To Your Children?"

A Social Democratic election poster prior to the June 1933 dissolution of the SPD: **Mothers, Is That Why You Gave Birth To Your Children?**

Langewiesche-Brandt, Ebenhausen near München, Germany

9. BLACKOUT!

[February – September 1940]

The day after my father had come home from the concentration camp, another one of my mother's sisters stopped by for a visit. Her name was Charlotte, but everyone just called her Lotte. Aunt Lotte lived on our street, too, eleven houses down from us in the direction of the park with the waterfall and the goldfish pond. Her apartment was on the second floor, which meant she didn't have to climb so many stairs, but it was in the rear house, so she didn't have a balcony as we did. She always said she'd be glad to climb more stairs in exchange for a better view, but I don't think she had much time for leisurely rest on a balcony. In fact, she spent every waking minute at her *Singer* sewing machine, turning the cloth and the patterns delivered to her each morning into skirts and coats by night time, although by then she was more likely to work on military uniforms. The factory paid her by the piece. If she got sick and couldn't work, she was paid nothing.

On this day, as I remember it, she came laden with gifts—a winter coat for me, a white shirt for my father, and a silk blouse for my mother. We all hugged her and everyone gave her a kiss.

"You must be working for Santa Claus these days," my mother said, admiring her new blouse, "but next Christmas is still ten months away!"

"Consider it a 'welcome home' gift," Aunt Lotte said. "I know you can all use it and it's from Liesel, too. She says 'hello.' But she couldn't come; scared to death of what Herbert might say."

My parents just looked at each other and said nothing about *that* subject. I think I told you already, Aunt Liesel was another one of my mother's sisters yet and she was married to my Uncle Herbert, the brown-shirt man.

"Maybe you can join us at the Baltic next July," my father said, quickly nudging the conversation in another direction. "Trudchen arranged for us to use the old apartment at Henkenhagen. Oma is coming, too."

"You know, I just might," Aunt Lotte said, as my mother poured coffee for her. "Four months of hard work and then we can *really* celebrate!"

Hard work began the very next day. It was my father's first day at his new job and he said we could walk together to my school, where he could catch the subway to Spandau. I knew he was right; Mr. Eisler had made us draw maps of the subway lines whenever we weren't too busy revising Germany's borders to the east.

It was snowing; so I put on my brand-new coat for the walk to school. It fit perfectly and made me feel proud. I wished I could show it off to Dieter, but I knew he couldn't come. He was still ill with scarlet fever and one could only look at him at the hospital through a pane of glass. My father put on his old raincoat, but he wore a fancy dark suit underneath, with a stiff white collar that my mother had starched and a dark blue tie. He also had shined his shoes till they mirrored his face, but he hid them under galoshes. We had fun walking to my school and even fed the gulls at the canal. We promised to report on the day's events at supper time.

Mr. Eisler had wiped clean the old bulletin board, at least most of it, so it looked like this:

1939
September 30   The war in Poland is over! Germany has won!

1940

******

All that empty space on the board, however, was short-lived. In the course of that spring, Mr. Eisler drew our attention to the north and west on his giant map and the board quickly filled up. First, Mr. Eisler introduced us to Denmark and Norway, our neighbors to the north. Like Poland, he painted them yellow too. Then he told us how Britain and France were setting out mines in the North Sea near Denmark and Norway, which kept poor Scandinavian fishermen from catching those wonderful herrings we all so loved.

"To protect the neutrality of these friendly neighbors and to get rid of those mines," Mr. Eisler explained, "the Führer had no choice but to send in our navy and our troops."

That evening, I proudly showed my father that I could spell *Scandinavia* and *neutrality* and my father was proud of me, too. He told me what he had done, in turn.

"Each Friday," he said, "I stuff paper bills and coins into little brown envelopes and hand them to the workers. There are over 600 of them. Just like Aunt Lotte, they are paid by the piece. Except the new Polish workers. They live in a dormitory, right at the factory, and they are paid nothing."

I knew about the Poles; I had seen them at the bakery store. They wore jackets with a big P on the back and the baker wasn't allowed to serve them until all the Germans had been taken care of. Just a few days ago, my mother had again been yelled at by someone when she said to a Polish woman "Go ahead; you were here first."

My father explained how he might figure the money going into an envelope.

"Seventy light bulbs sprayed red, times 5 Pfennigs a bulb, comes to 350 Pfennigs or 3.50 Reichsmark."

And that remark got my mother started with the multiplication table. Before many days had passed, I knew that 3 times 4 equaled 12, that 7 times 5 was 35, and that 12 times 12 came to 144.

"Won't Mr. Eisler be surprised when he tries to teach me multiplying in the next grade!" I thought.

My father also told me why his new workplace was called *Osram*.

"The base and filaments of light bulbs," he said, "are made of a thin metallic alloy, consisting of *osmium* and *wolfram*, two corrosion-resistant metallic elements. Together with the bulb itself, which contains a vacuum, this alloy produces a perfect glass-to-metal seal, regardless of the high temperatures a lighted bulb might take on."

Then my father helped me spell and write all the fancy words in his story, which reminded me of Mr. Eisler who was always doing the same thing.

******

Back in school, Mr. Eisler took the occasion of the latest military advances to teach us about Germanic poetry.

"Just as the Führer intervened to protect the Danes," Mr. Eisler said, "so have other Germanic heroes throughout history. Consider the splendid saga of Beowulf. This 8th century warrior delivered the Danish King from a man-eating monster, called Grendel, which had appeared for many years, night after night, striding out of the moors to ravage the King's palace and carry off his warriors. Indeed, Beowulf had to overcome Grendel's grandmother, too. She lived in a deep lake and tried her best to revenge her grandson's death. Eventually, Beowulf himself became King of the Geats, another Germanic people related to the Danes. After a long and happy reign, he had to fight a dragon to save his people, but he was wounded by the dragon's poisonous fangs and died. His body was burned on a great pyre."

"So you see," Mr. Eisler concluded, "glory can be achieved only through fearless courage. Beowulf's was a heroic age, full of great thoughts and great deeds. Just like ours."

Luckily, Mr. Eisler was able to provide current examples right away. To protect their neutrality, the German Armed Forces have now entered Holland, Belgium, and Luxembourg, he told us, and

Mr. Eisler wasted no time to paint them yellow on his map.

That night, when we listened to the news at home, Dr. Goebbels explained.

"Britain and France have dropped their mask," he said. "In the life-and-death struggle thrust upon the German people, our government does not intend to await an attack by Britain and France inactively, allowing the war to be carried through Belgium and Holland onto German soil."

Before long, Mr. Eisler turned our attention to France, where another *Blitzkrieg* was underway. On the large wall map, we followed each move by the German heroes who led the campaign, General Gerd von Rundstedt, General Fedor von Beck, and General Ritter von Leeb. And we added crucial new data to our own maps: Paris had 2.85 million inhabitants. The length of the Loire was 1,020 kilometers, that of the Rhone only 812 km, and that of the Seine a mere 776 km. And the highest point in France and even the entire Alps, was called Mont Blanc, some 4,810 meters tall.

But the high point of our year came just before we left for summer vacation.

"Paris has fallen!" Mr. Eisler exclaimed.

I so remember the day! There was wild rejoicing in the streets of Berlin. Church bells rang for 15 minutes. Flags were put out for three days. The 218th Infantry Division marched through the Brandenburg Gate. And Mr. Eisler got a new teaching device. He put up a large white screen in front of his map, placed a projector on his desk, and got ready to show us a movie!

We saw German tanks cross the bridges of the Seine and columns of German troops march down a tree-lined Champs Elysées and past the Arc de Triomphe. Then, in the forest of Compiégne—at the very spot where Germany was so humiliated after World War I, Mr. Eisler said—we saw General Wilhelm Keitel of Germany and General Charles Huntziger of France sign a truce!

Mr. Eisler was all too eager to elaborate. The French Armed Forces under Marshal Henri-Philippe Pétain were being disarmed, he said. Except for a southern portion, much of France was to be occupied by our troops. The French were to surrender all war materiel, gold, and foreign exchange, and they were to deliver coal and other raw materials to Germany.

As I left our classroom, grade report in hand, I cast a last look at the bulletin board. It seemed to have filled up in no time and looked this:

1940

April 9   German Army—supported by 1,000 aircraft and cruisers *Blücher, Gneisenau, Karlsruhe, Königsberg,* and *Scharnhorst*—enters Denmark and Norway, controls both countries by end of month

May 10	German Armed Forces enter Holland, Belgium, and Luxembourg
May 15	German Air Force destroys Dutch city of Rotterdam; Holland capitulates
May 18	General Gerd von Rundstedt's tanks pierce French lines along 100 kilometer front in Ardennes plateau; surprise move nets 12,000 prisoners
May 22	German forces reach the British Channel, trap 500,000 enemy troops in Belgium
May 26	British Expeditionary Force initiates retreat across Channel from Dunkerque
May 29	Belgium capitulates
June 10	Italy enters war on German side, attacks southern France
June 14	German Armed Forces occupy Paris!
	General Ritter von Leeb attacks Maginot Defense Line from rear
June 23	Truce signed with France! French Forces disarmed!

That evening, my parents made a big tent with our feather beds, placed the radio under it, and got the war news in their own way. According to the monthly summary by the BBC, broadcast in German, the British had sunk the German cruisers *Blücher, Karlsruhe*, and *Königsberg* during their Norway invasion. In addition, some 99 aircraft had attacked the industrial Ruhr basin on May 15, making this the first British air attack on Germany. Waves of British fliers had bombed Aachen on May 22, battling hundreds of Messerschmitt fighters. The British had captured Narvik, Norway's iron ore port, on May 30. Another first had come on June 21 when British bombers reached the Potsdam/Berlin area, a feat never achieved before....

I instantly thought of Frederick the Great and his beautiful Potsdam castle, *Sans Souci*. And I thought of all the pretty birds nearby on Peacock Island, which we had visited with Mr. Eisler. But the news continued.

On June 23, the very day France was defeated, the Royal Air Force had bombed the Krupp steel plants in Essen and the harbor in Bremen and had seriously damaged the German battle cruiser *Scharnhorst* off the Norway coast...In conclusion, Prime Minister Winston Churchill and General Charles de Gaulle urged the Free French forces to continue resistance…

My father turned off the radio and changed the dial to the *Deutschlandsender* [Radio Germany], where Uncle Walter announced the time once a day and every day. Precise to the second. But I wasn't worried about time. My report card had given me a 1 for punctuality, which was the best grade one could get. Fifty-six had gotten a 5, which was the worst grade and indicated the fact that he was always late. Naturally, he got acquainted with the Yellow Uncle just before school let out. But, as I said, I wasn't thinking about time right then. I was worried about the little red label that the Street Warden had put on our radio a long time ago when my father wasn't even there. My father saw me looking at it.

"Don't worry," he said. "Nobody can possibly know. This is our family secret."

"Punishable by death…" I thought. "Would they kill all three of us or just one?"

I felt my heart racing, as if I had run up all the stairs without resting. I was determined to be brave and hold back my tears, but a few squeezed out anyway, running down my cheeks like the sap from the acacia tree. I turned away so nobody would know.

******

Things got better the very next day when my parents, my grandmother, Aunt Lotte, and I took the train to the Baltic coast. Aunt Lotte told a funny story about Hermann Göring. Responding to rumors that British bombers had reached the Ruhr and even Potsdam near Berlin, the German Air Force Chief had said that no foreign planes would *ever* get to Berlin; if they did, everyone was free to call him Meyer.

"A nice name, Reich Marshal Meyer," my father said, but my mother told him to stop it.

We ended up in a small fishing village where my parents had spent their honeymoon. I had seen the pictures. Two dozen little houses, most of them recently whitewashed and covered with thick roofs of straw, were stretched out along a single dirt road paralleling a kilometer of beach. There were no streetcars shrieking, no buses honking, no church bells ringing, no swastika flags flapping in the wind. But there were hundreds of sea gulls circling, just as outside our balcony at home, inviting us to scale the dunes and look at their beach. And what a beauty it was! It was made of pure white sand and stretched out as far as the eye could see. I couldn't take my eyes off the waves, as they rose and crashed and rose again, revealing a million shades of ever-changing whites and black, of emerald green and the deepest blue…

We played for days at the beach. Always, my father and I got up real early to find the best spot. I helped him build our fort. We dug a big hole, half a meter deep and three meters square, with walls of sand all around. We collected large stones and used them to spell my name on one of the walls of sand:

H–A–N–S

Our little windmills and the red-and-blue flags went up on those walls as well. We placed the wicker seat with the tall back and roof in the rear and our blanket in front of it. All day, my grandmother sat on her shaded basket-chair doing her needlework.

My father and I made mud pies at the edge of the sea, went wading at low tide to look at the crabs and jelly fish, and played catch with the rubber disc. We gathered sea shells and looked for amber that was so plentiful that we could make a long necklace for my mother. Once, my father pretended to be a new kind of sea creature. With the rubber disc clutched between his teeth and me clinging to his back, we rode out of the sea and up the beach to surprise Aunt Lotte and my grandmother. My mother took a picture of us.

Evenings we stayed inside and played games. I liked playing "Hansa" the most. It was a board game with a map of Europe on it and the inscription 1245–1669. We rolled a pair of dice in a leather cup and moved colorful tokens of crystal, each representing a different ship of the famous merchant league. From Riga to Danzig and Stockholm, from Bremen to Antwerp and Venice we carried our wares, fighting pirates as we went. That's when my father told me the legend of Klaus Störtebecker, the most infamous pirate of them all. He sailed the oceans with his 12-man crew in a tall ship that had scary black sails and an even scarier black flag, showing white skulls and crossbones on it. For years, Störtebecker and his men terrorized the Hansa's merchant ships, stealing their cargoes and killing their crews. Then, finally, after a joint effort by all the members of the league, the pirates were caught. They were tried and sentenced to death by the axe in 1401. But Störtebecker was granted one last wish. So he made this request:

"Let all my men stand in a row. Once I am beheaded, if I can walk past any of them, let those go free."

The wish was granted and after the axe had fallen, a headless Störtebecker walked past one, past a second, a third, and a fourth comrade of his, apparently ready to go on—when a furious executioner threw a tree limb in front of his feet! That was the end of the other eight....

The day before we had to go home, we all took a horse-and-carriage ride to the next town. We found a toy store where my father bought me a pirate ship that came in a big box, labeled "Anchors Ahoy!" From stem to stern, not a single detail was missing: There was a crow's nest and there were cannons, there were sails and rigging and hatches, there even was an extendable plank and there were all sorts of figures representing pirates and their prisoners. I was so happy! And then we even went to a movie. It was a comedy, called *Quax, the Crash Pilot*. It featured an overeager Hitler Youth, played by comedian Heinz Rühmann, who wanted to learn to fly but who was incredibly inept. Thus, he always did precisely the wrong thing at a crucial moment—throw the stick out the window just before a stick-and-rudder landing approach or lose the landing gear on takeoff or forget to put enough gas in the tank. Although he caused his instructor's hair to turn gray prematurely, and although he crashed into many a barn, chimney, or tree, somehow Quax always managed to survive. My father and I died laughing, but my mother, Aunt Lotte, and my grandmother saw nothing funny in any of this.

That evening, black clouds moved in. Thunder rumbled by the time I went to bed in the little house with the thatched roof. Lightning flashed and crackled all around us. Then the earth seemed to shake underneath us; there were screams down the street. My father picked me up, and we ran out of the house. The cottage next door was all ablaze. People huddled in the middle of the street. Nothing could be done. In a few minutes, the house turned into a hissing pile of rubble. And then my father said a strange thing to me.

"That's what the tyrants would like to do to the whole world," he said.

I looked at him, and I saw the rain mingle with his tears.

"But you know what?" he asked. "The spirit of black, red, and gold, like the water running down our faces, is stronger than they. In the end, they cannot win. Water is stronger than fire."

******

By the time we got back to Berlin, everyone else seemed to be thinking of fire, too. In many apartment houses, boxes of sand had been placed on all the landings in the stairwells, precisely thirteen steps apart, and even more boxes had appeared in the attics. And the Street Warden told everyone to keep pails of water outside each apartment door to fight firebombs should the need arise.

And later that summer, on the first day of school, we were given a special demonstration in the yard. We all made a big circle around a fireman with a red helmet on his head. He held a red metal cylinder that was about 1 meter long and was called an *incendiary bomb*. When he pulled on a wire, the whole thing burst into a huge flame and he showed us how it could be put out with a single pail of water or a few shovels of sand. Nothing much to worry about there.

Something else seemed much more serious. The fireman told us of a "new secret weapon" the British were about to use. It consisted of an innocent-looking, chemically-treated piece of cardboard, he said, known to the experts as a "self-igniting leaf." Made of nitrocellulose, also known as guncotton, and mixed with phosphorous, the item was to be dropped from planes in a moist state. As it dries out, it bursts into flame unexpectedly, he said. To induce curious children to pick it up, the fireman warned, the piece carries a printed message. What we had to do or rather *not* to do was obvious.

Back in class, further training occurred. To everyone's surprise, each one of us was fitted with his very own *gas mask*, made of tight-fitting green rubber, giant glass eyes, and a silver canister filled with charcoal and such. The masks made us look like an army of scary ghosts. Mr. Eisler told us to carry our masks with us at all times.

"And, just for practice," he said, "you should wear the mask for at least 4 hours a day and you should sleep with it all night at least once a week."

"The hell you will," my mother said when I got home. "That man is insane."

But I wondered.

"What about the Montevideo mustard gas attack?" I thought. "And why was the man who owned the street-corner pub outfitting his horses with canvass masks?"

Nobody seemed to answer questions such as these, but when I thought about such matters and then remembered how Mr. Eisler had demonstrated the way people might *choke* to death during a gas attack, my eyes would well up with tears. I hated that.

I was even more concerned once I read the newspapers that were then delivered to our apartment door. According to the *Völkischer Beobachter* [People's Observer], British Wellington and Hampden bombers had reached Berlin on August 25 and again on September 4, only to be driven away by violent anti-aircraft fire. On September 11, however, the same paper said, British bombers hit the Reichstag and other inner-city targets, including the Brandenburg Gate, buildings along the Unter den Linden Avenue, the Academy of German Art, the House of German Engineers, and even the Catholic Saint Hedwig's Hospital. The German Air Force retaliated with a massive raid on London. Said Dr. Goebbels:

"Warsaw and Rotterdam have clearly revealed what effects our heavy caliber bombs have. If London wishes to taste a similar fate to the full extent, then let Herr Churchill and his criminal clique continue to send pirates at night to Germany!"

No one said a word about Reich Marshall Meyer, but I was worried, especially when the Street Warden came back and told everyone in no uncertain terms to black out all windows at night, lest we give aid to the enemy.

"We will have patrols in the street," he said to my father, "and I assure you: If we see the slightest bit of light coming from one of your windows, we will *shoot* into that window without warning!"

That was also the time at which my mother acquired a new habit. She was always after me to keep our apartment in the dark, just in case our shades didn't work perfectly. "Don't touch that switch," she would say. "Keep the lights out!" I must have heard her say it a thousand times.

Langewiesche-Brandt, Ebenhausen near München, Germany

The Enemy Sees Your Light!
Blackout!

10. THE PROPHETESS
[September 1940 – May 1941]

Because I was such a "talented and gifted child", as Mr. Eisler had put it, I moved directly from the middle of the second grade to the middle of the third when school resumed after our trip to the Baltic. As luck would have it, Mr. Eisler did the same. Thus, he was still my teacher in the late summer of 1940 when everyone's attention was focused on Operation Sea Lion, the distant battle for the British Isles. Naturally, Mr. Eisler had plenty of news to post on our bulletin board.

1940

September 4	German Air Force hammers South England airports and naval bases
September 11	German Air Force pounds London for 8 hours
September 27	Germany, Italy, and Japan sign Tripartite Friendship Pact
November 14	Five hundred German bombers destroy Coventry
November 20	Hungary becomes our ally
November 23	Romania becomes our ally

While German bombers pounded British cities, we learned that there were 8.41 million people in London, but only 1.11 million in Birmingham. Mr. Eisler used the occasion to show us how two numbers could be multiplied and he was so proud of himself when his superb teaching enabled me to show instantly that 8.41 times 1.11 equaled 9.3351. If the truth be told, I had learned the method a long time ago from my mother, but I didn't tell Mr. Eisler about that and let him think that he was the one who had awakened my innate ability. In addition, I knew, of course, that it was never wise to do or say anything that might spoil his good mood.

That day, Mr. Eisler was *so* happy about all the new friends Germany was making throughout the world. To learn about them, we drew maps of Italy and Japan, of Hungary and Romania. We learned that Rome had 1.66 million people and Milan 1.29 million, while Tokyo had 5.38 million and Kyoto only 1.10 million. Mount Aetna was 3,274 meters tall, topped by Mount Fujiyama's 3,778 m.

We also had a new subject, *Chemistry*, and it was quickly put to use in practical ways. Thus, Mr. Eisler brought in a blue bottle, labeled *Oxygen*, and, in no time at all, we knew everything anyone would ever want to know about "this wonderful colorless, odorless, and tasteless gas."

"Oxygen," Mr. Eisler said, "was first isolated in 1773 by a German pharmacist, Karl Wilhelm Scheele. The English claim the deed was done by an Englishman, Joseph Priestley, but that is an outright lie."

"At a temperature of 0 degrees Celsius and at a pressure of 760 millimeters of mercury," Mr. Eisler told us, "one liter of oxygen weighs 1,429 grams. That makes it slightly heavier than air, which itself is a mixture of mostly nitrogen and oxygen, plus trace amounts of other gases, and one liter of which, under the same conditions, comes to 1,293 grams."

"Ordinarily," Mr. Eisler continued, "oxygen makes up about 21 percent of the air, but what, do you think, will happen when the British attack us with incendiary bombs and poison gas? Picture yourselves *trapped* in a smoke-filled room or in an air raid shelter, with, say, mustard gas leaking in. Before long, the percentage of oxygen declines and once it's gone below 15, you are dead!"

"Unless, unless," Mr. Eisler concluded triumphantly, "you attach one of these little blue bottles to your mask. Then you'll be just fine for an hour or two."

He grinned, as we packed our gas masks and satchels to go home.

******

My mother met me at the school gate that day and she was furious when I told her what I had just learned.

"I'll have a talk with that dreadful man," she said angrily. "What does he think he's doing, scaring little kids like that!"

"I am not a little kid," I said, "and I'm not scared about anything."

We waited a minute for Dieter. He came from another room because he was still in the second grade. On the way home, we stopped at the hardware store and my mother bought a sun dial for our balcony. It was made of shiny brass and, just like my cuckoo clock, had Roman numerals on it, which pleased me to no end. It had an inscription, too.

"I only mark sunny hours," it said.

I could hardly wait for my father to come home and help me put it up with his magnetic compass. In fact, we met him in the street and he looked different. He wore a light gray uniform and a hat with a black visor that looked just like those worn by the streetcar drivers. He had an emblem above the visor, too, but it wasn't the Berlin bear. It was a big red cross!

"Vati has volunteered for the Red Cross," my mother said. "He'll work at the hospital on Saturdays and some evenings."

That explained that, but I wondered whether he knew about the oxygen problem. Maybe he should pick up some of those blue bottles at the hospital, I thought. On the other hand, oxygen did scare me, my protestations to the contrary notwithstanding. Mr. Eisler had said that things burn much faster and with a much brighter flame in pure oxygen than in ordinary air. So why would one want to run around with oxygen bottles when there was a fire nearby? In any case, I didn't get a chance to talk with my father about it, nor did we have time to put up the sun dial that day.

"Why don't you meet Eddy at the U-Bahn," my mother said to my father. "I'll stay home and wait for Rachel. Martel is coming over, too."

"Uncle Eddy and Aunt Rachel are coming to visit in a bit," my mother said, turning to me, and that was big news.

Aunt Rachel, I knew, was my father's sister and she lived in a faraway village in the district of Magdeburg where we had never been. Uncle Eddy used to live there, too, but now he was away, somewhere in France. They used to have two children, my cousins Hartmut and Gisela, but several winters ago, they both had died on the same day while skating on the frozen Elbe River. Ice fishermen had made a big hole and my cousins had sailed right into it and had never come back up. Being a big official in the Lutheran Church, Uncle Eddy himself had presided over the funeral service for his children.

"But today," my mother said, as if she were reading my thoughts, "is going to be a happier time. Uncle Eddy has to come to Berlin on some Army business, but he can't go anywhere else before he must return to Paris. So he and Aunt Rachel are meeting here for a few hours. We just arranged it all this morning."

Unfortunately, things didn't quite work out that way. Aunt Rachel never came. And Uncle Eddy—I remember only his horn-rimmed glasses, his jowly face, his green-gray captain's uniform, and heavy boots—Uncle Eddy only came by for about five minutes until my father told him to "get out and stay out." That night, I spied on my parents and Aunt Martel to gather up the information I needed to solve the mystery.

One part of the story was simple enough. Aunt Rachel, who had long and thick black hair, had been mistaken for a Jewish woman who had the gall to sit down in the double-decker bus on her way from the railroad station to our house. Before long, she had been dragged to a police station, where she had insisted that she was not Jewish in the least and that, moreover, her husband was Superintendent of the Lutheran Church in the district of Magdeburg, and was, at this very moment in our history, an officer of the Reich and as such deputy to no one else but the Commandant of Paris! A policeman was duly dispatched to our house to verify the story and that's where he ran into

Uncle Eddy storming out just as Aunt Martel arrived.

The next part of the story was much more complicated and, as usual, involved a lot of whispering. Nevertheless, over the years, I managed to put together the big picture. Way back in 1933, it seems, the new Hitler government had picked an obscure naval chaplain, Ludwig Müller, and made him head of the country's Lutheran Church with the title Reich Bishop. Other officials of the Church had quickly ratified the decision and a victory party had been held at the Sports Palace in Berlin, featuring a speech by Adolf Hitler, Luther's hymn, *A Mighty Fortress is Our God*, and the SA's favorite Horst Wessel song, *The Flag Held High…*

But a tiny minority of Lutherans had formed the *Confessing Church*, which sought to uphold the traditions of scripture, while opposing the "Aryanizing changes" proposed by Müller and his *German Christians*. Uncle Eddy, it seems, had quickly sided with the new Bishop and hung the swastika flag from his church tower and even behind the altar, right next to the crucifix. He had been rewarded with one of those new cars being built by Ferdinand Porsche and, more importantly, by being made one of several Superintendents of the Church, which had put him in charge of all the ministers in the Magdeburg district. When the war started, he had been rewarded again by being made Captain of the Army. All that had earned him Aunt Martel's undying contempt.

But the story got even juicier! On this very day, when my father, all dressed up in his Red Cross uniform, had met Uncle Eddy at the subway station, a disaster had occurred. My father had said "Hey, Eddy! Over here!" and Uncle Eddy, proudly wearing his Captain's uniform, had had a veritable fit.

"Is that how you salute a Captain? Show some respect to an officer of the Reich," he had yelled and then, right there, he had made my father lie down on the sidewalk and do a dozen pushups to teach him a lesson that he obviously needed to learn.

After that, it seems, they had walked silently to our house, climbed all those stairs together, and then my father had taken off his uniform and thrown Uncle Eddy out! Still, my mother sent Aunt Rachel a Christmas card that year, which I know because I slid it into the red mailbox at the corner myself, but we got nothing back in return, not for Christmas, not for my birthday, not for my mother's birthday later that spring.

******

On my mother's birthday, April 6, German troops entered the Balkans.

"At this very moment," said Radio Berlin, "swarms of Stuka dive bombers are pouncing like hornets on Yugoslav and Greek airfields and railroads, clearing the path for our tanks, infantry, and parachutists."

And, while we were eating breakfast, Dr. Goebbels made another speech:

"Soldiers of the Southeast Front! Since early this morning, the German people are at war with the Belgrade government of intrigue. We shall only lay down arms when this band of ruffians has been definitely and most emphatically eliminated, and the last Briton has left this part of the European Continent, and when these misled people realize that they must thank Britain for this situation, they must thank England, the greatest warmonger of all time. The German people can enter this new struggle with the inner satisfaction that its leaders have done everything to bring about a peaceful settlement. We pray to God that He may lead our soldiers on the path…"

My mother turned off the radio. She always did. My father sighed and, as usual, we left together for my school. Mr. Eisler was ready for us. Before long, his bulletin board filled up with the new events.

1941

February 14	Field Marshal Erwin Rommel's Africa Corps takes Tripoli and later all of Libya, even reaches Sollum, Egypt
March 1	Bulgaria becomes our ally
April 6	German forces enter Yugoslavia and occupy it in 11 days
April 6	German forces enter Greece; cross Metaxas defense line in short order, conquer the Thermopylae, the Isthmus of Corinth, the Peloponnesian peninsula
April 21	Over 640 German bombers destroy Plymouth
May 10	Over 500 German bombers raid London

Mr. Eisler lost no time to explain.

"The British," he said, "cowards that they are, always let others fight for them: first the Poles, then the Norwegians, then the Belgians, the Dutch, and the French, now the Serbs and the Greeks. But it won't work. We are on to them."

"In fact," Mr. Eisler continued, "while we Germans have been fighting a *Blitzkrieg*, the British have engaged in a *Sitzkrieg*." [While we Germans have been fighting a lightning-fast war, the British have engaged in a sitting-on-their-hands war.] Apparently, he thought this little rhyme was particularly clever.

Mr. Eisler also told us that Athens had 1.37 million inhabitants and that Mount Olympus was 2,911 meters tall. Above all, he focused on the war in the Peloponnesian peninsula, the home of *Sparta*.

"In ancient Greece," he said, "Sparta was a serious rival of Athens. The two city states fought the Peloponnesian War from 460-404 B.C. The Spartan lifestyle produced rigorously self-disciplined and self-restrained men. Their diet was austere, frugal, and simple. In the face of danger, pain, and adversity, they were courageous. Oh boys, *you* should have the Spartan character!"

We could tell that Mr. Eisler was on a roll. He was swishing the air with the Yellow Uncle and his eyes seemed to be covered with a strange glaze.

"The noble Spartans, you should know," he continued, "made up only 10 percent of the population. Other classes, such as the Helot serfs, made up the bulk of the people. For that reason alone, the Spartans had to be strong, which is why they had a strict upbringing. Right at birth, sickly and weak children were weeded out, taken into the mountains to die. Only the healthy and strong ones were brought up. Starting at age 7, they were taken from their parents and educated by the state. They were given nourishing but simple food, as I said before. In summer as well as winter, they got light clothing to wear and had to bathe in the river, regardless of the temperature. Sports and fighting became the main subjects of their education. They sang Homeric songs and rousing songs of war. Once a year, they were taken to the temple and whipped and they had to bear their pain without making a single sound. That made them ready to become good guards for supervising the Helots at work."

"Even Spartan women were tough," Mr. Eisler concluded. "When Spartan men left for war, the women pointed to their men's shields and said: 'With it or on top of it!' They wanted them to return victoriously, with shields in hand, or be brought back dead, lying on top of their shields, but having fought to the last drop of blood. Oh, how much we can learn from Sparta!"

******

When I told my parents about the Spartans, they were not impressed.

"That asshole," my father said and my mother told him not to use that word.

Then we listened to the BBC, as usual, under the feather bed. The top story was a great surprise. Rudolf Hess, after Reich Marshall Hermann Göring second in command to the Führer, had taken a Messerschmitt 110 and flown himself to Scotland! Berlin had already replaced him with Martin Bormann. In the meantime, the Royal Air Force had attacked the U-Boat docks at Bremen and Hamburg….

On the next day, Radio Germany confirmed the story. Said the announcer:

"On Saturday, May 10, at about 6 P.M., Party Comrade Hess took off from Augsburg for a series of flights from which until today he has not returned. A letter that he left behind unfortunately indicated, by its incoherence, symptoms of a mental derangement that permits the inference that

Comrade Hess became the victim of hallucinations. The Führer immediately ordered the arrest of the adjutants of Party Comrade Hess who alone knew of these flights and, knowing of their prohibition by the Führer, did not prevent or immediately report them."

That was also the day on which my father got a written order to appear at the Berlin headquarters of the SS! By 0800 hours the next day....

My mother said I didn't have to go to school that day and we just sat on the balcony and waited for my father to come back. We played "One-Two-Three." Our right fists went up in the air; then, almost faster than the eye could blink, our fists came straight down, went back up, and down, up and down in perfect unison, while we chanted "one, two, *three!*" But the last time down, the shape of our hands could change, and that would determine who won. If my mother kept her fist, but my hand turned flat, I would rejoice, for "paper can wrap up a stone." If my mother made a V, but I kept my fist, I also won, for "stones sharpen scissors." If my mother made a V, but my hand was flat, she was the winner, for "scissors cut paper."

"One, two, *three*," we yelled—my hand a little bowl, my mother making trembling fingers pointed to the sky. "Water beats fire," I roared, and I thought of my father at the Baltic Sea.

He looked ashen when he came.

"They wanted me to *volunteer* for the SS!" he said. "Put me in a room with a bunch of other guys, thanked us for volunteering and got ready to swear us in. 'Wait a minute,' I said, 'I'm not volunteering for anything; I was *ordered* to be here.' There was that long silence. 'My God, hush,' whispered the guy next to me, 'do you want to be shot?' But the man in charge was not perturbed. I was just the right age and just the right height, he said. 'Why not give it some thought?' But it was just a cruel game. I will never put on that black uniform, and he knew it."

My mother gasped and started to cry.

"They even gave me a second chance to volunteer," my father said, "and I fully expected to be shot when I said no again, but they wouldn't waste a bullet on me, had a much better idea. They need men to clear mine fields and get rid of duds. I was just made for it, they said. Needn't wear a regular army uniform, needn't carry weapons, can even spend three weeks in school: Crossen-on-the-Oder, six hundred hours, day after tomorrow."

"So it's a penal battalion and for the duration," he said, embracing my mother and me at the same time. We all cried.

******

"Do you think Eddy had anything to do with this?" my mother asked.

None of us knew the answer to that one, but my mother kept me out of school for a while and, two weeks later, we went to see my father. A soldier sat in the train with us. He had had a leave in Berlin. I looked at the medal pinned to his left breast pocket. It was an oval silver badge with a steel helmet at the top and below that were crossed swords, rimmed with oak leaves.

"It's a medal for having been wounded," he said when he found me staring at him.

"And having survived it all," he said to my mother. "That's a hell of a lot better than having met a hero's death, killed for Führer and Fatherland."

"I wished they'd shut up," he said, pointing to a group of Hitler Youth in the next compartment. They were singing *Lili Marleen*, the popular soldiers' song we always heard on the radio. But they weren't singing it as well as Lale Andersen did. She was my favorite singer. I loved her deep voice….

The Oder was the widest river I had ever seen. My mother and I sat on a big stone near the bridge and waited for my father. Tanks and big guns kept crossing the bridge; a group of boys in rags threw stones at them.

"Must be Polish," my mother said.

Under the bridge, a tug boat came into view; then long, flat barges loaded to the brim with coal. I had counted eight of them by the time my father appeared at the center of the bridge. He waved his arms wildly, and we ran up to meet him. The boys threw stones at us.

My father couldn't walk very well. He took off his boots. His feet were wrapped in bandages, and he took those off, too. His feet were dark brown.

"Iodine," he said, "The doctor put both of my feet into a pail of it, and that's only the end of the story. Wait till you hear the beginning."

He stretched his feet into the waters of the river.

"There is this lieutenant, you see, who runs our detonator class. One day, he asked whether anyone present could play the piano. I raised my hand. 'Good,' he said, 'you can go to the railroad station and help carry my piano. It'll come with the morning express. I want it in my house by noon.' But he didn't like the way we did it, using the army van. 'I said *carry* my piano,' he yelled. Are you too tender-footed to walk? I'll teach you to walk!' And I've been carrying the meals up to the crew on that mountain once a day ever since, and that's a three mile trip one way. Good for lots of blisters if the boots don't fit. And the doctor cures everything with iodine."

My mother burst into tears and my father hugged her.

"Maybe it won't be so bad," he said. "I might even be put to work in Berlin, defusing unexploded bombs."

That remark made my mother cry all the more.

"There, there," my father said, stroking her silky hair. "You should see how they treat the other guys! Some of them are said to be deserters, others are officers 'in disgrace.' They make them walk around the yard with a sign 'We will redeem our guilt with our blood!' And they are scheduled to be 'mine sweepers,' which means marching through minefields in front of everyone else, but the SS will escort them from behind and be ready, they say, to shoot anyone who might have the inclination to bolt."

"At least the war in the east is over," my mother said with a sigh.

A loud wail behind us made us turn our heads. There was that woman, all dressed in black, just a few meters away from us. She stood in the water up to her knees, her arms stretched out wide. She was staring at us as she spoke:

"I saw the seven angels which stood before God; and to them were given seven trumpets.

The first angel sounded, and there followed hail and fire mingled with blood, and they were cast upon the earth; and the third part of trees was burnt up, and all green grass was burnt up.

And the second angel sounded, and as it were a great mountain burning with fire was cast into the sea: and the third part of the sea became blood; and the third part of the creatures which were in the sea, and had life, died; and the third part of the ships were destroyed.

And the third angel sounded, and there fell a great star from heaven, burning as it were a lamp, and it fell upon the third part of the rivers and upon the fountains of waters; and many men died of the waters, because they were made bitter.

And the fourth angel sounded, and the third part of the sun was smitten, and the third part of the moon, and the third part of the stars; so as the third part of them was darkened, and the day shone not for a third part of it, and the night likewise.

And I beheld and heard an angel flying through the midst of heaven, saying with a loud voice, Woe, woe, woe to the inhabitors of the earth by reason of the other voices of the trumpet of the three angels, which are yet to sound!"

Deutschland Erwache!
Jeder deutsche Mann kann sich zur
Aufnahme in die Leibstandarte
SS "Adolf Hitler" melden.
Auskunft erteilt jede Polizei-Station.

Langewiesche-Brandt, Ebenhausen near München, Germany

Hitler's very own: A member of the SS in his black uniform. The SS = Schutzstaffel (Security Squadron) was founded in 1933. Long before it took on its murderous activities, the original 120-man squad focused on the Führer's personal protection and on ceremonial duties. The caption says:

Germany Wake Up!
Every German Man Can Now Volunteer for Admission to the SS Lifeguard Squadron 'Adolf Hitler.' Details Are Available at Every Police Station.

11. CEMETERY PLANTS
[June-December 1941]

Let me tell you about life in Berlin after we returned from saying good-bye to my father. I remember how annoyed Mr. Eisler was about my long and unexcused absence. Naturally, he promised to note that fact in my grade report. In retrospect, that was a small price to pay. Although we didn't know it at the time, we were not to see my father again for fully five years. As for Mr. Eisler, he urged me in no uncertain terms to catch up with the bulletin board and to learn all I could about the "glorious conquest of Crete by our brave paratroopers." Or else. I did my best, but I needn't have. As it turned out, Mr. Eisler forgot to examine me about Greece, because new events during the first week of summer turned everyone's attention to something else entirely. One Monday morning in June, our bulletin board read like this:

1941

May 20   German parachutists conquer Greek island of Crete

June 22   German Armed Forces launch Operation Barbarossa:

3 million men enter the Soviet Union along a 3,200 kilometer front, reaching from the Arctic to the Black Sea

Army Group North under Field Marshal Wilhelm Ritter von Leeb is to secure the Baltic coast and capture Leningrad

Army Group Center under Field Marshal Fedor von Bock is to take Smolensk and Moscow

Army Group South under General Gerd von Rundstedt is to conquer the Ukraine and Caucasus

---

Given the non-aggression pact with our friend Russia, the latest entries made no sense, but Mr. Eisler explained.

"It is a preemptive strike," he said. "That means the Russians were about to attack *us*, but the Führer spoiled their surprise by attacking first. Once again, the British tried to make others fight for them. For weeks, those Jewish Anglo-Saxon warmongers have goaded the Russians into concentrating lots and lots of troops on their western borders. This forced the Führer to establish a counterforce by withdrawing troops from France, where they might have been used to fight the British."

We got the point, but my thoughts were elsewhere. I thought of my father and our last meeting with him by the banks of the Oder.

"At least the war in the east is over," my mother had said.

******

We didn't know it then, but by the time our school closed for summer vacation, my father was already being marched through the minefields of the Ukraine, clearing the way for the regular troops. With SS guards right behind him, he certainly couldn't have expected ever to see us again. Meanwhile, Dieter and I were once again inseparable, trying to have fun. When it rained, which was often, we met on our balcony and studied Dieter's new *Max and Moritz* book, written and amply illustrated by Wilhelm Busch. It pictured the lives of two boys, about our age, who spent every waking minute playing pranks on people. Sadistic pranks it seems to me now! Once they came across an old widow whose livelihood depended on three egg-laying hens and a rooster. So Max and Moritz tied four pieces of bread to a single string and tossed it to the animals. Naturally, the chickens tried to eat the bread, but ended up gagging on the string and died miserably tied to each other, wings flapping desperately.

Poor widow Bolte, the sequel said, had no choice but to make the best of a bad situation. She decided to get at least something to eat for herself and her little white Pomeranian who had become the only companion in her lonely life. But while she was in the cellar, Max and Moritz climbed on the roof and, like anglers in a boat, managed to pull up all four roasts, right through the chimney, with a fishing rod. When Mrs. Bolte reappeared, her roasting pan was empty and her dog looked at her with big eyes. There she lost it and beat the poor dog to within an inch of his life! Up on the roof, Max and Moritz laughed and laughed.

And then there was tailor Bock who used to walk across a wooden footbridge every day. Max and Moritz sabotaged the bridge with a saw and the old man fell into the icy water and became dreadfully ill. That story brought us to teacher Lampel, who loved to smoke the pipe. Max and Moritz filled it with gunpowder, which made it explode, destroying the teacher's house and giving him near-fatal burns.

Dieter and I were just about to study the story of widower Fritz (who was permanently robbed of sleep after he found his feather bed filled with giant bugs), when my mother discovered us. She was very angry.

"There is enough cruelty in this world! I don't want you to read this dreadful book," she said. "Give it to me; it goes right into the kitchen stove."

"But you told me it is wrong to burn books," I said and that made my mother angrier still. I think that was the first and only time she took the carpet beater to teach me a lesson. But it didn't hurt, because, unlike Mr. Eisler, she hadn't made me pull down my pants. In any case, all was forgotten soon and by nighttime we were friends again.

I lay in bed, thinking of my father. I figured he wouldn't have liked the *Max and Moritz* book either. He had always insisted on being kind to older people, teaching me to offer my seat to them in the trolley car or the underground, just as he did himself. He also had always tipped his hat when passing them in the street, but I rarely wore a hat and only had to smile and say 'hello.'

******

On sunny days that summer, Dieter and I traveled around town. Our mothers had said it was all right; we were old enough.

"Just take the streetcars or the buses," they had said, "and stay away from the S-Bahn and the U-Bahn for now."

That didn't make much sense to us. Did they imagine we would jump on the tracks and get electrocuted? Still, we complied, although there were times when we were sorely tempted to get somewhere fast via the rapid electric train, known as the S-Bahn. And we were equally eager to try our luck with the U-Bahn, the name of which, in my view, made no sense either, given that the underground had above-ground, elevated sections in some parts of town. In addition, restricting us to streetcars and buses hardly made us safe. Our mothers never knew what we learned from the other boys, like standing on the streetcar running board as it approached its next stop, jumping off early, and hitting the ground running. That was considered a very manly thing to do, but we ended up face down on the cobblestones more than once before we had perfected the procedure and in those instances the wheels rolling by our heads could look pretty scary.

Talking about things scary, one day, when Dieter and I were hanging out at the dairy store, we overheard people discussing an "aerial mine." It hit the place like an earthquake, they said. But they hadn't seen it themselves; they had just read about it in the paper. So Dieter and I decided to have a look. We knew how to get there. For 10 pfennigs we could pick up the Number Six at the corner, ride all the way to the Cologne Station, take the next trolley to the zoo, and we would be there. Not that we cared about the zoo, at least not on that day, but the bombed-out department store was right next door. We'd been there with our mothers.

The conductor yelled at us for trying to board at the rear, pointing to the sign at the door: "Exit only." He yelled at us again when we didn't have the right change, and pointed to the sign over the window: "Proper change only." But he didn't scare us because he looked funny. His face was pink with sunburn, but he had big white circles around his eyes, apparently where sunglasses had been.

"What's the matter with you?" he asked. "Don't they teach you to read anymore? Your teacher ought to call on the Yellow Uncle!"

We knew then that it was hopeless to ask for a book of ticket stubs for our games. The square in front of the Cologne Station was busier than usual. Trolleys and buses came from all directions, honking horns and ringing bells and snaking their way through crowds of shoppers in the open-air market. They sold carrots and cabbages, sweaters and socks, herrings and hotdogs, and flowers, flowers, everywhere. All the vendors yelled at the top of their lungs, trying to catch the attention of every passer-by.

We had trouble finding the trolley to the zoo, because we were lost in a sea of benches and people, umbrellas and multicolored tents. When we got to the Number Nine, the driver yelled at us, too.

"Enter at the *middle*, you raving idiots! Can't you read?"

He closed the front door right in the face of an old lady who had wanted to get out.

"Jesus Christ, what took you so long making up your mind?" he asked. "Want me to be stuck here all day? If you can't walk, why don't you stay home?"

He jerked the trolley and sent everyone reaching for the leather straps.

The conductor was red in the face, not from the sun though, and *he* yelled at us, too, for not having bought tokens.

"This trolley takes tokens only. Says so right in front, can't you read? Stupid idiots! Your mothers ought to spank your butts raw."

"And what are *you* complaining about, you old witch?" he said, elbowing his way toward the white-haired lady at the front door.

"Missed your exit, did you? Makes my heart bleed! But let me tell you: You had your chance, what are you trying to do? Hold up the whole enterprise till sunset? Why don't you find a nice cozy spot in the cemetery where things aren't so hectic? You can feed the cemetery plants—from below!"

The people in the car laughed. But by then I was scared. I thought of my grandmother and wished we had stayed home. And I thought of all the things my father had said about being polite and kind.

******

The bombed-out department store looked like nothing we'd ever seen. The whole front was gone, and we could see all the floors at the same time. The building was like a giant's doll house, blue walls above green walls above pink. We saw the shoe department on the second floor, and the X-ray machine where we always looked at our toes. It was swaying in the wind, ready to tumble down momentarily. The toys were right above, some of the display cases dangled on the edge. There was a lot of rubble on the top floor, and it hid everything that might have been there before. More rubble lay on the sidewalk, and a torn poster that said: "Hush! The enemy listens in." A dog kept sniffing around our legs and a policeman told us to move on.

"It's the glass roof, that's what did it," one of the workmen said, "reflects the moonlight. How could the pilots miss seeing it?"

On the way back, we ran into the most amazing thing. One of the major avenues, the Charlottenburger Chaussee, had been completely covered with camouflage netting, reaching from tall poles on one side of the street to similar poles on the other. The netting contained thousands of fake fir trees, way above our heads; we figured it was done to confuse enemy airplanes, just like the netting over gooseberry bushes is designed to keep away birds.

And we were right. As our trolley passed the Column of Victory at the Tiergarten, we noticed even more of this foolishness: the golden goddess at its top had been painted a dull brown. "To keep enemy pilots from navigating by famous landmarks," a woman said when she saw us staring at the scene.

"You should go and look at the lakes at Staaken," she added. "They've been completely covered with wooden rafts that look like houses from the air. On one lake, they are even building decoys of all sorts of well-known government buildings! It's fun to watch."

******

When we got home, someone was pasting a new sign on the phone booth next to the trolley station. "FOR ARYANS ONLY!" it said. Across the street, workmen were tending to the little park, tearing out perfectly good pansies and replacing them with geranium plants. They also put notices on all the benches: NOT FOR JEWS. And the Wanselow kids were playing "Crete" in the middle of the street. They had little canisters, which shot objects into the air like a rocket. Each one went right up to the level of the third floor, unfolded a green parachute, and gently floated to earth, like our hero soldiers who had taken Crete.

Sometimes the Wanselows aimed their canisters right at old Mr. Joseph who was dozing in front of the pub, dressed in his usual Viking costume with a cap that had horns on the top. He always woke up with a start, and the Wanselows howled with laughter. They tried to shoot Dieter

akg-images, London, United Kingdom

and me, too, but we made it into the hallway before they could set their aim.

I went back down with my mother to help her queue for food. She stood in line at Meyer's vegetable store around the corner; they had a new shipment of potatoes and fresh fruit. I stood outside the bakery next to the pub and waited for the daily quota of bread. It was made of rye and there were crisp buns made of wheat. On this day, the lines were short, and I reached the door in a few minutes. I read the sign above the handle.

"Jews and Foreign Workers will be served only after all others," it said. "By order of the Municipal Government, City of Berlin." Unlike all the other signs I had seen that day, this one was made out in the old German Sütterlin script.

******

Later that summer, we went back to school and I found myself with a new teacher. His name was Mr. Barzel and, just like Mr. Eisler, he wore the Party badge in his lapel. He didn't have a large map, but he did have a bulletin board, which was empty when we arrived. In fact, it stayed empty for the rest of the year. But Mr. Barzel had lots of pictures on the wall where the map should have been. There was a snapshot of the *Graf Spee* being scuttled in the South Atlantic. And there were photographs of famous soldiers. I saw General Heinz Guderian, Field Marshal Walther von Reichenau, and General Erich von Manstein—all heroes of the Russian front, he said.

Beyond that, we didn't hear a word about the war at all. Mr. Barzel was much more interested in the *history of art*. Before it was time to go home for Christmas, he had taken us to Egypt, as far back as 4,000 B.C., then to Greece (1,000 to 200 B.C.), to Rome (200 B.C. to 500 A.D.) and on to Byzantium (500 to 1,000 A.D.). We had learned to draw pictures of Egyptian burial chambers and pyramids and temples. We had drawn Greek columns—Corinthian, Doric, and Ionic—and Greek vases and crosscuts and ground-plans of basilicas and cathedrals built over the course of a thousand years. I liked Constantine's Basilica the best.

Yet I missed the news. The Street Warden had come and exchanged our radio for the People's Receiver. Ordinarily, it cost 35 Reichsmark, but we got it for nothing. So we couldn't listen to the BBC the way my parents and I had done underneath the featherbed cover. But Dieter was still with Mr. Eisler and I borrowed his notes when school let out for Christmas. He had copied only a piece of the bulletin board, like this:

1941

September 19	German forces take Kiev; capture or kill 665,000 enemy soldiers
December 7	Japan attacks Pear Harbor, Hawaii; destroys 6 U.S. battleships, 188 aircraft, and 2,000 men
December 11	Germany and Italy, as allies of Japan, declare war on the United States

---

I also copied a few additional facts that Dieter had gleaned from Mr. Eisler, crucial stuff, all of it: New York had 7.89 million people, Chicago 3.62 million, and Los Angeles 1.97 million. Jointly, the Mississippi and Missouri Rivers were 6,418 kilometers long. Mount Whitney was 4,418 meters tall.

Just about then, around Christmas time, the Street Warden put up signs at the entrances to air raid shelters, saying "Jews and Foreign Workers Not Allowed."

"These people shouldn't mix excessively with the German race," the Street Warden said. He reminded us of a January 1, 1941 decree that all Jewish men had to add *Israel* and all Jewish women had to add *Sara* to their ID card names. "Together with the yellow star, that will make them much easier to spot," he said. "And look for the big letters the foreign workers have on their backs. You can't miss them," he added.

"That's so cruel!" Aunt Martel said to my mother. "You realize we now have 300,000 foreign workers in Berlin? I've seen the paperwork; they work in all the factories: at Siemens, Telefunken, and Borsig; at DMW [Deutsche Waffen und Munition = German Weapons and Munitions], at

Auto-Union and Dornier, you name it. They build locomotives, mortars, tanks, airplanes; yet are considered expendable, it seems! It's cruel as well as insane."

But she didn't say it out loud; as usual, the sisters were whispering and giving each other that knowing look. But Dieter and I had already noted foreign workers everywhere. The Street Warden was right; they were easy to spot by the large letters painted on the back of their jackets. B stood for Belgium, F for France, H for Holland, P for Poland, and, most recently, R for Russia.

We had also seen the consequences of the new September decrees: Jews aged 6 and above were made to wear a big yellow star on their clothes, the Star of David, "on a black background, affixed to the upper part of clothing," which made them conspicuous as well. Aunt Martel said they had special ration cards, too, stamped with a J. These cards were only good for a limited list of items and certain hours of the week, usually Fridays late.

On one such Friday, when the streets were obviously teeming with foreigners and Jews, I went shopping with my mother. Suddenly, out of the side of my eye, I saw something falling from a window across the street. People screamed. I heard a thud. She didn't move. She wore a long, white nightgown, and I saw her white hair turn slowly red and then her gown.

My mother grabbed me and took me home. I was scared and it felt as if my heart wanted to come out of my throat. In my bed in the dark, I heard red fire trucks hose down red cobblestones. I heard Mrs. Meyer whisper:

"You just watch it, the elderly will be next. They were going to take her to Moabit, you know." And I heard the voice of the streetcar conductor: "Cemetery plants ... cemetery plants ... cemetery plants."

An illustration from Wilhelm Busch, *Max and Moritz,* a children's book glorifying cruelty directed against the old and weak.

Otto Moravec, Vienna, Austria

12. MAGICIANS
[January-July 1942]

It was the last day of 1941. That's when my mother took me to my grandmother's place to celebrate New Year's Eve. All we had to do was walk down to the canal, feed the gulls, follow the footpath along the canal for a kilometer or so to the Glogau Bridge, and find Number 33 on the other side. Aunt Martel and Aunt Lotte were there, too, having just returned from the year-end service at the Martha Church down the street, and we all got quickly busy preparing for the New Year.

My grandmother put up colorful streamers and balloons, but she let me hand out the funny-looking pointed hats. Aunt Lotte took a moment to comb out the fringes of the rug, then spread out the Tarot cards on the living room table so she could read our futures. Aunt Martel collected a bunch of lead soldiers from the chest of drawers in her bedroom—the bottom drawer to be exact—to pursue the same goal in the traditional way. Near the hour of midnight, we would melt the soldiers and then each of us would pour a bit of melted lead into a pot of cold water where it would instantly freeze into a shape from which our future could be known. Clearly, it was just a matter of logic to interpret the meaning of those little chunks of lead. I had done it before. I would do it again.

My mother called me into the kitchen to help her with the doughnuts. She had already made the dough and, after I had sprinkled the table with a generous amount of flour, she rolled out the dough in the form of a large square. I then cut pieces from it, spooned a heap of raspberry jelly onto the center of each, and rolled my little pieces into balls. In the meantime, my mother brought a pot full of oil to a boil and we carefully dropped the jelly-filled balls into it, a few at a time. Eventually, I gave each of them a dusting of confectionary sugar and our feast was ready to be served!

While my grandmother was heating the cider and my mother helped Aunt Lotte with the Tarot cards, I retrieved my American Indian book from Aunt Martel's chest of drawers. I had left it there the last time we were there, along with all kinds of accessories. I loved Karl May and the stories he told about the Wild West. And I always pictured myself as Old Shatterhand, having adventure after adventure, and smoking the peace pipe with Winnetou, the famous Apache Indian chief. As I learned many years later, my adoration of Karl May was shared by many, including Kaiser Wilhelm II, Albert Einstein, Franz Kafka, Albert Schweitzer, and even Adolf Hitler who urged his troops to emulate the noble warriors depicted by May. Just imagine, those books sold over 100 million copies in the German-speaking world alone, making May (1842-1912) perhaps the most popular author in

German history—and all that despite the fact that he was a con man, writing his books in jail, while claiming to recount his own experiences in American places he had never seen. Somehow he made Winnetou a German national hero! But I digress.

On that New Year's Eve long ago, holding Karl May in my hands, I thought of abandoning my grandmother's pointed hat in favor of my Indian headdress. But I decided against it. For one thing, my colored chicken feathers were hardly worthy of the noble Winnetou whose outfit derived from the mighty eagle. More importantly, I had been warned not to wear Indian outfits anymore. Dieter and I had often played cowboys and Indians in the street, dressing up in turquoise jewelry and pretending to drink firewater, but the Street Warden had told us in no uncertain terms to stop all that whooping and dancing. He had even threatened us with jail.

"For one thing, we are at war with America," he had said. "In addition, we shouldn't glorify the non-Aryan races."

Still, I liked my Karl May. "His book is filled with pearls of wisdom," my mother had said, and I had marked one of them, right there on page 252:

"No soul ever came to earth unless it was first a spirit in heaven.

No spirit ever rose to heaven unless it was first a soul on earth."

When I showed the passage to my mother once again on that New Year's Eve, she said the strangest thing:

"Hansel," she said, "Heaven is going to have a precious gift for us this year. In a couple of months from now, you are going to have a little brother or sister! Then you'll have a playmate right in the family!"

What a surprise that was! To be honest, I didn't like the idea at all and I put it right out of my mind in any case, because it was time to pour out the lead. As far as I could see, my personal lead sculpture looked just like me, with a pair of skates underneath. I would certainly get a pair of skates pretty soon, I figured, just like the one I had seen at the department store.

******

Back in school that January, it was the fifth grade by then, Mr. Barzel focused our attention on *chemistry* and noted, with impressive logic, that all elements can be divided into two non-overlapping groups, metals and non-metals.

"Three quarters of all elements are metals," he said, "and the most important one of these is iron, which makes up precisely 4.7 percent of the earth's crust."

He also told us about iron ore and coke and blast furnaces and the fact that Germany had had 175 of them at the beginning of the war. We drew a picture of a blast furnace, in great detail, just as we had of Egyptian pyramids and Christian churches some time ago, and we wrote formulas for all the processes occurring inside such a furnace.

"At 1,200 degrees Celsius," Mr. Barzel said, "$CO_2 + C$ becomes 2 CO, while $Fe_2O_3 + 3$ CO produce 2 Fe + 3 CO_2."

But that was just the beginning of a long story. We also learned about copper, mostly found in the Rocky Mountains of the United States, in Chile, in the Congolese province of Katanga, and in Japan.

"We have some of it, too, right here in Mansfeld," Mr. Barzel said, "where it occurs in the form of $CuFeS_2$ and Cu_2S. But the Mansfeld mines do not produce enough copper to carry on the war, which is why you will see a lot of changes in the next few weeks. Many church bells will be dismantled and melted down. And so will all those copper tubs in the attics of your homes. And even statues will have to go."

He was right. In the park near our house, I saw them take down the statue of Bismarck, using a large crane, and they took that of General von Moltke as well.

By the time we got to lead (melting point a mere 327 degrees Celsius), I thought of New Year's Eve and the Gift from Heaven we were about to receive. And receive it we did. I had to stay with my grandmother and Aunt Martel for a while, which I didn't like at all because all my possessions were under my bed at home, and then my brother came home. I knew instantly that life would never be the same and I wrote to my father, telling him that Helmut was much too small and, therefore, quite useless as a playmate.

My father wrote back right away and promised to investigate, as soon as the war was over. I saved his letter in my little suitcase with all the other important documents of mine, but my mother wouldn't let me keep his stamp for my collection. She cut it from the envelope, put it in a bowl of warm water, and a miracle happened. The paper in back came off, but the cancellation mark in front came off, too. I had never seen *that* before, and I had been soaking a lot of stamps in my time.

"Surprised, aren't you?" she smiled. "These are special stamps for mail going to the eastern front. We can have only one stamp a month, and I need several of them to send Vati some cookies and a sweater. When we mail something, we put glue on the back, and a thin coat of soap over the top. The soap is invisible and if you do it right, the cancellation mark washes off along with it. Thus, we can be like magicians!"

******

This must have been the year for magic. Even Mr. Barzel was preoccupied with turning one thing into something else.

"From now on," he said one morning, "we'll spend one day a week fighting Wastefulness. And we will turn Wastefulness into crucial Raw Material, and Raw Material, in turn, into Victory for our fatherland!"

He took out a large map of the world and told us about the Anglo-American enemies. They were cutting off the sea lanes, he said, through which flow the iron and copper and lead our soldiers need to do their job. And through which flow the bananas and chocolate bars and oranges all children crave, he added.

And every Wednesday thereafter, dispatched by the bigger boys with the swastika armbands, we entered every house, climbed every last step, and knocked on every door in our streets. And out of the portals of every house emerged armies of little boys that carried, bit by bit, mountains of copper and iron, of textiles and paper, of bones and potato peels.

"All of these bits and pieces," Mr. Barzel explained, "the copper penny from the days of Frederick the Great, the old abandoned hammer and claw, the ragged coat, the box of grandma's letters, the pork chop bones, the potato peels—all of these will turn into ships and planes, new uniforms and soap, and even food!"

None of this made any sense to me, but I certainly wasn't about to let Mr. Barzel know that. In fact, as he droned on about the Raw Material Campaign, my mind drifted to more important things. I was looking out the windows across the room, as inconspicuously as possible, of course, and I was mentally turning the pages in my *Book of Clouds*, trying to identify the transparent clouds that were just then producing a stunning halo effect around the afternoon sun. Nobody else seemed to be aware of it and just when I had found the answer—*cirrostratus fibratus*—Mr. Barzel made us stand and sing *Deutschland Über Alles* [Germany Above All] and *Die Fahne Hoch* [The Flag Held High]. I was glad he didn't watch too closely because I didn't know the words. I merely moved my lips as in a pantomime, just as I did when my mother took me to church and everyone starting singing hymns.

******

One Wednesday, though, was different from all the others. It all started when I ran into Mr. Joseph on my way to the collection point, which was a big truck parked around the corner and across from Mr. Meyer's vegetable store. Mr. Joseph, as was his custom, was sitting on the sidewalk in front of the pub, holding a bottle of *Berliner Kindl* beer in one hand, while using his other hand to adjust his Viking cap with the horns on top.

"Collecting newspapers are you, kid?" he said. "I can give you a truckload of them. Come and see me at my place in an hour or so!"

"Thank you, sir. I'll be there," I said and when I got there, I was in for a big surprise.

He had a small apartment in our rear house, right on the ground floor, which we called *parterre*, and one of his little rooms was completely filled with dozens and dozens of bundles of newspapers! I didn't even try to count them; there were so many of them that it was almost impossible even to enter the room.

"There must be about twenty-five years' worth of news for you," he said in a rather matter-of-fact way, as if this sort of collection was commonplace. "They are all yours. Carry them off! It's time I made some room for myself."

And carry them off I did, some that Wednesday, more on the next two days after school, and all the rest on Saturday and Sunday as well. Mr. Joseph was pleased and so was I. Not only did I earn precious "honor points" at the collection truck, but I also made a crucial discovery: Buried within Mr. Joseph's mountain of papers, I uncovered fascinating stories about the past, stories that I had never encountered before, and many of which I quickly confiscated for my own purposes.

Every once in a while, I made a trip not to the collection truck, but to our apartment in the front house, where I deposited selected evidence under my bed for further inspection at night. My mother never noticed a thing; she was always busy with Helmut—changing his diapers and feeding him and cradling him and singing to him as she had once to me—but my very best friend Ludwig, which is what I had named my new canary, didn't miss a thing. He sat in his cage under the cuckoo clock, right next to my good old teddy bear, and he never failed to give me the attention I deserved.

But despite my occasional fits of jealousy, I can hardly have been an unhappy child in those days. In fact, I remember being very happy and excited about all the things I learned when I examined my newspaper hoard at night! The oldest paper I had kept was dated June 5, 1932. The front page talked about Franz von Papen who, it seems, was chancellor at the time. Inside, I found large ads by all sorts of political groups. One was called *Stahlhelm* [Steel Helmet] and it urged veterans of the World War to remember their "front-line experiences" and honor "German blood and soil" by fighting to restore the monarchy. I assumed they wanted the Kaiser to come back, just as my grandmother did.

Another page was "paid for by the Communist Party of Germany." The writer made fun of Hitler's "interminable speechifying, wild gesticulations, foaming at the mouth, shifty staring eyes, and monstrous fantasies." He also called him a "hoodlum representing the cesspool of humanity." And he urged everyone to buy copies of the *Rote Fahne* [Red Flag]. Wow! I was quite aware of the fact that my teachers wouldn't have liked that!

The next paper I had kept was dated December 6, 1932. I liked the date, because it was St. Nicholas Day, which is the day on which all German children discover how they will fare on

Langewiesche-Brandt, Ebenhausen near München, Germany

Christmas Eve. When going to bed on December 5, one puts a large red Santa Claus boot next to one's bed; mine was made of soft cloth and had white fleece inside. The next morning when they wake up, all the *good* children find their boots filled with cookies and other gifts. This is a sure sign that they will get mountains of toys and such on Christmas Eve. All the *bad* children, however, find their boots filled with coal or just plain empty, perhaps even with a Yellow Uncle sticking out of it. That is a sure sign that they will be punished by getting nothing for Christmas at all!

But that never happened to me. My mother said that it was a cruel thing to do, sticking a rod into the boot. In any case, that paper talked of a still different chancellor, Kurt von Schleicher. I had never heard of him. And the paper was filled with interesting notices, such as these:

The **KPD** [Communist Party of Germany] said: "Voters Decide: Hitler Dictatorship or Dictatorship of the Proletariat?"

The **Federation of Jewish Veterans** said: "Christian and Jewish heroes have fought together and are resting together in foreign soil. 12,000 Jews died in the war, but now blind hatred does not stop even before the graves of the dead. German women, don't allow them to make a mockery of the pain of Jewish mothers."

And right next to a most unflattering cartoon of Dr. Goebbels, the **Bavarian People's Party** said: "According to the Nazi leader Dr. Goebbels, 'the Nordic race represents the original and purest strain of humanity.' Bavarian kinsmen, have a look at this Nordic man! Then give this Superman and all his brown followers a clear Bavarian answer!"

I was tempted to cut out the Goebbels picture and paste it on the Goebbels Snout in our living room, but then my mother would have known. So I did the next best thing and pasted it on the flyer about the People's Receiver that the Street Warden had left with us. It turned out to be a beautiful work of art, I thought, and stored it under my bed as well. (Look at the previous page!)

I also found old issues of our current paper, the *Völkischer Beobachter* [People's Observer], published by the **National Socialist German Workers Party**. They were equally interesting. I selected crucial pages and put them in chronological order. Then I copied front-page summaries to my notepad to make everything look just like Mr. Eisler's bulletin board. I made one page for 1933 and a second one for 1934:

1933

January 30   President Hindenburg asks Hitler to become chancellor

Hitler swears oath of allegiance to Weimar Constitution

February 27   The Reichstag in Flames! Torched by Communists!

That's how the whole country would look if the Communists and their Social Democratic allies came to power even for a few months!

A cry of anguish goes through Germany:
Crush Communism! Smash Social Democracy!

February 28   Marinus van der Lubbe, Dutch Communist, arrested in Reichstag fire

March 5   Reichstag elections a Hitler triumph!

The distribution of the 648 seats:

National Socialists/Nationalists 341 = 52.6%

Social Democrats 118

Centrists/Bavarian People's Party 91

Communists 31

Others 67

March 24	Reichstag meets in Garnisonskirche, Potsdam cathedral
	With Communists absent and Social Democrats voting against it, two-thirds majority passes Empowerment Act, giving Hitler unlimited legislative powers
May 2	Trade unions outlawed; Social Democratic union leaders arrested
May 10	Communist Party of Germany outlawed!
	Social Democratic faction in Reichstag unanimously expresses confidence in Hitler, joins him in singing Horst Wessel song to unending applause and cheers.
	Jubilation in streets, SA bands march with drums and trumpets, flags held high, swords raised in salute, torchlight parades and fireworks at night
June 15	Social Democratic Party of Germany outlawed!
	Stahlhelm group merged with SA!
October 13	Reichstag dissolved! Führer holds all legislative and executive powers!
	National Socialist German Workers Party is sole legal party
1934	
June 30	Seven Storm Troop Leaders Shot! Response to Coup Attempt!
	By order of Adolf Hitler, the supreme conscience of the German people.
	Ernst Röhm, SA leader, personally arrested by Hitler in Munich, a suicide
	Other traitors killed include General Kurt von Schleicher, the Führer's predecessor as Chancellor, while resisting arrest, and Heinrich Klausener, chief of Catholic Action
	Viktor Lutze, new Storm Troop Chief of Staff, urges blind obedience, unquestioning discipline, exemplary behavior, end of moral debauchery
August 2	President Paul von Hindenburg dies at 86.
	Hitler takes Presidency!

I put my notepad under my bed, but not before carefully folding up a leaflet and hiding it inside. Issued on May 10, 1933 by the Communist Party of Germany, it condemned that day's actions of the Social Democrats as "a total betrayal of millions of followers." It equally condemned Adolf Hitler for having "betrayed the constitution and put an end to civil liberties." Examples included

- Nazi raiding parties to arrest left-wing deputies, as well as numerous literary figures, doctors, lawyers, and government officials
- Emergency decrees abolishing freedom of speech and the confidentiality of mail and telephone, while giving police unrestricted right of access to search, confiscate, arrest

Concluded the leaflet:

"As brown-shirt robbers and murderers act as police, enjoying the full panoply of state power, we can look forward to living in a world in which wild mobs break into our homes at night and drag defenseless victims to torture chambers."

That scared me and I regressed as usual, turning to Ludwig and Teddy to help me fall asleep. My mother came in, too, to say good night, and said she was proud of me for working so long and hard every evening. But I didn't tell her what kind of homework I had just done.

******

On the next day, Mr. Barzel had a surprise. He gave me an award for having collected more newspapers than any other boy in our school! I was the best by far among 851. My reward was a book, entitled *Cabin Boy Werner Franz*. It told the story of the Hindenburg airship that had gone up like giant torch while trying to land at Lakehurst, New Jersey, in May of 1937.

"I know you like history," Mr. Barzel said, pointing to my prize. "You'll find it interesting, and in more ways than one. The zeppelin was a wonderful German invention and it's fun to learn how it worked. But one cannot help but wonder: Did the Americans sabotage it?"

I hardly knew the answer and focused on the book's title instead. "Werner" and "Franz," I thought, were common first names; could "Franz" be a last name as well?

I asked Dieter after school, but he didn't know. He asked me to join him at the corner when we got home. I knew what he meant. Even though it was summer, he was collecting money for Mr. Eisler's winter campaign. In fact, after school each day, every corner, every trolley stop, every subway station in the 19th district was secured by Mr. Eisler's army of little boys. They shook their red and white collection boxes at every passerby.

"Won't you give for the Winter Auxiliary? Your pennies mean sweaters and gloves for the brave men on the eastern front!"

And they rewarded those who gave money with little wooden figures out of fairy tales, like Hansel and Gretel or Puss'n Boots.

While Dieter was shaking his box, I took a look at the poster column across the street. Such columns stood all over town—at street corners, at subway stations, in the middle of market squares.

They carried important announcements by the government or the latest news about the war or even an occasional commercial ad. Like the others, this column was a giant cylinder, 1 meter in diameter and 3 meters high, which, I figured, provided space for 1 times pi = 3.14159 meters (the circumference at the base) times 3 meters (the column height), or well over 9 meters squared. Yet most of that space was wasted on that day. I found only three items pasted to the column. One was a government order, dated February 10, which commanded all Jews to turn in luxury items, to wit bicycles, electric stoves, gramophones, hand mirrors, radios, and typewriters. And an April addendum banned Jews from using public transport. Then there was a news report, dated June 7, which told of the siege of Sevastopol, the Crimean fortress about to be captured with the help of our Dora gun, the world's largest mortar. And another report, dated June 22, told of the fall of Tobruk, Libya, to General Erwin Rommel's Africa Corps. There were 25,000 prisoners, it said, and Suez was next!

I wanted more news than that. So I persuaded Dieter to let me come to his place to listen to the real radio while his parents were still at the vegetable store. It was tuned to Radio Germany when we got there. Wilhelm Furtwängler was directing a concert in Nuremberg, Beethoven's Ninth Symphony, they said. We quickly found the BBC and listened to a report on the war in the air.

"In accordance with the Area Bombing Directive issued in February," the announcer said, "the Royal Air Force is now authorized to bomb industrial, military, and residential targets indiscriminately. And slowly, but surely, it is gaining mastery of the air. In light of diminishing German air defenses, the RAF carried out major attacks on Lübeck in late March….On May 5, during a raid on Kiel, RAF planes achieved a direct hit on the Battleship *Tirpitz*, while docked in the harbor. On May 30, some 5,000 Avro Lancaster and Halifax bombers rained loads of aerial mines and incendiaries on Cologne. Similar raids followed on Essen on June 1 and on Bremen on June 18…."

******

That scary news inspired us to follow our teachers' advice and use our summer vacation productively by "turning thoughtlessness into discipline!" As instructed on our last day of school, we walked the streets at night making sure they stayed *dark*. We wore green phosphorescent buttons on our lapels and handed out more to passers-by so we could all see each other on cloudy nights. And we roamed the streets searching for thoughtlessness: Light from a window, a match lighting a cigarette, a flashlight walking across the street—these were the enemies.

"If we keep this place absolutely dark, Berlin will be safe," Mr. Barzel had said. "Enemy pilots are lost without light. *So keep those light switches turned off!*"

"And our enemies are lost without spies," he had added. "You must unmask the spies. They listen everywhere," he had said, "in the subway, street, and bakery, even at home."

Like Mr. Eisler, Mr. Barzel welcomed any and all reports. There was one report, however, that he didn't get. One day, before they took the attic tub away, my mother tried to light the fire under the big copper tub in which she washed our clothes. But the coal would not light. Angrily, she used my wax-coated posters about the Fuel Thief, the whole pile of them. They worked like a charm.

But they had also been Mr. Barzel's favorites! During the summer, I was to put a poster on every door in our block: A picture of *Kohlenklau,* a fat little man dressed in black, with an evil eye, a stubbly beard and a moustache, tight-fistedly holding on to a sackful of stolen coal.

"His stomach growls, his sack is empty, and greedily he sniffs about…" the poster said.

Mr. Barzel never learned that the Fuel Thief, magically, had turned into fuel himself.

Da ist er wieder!

Sein Magen knurrt, sein Sack ist leer,
und gierig schnüffelt er umher.
An Ofen, Herd, an Hahn und Topf,
an Fenster, Tür und Schalterknopf
holt er mit List, was Ihr versaut.
Die Rüstung ist damit beklaut,
die auch Dein bißchen nötig hat,
das er jetzt sucht in Land und Stadt.

Fasst ihn!

In den Zeitungen steht mehr über ihn!

The Fuel Thief:
There he is again!
His stomach growls, his sack is empty,
and greedily he sniffs about.
From furnace and stove, from gas burner
and pot,
from window, door, and light switch,
he takes with cunning what you waste.
The armament industry is thereby robbed,
it needs even the little bit you have,
he looks for it now in countryside and city.
Catch him!
More about him in the newspapers!

Langewiesche-Brandt, Ebenhausen near München, Germany

13. THE GREIFER

[August 1942 – June 1943]

I have been thinking about the time when I learned the English language. It started near my 10th birthday, in 1942, when school reopened after summer vacation. That's when Mr. Barzel reminded us that we had successfully concluded our studies of German reading, writing, and grammar. He would now teach us a *new* language, Mr. Barzel said, and he promised to do so in no time at all.

"English is very easy to learn," Mr. Barzel said. "Using a dictionary and a grammar book, I myself learned it by reading a single edition of the London *Times*, every single word on every page. It took me a year, to tell the truth, but you can do no worse. When a year is up, you'll speak English, too."

He proceeded to hand each of us two books. The first of them was Langenscheidt's *Pocket Dictionary of the English and German Languages*, revised by Prof. Edmund Klatt. It was 1,061 pages long, but Mr. Barzel said we should focus on the first half that listed all the English words, along with their German equivalents.

"You will memorize one page a day," he said "and, by next summer, you will know two thirds of all the words."

The second book was much thinner. The *Summary of English Grammar* by Prof. Walter Fröhlich was a mere 97 pages long and was divided into parts that looked just like those in our German grammar book, ranging from articles and nouns to adjectives and irregular verbs and on to the tenses—present, past, future and even pluperfect.

To start things off, Mr. Barzel introduced us to a new version of the bulletin board, all written in English! By the time winter arrived, it looked like this and we could read every word:

1942

July 1	German Army conquers Sevastopol after 8-month siege, soon thereafter takes Voronezh and Rostov, advances into Caucasus
August 19	German forces reach Volga near Stalingrad
September 7	German forces occupy Novorossiysk
November 8	U.S forces under Lieutenant General Dwight Eisenhower land in French West Africa, Morocco, and Algeria

November 11	In response to U.S. moves, and at the request of Premier Marshal Henri Philippe Pétain and Vice Premier Admiral François Darlan of Vichy France, German and Italian forces occupy Southern France and Tunisia
November 19	Russian General Georgi Zhukov, in a North/South pincer move, attempts to trap German 6th Army at Stalingrad; the Führer forbids General Friedrich von Paulus to break out and retreat, orders Field Marshal Erich von Manstein to bring relief to encircled German troops

We were somewhat worried by the November events, but Mr. Barzel explained that temporary setbacks are inevitable in any war and should, in fact, be expected.

"One must not lose sight of the big picture," he said. "After all, German forces are holding a huge territory, reaching from the North Cape all the way to the Mediterranean Sea and Africa and from the Atlantic all the way to the Volga River and the mountains of the Caucasus."

Still, when I translated my notes for my mother—she had not been taught English in school—she was far from relieved. She had already read the same stories in the newspaper and she was crying.

"I just hope Vati isn't involved in this Stalingrad thing;" she said, "we haven't heard from him in weeks!"

Just then the door bell rang and Aunt Martel appeared. We all hugged and kissed, as we always did, and Aunt Martel promised me that she would stay overnight. I liked her to stay; we always had fun playing rummy till midnight, assuming, of course, that Helmut didn't steal the show.

"Been crying?" Aunt Martel said to my mother.

"I'm so worried about this Stalingrad thing," my mother said. "We haven't heard from Arthur in weeks, you know."

"And you wouldn't believe what happened today!" my mother continued. "We got a letter from Town Hall this morning. Our food and clothing rations will be cut, starting next month, they say, and you know why? Because we've been sending so many packages to Arthur, which is proof positive that we have more than we need! Also, they say, it's an insult to the Armed Forces, sending these packages, as if they didn't take care of their own! Oh, how I hate these people!"

"I'm not surprised," Aunt Martel said. "You'll hate them even more when you hear what I've to tell…. Later."

They looked at each other with that strange look I had learned to recognize and, sure enough,

Aunt Martel changed the subject by pulling a package from her bag, a gift for me. It was the watercolor box I had so admired in the store window last week, complete with three different brushes, ten colors, and six cardboard pieces showing faint outlines of scenes waiting to be painted. One of the designs featured a family of tigers in their natural environment; the others showed buffaloes and mountain goats, wolves and otters and deer.

I was elated, but, clearly, the gift was my clue to disappear. I knew from long experience that Aunt Martel always brought the most interesting news, but she was scared to death to relate it. Officially, she was still one of the confidential secretaries at the Customs Service, being so good at shorthand, fast typing, and such, but the Gestapo was running her office now and had moved her over to their headquarters at Prinz-Albrecht-Strasse 8, where she saw and filed and typed all sorts of super-secret reports. To hear about it, I just had to be patient and listen carefully from behind the kitchen door once the time was ripe.

"I better go and work on my vocabulary," I said, "but can we play rummy later?"

******

"Have you seen Herbert lately?" Aunt Martel said to my mother the moment I was out of sight.

"I see him sometimes," my mother said. "He's still strutting around in his SA uniform."

"Yes," Aunt Martel said, "but do you know what he really does at his fancy new office downtown? I found out; saw a report he wrote."

"You don't say!" my mother said. "A report he wrote?"

"Yes, indeed," Aunt Martel said and her voice became a whisper. "Ever since the big roundup of Jews last February, he's been a *Greifer* [grabber], in charge of catching Jews who've gone underground! Some of them manage to hide their identity and aren't wearing the star, you know. They rely on friends to feed them. They walk in circles all day at the zoo or some big park so that neighbors think they are just regular people who have gone to work….Herbert and his pals play detectives to flush them out!"

"Oh God!" my mother said with a sigh. "Oh my God! What does Liesel see in that man?"

"The sad thing is," Aunt Martel continued, still whispering, "until not so long ago, Jews could have gotten out of the country. All they had to do was make a tally of their assets for the Customs Service, hand over a big chunk of them to the government, and run."

Even I had heard about that. I had read an article in *Das Schwarze Korps* [The Black Corps], one of Mr. Joseph's newspapers. It had talked about the *Reichssicherheitshauptamt* [Reich Security Main Office] and its efforts, even in 1940, to "cleanse German soil" by urging Jews to emigrate.

"But that's easier said than done," my mother said. "What would we do in similar circumstances? Hope springs eternal! You know Mrs. Nussbaum, before she disappeared, she always said: 'How bad can things get? This is Germany, the country of poets and thinkers and great composers.' But that didn't help her any."

"Germany is also the country of great criminals," Aunt Martel said. "I'll tell you something because if I don't, I'll go insane, but, God oh God, keep it to yourself. They would *kill* me if they knew, literally *kill* me."

"You've heard of the Heydrich case, haven't you?" Aunt Martel continued. "Last May, the great Protector of Bohemia and Moravia was ambushed in Czechoslovakia and died soon thereafter. His SS pals gave him a big state funeral; you've read about it. What you don't know is what happened afterwards. The SS surrounded the village of Lidice, where it all happened, and executed every single man! Then they carried off all the others to the nearest KZ [concentration camp]. And *then* they leveled the entire village, made it disappear from the map! I saw the report."

My mother gasped.

"Just like the Romans with Carthage!" she said. (She had always been a history buff.)

"Precisely! And there is more!" Aunt Martel continued. "Last January, no other than Reinhard Heydrich had been in charge of a big conference at the Wannsee. That's where the SD has a guest house, you know. [SD = *Sicherheitsdienst* = Security Service] Heinrich Müller was there, the Gestapo Chief; so was Josef Bühler, he runs Poland now; and Rudolf Lange, he's in charge of Jewish transports when they get to the *Ostland* [Eastland, the German-occupied Baltic States]; and with them were a whole bunch of State Secretaries from the ministries. I filed the report."

"They wanted to figure out 'a final solution to the Jewish problem.' Years of harassment hadn't worked, emigration hadn't worked, even recent 'evacuations' to Poland and the Baltic provinces had been 'unsatisfactory.' Instead of haphazard measures, a *scientific* solution was needed, said the report. And you know what it is? Jews, along with Gypsies, the mentally retarded, the physically disabled, and other 'subhumans,' are to be done away with by *gassing* them! They've already made experiments with Zyklon-B, whatever that is. It's supposed to be an 'improvement' on the euthanasia hospitals!"

There was the longest silence. I thought of my gas mask. And of all the scary things our teachers had told us about choking to death for lack of oxygen. I felt my heart pound and tears well up. I bit my tongue lest I sniffle and be found out.

"Where?" my mother said finally. "At Oranienburg?"

"Maybe there, too," Aunt Martel said. "After all, it's Himmler's favorite KZ. But I read about some place in Poland; Auschwitz, they call it."

That did it for me. As often as we could, Dieter and I listened to the BBC to hear more about the story. And around Christmas time, our efforts paid off, sort of. The BBC reported mass killings of Berlin Jews at Riga and of others throughout the German-occupied East. But they talked about shootings; they didn't say a word about the gas.

******

When we returned to school in early 1943, after the Christmas holidays, a strange thing happened. There was no talk of war, nor of schemes to rid the world of Jews. Mr. Barzel was so happy: He had found a new way of teaching English! Having used German while drawing maps of all the countries on earth, he said, we were going to use *English* in our second geography course, dealing with cartography, climatology, and oceanography. Cartography came first.

"To understand cartography, also known as map making," Mr. Barzel wrote on the blackboard in English, "we must first realize that the earth was viewed as a plane by most people, at least till medieval times."

We all copied what he had written and then learned to pronounce and understand each of the words. All that was followed with another sentence and another still—day after day and week after week—until the lesson had been learned.

Before long, despite our flat maps, we viewed the earth as a globe, first through the eyes of Pythagoras, who speculated about the disappearance of ships beyond the horizon at sea, as early as the 6th century B.C., then through the eyes of Magellan who circumnavigated the earth in 1519-21, and, finally, through the eyes of "pure logic," as Mr. Barzel liked to put it.

"Think about it," he said. "If the earth were a plane, "the sun would reach its highest point everywhere at the same time, but it doesn't. In addition, there would have to be several polar stars and that isn't the case either. Elementary, really."

He shouldn't have said "elementary," because I hadn't understood his points, but I certainly wasn't about to reveal my stupidity. In any case, Mr. Barzel turned to meridians, "imaginary great circles on the earth's surface passing through the North and South geographic poles." All points on either half of such a circle, he told us, have the same longitude. And he told us of other imaginary lines that encircle the earth parallel to the plane of the equator and that are used to determine latitude, "the angular distance north or south of the earth's equator, measured in degrees along a meridian."

"While it is natural to count latitude from the largest parallel, namely, the equator," Mr. Barzel said, "the position of 0 degrees longitude is totally arbitrary. That longitude line goes through Greenwich, near London, now. It went through Paris and other places before that, and it may well pass through Berlin after we win the war."

We also learned of three different ways of projecting the globe or parts thereof onto a plane, which took us right back to the flat maps we had been studying all along. I liked the azimuthal equidistant projection best. But Mr. Barzel said that conical and cylindrical projections were just as valid. We were still speaking English at the time.

******

It was just about then that the Street Warden paid my mother another visit at home. It concerned me. Although I was too young to join the Hitler Youth, he said, she should seriously consider signing me up for the *Jungvolk*, which was the kindergarten version of the real thing, although he didn't describe it in just these words.

"If he joins now," said the Warden, "he doesn't have to wait till he is fourteen to have all of the benefits. He can start his athletic training now, go on educational trips, and even get extra clothing rations for the uniform and all."

My mother told him she would read the brochure, but she told me that I would join over her dead body. That was fine with me; the Hitler Youth guys always scared me. I was equally scared by the speech Dr. Goebbels made on the radio soon after the battle of Stalingrad.

"From now on, there will be Total War," he said. "Total War means Shortest War. There will be no more 'bourgeois squeamishness.' Every German, high and low, must sacrifice for the common cause. Now people, arise, and storm, break loose!"

I had no idea what he meant, but it sounded ominous. That's why Dieter and I turned once again to the German broadcasts of the BBC. We even found another station that had good news. It came in from Switzerland and was called Radio Beromünster. My mother didn't know what we were doing, nor did Dieter's parents, but their wonderful radio was just too tempting. In addition, the BBC was then mixing the news with a new type of music, called *jazz*, which we liked. While listening to Benny Goodman, Glenn Miller, and, of course, Duke Ellington, these are some of the stories I wrote down in my notebook, none of which appeared on Mr. Barzel's bulletin board:

1943

January	British Lieutenant General Bernard Montgomery defeats Field Marshal Erwin Rommel's Africa Corps in Libya, conquers Tripoli
February	After fierce winter battle at Stalingrad, German 6th Army capitulates, Russians take 100,000 prisoners, then retake Kursk, Krasnodar, Rostov, Kharkov

March	U.S. and British forces occupy Tunisia
April	U.S. and Britain officially announce the use of a new weapon, called *radar*, in war against German submarines, thereby gain upper hand in Atlantic; furious Hitler replaces Navy's commander-in-chief, Grand Admiral Erich Raeder, with Grand Admiral Karl Dönitz
May	Last remnants of German Africa Corps driven from North Africa

One day in May, when I got home from yet another secret after-school session with Dieter, Aunt Martel was there. She had brought a stuffed toy monkey for Helmut and placed a mysterious box on my bed. I quickly stashed away my notebook and read the label.

"Easy Weaver," it said in giant red letters at the top and "Hardwood Weaving Loom with Beautiful 100% Wool Yarns and Accessories" was printed underneath.

"Now you can make scarves, placemats, potholders, and all sorts of nice things for people," Aunt Martel said, standing in my bedroom door.

That did sound like fun and I thought of my grandmother's birthday coming up soon. But I was too tired from a long day of school and play to try my hand at it right then. In fact, I remember lying down on the living room couch right after supper, with Teddy at my side, and only half listening to Aunt Martel's terrifying news. They probably thought I was asleep and didn't bother to send me out of the room.

"Came across another document from Herbert's office," Aunt Martel said to my mother. "From last February, a proud report on the successful conclusion of the *Fabrikaktion* [factory action]. They tallied 7,000 Jews still working in Berlin factories and arrested them all. To make Berlin 'judenrein' [cleansed of Jews] in time for the Führer's birthday. Replaced them with French and Ukrainian workers."

"Where do they take them all?" my mother said.

"Not sure," Aunt Martel said, "but I do know one thing. They are put on freight trains at the Grunewald Station, nicely away from the center of town, so hardly anybody sees them being shipped out."

I heard my mother's and Aunt Martel's voices drifting away, as I listened to soft music on the radio in our living room: *Es steht ein Soldat am Wolgastrand* [A Soldier Stands at the Volga's Bank] and *Tapfere kleine Soldatenfrau* [Brave Little Soldier's Wife] and, longingly, *Komm zurück* [Do Come Back]. I heard voices, too. "Victorious retreat," they said and "Anglo-Saxon terrorists" and "now in the air, passing Hamburg, heading southeast ..."

Teddy and I promised to tell each other our dreams. Strange, looking back at it now, I was a big boy by then, well over 10 years old, but I always regressed at bed time when I met my little stuffed bear.

I was running across the street, dragging Teddy behind me. My heart was racing. Uncle Herbert was chasing us with a whip. I only had my nightgown on, but Teddy was completely dressed, with socks, shoes, and shirt; leather pants and coat. But I wasn't looking at Teddy. My eyes were fixed on the whip and then on the big locomotive hissing and screeching and catching up with us and then on a parade of fire trucks racing toward the bridge with their sirens howling ...

"Wake up, wake up!" my mother shook me. "The alarm! The alarm!"

I was in my bed, and the dark room filled with the wailing sound of the air raid siren. I heard the door of the cuckoo clock open and I jumped out of bed and into my clothes before the clock had a chance to strike three.

I grabbed Teddy, my suitcase full of games, my gas mask, and a flashlight. My mother brought Helmut, but Aunt Martel was gone. We ran down the four flights of stairs. In the semi-darkness, we bumped into neighbors coming out of apartments and ran into sandbags and pails full of water standing next to all the doors. It happened every night then.

Down, down, down the avalanche of people fell—through the hallway, faster across the back yard and toward the open cellar door. The sky was crisscrossed with search lights. There was a bright flash somewhere as we went in.

Inside, the cellar was brightly lit. All the children raced for their bunk beds, ready to sleep or start their games. Teddy and I looked at our stamps: We loved the ones from Thurn and Taxis, the old Regensburg duchy; we also liked to look at the more recent stamps from the Weimar Republic in the 1920's with all the big numbers on them.

All was quiet outside.

When Dieter reached up the jar of white glue from his bed below, I put the stamps away and took out the *Flora and Fauna* book. He had won it collecting a hundredweight of newspapers. We were slowly filling up the blank spaces in the stories with the glossy color pictures we got for bringing in copper or aluminum. The first picture was of an elk. He stood in a brook in the forest. The doe pictures were missing, but I had the one of the mountain goat standing at the edge of a cliff. As I looked at it, there was a loud bang, and the lights flickered. The part with all the foxes was complete; one of them had a rabbit in its mouth. I had the Alpine hare, too. It was cute, all white with a pink nose. Teddy helped me glue in the moles and bats, then the turtles and snakes, but the lights went out just when it was Dieter's turn to do the frogs and salamanders.

It stayed black and I felt scared when all the noise started, but my mother held on to my shoulder with her hand. Helmut sat on her lap. We heard cracks like thunder, and the earth shook. We heard a shower of broken windows landing on the pavement above. What were people thinking? They were supposed to leave all their windows open precisely so they wouldn't be shattered by sudden changes in pressure made by exploding bombs.

The lights came back and I saw Mrs. Meyer sitting in the farthest corner, as usual. She had given up on darning Dieter's socks. I could hear her pray. Mrs. Wagner screamed when we heard the whistle bomb, and all the women sitting shoulder-to-shoulder on the benches across from us brought their heads to their knees at the same time. I refused to duck; it didn't make any sense. For one thing, they had put new steel plates in the ceiling and set up rows and rows of steel columns to hold them up. If the ceiling caved in, nevertheless, why would one be safer with one's head on one's knees rather than held high? Still, Dieter buried his head under a pillow; he didn't understand. But the explosion was farther down the street. We heard the sound of a building crashing.

All the women across from us resumed their needlework, as if in unison, just as they had bowed before the whistle bomb. One woman wore a helmet; another one had purple shoes; there were no men. Men fought the war in faraway places or manned the anti-aircraft guns and search lights in the gardens outside. Or they sat in fire trucks on the street corners. I decided to ask Mr. Meyer tomorrow about the whistle bomb. Mr. Barzel had told us that hearing it was a sure sign that it was headed somewhere else.

"Only when it's precisely coming towards you, then you can't hear it," he had said.

******

During the last weeks of spring that year, Dieter and I and all the other boys played a new game, finding shortcuts on our way to school. So many houses had disappeared, or rather turned into giant piles of rubble, that any enterprising group of boys could make new footpaths through the debris and follow a straight line to school, rather than the zigzag paths of ordinary sidewalks. And so we did. Climbing over rubble and around craters filling up with sewage and buzzing with flies, we made our own paths to school. And while we were at it, we collected sacks full of silvery shrapnel, with twisted sharp edges that reminded us of the lead sculptures we made on New Year's Eve and that some of us made again and again until the future turned out right

We also saw how lucky we still were. Other families now lived in drafty bombed-out shells of houses, with plywood or carpets nailed over window holes, or even in cellar holes from which house numbers stuck up like submarine periscopes.

As for me, I made a point of finding the big signs that, like gargoyles on churches, had once decorated the roofs of tall apartment buildings before they tumbled to the ground. I found the Continental Tires sign, but Dieter was saying Con-TEEN-ental, which was clearly wrong. I also found the broken and twisted ad of the Juno Cigarette Company. I had often noted it, because it rhymed and especially because the verse made little sense:

Aus gutem Grund ist Juno rund

"We have good grounds for making Juno round."

And behind the gutted Geyer Works, across the street from us, I found a giant version of a sign that was also pasted to every store window and bus and streetcar and subway train across town: "Hush! The Enemy Listens In." And further down the street, a group of women was cleaning up the mess left behind by a house that had collapsed. They didn't have any tools, just picked up the pieces, one brick at a time. It seemed so futile.

Just then I spotted Uncle Herbert coming around the corner near the pub. He was walking with a German shepherd by his side and swinging a whip with his right hand.

DEFA-Stiftung/Klagemann, Eberhard, Berlin, Germany

Cleanup after an air raid

14. CHRISTMAS TREES
[July 1943]

By the summer of 1943, just as Mr. Barzel had once predicted, I could read and speak quite a bit of English. My Aunt Martel, I remember, surprised me with a special gift, an English-language copy of *The International Cloud-Atlas*, published in 1896, which I could easily decipher. The atlas featured the work of Luke Howard, an early 19th century Englishman who had created the system for classifying clouds using Latin names. He described the three most common shapes as *cirrus* (curl of hair), *stratus* (layer), and *cumulus* (heap). He also defined four compound cloud forms that derive from the three primary shapes, using terms such as *nimbus* (rain) to create words such as *nimbostratus*. But receiving my new atlas was only the first of several pleasant surprises.

Just before school let out, on my grandmother's birthday to be exact, a delegation from Town Hall appeared at her doorstep and presented her with the silver edition of the Mother's Cross. I know because I was there, and just about ready to put whipped cream on top of my favorite gooseberry cake, when they rang the bell. I suppose Aunt Martel wasn't too happy about the interruption either, lest her coffee get cold, but then it wasn't real coffee anymore; hers was *Ersatz*, a common substitute made of barley. In any case, the men read a citation, honoring my grandmother for having given birth to six Aryan children and even citing the Führer on the subject: "Each mother who has given birth to a child has struck a blow for the future of our people." The men also gave my grandmother a brochure written by District Leader Dr. Goebbels and stating that as of June 19, 1943, Berlin was free of Jews.

That was supposed to make us happy, I suppose, along with other bits of information, such as these: If she had had 8 or more children, my grandmother would have been eligible for the gold version of the Mother's Cross, but even the silver edition carried great privileges. When wearing the cross, my grandmother was entitled to going to the head of any queue, being served first at government offices, on public transport, at mass events, and, of course, grocery stores. Moreover, she had to be greeted with a snappy "Heil Hitler!" by all members of the Hitler Youth.

In fact, my grandmother was glad when the men were gone. She tossed their brochure into the wastebasket and let me examine the medal. It looked similar to the iron cross awarded soldiers, but my grandmother's cross was dark blue rather than black and the lower section was longer than the other three. A swastika in the center of the cross was surrounded by a burst of silver sunrays.

My grandmother said I could take the medal home and keep it, for all she cared, but my mother wouldn't let me.

******

Another surprise yet came on our very last day of school.

"This spring, you've done exceptionally well with the raw materials campaign," Mr. Barzel said, "The nation is proud of you and that is why Mr. Werner is here."

"Thank you, thank you, at ease," Mr. Werner said when we jumped to our feet. "First, I have a gift for each one of you. Then, the three best collectors will get a special reward."

He opened a box and handed each of us a Swiss Army knife, complete, as I later found out, with thirteen attachments, including, besides the obvious, a saw, a toothpick, tweezers, and a wire stripper. And then he read off three names—names rather than numbers, mind you—mine included.

"I have a special surprise for you three," Mr. Werner said. "As you probably know, the Strength-Through-Joy organization has been doing wonderful things for people for many years. Using the beautiful steamship *Wilhelm Gustloff*—named after the Swiss National Socialist leader who was assassinated by a Jewish student in 1936—we have organized marvelous ocean cruises for those who have worked faithfully for the fatherland—cruises to Scandinavia, the Mediterranean, and South America. With the war going on, we can't go that far anymore. For the time being, the majestic fjords of Norway, the sunny Atlantic islands of Madeira and Tenerife, and such exciting foreign cities as Montevideo, are equally out of reach. But we can go to nearby places—not by ship, of course, but certainly by train. And the three of you, along with some boys from other grades, are going to go to the Spreewald!"

I had heard of the place. The area, many kilometers south of Berlin, was the birthplace of the Spree, one of Berlin's two rivers. My parents had been there when they were young; I had seen pictures.

At first, I didn't like the idea of going away all by myself, or rather with a bunch of scary Hitler Youths, and, furthermore, Dieter and I already had other plans. But I changed my mind on the way home from school when I found out that Dieter had won the trip as well. He had helped me carry that ton of newspapers from Mr. Joseph's apartment and had thus been equally productive. The deal was sealed when our mothers agreed.

"Being away from the city for a couple of weeks will do you both a world of good," my mother said.

"It'll be exciting!" Mrs. Meyer added. "Haven't you just studied the Florida Everglades? They say the Spreewald is just like that!"

And thus began our trip to the magical land of shallow waters and tall trees. For days, we gathered right after breakfast at the launching site. We got into the flat-bottomed, square-ended boats and punted our way through an endless labyrinth of slow-flowing waters—brooks and ponds, covered with forest growth so dense that it had to be parted to let us through. A woman in colorful costume stood at the end of each boat. She pushed a long pole against the bottom of the shallow waters and thus propelled us toward ever-changing mysteries: We were explorers, going through the swamps of Georgia. Saxon vines turned into Spanish moss, and the protective cries of mother storks into the battle-cry of Indians. On we pressed, from Georgia's swamps to Florida's Everglades, from the jungles of the Amazon to the steaming world of the Congo. Lizards sunning themselves on stones were crocodiles out to devour us. Tiny fish became sharks, gentle winds turned into mighty hurricanes…

At night we slept. No sirens wailed.

On some days, when thunderstorms lingered, we stayed in our youth hostel and did other things. Naturally, I studied my cloud atlas. "Thunderstorm clouds (*cumulonimbus incus*)," it said, "form when rapid updrafts within *cumulus congestus* clouds rise into the upper atmosphere and spread out into mushroom-shaped anvils. They always produce lightning, heavy rain, and large hailstones; sometimes even tornadoes."

Dieter had a jigsaw puzzle of the Amazon rain forest. There were 1,000 pieces, waiting to be turned into a colorful scene filled with strange wild plants, exotic birds and butterflies, monkeys swinging from vines, and snakes, frogs, and creepy crawlers wherever one looked.

We also played with my rubber stamp kit, a brand-new gift from Aunt Martel. It had multi-colored ink pads and lots of rubber stamps for different Egyptian hieroglyphs. Using a booklet with a key, we practiced writing and deciphering secret messages in the ancient, mysterious language of the pharaohs.

The other boys played "Scapa Flow." It was a board game that I once owned myself; a gift from Uncle Herbert, but my mother did not want me to play war games and had thrown it out. It had a map of the North Sea and the British Isles, similar to the one we once drew in school for Mr. Eisler. There were lots of submarine tokens and battleships, bombers and fighter planes in the game. The idea was to make Anglia submit to Teutonia.

******

On the day we were slated to go home, I wrote in my diary that I had had the most wonderful time of my life and that I had actually seen *cumulus humilis, cumulus congestus*, and *cumulonimbus incus*. It was dark by the time we climbed onto the Dresden-to-Berlin express. In the third-class compartments with all the wooden benches, every seat was occupied, mostly by soldiers heading home for a brief respite from some faraway front. Some soldiers were sitting on suitcases in the aisles; others were standing, holding on to ceiling straps.

But *we* didn't have to stand. We were led to the second-class compartments where all the seats were covered with upholstery and that were reserved for military officers and, occasionally, for travelers with special tickets, such as those given to us by the Strength-Through-Joy people. Unfortunately, Dieter got the last seat in one car and I was told to move on to the next one, closer to the front of the train.

My compartment was mostly empty; except for a woman and two Army officers—a lieutenant and a colonel—I knew it because we had learned to recognize the insignia in school. The woman was trying to sleep. The colonel was straining to read a newspaper in the dim nightlights that illuminated the compartment. The lieutenant smoked a lot and the smoke bothered me. I sat next to the window across from him and watched shadowy trees fly by and an occasional house. I listened to the thump-thump-thump of the wheels on the tracks. I stared at my face and the rest of the scene as it was reflected in the window glass. There I saw the lieutenant, drawing another cigarette from his pack, groping for a match, then lighting it, and blowing puffs of smoke into the air. I thought of smoky fire bombs and our air raid shelter and I wondered whether my mother and Helmut were still alright.

Half-way to Berlin, for no apparent reason, the train stopped. A conductor said there was an air raid in Berlin. We'd go in right after the all-clear.

"All dark, all dark!" he yelled, going from one compartment to the other.

But the lieutenant kept lighting his cigarettes. I thought of Mr. Eisler and how he had sent us out into the streets at night to stamp out every last light that enemy pilots might see. Certainly, a lighted cigarette would qualify. But I said nothing.

We listened to a nerve-wracking hum of engines overhead, droning like mosquitoes high up in the sky. And suddenly, dozens of lights flashed all around the train.

"My God," the woman said, "they are going to parachute right into us!"

Parachutes, each sparkling with a thousand lights, it seemed, hung overhead, motionless. The train stood in a landscape as bright as day!

"Christmas trees, just Christmas trees," the lieutenant said. "Nobody's going to get us."

The suspense was awful. My heart was beating in my throat; each breath felt like it might be my last. I heard the sound of machine guns. An airplane veered off to the right, just missed the trees at the edge of the meadow. I felt blood trickle down my cheek; glass splinters lay in my lap.

When I dared open my eyes, I saw the lieutenant slumped in his seat across from me. He didn't move. Dark blood poured from his mouth, slowly spreading over his chest, flowing over his medals, soaking his pants, the upholstered bench, dripping to the floor. And I saw something even more incredible: two fingers lying on the floor, still clutching a cigarette....

I felt tears pool in my eyes. My vision glazed, I saw nothing at all, except the tailor cutting the little boy's thumbs in the *Struwwelpeter* book.

"He's dead," the colonel said to the woman.

"Are you all right?" the woman said to me, but I couldn't respond. I felt frozen in place, I couldn't feel anything, I couldn't move.

******

I don't remember what happened next. But I do remember the nice lady from the Red Cross who took me home from the train station the next morning. She couldn't call my mother very well; nobody in our apartment house had a telephone. So she just went with me on the subway, but I was so afraid of what I might find at the other end! I stopped half-way up the stairs leading to our street. My heart kept pounding, and I couldn't hold back the tears. The scene swam before my eyes, but I could see enough: Our house was still there.

My mother screamed when she saw me all bundled up with bandages, but the Red Cross lady explained. They put me to bed and I fell asleep almost at once. I heard them talking, but nothing made sense.

"Lost memory" someone said and "it's natural."

Langewiesche-Brandt, Ebenhausen near München, Germany

Strength Through Joy
A drawing of the 27,000 ton Strength-Through-Joy ship Wilhelm Gustloff, entering a Norwegian fjord, along with Travel Savings Certificates

15. TRAITORS EVERYWHERE

[August – October 1943]

For a few weeks after my trip to the Spreewald, my mother kept me with her at all times. She said she needed me to help with Helmut who was just learning to walk, but I knew better. She was worried about me because of those Christmas trees and all, which is why she kept hugging me for no apparent reason. But I was *fine.* The little cuts and scrapes on my face had long since disappeared and I was eager to see Dieter again at some time other than our nightly trips to the air raid shelter.

My mother said Dieter could come up to our place; she had bought us a whole bunch of toys so we would have something interesting to do. The toys came in several boxes. One of them contained a marvelous medieval castle with four movable towers, all sorts of walls and staircases, a working drawbridge, and an army of knights to keep the enemy out. Another box contained a woodcraft construction kit. The kit came with plenty of laminated wood, sandpaper and glue—I so liked the owl on the yellow tube of *Uhu Alleskleber* glue!—and there were plenty of suggestions as well. I chose to build models of dinosaurs; Dieter worked on a Mayan temple. First, I started with *triceratops*, the one with the three-horned face. Then came *stegosaurus*, the "roof reptile," followed by *tyrannosaurus rex*, the largest meat-eating dinosaur that ever lived. It weighed 7 tons, my booklet said, was over 13 meters long and over 5 meters tall. The *diplodocus* even weighed 11 tons, in reality of course, and was twice as long and over twice as tall. I had fun building its whip-like tail. Still, my favorite creation was a smaller creature, called *velociraptor*, which lived some 80 million years ago in the Gobi Desert of Mongolia. I always found Mongolia fascinating. Mr. Eisler had told us that Outer Mongolia now was under the control of Russia and that its capital was Ulaanbaatar. It had almost 2 million inhabitants.

In the meantime, Dieter built the pyramid temple El Castillo, located somewhere in Mexico, where people worshipped the god Kukulkan some 1,500 years ago. Dieter was only half done with the Temple of the Warriors at Chichen-Itza when I finally got permission to go down to his place.

When his parents were gone, we made a beeline for the radio and we quickly updated my secret notebook with the latest summary of events, as reported by the BBC.

1943

July   The world's greatest armored battle is raging around the Ukrainian
              city of Kursk, involving over 6,000 tanks

	Field Marshal Günther von Kluge loses 250,000 men
July	A 2,500-vessel invasion fleet, carrying British, Canadian, and U.S. troops commanded by General Bernard Montgomery and General George Patton, lands on southern Sicily, takes the island within 5 weeks
August	Nearly 600 British bombers attack Germany's super-secret rocket research center at Peenemünde on the Baltic Sea, where German scientists have developed a pulse-jet-powered Flying Bomb, called V1, and a faster liquid-fuel model, known as V2; V stands for *Vergeltung,* the German word for *revenge*

We didn't think our teachers would fill us in on such news; so we decided to make appropriate entries on Dieter's European map, which we kept under his bed. Using my hieroglyphic rubber stamps, we put a red stamp on Kursk, a blue one on Sicily, and a green one on Peenemünde on the Baltic coast. We were so pleased with our cleverness.

And we were very surprised when we walked to school the next day, for the first time in weeks. So much had changed! Many more buildings had turned into mounds of debris or just into empty skeletons with scorch marks around all the window holes. In some streets, in fact, not a single structure had been left unscathed. And everywhere we ran into little groups of Russian POW's, cleaning up broken concrete and bricks and plaster and strips of wallpaper that had spilled onto the sidewalk and even into the street. We could tell they were Russian by looking at their brown army coats—the German ones were green and gray—and at the funny hats they wore with the dangling earflaps, and, of course, by noting the big R on everybody's back.

At one street corner, they were loading plumbing fixtures onto a truck, along with pieces of furniture, upholstery ripped open, a twisted street lamp, and the sad remains of a chandelier. At another, they were reclaiming bricks, stacking them into neat piles and making the sidewalk passable. We watched a streetcar there, too. It was stuck because the metal arm coming out of its roof had become separated from the overhead wires which were sparking like crazy. The conductor had come out, trying to push the arm back to its proper place with a long pole. We waited to see whether he would get electrocuted despite the fact that the pole was made from wood. He wasn't and we went on. Some of the ruins, we noted, now had messages on them, written in chalk.

"Everyone saved from this cellar" one sign said.

"Mrs. Schmidt, where are you?" said another. "Come and stay with me. Heta Burg."

******

Back in school, just as I had expected, Mr. Barzel had nothing to say about that summer's events in the war. Without delay, he took up our language instruction and this time its focus was *Caesar.* He pronounced the name KAH-E-SAR and said that's what the Romans did, which also explains why our emperor was called a Kaiser.

"As to Caesar, he undertook two trips to Britain, in 55 and 54 B.C.," Mr. Barzel said, "to punish the Britons for helping the Continental Celts. Eventually, many years later, Britain became a Roman province, too. That's when many Latin words were brought into the English language. Some show up in names of towns; others, in words of daily life."

"Thus," Mr. Barzel continued, "Latin words like *castra, colonia,* and *portus* appear in Lancaster, Lincoln, and Portsmouth. Words like *strata, vallum,* and *milia* show up as street, wall, and mile."

"But enough of that," Mr. Barzel said. "This fall, we will learn why Caesar did not live to see Rome triumph over Britain. The reason was a simple one: *He was betrayed and murdered by his own friends!*"

Mr. Barzel told us about Brutus and his pals, stabbing Caesar during the Ides of March, and he told us of Schiller's play, and of Shakespeare's.

"But nowhere," Mr. Barzel concluded, "is the story of this treachery more beautifully told than by William Shakespeare and to that story we now turn."

Before we knew it, Mr. Barzel handed out copies of Shakespeare's *Caesar,* asked us to turn to Act III, Scene II, and told us to memorize Mark Antony's eulogy by the end of the week. We would talk more about betrayal then. But we didn't talk much about Brutus and Caesar.

"Betrayal is a terrible thing," Mr. Barzel said, "yet it is happening all around us. At this very moment in our history, military men who pretended to be his loyal friends, just like Brutus once was to Caesar, are betraying our Führer. I have put two examples on our bulletin board."

And so he had. When he pulled away the cover sheet, we saw this:

1943

Betrayal # 1:   On September 19, a so-called Union of German Officers broadcast an appeal from Moscow, asking our brave soldiers to stop fighting on the eastern front. The appeal was made by generals captured at Stalingrad, including Field Marshal Paulus, General Strecker, and General von Seydlitz, the very ones who had disobeyed the Führer's orders not to capitulate.

Consequence:	The Stalingrad betrayal allowed Russian troops to break through German lines, forcing German troops to relinquish the Donets Basin and even give up Smolensk.
Betrayal # 2:	On July 25, Marshal Pietro Badoglio staged a coup in Italy, formed a new government, arrested Benito Mussolini, and dissolved the Fascist Party.
Consequences:	On September 3, which was their 4th anniversary of war with Germany, British and Canadian troops under General Bernard Montgomery, facing minimal resistance, were able to land at the tip of Italy's Calabrian peninsula, opposite Messina, Sicily.
	On September 8, the Badoglio traitor surrendered Italy to the Allies; asked Italian forces to prevent trains, ships, and trucks from carrying German soldiers and supplies; sent 24 Italian warships to captivity in Malta. In response, German troops occupied Northern Italy and imposed martial law.
	On September 12, German paratroopers, led by SS Lieutenant Colonel Otto Skorzeny, rescued Benito Mussolini from the Gran Sasso d'Italia hotel in the Abruzzi Mountains.
	On September 13, Benito Mussolini formed a new National Fascist government in Northern Italy
	On October 13, Marshal Pietro Badoglio's government in Southern Italy declared war on Germany.

"Such," said Mr. Barzel, "are the terrible consequences of betrayal in our time. But be assured, the cowardly treachery of Pietro Badoglio will not be tolerated. The Duce's National Fascist government will punish these traitors pitilessly."

"And you can help!" Mr. Barzel continued. "You can help counter treachery by joining the new campaign to Fight Waste! You will get instructions tomorrow. As you will see, and already know, fighting waste saves crucial raw materials and thereby strengthens our troops in the East, in the South, and wherever they are called upon to defend our fatherland."

He opened up the cabinet holding the record player and made us stand while he played Italy's Fascist anthem, the *Giovinezza*. Then he gave each of us a leaflet to take home.

"YOU ARE A TRAITOR," it said, "if you listen to enemy broadcasts, if you believe in enemy slogans, if you spread enemy propaganda, if you follow enemy instructions, if you make a pact with the enemy. Even if you carry the mask of an upright citizen, of a friend of humanity, you won't elude us. We will grab you, quickly and firmly… TRAITORS BELONG ON THE GALLOWS!"

******

On the way home, Dieter and I worried about our listening to the BBC. Would they hang us children as well? And we discovered a new placard on the poster column:

TO THE PARENTS OF BERLIN'S YOUTH!

The enemy's aerial terror does not show the slightest consideration for the civilian population. The Anglo-American gangsters of the air are carrying out a brutal and sadistic war of annihilation against defenseless women and children. My concern about Germany's youth, about its health and life, requires special measures.

Therefore, as of this moment, Berlin school children can be evacuated to safer places in the districts of Brandenburg, Pomerania, and East Prussia, where they can continue their education. I expect parents to take advantage of this opportunity. Their willingness and understanding will contribute to a frictionless process and allow us to safeguard our children from the consequences of the enemy's terror.

The Reich Defense Commissar for the Reich Defense District Berlin
Dr. Goebbels, District Leader and Reich Minister

That was scary stuff. Somehow, that message shook me even more than the prospect of hanging from the gallows. Despite all the dangers present in Berlin, *I didn't want to leave home, not ever again*! Without my mother, I felt, it would only be a matter of time—hours at most—before I would sink into a delirium and die.

A whirlwind of frightening thoughts danced through my head. I thought of the BBC story of a few days ago, about Armament Minister Albert Speer touring Essen, Dortmund, and Wuppertal—all of them devastated by the Royal Air Force earlier in the year. He considered Wuppertal beyond rebuilding, they had said. And they had quoted Prime Minister Churchill's promise: "Every corner of Germany will be bombed as thoroughly as the Ruhr has been…"

And that bombardment, the BBC had said, would be an all-day affair; the British at night, the Americans during the day.

And I had another even more frightening thought, something of an epiphany in fact. I remembered all the bombing stories they had told us at school about times when the shoe was on the other foot: How Germany's *Condor Legion*, way back in 1937, destroyed Guernica from the air on Franco's behalf, how Germany's dive bombers annihilated Warsaw in 1939, not to mention other cities, like Rotterdam and Coventry in later years. But what had Spanish and Polish and Dutch and English children ever done to me? Wouldn't justice demand that I be killed in turn?

Just then, across the street, I noticed firemen who were *still* pumping air into the cellar of a collapsed house! I wondered whether they could hear the people trapped underneath. I heard a strange roar in my head and felt dizzy. I couldn't breathe right and my heart seemed to jump. I ran home and my mother promised she would never send me away.

akg-images, London, United Kingdom

Children walking to school amidst ruins. Note the poster column in the background, a favorite source of news.

16. FIRESTORM
[November 1943 – February 1944]

You may think that the stories I have told you so far are pretty grim. One wouldn't wish those experiences on anyone, certainly not on a child. You would be right, of course, but so much worse was yet to come! Starting near the end of 1943, our life became a lot scarier still as a result of events that unfolded in rapid succession. In December, just before school let out for Christmas, Mr. Barzel decided to teach us one last lesson. It all had to do with *phosphorus.*

"Phosphorus, symbolized by P," he said, "is a highly reactive, poisonous, nonmetallic element occurring naturally in phosphates."

He paused long enough to write relevant formulas on the blackboard, like this:

Examples of Phosphates: $Ca_3(PO_4)_2$ or $Ca_5F(PO_4)_3$ or $Ca(H_2PO_4)_2$

"Phosphorus," Mr. Barzel continued, "can exist in any one of three allotropic forms: white/yellow, red, and black."

Again he paused, waiting for us to consult our dictionaries, as we had been taught, and to translate "allotropic forms" into something more manageable, such as "molecular structures," perhaps.

"Phosphorus, atomic number 15, atomic weight 30.9738, valence 3.5, specific gravity 1.82," Mr. Barzel said, "is an essential constituent of protoplasm—the complex, semi-fluid, translucent substance that constitutes the living matter of all plant and animal cells."

"But," Mr. Barzel said, "we are not going to pursue biology today. We are going to consider the industrial uses of phosphorus, its use in the manufacture of matches, fireworks, fertilizers; its use in substances that protect metal surfaces from corrosion and, above all, *its use in the making of incendiary bombs.*"

"It is in the latter use that the white/yellow version is most important these days. That wax-like substance is highly poisonous, glows in the dark, and most importantly, catches fire at 60 degrees Celsius. It must, therefore, be stored under water, which brings us to the most crucial lesson of all."

"It is a matter we cannot bury and ignore, that we must proclaim out loud," Mr. Barzel said with a quivering voice. "In light of the Anglo-American atrocities that are visited upon us night after night, we must be on permanent alert for our self-protection. You may well come into contact with phosphorus one of these nights and the only thing that will save you from terrible burns is having a sponge ready and a pail full of water nearby. Or you might drape your heads in wet towels as you sit in your shelters. Always remember: *Phosphorus Hates Water.*"

"Actually," he said, writing on the blackboard as if it were an afterthought, "combustion creates whitish phosphorous pentoxide, P_2O_5, which, in turn, combines with water to become phosphorous acid, H_3PO_4. Phosphates, in turn, are nothing else but the salts of this acid!"

And that concluded our last lesson of the year. I showed my notes to my mother when I got home, but she said Mr. Barzel was a sadist, scaring little boys like that, and I shouldn't give the matter a second thought. But the night came when I did.

******

I was freezing at the time. My mother kissed me good night, and I climbed into my featherbed. There was no heat in the room; our winter ration of coal had long been used up. Yet I knew that I would be warm soon, deep down in my featherbed castle. I snuggled up to Teddy the Bear—it didn't matter that I was already eleven years old. My Teddy was always ready to talk or play, sleep or growl, helping me to be less scared. That night, we decided to talk.

"What a waste," I said, "I walked all that way to school in the snow just to end up spending five hours in the air raid shelter! We should have gone tobogganing instead."

Teddy agreed. He always did. So did Ludwig who chirped in the darkness across the room. Some people say canaries are quiet in the dark, but that just isn't so.

I couldn't sleep. My mother was fussing with Helmut in the next room; soon he was going to be two years old. I thought of Dieter and how we couldn't get the BBC anymore. His radio was just squealing whenever we tried and ours was long gone. Dieter said he had heard his father talk about someone jamming the frequency. I crawled out of bed and checked the last entry in my secret notebook. It was almost three months old.

"**November 6** Russians take Kiev," it said. I knew about Kiev; it was the capital of the Ukraine and it now had a red hieroglyph on Dieter's map….

I heard airplanes droning in my head and machine guns firing and I saw the lieutenant sitting across from me patting his pockets for a book of matches and suddenly lying in a pool of clotting blood. I woke up with a start. That's why I was wide awake when the sirens screamed.

******

Down in the cellar, someone had turned on Radio Germany. They played martial music and gave a bulletin. A thousand enemy bombers were headed for Berlin, they said.

"Take cover in the nearest shelter and do so *now*!"

Someone got up to turn the radio off. The silence seemed strange, but we all knew it wouldn't last. I saw Mrs. Meyer praying in her corner; she always did. And she didn't wear a wet towel around her head; nobody did. Nor did I see any pails of water in the room or wet sponges in everyone's laps. I found an old newspaper on my bunk bed.

"December 26," it said. "*Scharnhorst* Sunk in Heroic Battle of North Cape. Battleship had crew of 1,800 men. All but 36 lost."

I turned to my rug hooking kit, but my heart wasn't in it. I was trying to put three wooly sheep on a simple blue and green background. One of these days, it would make a fine present for grandma.

Dieter was toying aimlessly with the wooden blocks he got last Christmas. There were forty-four of them, meant to be made into a crèche. He had Joseph, Maria, and Jesus, the three kings, and all sorts of animals and trees. It seemed odd putting up a nativity scene, it being February. My attention was diverted when I heard Mrs. Meyer talking with my mother about a new kind of incendiary bomb her sister in Hamburg had written about.

"They had terrible attacks last July and August," she said. "Those bombs sprayed some people with phosphorus and they couldn't get it off: Gerda says they jumped into the canal or rolled in the sand to kill the flames, but the moment they stopped, the fire came back."

"My brother wrote me, too," Mrs. Wagner said. "He's a fireman and he had never seen anything like it. Entire sections of the city turned into a sea of flames, over a kilometer high. The fires blazed so intensely, he said, they couldn't do a thing."

"In fact," Mrs. Wagner added, "those phosphorous flames suck all the oxygen from places nearby and you'd be stupid to go near them. And worse! About an hour after the all-clear, a huge wind came up, pushing 1,000 degree flames around like a hurricane. They measured speeds of 150 kilometers per hour, he said."

There was a moment of silence and then we heard the familiar drone of aircraft, the thunder of guns, someone whimpering in the next room. Our house above us trembled as if in an earthquake and then more silence.

"Actually," someone said, "the cellar is the safest place to be, safer than sleeping in bed. Most people die in bed, you know."

"Idiot," said someone else.

More silence still. I thought of the lieutenant in the train; he hadn't died in bed.

"You heard about the zoo?" Mrs. Wagner said, interrupting everyone's thoughts. She didn't wait for an answer. "The other day, they damaged some of the cages during the raid. Some of the wild animals got out and the guards had to shoot them as they ran. A crocodile even made it into the Spree. They shot that one, too. But they hushed it all up."

"Shut up, just shut up, we don't want to hear about it," Mrs. Schmidt shouted, and the lights went out. Darkness and silence…

I thought of the women in the bakery. They had talked of people being buried alive when their house collapsed on top of the shelter. Hot water pipes burst and some must have boiled alive, they said. But that was no problem here, I thought. We only had cold water in this house.

But then I had a second thought. In my mind, I pictured the water pipes near the ceiling, now hidden in darkness. What if they burst and the cold water had no place to go and the water covered the cellar floor and started to rise and rise higher until everyone drowned?

I looked at the gas pipes. What if they burst and our gas masks didn't work? And what if someone lit a cigarette, just then, and we were all torn to pieces by a giant explosion?

And again I thought of the women in the bakery who had talked of people burning to death after the phosphorus seeped down from above. I pictured the fire slowly creeping up to them with all the exits blocked. I pictured people pressing against a brick wall, their feet burning first, bubbles forming on their skin and flesh sizzling, just as Mr. Barzel had described it to us….

Then I decided not to think of anything, to empty out my mind, but, of course, it didn't work. I pictured Mr. Barzel at school last week, giving us a lesson in the "science of bombing."

"If you see an enemy airplane straight overhead," he had asked, will you be safe?"

"One may think so," he had said, "given the scientific fact that the bombs it carries have the same speed as the plane; thus, if they are released over your head, they are bound to continue in the direction of the plane, their path being modified by air resistance and possibly the wind, of course, but they certainly won't go straight down."

"So, standing right underneath the plane, will you be safe? Far from it," he proclaimed triumphantly. "The plane could have released its bombs *before* it got to the spot above your head and even if it hasn't, there could be other planes releasing their bombs far away and heading for the very spot you occupy. So, don't stand there and gawk!"

So much for emptying my mind….

Someone sobbed softly when the all-clear siren came on. People dragged themselves back to their feather beds, but not in darkness. When we opened the shelter door, the sky shone brilliant red, like sunset in hazy summer. Two hours left till daybreak.

******

My mother put Helmut in his crib, and we opened the balcony doors. A hot wind had come up, unlike any we had ever felt. To the east, beyond the gardens, we could see the silhouettes of houses in flames. Down the street, sparks shot up above the roofs and rained onto the sidewalks. Smoke billowed through gaping window frames. There was a smell, like tar burning.

"My God, those poor people," my mother said.

I thought of my grandmother. She lived just beyond the mile-long flame to the east. But I didn't say a word. No one had a phone. We didn't discover it until I had dressed for school the next morning: A molten piece of metal lay on the carpet. There was a hole in the ceiling where it had come through. I noticed the silence and removed the cloth. My canary, in its cage, was dead.

******

Our next walk to school was a somber occasion. There were giant craters in the road and dead bodies floating in the canal. To this day, I don't know how they got there. Perhaps the stories about phosphorus were true. In any case, when we turned the corner at Stuttgarter Strasse, we saw that every house had burned, leaving only bare walls standing, with black holes where doors and windows had been. At one place, we encountered the smell of charred flesh, animal or human, we didn't know. It was overpowering. We had smelled it before when corpses were decomposing under ruins because the rescuers hadn't come in time.

A policeman told us to move on. A crew of Italian traitors was about to fix the road, he said. I noticed the smoke coming out of their mouths as they were breathing the cold air.

akg-images, London, United Kingdom /RIA Novosti

Street repair after air raid

17. THE BIRTHDAY
[April 1944]

Today I am going to tell you about one of the worst days of my life. For three decades, I didn't talk about that day at all and, according to my mother, I wasn't supposed to. "Now, Hansel," she had said one day that spring, "we will never raise the subject again." And we didn't, neither between us nor with any other member of the family…. Of course, my mother wasn't always right; I know that now. It is better to talk about some things, but it can be difficult, even fifty years after the event.

The day before it happened, we went to see Uncle Kurt. He had gotten a leave of absence from the eastern front, where he was flying a *Messerschmitt ME-109*, and we all agreed to meet at my grandmother's place. That made sense because his parents had long since died and he liked to hang out at my grandmother's because she was his aunt, which means he wasn't really my uncle, although I called him that. He was actually Aunt Martel's and my mother's cousin, but I couldn't very well call him *that*.

On the way to my grandmother's place, my mother, Helmut and I stopped at the poster column near the canal. It held only two pieces of news and one of them was three weeks old:

"March 30," it said, "Today, the Führer summarily dismissed Field Marshal Erich von Manstein and Field Marshal Paul von Kleist, both for disregarding the Führer's stand-fast order in the Ukraine. Despite Russian advances, following these acts of disobedience, the German armed forces scored numerous victories during their retreat."

The other poster seemed much more recent and looked like this:

Since November 18,
the Anglo-American pirates of the air have
killed 6,100 innocent women and children in Berlin
and have seriously injured 18,400 more.
Now, more than ever, the War Fortress Berlin cries out:
Hail to the Führer!

Uncle Kurt was already there when we arrived at my grandmother's apartment. He wore his uniform, and I instantly spotted the new Iron Cross on his chest. In fact, his being a hero was the reason for his being here. A week's leave was part of the reward.

Uncle Kurt let me examine the medal and I told him about my grandmother's Mother's Cross, which was so much prettier, but I didn't tell him that part. He also let me read the citation, which he fished out of his pocket.

"In the name of the Führer and Supreme Commander of the Armed Forces," it said, "I hereby confer upon Corporal Kurt Förster, Staff Company II/Fighter Squadron 300, the Iron Cross First Class with Swords. Signed at Division Fighting Position, on April 15, 1944, by Gutemann, Colonel and Division Commander."

There was also an official seal depicting an eagle, with wings spread wide, clutching a swastika. When I looked up to return the document, I saw Uncle Kurt holding Helmut in his lap and I read the inscription on the buckle of his Air Force belt.

"God With Us," it said.

Uncle Kurt was rocking Helmut on his knees and reciting an old German children's rhyme. "Hop, hop, goes the rider—when he falls he cries—if he falls into the ditch, the ravens will devour him—if he falls into the swamp, the rider goes kerplunk!"

That was the occasion to part his knees and let the child fall to the floor—ever so gently, to be sure—amidst great laughter all around. Helmut couldn't get enough of it.

"One more time, one more time," he kept begging.

Just then, my mother called us to the table for our evening meal and I noticed Uncle Kurt insisting on the same ceremony that my father had taught me. We men had to stand at the table until all the ladies were seated, and then we sat patiently with our fingertips on the table's edge until all the ladies had taken their first bite, and then we ate our sandwiches, always using fork and knife and never touching any food by hand, and later we cleared the table and washed the dishes in a big enamel basin in the kitchen with water brought to a boil on the gas stove, and then we dried the dishes with a towel, while the ladies chatted in the living room. To Uncle Kurt, as for my father, proper etiquette was very important.

"The ladies of the house did the cooking," he said to me. "It is only right that we do our part by cleaning up afterwards."

Uncle Kurt was equally gallant later when he insisted on walking us home in the dark along the canal, but we weren't quite ready to go as yet. I first had to inspect my latest gift—Aunt Martel never failed me on that account. This time, she had bought me a fingerprint kit, complete with dusting powder, dusting feathers, a magnifying glass, 32 classification cards, and a booklet explaining the entire procedure. Naturally, I took everybody's fingerprints before the evening was spent.

I also took a few more minutes in Aunt Martel's room. She thought I was studying her jewelry case, as I often did, filled, as it was, with a treasure of glistening brooches, ear rings, and pearls. On this day, however, I do not know why, I had another plan. I knew the key was in Aunt Martel's purse and the purse was in her room. I took the key and opened the glass door to her secret cupboard. I didn't care about her love letters; everybody knew about those. I wanted a closer look at the chocolate hussar!

He sat on a magnificent horse which was chocolate, too. And he had been sitting there for twenty-six years, ever since 1918. I was surprised how heavy he was. He seemed to weigh a pound, and he made my mouth water. Nothing was left out, not one button on the uniform, not even a nail on the horse's hoofs. I thought of biting off a leg, but knew it would be too obvious. The horse wouldn't stand straight. I bit off the soldier's head instead!

Aunt Martel didn't notice a thing, at least not on that day, but when I went to bed later that night, I told Teddy the Bear what I had done. We worried about the next day when Aunt Martel would come for a visit, and we had trouble falling asleep.

Two fierce-looking Chinamen, in flowing gowns, came through the balcony door. They bound me, hand and foot, to the four posts of Aunt Martel's bed. They tied up Teddy, too. "Pleasant dreams," one of them said, and he attached a strange-looking gadget above my head. As in the movies we had seen at school, he took a puff from an opium pipe.

A drop of water hit me in the middle of the forehead, followed by another and another still. I heard a thousand drips, in a thousand places; water upon forehead, water upon water; I saw dark Bedouins on camels racing through the dunes carrying off blonde slaves; water upon forehead, water upon water; black men in the jungle danced around a boiling kettle filled with white explorers; water upon forehead, water; I saw the sky become a burning fire, and it fell into the water. Water became blood!

I woke up with a start. I saw the cuckoo clock and heard rain. All the pots on the floor were filled to overflowing. The entire ceiling was dripping, because half the roof had burned some weeks ago and the shrapnel made new holes every night.

******

The next day was going to be special, in a strange sort of way. Mr. Eisler was sick and we had been told that the 7th and 6th grade boys would all be joined together in Mr. Barzel's room. Thus, I was slated to be in class with Dieter for the first time since the middle of 2nd grade when I was skipped to grade 3 and he wasn't.

Dieter and I took the long way to school that day, east through the gardens and later across the canal on the trolley bridge. We could find more shrapnel that way. Our teachers always told us not to touch the stuff, but we knew perfectly well what was and wasn't dangerous. We had seen the demonstrations in the school yard. Mr. Barzel and Mr. Eisler, certainly, always exaggerated, even told us not to pick up toys and pencils lest they explode in our faces.

"The terrorists are capable of anything," they had said.

When we got to school, we remembered what day it was. The school was decorated with flags, one from every window, and there were nearly a hundred of them. Mr. Barzel called on Thirty-One to recite the story.

"Our beloved Führer, Adolf Hitler," he said, "was born in the Austrian village of Braunau on the Inn River on April, the 20th, 1889. When he was a little boy, he shed tears about the senseless boundary line that separated the Germans in Austria from the Germans in Bavaria. He swore that this boundary line would go, that one day all Germans would happily live together in a nation united. Fifty years after his birth, Adolf Hitler's great dream came true. Greater Germany became a reality. But," Thirty-One droned on, "Adolf Hitler did many other heroic deeds as well..."

Nobody listened, not even Mr. Barzel. He kept smiling at *me*. He had been especially nice to me for a week, even told me I could have my lunch in the classroom and that I didn't have to go down to the yard.

"Too easy to catch cold down there," he had said.

But I knew better. He was still thinking of my *mother*. She had come to meet me every afternoon with Helmut, but Mr. Barzel kept appearing from nowhere, almost stumbling in his eagerness to catch up with her, and insisted on walking us home. That spoiled the whole fun. Come to think of it, she must have been a very beautiful woman. Men's jaws dropped wherever she appeared; even I had noticed that. But when Mr. Barzel asked my mother to visit his apartment after school, she stopped meeting me.

That's why Dieter and I walked home alone that day, and this time we took the regular route. The city had certainly changed a lot since first grade. Plywood, cardboard, and X-ray film had replaced the glass windows in the buildings across from the school. The big cigarette ad at the corner was half gone. "WHY IS JUNO ROUND?" it still asked, but the answer was missing. And all the tall brick buildings on either side of Stuttgarter Strasse had turned into hollowed-out skeleton houses with black scorch marks on all the walls.

Except that something was different on that day! While we had been at school, a rare spring snow storm had swept over the city and left a few centimeters of white fluff on all the sidewalks and roads. Even as we stepped out of the school gate, big round flakes of snow were still drifting down like cherry blossoms, sticking to our clothes and the walls of ruins, covering the scorch marks around all the empty window holes, covering the craters and piles of reclaimed bricks, covering the iron railing along the canal that had not yet been ripped out to make guns, and even covering the inscription on the block of cement on which Bismarck's statue once stood. But I knew what the sign said, I had read it dozens of times on my way to school:

"We Germans Fear God, But Nothing Else in the World—Otto von Bismarck, February 6, 1888."

******

We stopped at the center of the footbridge to feed the gulls. They flew down from the black gutted houses along the canal, now dressed up in fluffy white. Their cries mixed with the air raid sirens.

"A birthday party coming right up," Dieter said, and I knew he meant the planes. We also knew that there was no need to hurry. The sirens were always early, we had heard the story on the radio a thousand times; the planes were still "over Hamburg, going southeast ..."

A plane came out of nowhere! It flew low and fast along the canal and its wing tips almost touched the crowns of the linden trees. They had new green leaves, covered with a dusting of snow. I saw red-and-yellow tongues flickering along the wings, bullets stitching their way across the bridge.

One plane, a burst of thunder, a single cry on Dieter's lips.

I saw his head, half gone, half turned into a bloody mess. I saw the flutter of his hand, his body jerk, snow turning red. There was no solid ground beneath my feet, I could not breathe, my mind was numb, my body turned to stone. I couldn't move; my words, they wouldn't come. A streak of lightning flashed inside my head, I thought I'd fall, a bolt-struck tree. I shut my eyes, I opened them; I heard gulls fly overhead in raucous rage....

And the red snow at our feet started to melt and the bridge turned, upside down, right side up; I knew Dieter was lost; upside down, right side, my legs carried me down the steps; faster turned the bridge, and I raced to the corner pub that wasn't there; upside down, and I passed the acacia tree; faster and faster spun the bridge—till my legs collapsed at my mother's feet.

Ronnie Olsthoorn, United Kingdom

A Spitfire ready to attack

This 1940 version had a maximum speed of 367 mph. Its machine guns—four on each wing—were sighted so that the bullets from all eight converged at a distance of about 250 yards.

18. THE PLOT

[May – July 1944]

After Dieter's funeral, my mother kept me home for almost two months. I don't know how we got away with it, nor do I remember much of what we did. I do remember dreaming up vague illnesses, like headaches and stomach pain—anything but the truth: I simply dreaded crossing that bridge on the way to school. But clearly, my mother knew what was going on. When she offered to walk me to school and back, I returned for the last week before our summer break. Little had changed. Our school was still standing, untouched in a sea of rubble. Mr. Barzel was still there and his bulletin board was brimming with news I had missed:

1944

May 9	Russian forces take Crimean city of Sevastopol
June 3	Field Marshal Albert Kesselring, Commander-in-Chief of German forces in Italy, receives the Führer's permission to give up Rome; American forces occupy Rome
June 4	Western allies invade the Le Havre/Cherbourg area of Normandy, using an estimated 10,000 airplanes, 80 battleships, 4,000 transport ships, 2 million men
June 18	The Führer orders the Cherbourg garrison to fight to the death 22,000 U.S. soldiers killed
June 29	Lt. General Omar N. Bradley takes Cherbourg, capturing Lt. General Carl Wilhelm Schleiben, garrison commander, along with 30,000 German troops
June 30	Two thousand V1 rockets launched against London in revenge

---

Mr. Barzel had saved me a newspaper clipping that explained what had happened in Rome. "There was danger that Rome, one of the oldest cultural centers of the world," the paper said, "would be directly involved in the present fighting. The Führer has ordered the withdrawal of German troops to the northwest of Rome to prevent the destruction of Rome. However, the struggle in Italy will be continued with unshakable determination to break the enemy attacks and to force final victory for Germany and her allies…This year of invasion will bring Germany's enemies an annihilating defeat at the most decisive moment."

I decided to pay more attention to the news over the summer and to make new entries in my notebook, but I only did it once, using a new *Pelikan* fountain pen Aunt Martel had given me.

"**July 11**   Red Army takes Minsk, capital of White Russia; 70,000 Germans dead," I wrote and then I quit.

I kept thinking of Dieter and how we had done this sort of thing, but what was the point? And I wondered what had happened to the secret map we had stashed under his bed.

There was one piece of news, though, that I couldn't escape. Nobody could. It happened on July 20, 1944, another date firmly lodged in my memory. I even remember the time; it was 18:25 hours, when Berlin Radio stopped Zarah Leander in the middle of her song, *Einen wie Dich* [A man like you] and made the surprising announcement:

"At 12:42 hours today, at his East Prussian headquarters of Rastenburg, an attempt was made on the Führer's life with explosives… The Führer himself suffered no injuries beyond light burns and bruises. He resumed his work immediately and, as planned, received the Duce for a lengthy talk."

By 0100 hours that night, the alleged perpetrator, Count Schenk von Stauffenberg, had already been executed and the Führer himself appeared on the radio:

"A tiny group of ambitious, irrational, and criminally stupid officers without conscience hatched a plot to get rid of me and to eliminate practically the entire leadership of the German army. They are a small gang of criminals who will be hunted down mercilessly."

******

Men in black clothes emptied buckets of earth on top of me; and, each time, I felt pain in my stomach and my breath went away. It was as if someone had sat an anvil on my chest. I wanted to scream, but I couldn't make a sound. I wanted to open my eyes, but I didn't dare. I knew they had flowers, tons of flowers, to dump on top of me if I even blinked.

My mother said I had just been dreaming of Dieter's funeral, but I wasn't so sure. I caught a glimpse of memory, like light under a door, I trembled, I whimpered, I felt darkness all around. My mother gave me peppermint tea and said "There, there."

When I woke up, Aunt Martel had come; she was talking to my mother. As usual, they were whispering, but I heard some of it.

"I'm going to quit this job," Aunt Martel said. "I simply can't take it. I gave them notice yesterday. Lucky I am not a man or they would send me into the Russian swamps with Arthur. Hell,

I don't care; they can just find another confidential stenographer."

When I stirred, they changed the subject.

"Aunt Martel has the day off and she'll take you to Kranzler's," my mother said. "A little outing will do both of you a world of good."

I liked the idea. We had gone to Berlin's favorite coffee house before, although it had been quite a while. They would probably serve Black Forest cake and, perhaps, even whipped cream. They might also have *Schiller locks*, shaped like the locks of hair worn by the people in history books: British judges, French philosophers, and German poets. These white, brittle pieces of sweetness were almost as good as chocolate hussars. But even if the café should be out of locks, it would surely have *Americans*—those saucer-shaped pieces of cake with black chocolate frosting on one side and white vanilla coating on the other, a vivid reminder, Mr. Eisler had once said, of the mixture of black and white people in America. I always wondered where the Red Indians fit in.

Aunt Martel liked the coffee they served, even though it was now made of roasted barley.

"What happened to the chocolate hussar?" I asked after we sat down. "I'm sorry."

"Oh, it's all right," Aunt Martel said. "I should have just given it to you last Christmas, I should have. It'll just burn up one day, along with all the rest."

"I was engaged to Walter when he gave it to me," Aunt Martel continued. "Before the war—the *first* war—Walter was a customs man, too, you know. We worked in the same office. He brought in the smugglers, and I took it all down; the questions, the answers, even the hearings in court. He was a good man; he couldn't have hurt a fly, but then the war killed him."

As if she needed to prove the point, Aunt Martel fished a piece of paper from the depths of her pocket book.

"Look here," she said, "I still have the citation he got for his wounds."

I unfolded the paper, turned yellow over time, and read it.

"Certificate of Ownership," it said. "In the Name of His Majesty the Kaiser and King, the Medal for Wounds Suffered in Battle, rendered in black, is hereby awarded to Lieutenant Walter Henle, born November 19, 1880 at Schweidnitz, Silesia, now of the Royal Prussian Infantry Regiment Nr. 52 at Alvensleben, 9th Company. Signed in the field, July 28, 1918, Steinkopf, Lieutenant Colonel and Regimental Commander"

What could I say? I had heard of Schweidnitz. That's where grandma was born as well. And I knew something else. As Mr. Barzel had taught us, Schweidnitz was also the birthplace of the Red Baron, officially known as Baron Manfred von Richthofen, who buzzed World War I battlefields in his red Fokker triplane and downed a record 80 enemy aircraft in the process. That made him the war's top fighter ace. Just like Aunt Martel's Walter, he, too, had died in 1918, but I decided not to mention any of it. The steel cables in front of the café were making a racket again, and Aunt Martel looked up. There were tears on her face.

"We were going to be married, you know. Twenty-five years ago this month. Any day now, we'll meet again."

"Will you walk to school with me this fall?" I asked suddenly. "I don't want to walk alone anymore."

"Sure," she said; and she looked just like my mother. "A little walk each morning will be good for me and, besides, I like to feed the gulls."

"I don't want to feed gulls," I said. "Not ever."

"I didn't think," she said softly. "I'm sorry."

She took my hand, and she looked just like my mother.

"Walter and Dieter, they are together now, just as we are. They're in a much better world, I am sure."

We watched the traffic outside. A man opened the door with a loud noise, and the wind came in and picked up our napkins.

"Attention! Attention!" he said. "The would-be assassins of our beloved Führer, Adolf Hitler, to wit Brigadier General Ludwig Beck, General of the Infantry Friedrich Olbricht, Colonel Claus Count Schenk von Stauffenberg, Colonel Albrecht Knight Mertz von Quirnheim, and First Lieutenant Werner von Häften, have now been executed. Heil Hitler!"

"You know what?" Aunt Martel said, changing the subject with fierce determination. "They're having a new production of Hansel and Gretel across the street. Someone turned it into a musical. Let's go to the theater!"

And so we did. Outside, the sun had just set and the wind was blowing hard. The anti-aircraft blimps in the sky were struggling to escape the steel cables holding them to the ground.

******

In the middle of Act II, the sirens wailed and everything came to a halt. Spectators, musicians, and actors alike followed the white-and-blue air raid shelter signs to a huge bunker in the ground. That much I remember, but the rest of that night, and how we got home, is something like a blur. I do remember being shocked to see all the actors up close. They had looked so lovely on the big stage; yet they seemed positively grotesque when we came face to face. I had never seen theatrical make-up before!

I also remember leaving the theater in search of the subway station, but then, suddenly, we seemed to stand at the edge of a cliff, ready to fall into a bottomless pit. Nothing had prepared me for the scene we encountered out there in the starlight—not the lieutenant in the train, not even

Dieter on the bridge. How could anything be worse?

We were coming face to face with the fact that the possibilities of horror had not yet been exhausted. We saw a house in flames and helmeted firemen and soldiers in SS uniforms and Hitler Youths, all of them busily hauling *corpses* to the middle of the street, stacking them up, two, three, and four layers at a time, many of them charred beyond recognition, some reduced to half their normal size like some of the mummies I had seen in the Egypt exhibit near our school, others looking almost untouched, but overcome, perhaps, by carbon monoxide in some closed cellar nearby, but rapidly stiffening even then and beckoning us for help with claw-like hands....

We stood in silence, our hearts beating in our throats, smoke stinging our eyes, our hands clutching for support. And we stumbled and tripped over soft yielding bodies with torn clothes, trying not to step on faces, blinking away a flood of tears...

And around the corner, just next to the U-Bahn sign, there lay a figure, all doubled up, in a pool of liquid that was still feeding small bluish phosphorous flames. I saw a wedding ring glimmer on a charred hand.

After an air raid

19. BURIED ALIVE

[August – September 1944]

In the summer of 1944, when I was in the 7th grade, we got a new teacher whose specialty was *logic*. On his very first day of school, Dr. Neumann drew a graph on the blackboard like this and presented us with a puzzle:

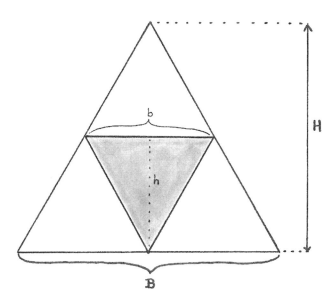

"Given an equal-sided triangle with base *B* and height *H*," he said, "I want you to find the *largest possible* second triangle—such as the shaded one here—that fits into the original triangle in such a way that its peak is found at the center of base *B*. Describe the shaded triangle's base *b*, height *h*, and area *a* in terms of *B* and *H*."

"It's just a matter of logic," he said reassuringly. "You have until tomorrow to find the answers."

I did find the answers [$b = \frac{1}{2} B$ and $h = \frac{1}{2} H$ and $a = (B\,H) / 8$], but I was considerably less certain about another puzzle Dr. Neumann asked us to consider in the coming weeks. Oddly enough, it involved the bulletin board, which looked unlike any of the other ones we had seen:

August/September 1944

Western Front	**Eastern Front**
1) General Dietrich von Choltitz, commandant of Paris, is ordered by the Führer to destroy the city as Western Allies approach; instead he surrenders it	1) 38,000-member Polish Home Army, under Lt. General Tadeusz Bor-Komorowski, stages uprising in Warsaw
2) Radio Berlin announces: General Charles de Gaulle, President of the so-called French Committee of National Liberation, upon entering Paris, said: 'France will take her place among the great nations which will organize the peace. We will not rest until we march, as we must, into enemy territory as conquerors.'	2) After victories in the Baltic states and the Ukraine, which have pushed German troops out of the last Russian town, Russian armies occupy Rumanian capital Bucharest, then Bulgarian capital Sofia, and are racing towards Hungarian capital Budapest
3) British troops occupy Belgian port of Antwerp and capital city Brussels	

"Think of the bulletin board as an oracle," Dr. Neumann said. "What, do you think, it is telling you? Do the math; it's just a matter of *logic*."

When I got home, Aunt Martel was there and I could see that my mother had been crying, but they said it wasn't because of my father. My mother said Dr. Neumann was a brave man, or perhaps just suicidal, and then I knew what she meant. No one I knew had ever come so close to saying that Germany was losing the war.

My mother insisted I go to bed right away; she wanted to talk with Aunt Martel. I took the box she had brought—it was labeled *Spy Science*—and disappeared as requested. The box was filled with fun things. There was a booklet about passing on classified information, which explained Indian smoke signals, the Morse code, and more modern encoder/decoder wheels. A copy of such a wheel was included. There also was a bottle of invisible ink, a spy pen, an ultraviolet decoder light, and a message code book. And there were instructions on listening in on secret spy meetings, along with a stethoscope one could place discreetly on a wall.

"Even the slightest voice can be heard distinctly," it said.

Naturally, I tried, but all I could hear was my mother and Aunt Martel whispering in the next room. Just like my mother and Mrs. Nussbaum had done, just like my mother and Mrs. Meyer always did.

******

I was still wide awake when the sirens went off. It wasn't even midnight yet. As usual, we raced down the stairs, across the yard, into the cellar, catching a passing glimpse of the searchlights crisscrossing the sky. Because Dieter was gone, I decided to sit with Helmut on the bench along the far wall, my mother on one side, Aunt Martel on the other. There was a new sign across from us. "No Talking," it said, "Preserve Your Oxygen," but nobody paid any attention to that.

In fact, before all the noise started on the outside, Mrs. Wagner said something about the plotters having been brought to justice and that did not go well with Aunt Martel.

"You idiot, you stupid, jabbering idiot," Aunt Martel hissed.

That certainly got everyone's attention and, just for a moment, we all sat in stunned silence.

"Hush," my mother whispered under her breath, but there was no stopping Aunt Martel then. It was as if someone had thrown a switch inside her head and there was no way to put it in reverse.

"What do *you* know about justice?" Aunt Martel continued. "Nothing, nothing at all! But let me tell you, because I just quit a lifelong job in our great Ministry of Justice. In the 20's, we used to go after maniacs who cut little boys to pieces in dark cellars and strangled women in abandoned houses. We caught smugglers arriving at deserted beaches with loads of opium, and we prosecuted rich businessmen who never paid their taxes. But how things have changed in the Thousand Year Reich! We turned the Customs Service into secret police, spying on perfectly decent people who sold their belongings to move abroad. They became 'smugglers' because they were Jews. And now we look greedily at the elderly, move them into government 'homes,' and arrange to collect their savings right after they 'fall asleep'."

"*Like dogs in a pound, that's how they fall asleep,*" she thundered, "and you all know it. Moabit! Hadamar! Must I say more?"

"Hush, hush," my mother implored, but Aunt Martel was on a roll. Some engine inside her head was roaring, even accelerating.

"Yes, I'll say more," she continued. "Last week, I discovered a metal box in my boss's desk. 'Nuremberg Fine Cookies,' it said. My mouth watered. I lifted the cover. The box was filled to the top with gold teeth."

Just then, the lights went out; I had never heard such deafening silence.

"And there is this little room," Aunt Martel's voice continued in the dark, ever so quietly yet so distinctly, "right in the Plötzensee jail, I see it now: thick, white-washed walls; barn-like rafters in the ceiling, two narrow windows in one wall, close together, tall, rounded on top, like stained-glass windows in a church, but without the colored glass. A wooden beam stretches across the room *and there were six meat hooks in the beam ready for the traitors!"*

"And there they hanged them with piano wire, do you hear, not even rope, and the film crews were there to make pictures for the Führer and to record the sound."

Aunt Martel had just signed her death warrant. Even I knew that. The silence was so loud, we hardly heard the noise. But we felt the plaster in our throats, and the earth shake under our feet. I felt my mother's hand on my shoulder, and she promised we would live.

******

Someone had a flashlight and we watched its little circle of light move to the ceiling, catching clouds of tiny particles in its beam, examining the iron plates, still holding, probing the columns of steel, still standing, their red paint turned white from all the dust. Wood splintered with a loud crack and we heard the thunderous noise of walls collapsing, taking down another part of our house and stacking another pile of masonry on top of us.

The air seemed acrid, even smoky—I had forgotten the gas mask, I suddenly thought—I felt a gritty mess on my teeth, my nose turning raw. Panic rose within me, choking me at the throat. And a paralyzing thought flashed through my mind: What if they use the flamethrower to kill the maggots and the rats and the flies, as they often did before digging out the dead, *when we aren't dead yet?*

Fred Wagner climbed onto the stationary bike that had been placed in our cellar for just this occasion. He started cycling and, as promised, the bike's dynamo made light in the lantern above his head and I could see his Hitler Youth uniform. It was an eerie scene. Everyone looked like the people inside the wind mill we had visited at the Baltic Sea, as if covered with a thin layer of flour ground from the sacks of wheat kernels the miller was forever funneling into his machine. Aunt Martel wasn't talking anymore; she was holding on to Helmut, now stroking his hair with her left hand, then blowing off the dust from the top of his head with tiny puffs from her lips. My mother held me to her breasts, saying something I couldn't understand, in a quiet, reassuring voice.

******

"Maybe this is the time to use that sledge hammer?" Mr. Joseph asked.

"God no, don't you dare!" said Mrs. Schmidt. "It would just be our luck to drown in here."

I knew what they were talking about. Earlier in the year, big holes had been made into all the cellar walls along our street to connect the cellar of each house with the one next door. Then the holes had been closed with a thin layer of bricks, which could easily be smashed with a single sledge hammer blow. That way, it was thought, people buried in one cellar could escape to the neighboring one and easily walk up the neighbors' cellar stairs. Brilliant.

Except for one thing. What, people asked, if the neighboring cellar was filled with poisonous gas or smoke or phosphorous flames or water from burst pipes? Those who would yield that sledge hammer would be opening Pandora's Box.

"At least we should be making some noise down here so they know we are alive," Mr. Joseph said, and everyone agreed to that. Mr. Joseph would be first; others would relieve him later on. He picked up a wrench and started hitting on a copper pipe. A sharp metallic sound filled the room; it would be difficult for rescuers to miss it.

Clank, clank, clank.

Just then the light went out; Fred had gotten tired. Sitting in the dark, I counted my pulse, listened to low murmuring voices, my own breathing. Was I still breathing? I had to pinch myself to prove that I was still there.

Clank, clank, clank.

The air seemed to thicken, my eyes grew heavy. If we could only open that door, I thought, longing for a breath of fresh air. Helmut was crawling across my lap towards my mother; she straightened out our hair right there in the dark.

Clank, clank, clank.

I thought of the time when Dieter and I had played "flamethrower" in the street. We each had a swastika flag, attached to a pole, and with all of our might, we threw the pole into the air, like a spear, again and again. Each time, the red-and-white flag fluttered in the wind, like a burst of red-hot flames. But then the Street Warden had come and put a stop to it. He had told our mothers, too.

"Your sons are desecrating our nation's flag," he had said.

Then I noticed the silence. Mrs. Schmidt did, too.

"Don't stop! Don't ever stop!" Mrs. Schmidt cried out to Mr. Joseph. "Let someone else do it for a while. Just when we stop, they listen and decide it isn't worth it to dig."

Clank, clank, clank.

The light flickered on and off. Someone was riding the bike again and my mother had to take Helmut to the toilet in the next room. I was scared when she was out of sight, but Aunt Martel was there.

"I am thirsty," I said and looked at my watch.

Twenty-one hours had passed; it didn't seem possible. The sun must be setting, I thought, and I tried to picture the rescue workers on the outside, getting too tired to go on. I also remembered Mr. Eisler's oxygen lesson and wished I could make time stop before there was nothing left to breathe.

Clank, clank, clank.

Maybe time did stand still or I did fall asleep. I remember Aunt Martel handing me a bottle of green soda, with woodruff, just as I liked it, and my mother and Helmut coming back. And then I remember a big crash near the door, waking me up with a start, turning my blood to ice, as I was sure that now, finally, Death was knocking at the door. But it wasn't Death. It was Air and Light rushing into the cellar with a big bang and announcing that there *was* another day.

When they dug us out, fifty-five hours had passed and the sun was rising. It promised to be a fair day; the clouds were so pink. And I could see the clouds because our house and the acacia tree were gone, as if a giant eraser had rubbed out their places against the sky.

But down the street we saw the most ghastly of sights: piles of corpses being cremated right there in the open where would-be rescuers were still delivering them. Helmut and I were clinging to my mother and didn't say a word. Aunt Martel stated the obvious.

"That could have been us," she said. "Adolf has certainly kept his promise: 'Give me ten years and you will not be able to recognize Germany!'"

**Cremating corpses
after an air raid**

akg-images, London, United Kingdom

20. CRICKET SONG

[September 1944]

Let me tell you what happened after the bombing of our house and also what did *not* happen. Nobody, it seems, reported Aunt Martel's outburst to the Gestapo; she got away with it. In retrospect, this is truly surprising; she certainly tried her best to commit suicide that night in the cellar and everybody knew it. As for the rest of us, the Red Cross people said we were lucky to have sustained a 100 percent loss rather than a partial one. This way we were eligible for the special ration of Rhine wine, oranges, and chocolate. I made sure not to tell them that I still had my little suitcase with Teddy the Bear, my postage stamps, the inflatable rubber ball, and lots of secret notes. Yes, I was still very good at regressing: I still clung to my bear, even at age twelve.

And no, they said, my father could *not* get a week's leave, as was customary in such cases, because he was on the eastern front and all leaves there had been canceled until further notice. In addition, being in a penal regiment, they didn't think he would get a leave anyway.

However, they said, there was also good news. Because my mother had such a small child, and they were talking of Helmut rather than me, a wonderful new home was waiting for us at Elbing in East Prussia. They gave us railway tickets, but my mother had other ideas, although she was more than ready to get us out of Berlin.

"No way are we going east," my mother said to Aunt Martel. "By the time we get there, the Russians will be there, too."

Aunt Martel said she would stay to take care of my grandmother; we should come along for at least a day or two until we had made our plans. We agreed, but first my mother went to the public phone booth at the street corner and called Aunt Rachel in Ziesar, which was pronounced tsee–ay–zar with the stress on the second syllable. When measured by a straight line on the map, Ziesar was about 80 kilometers to the southwest, rather than 440 km to the northeast, as Elbing was. Aunt Rachel agreed to let her brother's family join her at the parsonage, at least as long as Uncle Eddy was still at the western front. He wasn't in Paris anymore, she said, but had moved on to Lyons last she knew.

On the very next day, we said a teary goodbye to my grandmother and Aunt Martel. Then we traded in our Red Cross tickets at the railroad station and stood in line for the train to the west. Things certainly had changed since the day some years ago when my father had come home from the concentration camp. Most of the outer station walls stood there as before, but all the windows were broken and the giant glass dome had long since been blown to bits. The big clock near the roof was dead, too. The hour hand was pointing to 11, the minute hand was gone.

When the Magdeburg express finally inched its way along the platform, the train whistle shrieked and the locomotive hissed as before, but otherwise things looked very different, indeed. For one thing, the train was a curious mixture of freight and passenger cars. For another, there were hundreds of people not only inside it, but also clinging to every available spot on the outside. Some people lay on the roofs, others perched on running boards; others sat in the open sliding doors of box cars, with their feet dangling in the wind.

Still, somehow we made it onto the train and then on to Potsdam, Brandenburg, and, finally, Genthin—the 'Home of *Persil*,' a detergent ad said—where we switched to a much smaller and almost empty train for our journey's final leg. The land we passed was flat, covered with pine forest or recently harvested fields or meadows filled with sheep, and crisscrossed now and then by sandy roads.

When the train stopped, my mother, Helmut, and I were the only passengers left. We still seemed to be in the middle of fields—from our window, I saw cows grazing and wagons being drawn by horses—and, when the conductor asked us to disembark, I looked in vain for the kind of arrival hall I had seen in Berlin. There was hardly even a platform, just a short strip of gravel next to a small, red-brick station house, which had a big round clock sticking out from its side. That one was working. Near the front of the train was a pump, where the locomotive took on water, and that's where I also spotted the sign.

"Ziesar, Founded in 948," it said. Wow.

We walked to the front of the station house and stared at the long sandy road leading away from it and towards a distant grove of trees above which three towers could be seen. Two of them looked like they belonged to some ancient castle, the kind I had seen in my fairy tale books; the other one was almost certainly part of a church. The conductor saw us hesitate and offered to help. He knew Aunt Rachel, he said, although he called her 'Mrs. Superintendent,' and he told us what we had to do.

"Just follow the sand road along that row of chestnut trees," he said. "When the trees end and the cobblestones begin, you are on Breite Weg; that's the main street. Follow that one past Castle Street on the left, past School Street on the right, till you reach Cloister Street, also on the left. That takes you right to the church and the old monastery. You can't miss it; it's not far, one kilometer at most."

And thus we made our way to Cloister Street Number 3, through a sleepy little village filled with tiny, look-alike houses, all precisely two stories tall, with walls made of weathered oak beams surrounding squares of red brick, with flowers dripping from window boxes, with steep roofs covered with tiles of red clay, and not one of these houses had burned down! We walked past a bakery store on the right, a shoe store and grocery on the left, a pharmacy with a giant black eagle above the door and a butcher shop with the sign of a fat pink pig, both on the right, a tobacco store on the left and the Town Hall on the right, and we saw no ruins anywhere! Children played in the middle of the cobblestone street, where horses pulled wagonloads of harvested loot and all the farm houses sat side by side, each with a giant gate offering a passing glimpse of crowded backyards, filled with hordes of chickens and geese and even an occasional ox, and nowhere did we see a single car!

Aunt Rachel, it turned out, lived all alone in an ancient monastery, right next to the church. The place had long ceased to be inhabited by monks and nuns, and it had been thoroughly remodeled just before the war to create a respectable home and office for Uncle Eddy, Superintendent of the Lutheran Church. For the purpose, two large buildings had been joined together and no fewer than thirty rooms had been outfitted with modern conveniences, ranging from electric light and telephones to central heating and indoor bathrooms, complete with running water, cold and hot. There was also a giant garden behind the remodeled mansion, filled with row upon row of apple, pear, and cherry trees, peach, plum, and walnut trees, along with bushes of gooseberries and red currants and beds of strawberries, carrots, cabbages and so much more! Naturally, all this called for lots of help, and the Church had provided its Superintendent's wife with three full-time servants, seven days a week.

But we knew none of this as we approached our new home. What we did see, before all else, was the massive tower of the church, probably 40 meters tall, and constructed in a most peculiar way. The lower three quarters of the tower consisted of a rectangular structure, made of large field stones encased in mortar and capped by a steep two-sided slate roof that rose to a central pinnacle from each of the rectangle's two longer sides. As a result, the rectangle's two shorter sides were somewhat taller, each rising to meet the line of the roof and a cross at the highest point. Just below the slate roof, four tall openings, rounded at the top, appeared on each of the structure's longer sides and two such openings appeared on each of the shorter sides. But a second and much smaller tower, this one made of metal and round and housing a bell, was embedded in the center of the slate roof and rose, perhaps another 10 meters, past a circular series of columns to a steeply pointed roof of its own.

The church itself, laid out in the form of a cross and still mostly hidden from our view by all the trees, was attached to the tower on the right. Aunt Rachel's monastery house was similarly attached on the left. Unlike the other houses in town, hers had yellow stucco walls, some of them overgrown with dark green moss, others hidden behind wooden scaffolding supporting an abundance of green leaves and large clumps of deliciously looking blue grapes. Pigeons were cooing in the gutters and a family of ravens announced our arrival.

Aunt Rachel must have heard the cawing; she appeared at the door before we could ring the bell. She was surprised that we had come so soon and led us to a small back room that overlooked the garden.

"You can have this one," she said, rather abruptly. She hadn't even said hello.

There were pretty curtains on the window, and I saw two beds and a crib, a chest of drawers and an armoire, all painted white. Right next door, there was also a bathroom with a flush toilet, a sink, a mirror, and an enamel tub. I couldn't believe that there was such a thing as hot running water!

I don't remember much of what happened next, except for meeting Mrs. Zweig, the cook and gardener, who took us to the kitchen to serve bread and cheese and a wonderful mixture of minced onions and tomatoes, along with a glass of chocolate milk.

"The Mr. Superintendent, he always sends us cocoa from France," she explained with a smile.

"Does he now?" my mother said, and then she put Helmut and me to bed.

We were exhausted, and I must have fallen asleep in no time. But later that night, I woke up with a start. Perhaps it was because Helmut kept coughing or because my mother was snoring. But my heart was pounding and I felt that I couldn't breathe. I stared at the clock on the night table and waited for the air raid sirens. The time was just right. And I kept hearing a frightening noise. It surrounded the house and swallowed the trees. It moved across the fields. It was in the air. It was everywhere, and it wouldn't stop.

I looked out of the window and saw nothing but darkness. No moon, no stars, not a single searchlight in the sky. My mother woke up and said it must be the humming of telephone wires, and I should go back to sleep. But I hadn't seen any telephone wires, so how could I sleep?

City boys don't know about crickets.

******

The next day, while Aunt Rachel introduced my mother to Erna, the house cleaner, I decided to check out our new surroundings. I started with the second floor, which had a long corridor, with shiny oak flooring, and lots and lots of doors, all of them closed. I opened the first one and found myself in a large room with two windows, shades drawn, half covered with heavy curtains made of fancy brocade, and sun rays making their way past the bottom of the shades to a big Persian carpet in the center of the room. The room, it seemed, was some kind of sitting room, elegantly furnished with all sorts of pieces of furniture, every one of which was made of *mahogany*, the reddish-brown wood we had once studied in school, and many of which featured elaborate carvings, usually of plants that I could not instantly identify.

The next room was almost a copy of the first, except that there was a large table in the middle of the room, surrounded by eight chairs, and all the furniture was made of *cherry wood*. By then I understood what was going on. I inspected thirteen rooms on the second floor and every one of them could easily be identified by a particular theme. There was a bedroom with lacy curtains and furniture of *birch*, a second bedroom featuring only *walnut* wood. There was a smoking room, filled with *black leather* chairs and a black leather couch and a little table with a chessboard standing in-between. Even the pieces were set up, as if they had been abandoned in the middle of a game. One could imagine a "check" or "gardez" still sounding in the room.

I found Uncle Eddy's study, too. Two of the walls were covered with shelves overflowing with books; his desk was covered with a large white sheet. The other wall, across from the windows, had two large pictures on it; I had seen them both in Berlin. One pictured Martin Luther; the Great Reformer; the other one showed the Wartburg, the famous castle where he once hid from the Pope, translated the Bible into German, and had many a fight with the Devil himself. Once he threw a bottle of ink at Satan, and visitors can see the splotch on the wall, I had been told, to this very day.

I had just finished inspecting the music room, complete with Steinway piano and violins and flutes in a glass case, when Aunt Rachel caught up with me. She was not happy.

"What do you think you are doing?" she yelled. "These rooms are not to be touched until Uncle Eddy gets home! Don't you ever go up here again!"

"And wipe that stupid grin off your face," she added.

I knew what she was talking about. It had become a habit of mine to laugh at anyone who was attacking me. It wasn't very smart, but I just couldn't help it.

"Come down with me and I'll give you something useful to do," she said firmly, and down we went. Aunt Rachel told my mother what I had done and explained to her as well that our room was our room, but the rest of the house was taboo.

"Except for the bathroom and the kitchen, of course," she corrected herself.

"But even there," she continued, "as you well know, 'too many cooks spoil the broth.' It's *my* kitchen and I will be the one who tells Frieda what to do. Which reminds me, I got to check out what she's up to in the garden…" and out the front door she went.

My mother cried; she always cried, it seemed. I told her what I had found upstairs. And, rather than chiding me, she agreed to be my ally. We decided to inspect the downstairs *together*, while Aunt Rachel was checking up on Mrs. Zweig and Helmut was still asleep. My mother was so much fun!

But we didn't get to see much before Aunt Rachel was back, just two of the rooms. One of them was empty, except for lots of paintings on the walls; we later named it "the gallery." The other one had ornate tablecloths hanging from all the walls, and there were glass display cases filled with Greek vases and Chinese porcelain and all sorts of pieces of pewter. There were also unopened boxes on the floor in the middle of the room. They had been sent from Paris; the stamps and Uncle Eddy's return address made it very clear. We called that room "the museum."

Like two conspirators, we made it back into our room just before Aunt Rachel entered the house.

She had a project for me, she said, at least until I was enrolled in school in the coming week.

"Frieda is harvesting the apples this week," Aunt Rachel said to me, "why don't you go in the garden and help her."

"First, we fill up the baskets," she continued without waiting for my response, "then we bring them into the cellar and lay the apples on the shelves along the walls. Frieda will show you, but be very, very careful when you handle the fruit. Treat each apple with the utmost of care. Like a raw egg. There must be no dent of any kind or the apple will rot in no time."

I was more than glad to oblige, and the project turned out to be fun, too. For one thing, I learned all about the garden, which was amazingly huge. And I loved climbing the trees. The walnut trees were the best, because their branches were so incredibly supple, as if they were made of rubber. I could climb along the trunk to the top of the tree, then crawl outwards along a branch, and that branch would gradually bend downward under my weight, deposit me gently on the ground, and snap back up to its original place. That was not something one could do with any other type of tree!

Mrs. Zweig taught me how to harvest the apples without bruising them. She also showed me how to deposit apples carefully on the cellar shelves, where they might, with some luck, last through the winter and even longer, perhaps even until a new harvest came along.

I didn't like being in the cellar, though. It made me think of air raids and I couldn't breathe. It also scared me to realize that there were no reinforcements and supports of any kind. If this house were ever to be bombed, everyone in the cellar would surely be crushed or burned. I made a mental note that this cellar was no place to be.

Mrs. Zweig also taught me something else, although, perhaps, inadvertently. While I was sitting in the apple tree, she introduced me to 'Mrs. Pastor Jahn' who had come into the garden and who, she said, was the wife of the minister currently taking care of the church. They were living in a tiny two-room cottage on the other side of the church, which I had seen but imagined to be a barn because it was so small and also had a thatched roof. In any case, according to the rules of the local church, I was told, Pastor and Mrs. Jahn were entitled to *some* of the fruit that the monastery garden produced, but only to the 'drop fruit,' which was the fruit that accidentally fell off any one of the fifty trees and was lying on the ground. That's why Mrs. Pastor Jahn walked though the garden once a day with a basket in her arm. When I heard the story, I thought of all the times my mother had told me to be kind and willing to share. So I violently shook the tree in which I was sitting and a shower of apples fell to the ground, all bruised. Mrs. Zweig laughed and said I was a good kid. I wondered what Mrs. Pastor Jahn would do when nobody was looking.

******

The next day was Sunday and, right after breakfast, the bell called everyone to church. I was surprised that the bell was still there and hadn't been melted down. In any case, none of us went to the service.

"Pastor Jahn is boring, nothing like Eddy," Aunt Rachel sighed and that was it as far as she was concerned.

"Feel free to go," Aunt Rachel said, looking at my mother.

"But allow me to give you just a bit of friendly advice," she added. "Forget about that *Nivea* cream and all that powder and lipstick and perfume you are using. People around here don't go for all that big-city stuff. They are liable to call you a whore."

"What's a whore?" I asked, but neither my mother nor Aunt Rachel would answer me.

"Well, thanks a lot," my mother said to Aunt Rachel and turned to me. "Why don't you go and explore the village, Hansel. I bet it'll be fun! Today you have all day; tomorrow we'll have to sign you up for school."

Once again, I was glad to oblige, but not before getting some pointers from Mrs. Zweig who was sitting in the kitchen laying out Tarot cards for a woman I hadn't met.

"That's Irma," Mrs. Zweig said, "she's in charge of washing and ironing. She also helps with the canning and such, but she's just visiting today. She's not working on Sundays."

"Now you won't tell on us about the cards, will you?" Irma said to me. "The Mrs. Superintendent, she doesn't like this satanic stuff."

"Not if you tell me how to get into the castle," I said with a wink. "My Aunt Lotte back in Berlin told me all about those cards; I think they are neat."

I followed their advice and took the shortcut to the castle, right down the narrow path along the brook behind our house. A little sparrow moved before me, darting from willow tree to willow tree as I went, almost like a scout.

The castle wasn't anything like the one in Berlin where the Kaiser used to live. There were no gardens, fountains, or statues. There were no people standing guard on polished floors, eagerly outfitting visitors with oversized shoes made of felt, lest they make a scratch. There were no gilded ceilings, fancy tapestry, and fine pieces of furniture. There were no vases filled with flowers, display cases filled with jewelry, or giant windows covered with curtains of lace.

In fact, the castle that I found was not remotely of the kind I had seen in fairy tale books. There was a giant circle of sixteen houses, tightly joined together like Aunt Rachel's monastery house, but ranging between two and four stories in height, all made of yellow-painted stucco and capped with steep roofs of reddish clay tiles. If one entered the circle of houses through a tiny unlocked gate, one came face to face with the first of two round towers. This one, the taller one, was almost entirely made of red brick, completely windowless, and topped with a structure resembling a bishop's cap. And if one dared enter the tower through a tiny wooden door, one discovered it to be hollow, except for a creaky old spiral staircase that swayed back and forth when anyone stepped on it and that, by this very fact, invited naïve little boys to a climb to the very top. And from the very top one could recognize that the entire village, in turn, formed a tightly packed circle, with not a single structure beyond its outer rim. And all around one could see a long summer dying; although it was still warm and there hadn't been a killing frost. The grass was brown, the fields were being plowed, the red oaks were turning yellow, and cloud-shaped shadows were racing across the land …

Looking straight down, one could also see that the castle was, in fact, a working farm, with most of the buildings being used as barns. Some were being filled with hay at that very moment; others, just as clearly, were the homes of horses or cows, pigs or sheep. And if one dared, one could retrace one's steps, climb down to the ground, and investigate the second tower that stood outside

the circle of castle barns. That tower was not as tall, but was also made of bricks, with a steep triangular structure at its top, and a stork's nest on top of that.

I did all this, of course, and when I opened the heavy door to the second tower, I found it to be just as empty, silent, and windowless as the first. It was emptier, perhaps; there wasn't even a spiral staircase there. Still, I saw that weeds had invaded the inside; one wall was overgrown with ivy. I heard water dripping, somewhere in the dark. Just then, the sun caught me from behind and made long, scary shadows in front of me. And as it burned away the ghostly mist, I could read the signs someone had scrawled on the opposite wall:

"This is where Prussian kings fed their prisoners to the rats"

and

"This is where Hans Edler zu Putlitz was eaten by rats"

I took a step to get a better look and almost stumbled over a broken trap door pretending to cover the cellar steps. I looked into the black abyss and smelled dampness and decay coming from below. I stared into the depth and waited and stared some more. I could swear I saw something move. I wasn't about to stay long enough to make sure. I turned to see the sun sinking lower and lower in the southwest and I saw a quarter-moon rising in the southeast. I heard frogs making scary noises along the brook as I ran home.

21. VILLAGE IDIOT
[September 1944]

As you can imagine, it takes a while for a city boy to get used to the ways of the countryside. I made new and surprising discoveries every day, even of things that seem so utterly obvious in retrospect. I remember the Monday morning on which we were scheduled to register at the local town hall. Right after breakfast, Mrs. Zweig took a step ladder and a bunch of tools and disappeared into the garden. Aunt Rachel said she would have to go as well to supervise the pruning of the fruit trees. She put on a pair of yellow rubber gloves and pulled a huge pile of burlap from a closet.

"We do that every fall," Aunt Rachel explained. "Proper pruning makes for healthier trees and bigger fruit next summer. We also wrap the trunks with plenty of burlap; otherwise the rabbits and squirrels gnaw at the bark all winter, which can easily kill a tree."

I followed them into the garden and that's when I first noticed that different kinds of trees had different types of bark and that none of them was endowed by nature with the sooty kind of coat that was common in Berlin. Obvious, of course! Nobody in Ziesar burned the low-grade lignite coal that everybody used in Berlin.

I remember something else about that day. It had only been 8:30 or so in the morning when I had had the epiphany about the trees, and we didn't have to be at the Town Hall till 10. That was my chance to sneak into Uncle Eddy's study and have a look at his massive dictionary. It sat on a little table all by itself and one couldn't miss it. Given my mother's unwillingness to explain it, I was determined to look up the word "whore."

Unfortunately, even the gigantic book was of little help. For one thing, it offered three answers:

1) a person who accepts payment in exchange for sexual relations
2) a person considered sexually promiscuous
3) a person considered to have compromised principles for personal gain

In addition, the book spoke in riddles. What were sexual relations? What was promiscuous? I looked up the latter and got the same kind of double-talk:

"Promiscuous," it said, "having casual sexual relations, frequently with different partners." So what did all that have to do with my mother putting on lipstick and using perfume and *Nivea* cream? I knew less than before! So I sneaked back down and asked my mother: "What are sexual relations?"

"Hansel!" she said, "What on earth makes you ask such a thing? Not now, please, we have to be at the Town Hall in ten minutes."

And that was that. Grown-ups were weird. They never gave a straight answer, not if they could help it.

******

The Town Hall was just around the corner on Breite Weg; we had passed it on the day we arrived. I noticed that a special tree was standing in front of it. I could tell that it was special, because it was standing in a raised bed cut out from among the cobblestones and it was surrounded by four small posts which were linked with an iron chain. The arrangement looked just like the exhibits I had seen in museums in Berlin. In fact, there was also a bronze sign.

"1,000-Year Oak, Symbol of the Destiny of the Third Reich," it said.

I got the point. The Führer had promised that his government would last a thousand years, but the oak, of course, was much younger than that.

"Come on, Hansel," my mother said. "Take Helmut's hand."

We climbed up the steps and my mother talked to the receptionist about residency papers and ration cards. She also gave her the *Bombenschein* [bombed-out certificate] which the Red Cross had given us and which proved that we had lost everything. Meanwhile, Helmut and I inspected the hunting trophies on the walls and the shelves filled with rows of pewter jugs and bright earthenware plates. Across from them was a row of wooden pegs; one of them held an umbrella, another one the jacket of an SS uniform, and a third one the associated cap with the skull and crossbones. There was a large poster on the wall as well; it pictured an infantryman moving forward with gun and fixed bayonet, but at that very moment being knifed in the back by a shadowy figure with the Star of David on its sleeve. "The Betrayal of Judas," the caption said, "A woodcut by Willy Knabe."

"You are all set," I heard the receptionist say, as she handed my mother a piece of paper, "but you should also see Dr. Dietrich, right through that door."

"Dr. Dietrich, Mayor," the sign said. We found him sitting behind a marble-topped desk, his glasses floating at the tip of his nose. A big bottle of black ink sat on one end; a stack of papers lay on the other. A small photograph in a green frame stood in-between. I recognized the man in the picture; he had been hanging on the wall in Mr. Barzel's class. Baldur von Schirach was his name and he was a leader of the Hitler Youth for many years until he became District Leader of Vienna. I knew all about that, too. As Mr. Eisler had told us, the Führer abolished all the old states—Prussia, Saxony, Bavaria, and so on—and divided Germany into Administrative Districts, each of which was governed by a *District Leader* who was directly responsible to the Führer. That thought drew my attention to the picture of Adolf Hitler that hung on the wall. It was a painting, similar to many photographs I had seen, in which he wore a brown uniform, black boots, and a swastika armband. Dr. Dietrich was dressed in pretty much the same way, but I saw three stars on the collar of his uniform, which made him an SA captain.

"Good morning," my mother said, "we are supposed to see you. Coming from Berlin, just got our residency papers."

Dr. Dietrich jumped to his feet, clicked his heels, raised his right hand, and said sharply:

"Heil Hitler! That's how we do it around here. You better take heed!"

He sat down and took the papers from my mother's hand.

"May we sit down?" my mother asked.

"Of course, that's what chairs are for," Dr. Dietrich said, without looking up.

I noticed a framed sign on the wall. "The Jews Are Our Curse," it said.

"All right then," Dr. Dietrich said, finally, "welcome to Ziesar."

"And here is your work assignment," he continued, looking at my mother. "You will work at Steinert's, part-time, because of the small child. It's a ceramics factory, right here at the edge of town. Used to make flower pots, vases, and the like; they make insulators for electric and telephone lines now. You can take the baby along. It'll be an easy job, you'll hardly have to do a thing, mainly keep an eye on a bunch of Italian traitors, Badoglio bastards all of them and lazy as can be."

He handed my mother a white card.

"And we, young man," Dr. Dietrich concluded, looking at me, "will meet again in school, at the end of School Street, tomorrow at eight."

Dr. Dietrich explained that he was also the school principal and I would learn all there is to know about the school in the morning.

"What do you want to be when you grow up?" he said as we were about to leave.

"I want to be a pilot," I said, which surprised me and my mother alike. Where did *that* come from? I certainly didn't know.

"An excellent choice," Dr. Dietrich said before I could think about it. "The Air Force needs well educated young men and you are on your way."

"Which reminds me," Dr. Dietrich added, looking at my mother and me, "I have some welcome presents for both of you."

He gave my mother a little radio, the familiar Goebbels Snout, although, of course, he didn't call it that. He also gave her a pamphlet about the history of Ziesar. In turn, he gave me three books. One was called *The Cossacks*, the next one, *Opossum*, and the third one, *The Olympic Games of*

1936, which was full of pictures. Helmut got nothing.

I spent the rest of the day examining our new-found treasures. As expected, the radio only worked with German stations; I managed to tune in Radio Berlin, Radio Germany, and Radio Hamburg. No luck with Radio Beromünster or the BBC.

My mother's pamphlet was more interesting. It was filled with colorful drawings and said that Ziesar had been founded almost 1,000 years ago, in the year 948 to be exact, by a man called Clio who built an early version of the castle. Eventually, it had seven towers. By then, the town had made an alliance with the Bishop of Brandenburg, which was the occasion of putting a red-brick bishop's cap on top of the tallest castle tower. Later still, the allies successfully battled the Slavs, while Zisterzienser nuns and monks lived in the cloister. More recently, Frederick the Great built a fancy house in town and he stayed there whenever he inspected his troops nearby. And Queen Luise stayed at the local inn, called the *Prince of Prussia*, and never missed a chance to drink tea at the *Alte Post*. In our day, the pamphlet concluded, Ziesar was linked to the rest of Germany not only by rail but, more importantly, by the Führer's Road, the *Autobahn*, which was a mere three kilometers away. There was also a picture of the ceramics factory where my mother was scheduled to work. I showed it to her.

It took much longer to examine my three books; in fact, I didn't finish doing that till Christmas, some 3 months later. *The Cossacks* told the story of great cavalry men, living mostly in the Ukraine. The word itself, the book said, came from the Turkish *qazaq*, which meant *adventurer*. Nowadays, the Cossacks were excellent hunters of Bolsheviks, Gypsies, and Jews, the book said.

The *Opossum* book described life in the Southern United States. The hero was a white rancher who had lots of black slaves. One day, he decided to teach his teenage son about sex and "they had their way with a beautiful slave girl in a freight car parked at the railroad station." The girl pleaded with them to leave her alone, having just been married, but they persisted. I read the above passage and I read it again, but I didn't understand the story at all, and when I asked my mother, she was angry and threw the book away.

She did let me keep the Olympics book, however, and Helmut and I had fun with it. When we first looked at the pictures, and there were over 200 of them, they all seemed fuzzy and unclear. But once we put on a special set of glasses, which were embedded in the back of the book, a miracle happened. Everything appeared in three dimensions and looked as alive and close as it would have if we had stood right there, taking the pictures ourselves! In fact, I liked my book better than the film about the XI Olympic Games in Berlin, which had been made by a famous woman, Leni Riefenstahl, and we had seen at school in Berlin.

******

It was easy to find the school the next morning. It was a big building made of red brick, just as in Berlin, but it wasn't as tall. Nor were there any ruins all around, just meadows and hundreds of white sheep grazing in the rising sun. Dr. Dietrich stood at the door, waiting for me. He was again dressed in his uniform, but he also had a Yellow Uncle in his hand. I knew he was in charge. He took me to his office and explained that I would once again start at the beginning of 7th grade, because their school year began in early fall rather than on January 1, as in Berlin. He also said that he had seen my excellent record and was very pleased.

"You will have 12 subjects, 3 hours per week each," he said, "Mondays through Fridays 8 to 15:30 and 18 minutes for lunch."

He handed me a card, which listed the subjects like this:

German, English, Latin;

History/Contemporary Issues, Geography;

Biology, Chemistry, Physics;

Mathematics;

Music, Religion, Sports.

Note: Students are also graded on Conduct, Industry, Attention, Penmanship, and Orderliness in Textbooks and Notebooks.

Then Dr. Dietrich took me to my classroom where everybody stared at me, but I pretended not to notice. In the back of the room, I saw the pictures of two men, one of whom I recognized immediately. I had never seen the other one, but the captions underneath both were clearly visible, even from the door. Frederick the Great (1712–1786) said the first one; Immanuel Kant (1724–1804) said the other. There was smaller print as well, but I couldn't read that until later in the week when I had time to explore.

"Frederick the Great (1712–1786)," said one of the labels, "Won the War of the Austrian Succession (1740–1748) as well as the Seven Years' War (1756–1763) and, thus, brought Prussia great military prestige throughout Europe."

"Immanuel Kant (1724–1804)," said the other label, "German philosopher whose synthesis of rationalism and empiricism marks the beginning of idealism; put forward a system of ethics based on the categorical imperative."

But, as I said, all that came later. At the moment I entered, when all the farmer boys looked me over, my attention was riveted to something else entirely: The teacher I was about to meet was a *woman* and there were also lots of girls in the class. I had never seen anything like that in Berlin!

"Unlike in Berlin," Dr. Dietrich said, interrupting my thoughts, "you will have many different teachers here, each teaching a different subject. This is Mrs. Dr. Dietrich; she's in charge of biology."

I sat down as in a dream. I kept looking at the girl with the black braids. She sat across the room, and I wondered whether Snow White might have looked like that, or Sleeping Beauty. I found out later that her name was Helga.

In the meantime, Mrs. Dr. Dietrich talked about Germany's birds. Her words, hypnotically and rhythmically, washed over my mind like the distant waves on the Baltic coast, almost, but not quite, putting me to sleep. I kept staring at Helga, and I didn't even take notes.

"For a century now," said Mrs. Dr. Dietrich, "voices have been raised around the world about the possible extinction of animal species due to the actions of people. The most infamous example is the American buffalo. At one point, hundreds of thousands of them were roaming the prairie; now hardly any are left—all because of conscienceless hunters, who lack feeling for these creatures, and because of meat producers, who have an insatiable hunger for profit. Similar stories could be told about bears, wolves, and wild cats. In some countries, there are even bounties for birds of prey, which leads to the coldhearted murder of eagles, owls, and ravens."

"But not in Germany!" she exclaimed, almost awakening me from my trance. "Under the leadership of our Führer, we have established nature reserves and taken resolute measures to preserve the animal kingdom. To give just one example, our government has established breeding colonies for 12,000 pairs of seagulls on Borkum and Sylt, which yield 30,000 eggs per year, which are nursed into new seagulls. And that's what we will talk about in the coming months: Germany's birds. Before the year is over, we will have studied 25 different types, including," and now she read from her notes, "eagles, hawks, falcons, buzzards, and owls, then herons, storks, cranes, snipes, and ducks, then swallows, seagulls, swans, and geese, and, finally, woodpeckers and cuckoos, ravens and crows, larks and thrushes, nightingales and sandpipers, and doves, partridges and pheasants. Surely, you have seen the storks at the castle? Did you know that the adults have a wig span of 2 meters? That's more than the height of the tallest man!"

Snap! went the Yellow Uncle on the desk... I was wide awake then.

"There will be no more classes today," said Dr. Dietrich, who had somehow come back into the class while I was daydreaming. "You will form groups of 10 and collect chaff for victory."

Everyone seemed to know what to do. Mrs. Dr. Dietrich told me to follow one of the big boys;

and out of the back door we marched, right into the fields behind the school.

There, outside, I heard the sound of huge swarms of bees, but they were really formations of bombers, way, way up in the sky, heading for Berlin, the sun reflecting off their canopies and propellers, glittering, shimmering, and making my mind spin.

I saw bullets stitching their way across a bridge and little blue flames feeding on the melted fat of a corpse lying on the sidewalk; I felt choking plaster dust in my throat and my heart pounding. My thoughts were too terrible to utter aloud, my images too horrible to describe....

And the others kept pointing at me. As I dodged thistles and nettles and bumble bees, I didn't keep up with the general line of advance. Also I didn't know what to do, since I had never heard of *chaff* before.

Before long, everyone was gathering up silvery strips of aluminum that were draped over all the potato plants. I did the same, but I couldn't figure out who had spread all this Christmas tinsel and why. I asked the big boy leading our group, but he just laughed and repeated my question out loud. Everybody stood around me in a circle and whispered, even the pretty girls in their Jungmädel uniforms [Jungmädel = junior division of BDM, the female equivalent of the Hitler Youth, consisting of "Aryan" girls aged 10-14]. Then someone said I had just gotten a new name and one of the big boys bent back the little finger of my right hand till it hurt and another boy did the same thing with the left hand. Without letting go, they pulled me across the field and lifted me across a fence that said "Beware of the bull." They all chanted "Village idiot, village idiot, village idiot ..."

******

Aunt Rachel was not happy when I got home and tracked all the dirt through the house, even though I had washed off the green cow dung under the garden pump before I went inside. She said she hoped I hadn't similarly annoyed Mrs. Dr. Dietrich. After all, she was the Mayor's wife and also the sister of the District Leader of Magdeburg, a most important man.

My mother didn't like what Aunt Rachel had said and took me into our room. While I was in school, my mother had bought a large mirror, and there were blankets on the bed. She had a new pair of pajamas for me, too. I put them on and looked at myself in the mirror. Then I turned up the brims of my leggings as far as they would go until I had two puffy rings of cloth above each knee. I liked the way I looked. Just like the prince in my old *Cinderella* book. In my mind, I pictured Helga as my princess.

That night, I had nightmares and ran into the cellar to check out once again how safe it was. My mother took me to Dr. Weiss, right there in the middle of the night. Unlike Dr. Dietrich, Dr. Weiss was a real doctor and lived just down the street from us. He said my pulse was far too high and gave us a bottle of Valerian, a water-like liquid, which, he said, we should use with the utmost of care.

"Give him precisely three drops on a spoonful of sugar whenever he's upset," he said. "Don't give him more than that; we don't want his heart to stop."

That remark scared me to death and caused me to make another trip to Uncle Eddy's dictionary when the first chance arose.

"Valerian," it said, "from the plant of the genus *Valeriana*, widely cultivated in Europe and Asia for its small, fragrant white to pink and lavender flowers. The rootstalk of the plant can also be turned into a powerful sedative, used in medicine."

I knew what to do. Three drops per day in sugar. No more, lest my heart stop.

Ziesar's history

22. CHRISTIANITY

[October – November 1944]

In the weeks that followed our night-time visit to Dr. Weiss, many things happened that upset me. Unfortunately, my mother was less than forthcoming with my Valerian drops. She thought they were much too dangerous and said Dr. Weiss was a quack. As I soon discovered in Uncle Eddy's dictionary, the word referred to either "the characteristic sound uttered by a duck" or to "a charlatan who pretends to be a physician and dispenses medical advice and treatment." Accordingly, I did a little bit of investigating by looking more carefully at the white enamel sign outside Dr. Weiss's office.

"Dr. med. Werner Weiss," it said, "Specialist in Dermatology and Venereal Diseases."

As usual, this raised more questions than it answered. As was to be expected, too, my mother wouldn't explain, which only increased my curiosity. But, alas, I had to wait for my explanation because my mother was clearly too busy with other things. She had started her job at the ceramics plant and her assignment to the "Strike Force for Total War" soon got her into trouble with Aunt Rachel.

It all started when my mother discovered that there was a prisoner-of-war camp outside the village and it was from there that military guards, carrying rifles with fixed bayonets, marched a contingent of Badoglio Italians to the ceramics plant each day. My mother was to watch over their work inside the plant, which proved difficult because she spoke no Italian, and the Italians spoke no German. Nevertheless, they managed to communicate using sign language, and one thing quickly became clear: The prisoners received no medical attention and very little food. In fact, they were starving.

"That's not a problem that concerns you," one of the guards said to my mother. "Those lazy bastards are lucky to be alive. Nobody is more despicable than an ally who has changed sides."

My mother's German coworkers echoed the thought, which was supposed to be a direct quote from the Führer. And, as if it made matters better, my mother's coworkers pointed out that other POWs at the camp were much worse off by far.

"You should see the Russians," said Mrs. Mertsch, "they are positively emaciated. Their clothes are in tatters and they sleep on the ground, wrapped in filthy blankets. Last spring, the SS was still in charge of the camp and they always had their fun with the prisoners. Sometimes they made them strip and sing for hours on end, threatening to set the dogs on them if they stopped. At other times, they made them do knee bends or goose-step in rapid time, hitting them with rubber truncheons if they failed to do it right. Frieda, that's my daughter, told me all about it; she's a secretary at the camp."

"But it's not all bad," interjected Mrs. Krohn. "Don't exaggerate. My daughter works in the camp, too; she's a cook. She says they also have Americans, and some English and French, and *they* live like kings. They don't have to work, you know, lie in the sun all day with their hats over their eyes or play ball or cards and they even get letters and Red Cross packages! It's a long holiday for them."

"For all we know," added Mrs. Ernst, "those Russians were being punished for trying to escape or to murder a guard. You got to have discipline in a place like that."

Well, my mother didn't buy that story and from that day on she sneaked all sorts of food out of Aunt Rachel's pantry and fed it to her Italians at work. She brought them other supplies as well, such as band-aids and bars of soap and even some clothes—until Aunt Rachel discovered it.

"Are you out of your mind?" she screamed. "Do you realize what you are doing? You are aiding and abetting the enemy in a time of war! THAT'S HIGH TREASON! We could all get killed over this! Stop it right now or you are out of here!"

I don't remember exactly what happened next, except that my mother said something sarcastic about "good old Christianity at work" and she wasn't referring to herself and that made Aunt Rachel get red in the face. One would have thought that things could hardly get worse, but I managed to arrange that on the very next day when my eagerness to hear the latest news about the war led me back into Uncle Eddy's study, where I had seen a really fancy radio set. I managed to tune in the BBC and found it not jammed. I listened to the monthly summary of events:

October/November 1944

- V2 rockets, traveling at supersonic speeds, now launched against Britain from Holland
- Field Marshal Erwin Rommel, the desert fox, apparently implicated in the July plot, dies mysteriously, but still gets state funeral
- Marshal Tito captures Belgrade
- Aachen surrenders to U.S forces
- The U.S., U.K., and U.S.S.R. recognize the new Italian government under Premier Ivanoe Bonomiä
- German positions in Holland and Belgium increasingly untenable
- Russian troops near Warsaw

- Russian troops take Lithuania
- Russian troops near Budapest
- A joint U.S. Army/Navy statement holds it "entirely possible for Hitler's flying bombs to reach the United States from Europe"

Unfortunately, Aunt Rachel caught me in the middle of the report. To make matters worse, she also saw that I had rummaged through one of Uncle Eddy's huge packages and had discovered its contents: bottles of French champagne, cognac, and gin; a box of cigars; all sorts of satin underwear, silk stockings, and a silver fox fur coat! That's when she screamed a lot and told us to take our things and get out.

"You and that son of yours are just as crazy as Arthur," she said to my mother. "You are jeopardizing my life and Eddy's as well. That's unforgivable."

But she still gave me a good-bye present, taken from Uncle Eddy's study, a beautifully bound copy of *Dr. Martin Luther's Catechism, With Bible Sayings, Gospels, and Epistles*, 16th edition, Breslau, 1885.

******

My mother thought of reminding Aunt Rachel of the document she had received from Dr. Dietrich. As usual, I had made a copy of it:

PLACEMENT OF BOMBING VICTIMS IN THE VILLAGE OF ZIESAR

To: Mrs. Superintendent Rachel Lichtenberg, Ziesar, Cloister Street 3

According to laws and executive orders promulgated on 1 September 1939 and 19 August 1943, the following rooms are sequestered:

1 bedroom, plus necessary common rooms (bathroom, corridors, kitchen, living room) and are to be made available forthwith to the family:

Gertrud, Hans, and Helmut Keller.

Legal recourse against this order does not exist.

15 September 1944
Dr. Dietrich,
Mayor, Village of Ziesar, District of Magdeburg

But Mrs. Zweig told my mother to go back to the Town Hall and talk to the housing officer, which we did, dragging Helmut along. Like Aunt Rachel, he was screaming, too.

"Now you aren't Catholic, are you?" the housing officer asked after my mother had inquired about another place to live. My mother shook her head.

"Then you are in luck," he smiled. "You'll fit right in at the Albrecht place. You can live above the butcher shop, on Breite Weg, Number 29."

The place was easy to find, being on the main street and having a sign with a pig hanging above the shop window, which we had noticed even on the first day while marching into town. We walked into the shop and met Mr. Albrecht himself. He had bushy white hair, bright blue eyes, and was huge. He must have been nearly two meters tall and may well have weighed three hundred pounds. He was also short of breath, and his face was red. We caught him in the middle of weighing sausages on an old rusty scale that was hanging from chains fastened to the ceiling. When he learned who we were, he stopped and took us to a room above the shop. Two windows faced the street, right above the entrance to the store. We had pretty lace curtains, two beds, a small table, and two chairs. There was a walk-in closet, too, and I saw a stool in the corner with a ceramic wash basin and a water pitcher. The smell of freshly oiled floors hung in the air.

Swarms of flies were buzzing about the room and I noticed honey-colored flypaper dangling from the ceiling and the fact that the windows, unlike Aunt Rachel's, didn't have any screens. Helmut was climbing onto one of the beds.

"The pump's in the backyard, the latrine's out in back—way back, near the fields—and there's a little kitchen through that door," Mr. Albrecht said, pointing to a small opening in the back of the room.

My mother and I had a look and found a second room, tiny, windowless, and nearly empty, except for an aluminum pail, a broom made of straw, and a black cast-iron stove. The stove stood on a shiny sheet of aluminum that was nailed to the floor. Another such sheet was nailed to a spot near the ceiling where the stove pipe disappeared into the wall.

"That stove can get pretty hot," Mr. Albrecht explained when he saw us stare at the aluminum. "We don't want to burn the house down. But you'll have to get your own firewood eventually. Until you do, feel free to use the pile in the backyard."

"Or, if you prefer," Mr. Albrecht added, "you can also use the big kitchen downstairs, but then you'll have to share it with two other bombed-out families. They are from Cologne, a bunch of Catholics, I'm afraid. Sure am sorry about *that*; let me know if they give you any trouble."

He turned to leave, but stopped at the door and grinned at my mother.

"You know the joke about the whales, don't you?" he asked, "Used to be my father's favorite:

The moon sails in the sky, the sheep graze down below, the whales live lower still, their shit drifts lower yet. *But Catholics are lower than whale shit!*"

He laughed so hard, his whole body shook. I saw ripples flowing over his belly like waves on the ocean. After he left, my mother sat down at the table and cried.

******

I took the pail and went to explore the back yard. The water pump stood next to the back door. It was all dressed in straw, to keep the water from freezing in the winter, Mr. Albrecht said. The handle was rusty and the pump made a squeaking noise when I filled up our pail.

I also found the big pile of firewood. It was really tall, stacked up to look like an Egyptian pyramid. Mr. Albrecht said he'd teach me how to build one just like it. All I had to do was to get lots of small trees from the forest; I could borrow his hand cart and a saw. And he'd teach me what to do next, he said, pointing to a chopping block with an axe stuck in it.

I had a look at the outdoor toilet next—way out in back, just as advertised. It consisted of a small wooden shack with four doors, each of which had a hole in it near the top, in the form of a heart. Inside each of the four cubicles was a wooden bench with a circular hole, no cover, and a bad smell. There also were piles of newspapers, some of them cut into little rectangles, to serve as toilet paper. And, again, there were swarms of flies, but I saw no flypaper there. I opened one of the doors a second time and made it slam against the door frame with a bang.

"Gets pretty cold in the winter out here," Mr. Albrecht said, just in case I was having too much fun, "but at least those damn flies will be gone."

After Mr. Albrecht had disappeared, I slammed the toilet door a few more times and then sat down to examine one of the newspaper piles. There were lots of copies of *Der Angriff* [The Attack], a military paper I thought, and they featured many an article about Berlin. One of them showed photographs of the *Tiergarten*, Berlin's central park where dozens of marble busts of the *Hohenzollern* dynasty were lined up along its central boulevard. Berliners referred to it jokingly as *Puppenallee* [Avenue of the Dolls]. Dieter and I had been there. I almost cried at the thought, but was determined not to lose control of my feelings again, not ever. So I held back my tears and examined another issue of the same paper instead. It reported that there had been 160,564 Jews in 1933 Berlin, only 140,000 by 1937, then 75,000 by 1939, and none at all by 1943. I took the article to my mother, but she wouldn't read it, which inspired me to make it the first item in a new secret stash I created under my new bed. As I told you, it was the sort of thing Dieter and I had always done: gather evidence about all the things the adults refused to discuss.

Later that day, Mr. Albrecht showed me how the household waste water should be dumped into the side street, where it would run downhill to open fields, just like the effluent from his abattoir, where he slaughtered, he said, cows and pigs and sheep and an occasional horse. The place was spanking clean, covered with white tiles on all the walls and floors, and filled with all sorts of shiny machinery to make sausages and smoked pork chops and such. I saw a vat full of discarded horns and rolls and rolls of cowhide, preserved in salt.

When I finally returned with my pail of fresh water, my mother was talking with Mrs. Albrecht who had a son, she said, fighting somewhere in Italy. She hadn't heard from him since Naples, and my mother told her about the Italians at the ceramics plant and about my father from whom we hadn't heard in many months. They both cried, but then Mrs. Albrecht told my mother to come down for lunch till we got settled in. On that day, we had a choice, she said: salt potatoes with gravy and Kassler or rye bread with lard and smoked sausages.

"Whatever's left, you can take to the ceramics plant," she whispered.

I knew my mother was very happy about that. I also knew about the delicacies waiting for us. I had watched my grandmother make both.

"Salt potatoes are regular potatoes that are peeled when raw and then cooked in salt water," I explained to Helmut, although I wasn't sure he understood a word I said.

"Kassler is smoked pork, and lard is made by melting a chunk of suet till it spreads like hot butter and, if you are lucky, leaving in the greaves."

After lunch, Mrs. Albrecht gave my mother a bowl of oatmeal cookies and my mother told me to divide them evenly between Helmut and me. I counted thirteen and said that an even division of an odd number was logically impossible. My mother ate one of the cookies and told me to try again.

She also told me to say "thank you" to Mrs. Albrecht, but I refused. That was a problem of mine going back several years, to a day when we had had a family gathering at our apartment in Berlin. Aunt Martel had brought me a bar of milk chocolate, an extremely rare delicacy in those days, but when I had started to eat it, contrary to earlier instructions I should add, my mother had told me to share it with all the guests around the table. That was a bad idea in my view because such generosity would leave exactly nothing for me. Still, my mother had insisted, which had led Aunt Gerda to ask my cousin Werner to share his cookies as well. And then to make matters even worse, my mother had asked me to say "thank you" for one little cookie. It had just been too much for me and my feeling of outrage had stayed with me ever since.

******

The day after we moved in with the Albrechts, I went back to school. Our first subject of the day was religion, taught by none other than Pastor Jahn. He and I, it seemed, were destined not to get along. He asked me for my name, which was nice and seemed to indicate that I wouldn't be viewed as a mere number, as in Berlin. But when I said "Hans," he was annoyed and wanted to know my *middle* name. I didn't have one and tried to explain. My father had a middle name, Oskar, I said, and my mother had a middle name, Anna, but my parents had decided that giving *two* names to children was an unfortunate sign of ambivalence. It was vastly preferable to make up one's mind and come up with a single name, they had said, and that's why they had just called me *Hans* and my little brother *Helmut* and that was that.

Pastor Jahn didn't like my explanation at all and intimated that I was on the verge of being insolent, which I must have confirmed by grinning and saying that *Jesus* didn't have a middle name either. Pastor Jahn shot an angry look at me and then changed the subject. He gave us each a sheet of paper which, he said, contained an excerpt from Romans 13:

"Let all people be subject to the governing authority that has power over them. For there is no government authority except from God, and wherever governmental authority exists it has been instituted by God. Those who therefore resist such authority resist what God has appointed, and those who resist will call judgment upon themselves."

Pastor Jahn said that a very important lesson was to be learned here and that the July plotters who had tried to kill our Führer had clearly ignored that lesson.

"What is that lesson, do you think?" he asked.

I decided to answer him and said: "That the Führer has been put there by God…"

But before he could reward me with an emphatic "excellent," I continued: "…and that Stalin has been put there by God and so also Churchill and Roosevelt."

Pastor Jahn was not happy. He said I was an impudent brat and that God, the Almighty Father, would surely punish me for such impudence. That remark did something to me. In a fraction of a second, my mind was deluged by images of a cruel world that I had barely left behind: a world in which fire and destruction rained from the sky, charred corpses piled up in the streets, and mothers and children were buried alive in dark cellars.

"So how could God, the Almighty Father," I thought, "look down upon such madness and not take a hand? If he was really almighty, why hadn't he stopped the plane that killed Dieter—surely not a task too difficult for an Almighty God? Or had Dieter, perhaps, committed a sin that I didn't know about, a sin so grievous that it had to be punished by death?"

But I said nothing. Yet I felt such incredible *rage* against Nazi Pastor Jahn and didn't know what to do with it. I almost felt that I was outside my body, looking down upon the classroom scene, when I said:

"So, who exactly is going to punish me? Which one of our three Gods? God, the Father; or God, the Son; or God, the Holy Ghost?"

The room was silent and Pastor Jahn was beside himself. His ears turned bright red and his lips quivered.

"I will pretend you haven't said that," he said finally, with great effort and a very calm voice. "And we will use the occasion to talk about the Holy Trinity."

"There is *one* God and only *one* God," Pastor Jahn continued, "but he appears to us in different forms on different occasions, sometimes as the Father, at other times as the Son, and at still other times as the Holy Ghost. Indeed, you have learned something similar in your science classes. Think of all the water we have on this earth, formula H_2O. Do we encounter it only in a single form?"

"Of course not," Pastor Jahn answered his own question. "Often water appears in liquid form, as you see it in rivers and oceans around the world or when you work that pump in your back yards. But just as often, you meet water in solid form—surely you have seen ice on winter ponds where you skate. And you have also met water in gaseous form—think of steam coming out of locomotives or of all the clouds in the sky. Still, always, it's H_2O."

"So, is the Father the ice and the Son the liquid and the Holy Ghost the steam?" I asked.

That's when Pastor Jahn really lost it. He said something about "rotten city kid" and told me to get out of the room. I obeyed gladly. At first, I lingered in the corridor, where I listened to the secretary's typewriter rattling away in the principal's office and to the murmuring voices coming from all the other classrooms. They reminded me of the rumbling of the subways under our street in Berlin. Then I discovered another picture of the Wartburg with a saying from Martin Luther printed underneath.

"Martin Luther on the Jews," it said. "Their synagogues and schools ought to be set on fire, their houses be broken up and destroyed, and they ought to be put under a roof or stable like the Gypsies, in misery and captivity, as they incessantly lament and complain to God about us."

Then I went home. And in my mind I challenged the Almighty to reveal himself. I kept looking for a burning bush. I picked up branches lying under trees and threw them back on the ground, daring them to turn into snakes. I told God that when he punished Dieter he had also punished Mrs. Meyer and Mr. Meyer and me and that just wasn't fair. Whatever it was that Dieter had done, it wasn't our fault.

God didn't answer me.

A poster of the Strike Force for Total War, which demanded that all women pitch in: **You, too, Should Help!**

Langewiesche-Brandt, Ebenhausen near München, Germany

23. LICHTKIND

[December 1944 – January 1945]

The issue of God responding to us came up again in Pastor Jahn's class soon after my initial run-in with him. Unfortunately, that lesson got me into trouble again.

"It is a central tenet of Lutheranism," Pastor Jahn said, "that Faith is vastly more important than Good Works. You can't ingratiate yourself with God by doing good deeds. God is not some Jewish trader who gives you one thing if, and only if, you give something else in return. Our Heavenly Father takes a personal interest in your affairs—not because you have proven yourself to be worthy, but simply because you are his children whom he loves. There is no *quid pro quo*. All you have to do is *believe*. Talk to God in prayer; ask him for what you need, and you shall receive. Prayer works!"

"Are you sure?" I asked impudently. "What about all the people who pray for their husbands and fathers and brothers fighting on the eastern front? Could we conclude that those who died had relatives who didn't pray or didn't pray enough?"

Pastor Jahn gave me a withering look. I suppose he had never met such an angry child before.

"If you truly believe and pray, thou shalt receive," Pastor Jahn insisted, but I wouldn't let it go.

"That would be easy to test," I said. "Why don't we ask everyone in Ziesar whether they prayed for someone in the war and whether their loved ones are still alive? Then we can see how often prayer worked."

"Thou shalt not tempt the Lord!" Pastor Jahn thundered, but there was no stopping me then.

"Don't the Russians and the French and the English pray, too?" I asked. "Then why does anybody die on either side? Do only those who aren't prayed for die?"

That's when Pastor Jahn came after me with the Yellow Uncle. He said something about my being a "satanic child," but I don't remember the details. My mind went somewhere else. I was thinking of Dieter and how Mrs. Meyer had always prayed so much in the air raid shelter. I have no idea whether he hit me or how much. I didn't feel anything.

******

That afternoon, we had our Contemporary Issues class with Dr. Dietrich. He said that his classes were the most important ones in school because he taught us to be good Germans. He made us stand at attention when he entered the room, and he made us face the big poster on the front wall. "A German Says Heil Hitler," it said.

With our right hands raised, we sang "Germany, Germany above all," every single verse. And Dr. Dietrich made sure that we didn't rest our tired arms on the shoulders of those who stood in front of us.

A large map hung on the wall across from the windows. The map had pins in it with colored heads. They marked the position of German troops: from the North Cape of Norway to the deserts of Tunisia, from the Channel Islands to the Caucasus. The front lines were somewhat out of date, but Dr. Dietrich explained that the positions on the map would be recaptured soon, which is why he didn't bother moving back the pins.

"There is no way the enemy can win this war," he said.

He had been in France, England, and even in America, in the '20s, when he was working on his Doctor of Geography degree, he said. He knew the mentality of the enemy.

"The French are corrupt and disorganized," he said, "and that's why they have lost the war already, just as they lost the last one and the one before that. When you get to the next grade, you'll read Emile Zola. He wrote all about their corruption, in a book called *J'Accuse*."

Dr. Dietrich also told us why the French government could never get anything done.

"There is a basic flaw in their system," he sneered. "Elections follow elections; they hold endless debates on everything. It was the same, of course, in the Weimar Republic, and that's why the Führer put an end to the black, red, and mustard flag."

"The French do have the meter, though," Dr. Dietrich continued, "the only true meter. It's a metal rod, made of platinum, and it lies in alcohol with a thermometer attached so it won't contract or expand. That's very important, for nobody would otherwise know what a meter was. Someday, we'll move it to Berlin, and then you can look at it. Why should all people go to Paris to check their measuring sticks?"

Dr. Dietrich also told us that German troops had left Paris for a while, but the French didn't know the whole story:

"The whole city is mined; dynamite has been placed everywhere. And just when the French get ready to celebrate, the Führer presses a button, and all goes up in smoke!"

"The English," Dr. Dietrich continued, "the English aren't any smarter. They even *look* stupid with their helmets shaped like soup dishes. They don't even have the decimal system, they drive on the left side of the street, and all their windows are warped and won't shut. They don't have fir trees at Yuletide, either, just mistletoe. And men can often be seen walking to a lady's *right*!"

"What's wrong with that?" he asked and pointed to Gertrud Kleist.

"A gentleman always walks to a lady's left so as not to injure her when he draws his sword in her defense," Gertrud answered.

That was certainly news to me.

"Excellent," said Dr. Dietrich, and he moved on to discuss the Americans.

"Every year, fewer storks return from Africa; have you ever asked yourselves why?" he asked. "Because the blacks shoot at the harmless white birds!" he explained. "Some of the storks fly around for weeks with broken arrows in their bodies, and they can't make it back across the Mediterranean Sea. It's a shame, and it tells us a lot about the intelligence of African natives. That will be the downfall of the Americans. Their blood is all mixed up with that of the inferior African races; their brain power is ever decreasing."

Dr. Dietrich was on a roll.

"Now consider the eastern front," he said, and the Yellow Uncle swept across the map. "There has been much talk recently about the large number of Russian tanks. And it is true; they produce three tanks while we make one or two. But you should *see* their tanks!"

"Unfinished, unpolished, rusty even as they leave the factory! A veritable monument to the stupid, depraved vodka drinkers who produce them! In contrast, our tanks are made to last. German quality! Everything is perfect, inside and out, right down to the little brass signs that tell the soldiers where to put their caps and gloves and water flasks."

"Yet they have three tanks for our two. What then is the proper response?" Dr. Dietrich asked, and he pointed to Gertrud Kleist once again.

I liked her long braids and kept looking at her breasts, but my thoughts were quickly interrupted.

"The German troops must retreat temporarily," Gertrud answered, "while production is being reorganized."

"Go on, go on," prompted Dr. Dietrich.

"For every tank we produce we can also produce a hundred bazookas; and a hundred such *Panzerfausts* can stop an army of Russian tanks," Gertrud explained.

I figured that all this must have been discussed before.

"Superb!" said Dr. Dietrich, almost dancing for joy on his podium, "You have done your homework well."

Then Dr. Dietrich held up a newspaper.

"Seven hundred fifty-two Soviet tanks destroyed!" the headline said.

"We'll show that eastern vermin!" Dr. Dietrich yelled. "We'll show those Marxist sows!"

That's when the bell rang. Dr. Dietrich told us to chew our lunches well.

"Every bite thirty-two times," he said, "once for every tooth."

******

Fritz Hebbel shared his lunch with me. He was a little older than I, but I knew him because his mother was working with my mother at the ceramics plant. His father was a farmer; so Fritz had plenty of good things to eat, like bread and pork sausage. I let him drink out of my bottle of pop that tasted like woodruff.

I was glad we didn't have to walk in a circle as in Berlin. We could do more interesting things, like setting leaves on fire with sun rays captured by a magnifying glass or burning yellow sulfur powder that we stole from our chemistry lab. I liked the blue flames; I also liked making deals.

"Sure would like to borrow your magic lantern tonight," Fritz would say.

"Sure would like to have a liverwurst for supper," I would reply.

"Could be done," he would say.

Aunt Martel had sent me the lantern for Christmas and it had made me pretty popular. The *Laterna Magica* was a projector that only required a light bulb and an electric outlet to work. It came with hundreds of color slides, depicting scenes from fairy tales and the Old Testament mostly, and it could project them on any white-washed wall. Fritz wanted to treat his girl friend Gisela to a private showing.

After lunch, we had a lesson in the German language. Dr. Dietrich told us about *words*.

"There are three types," he said, "Germanic words, foreign words, and borrowed words. It is very important to recognize which is which and to use Germanic words whenever possible. Our language, just like our blood, must be kept pure. The Aryan race can be ruined by contamination with the blood of inferior people. That much is obvious. But our race can also be destroyed by the language of the inferior ones. The effect is subtle, but just as real. If we talk as our enemies do, we will soon think as they do. We will be as corrupt as the French, as stupid as the English, as sloppy as the Russians."

He called on Helga to name *Germanic* words.

"Adolf," she said, "the noble wolf. Herbert, the glory of the army. Gertrud, the spear maiden."

"Splendid, splendid," said Dr. Dietrich.

He asked me for a *foreign* word.

"Stop," I said, and I suddenly realized why all the STOP signs had been changed to read HALT.

"Splendid, splendid," said Dr. Dietrich, "but who can think of a *borrowed* word? It is the trickiest of them all. Like a spy, it looks like one of us, but it is one of theirs."

Only Rosel raised her hand.

"Nose," she said.

"Exactly," said Dr. Dietrich, "and that's another kind of word one should replace. 'Facial bay' or 'blow horn' might be good."

Dr. Dietrich also taught us new, *National Socialist* words, like *artfremd* [racially alien] and *Einsatz* [strike force] and *Garant* [pledge] and *Gleichschaltung* [being on the same circuit, the equalization of everyone's thinking] and *Kessel* [cauldron, a group of forces encircled by the enemy] and *Scholle* [holy soil] and *Untermensch* [subhuman] and *Volksgenosse* [racial comrade].

"To be a racial comrade," Dr. Dietrich explained, "one must be purely Aryan, of course. One cannot be a *Mischling* [mixed race person], such as a quarter or half Jew. Nor can one be a *Geltungsjude* [a legally Jewish person], such as a person who has married a Jew or joined a synagogue."

When my mother saw my notes, she said Dr. Dietrich was stupid and I should forget about this revolting jargon. Still, that night, I turned off my mother's snoring by tapping on her blow horn.

******

Christmas 1944 was a sad affair. We didn't have a tree and my father and grandmother and Aunt Martel were all far away. We were cold, despite the fact that we had lots of blankets on our beds. My mother sang songs for us. *Oh, Tannenbaum* [Oh, Christmas Tree]…*Stille Nacht* [Silent Night].… *Süsser die Glocken nie klingen* [Never the Bells Sound Sweeter]… *Leise rieselt der Schnee* [Softly Falleth the Snow].…

I only half listened. I kept staring at the louvered closet doors across the room, waiting for evil witches to emerge to join the dragons beneath my bed. I kept thinking of the newspaper I had just read, about the German offensive in the Ardennes, commanded by General von Rundstedt, which would reverse the war in the west, the paper had said. I pictured the stories in my mind: soldiers battling one another in knee-deep snow, General George Patton's tanks sliding down steep and slippery hills like children's sleds, General Hasso von Manteuffel's men standing on ground so hard they had to use dynamite to dig trenches…And I had nightmares of airplanes strafing people on the ground and of Dieter standing with me on the bridge.

Apparently, I got up in my sleep and tried to climb out of the window, but my mother caught me. Dr. Weiss said not to worry; it was a case of somnambulism, I was just being attracted by the moon. My mother gave me two Valerian drops.

******

When we returned to school after Christmas, Dr. Dietrich looked at my chapped lips, which must have been unusually red, and accused me of wearing lipstick.

"Disgusting," he said.

Then he made us sing a new song.

"To Adolf Hit…" and then came a long pause, "…ler we are sworn…"

For some reason, the pause was very important. We never learned why. But Dr. Dietrich did tell us about the day he first saw the Führer.

"It was in Berlin," he said, "in the early '30s. A hundred thousand people were packed into a small square. The sky was overcast; it drizzled now and then. We waited for hours. By the time he came, we were cold. He appeared on the platform and just stood there. He didn't move until everything was quiet as a mouse. Then he raised his hands, and he talked:

Of the shameful Treaty of Versailles.

Of colonies stolen from us.

Of hunger stalking in our midst.

His eyes were everywhere, his voice rose up mightily, and his words moved our hearts.

'Do you want jobs?' he asked. 'Do you want food?'

And just then the clouds parted, and a single beam of sunlight fell upon the Führer. Like a consecration! We were seized by a feeling of incredible joy. We fell into each other's arms, perfect strangers, and cried."

"A few years later," Dr. Dietrich continued, "I had the great honor of meeting the Führer in private. 'This was the most beautiful day of my life,' I wrote in my diary. We were at the Party Congress, in Nuremberg. He shook my hands with the strength of steel. His eyes looked through me as if he could read my thoughts. They were the eyes of Odovakar, conqueror of Rome, and the eyes of Frederick the Great, marvelous dark blue eyes. And later! I wish you could have seen him at the airport, how he walked to the plane, firmly, then waved. The engines roared, and off he went into the clouds. Like a prophet!"

"And that's what we should celebrate at the time of winter solstice," Dr. Dietrich continued, "the appearance among us of the incarnate light, the *Lichtkind*, the Child of Light."

Dr. Dietrich said we had wasted enough time listening to crazy stories about that Jew in a manger. He had a better project for us. We should all go out and ask people about the Führer. Dr. Dietrich wanted a written report from each one of us within a week.

******

I decided to interview all the store owners.

The lady in the shoe store said she had never seen Adolf Hitler herself, but that the Führer, obviously, was a genius.

"Marvelous, the way he built the Autobahn," she said, "and how he sandblasted all the old castles to make them look like new, simply marvelous."

The baker said the war was bad, but it wasn't Adolf Hitler's fault.

"Sometimes a nation has to go through a painful process of cleansing itself," he said.

I didn't understand what he meant, but I wrote it down anyway. The baker also said the Führer was very, very smart.

"He got rid of the depression, just like that. And right now, just as in our school, all the gymnasiums in the country are stocked with canned food," he said. "That way, we can carry on the fight for years to come. Marvelous."

The lady in the tobacco store, which was right across the street from us, said that the war was going badly, but it wasn't Adolf Hitler's fault.

"He is too trusting," she said, "shouldn't have relied on the Italians and Rumanians. A bunch of gypsies, that's what they are!"

Like Dr. Dietrich, Mr. Albrecht had seen Adolf Hitler, too, but he didn't agree with Dr. Dietrich at all.

"Saw the little shrimp in Berlin," he said, "the day I bought my smoking chamber. Waddled like a duck. His shoulders drooped. He looked at me with those cold fish eyes of his and didn't say a thing. Sure does a lot of hysterical screaming on the radio, though."

I watched Mr. Albrecht hang up the liverwursts, then the braunschweiger. My mouth watered. "He's a Catholic, too," Mr. Albrecht added. I left for the grocery store.

"The day Adolf Hitler took power," the grocery lady said, "my husband stood in the yard and shot all the brown chickens. He pretended they were brownshirts, shot them all, one after the other. Never had brown ones again either."

"And was he ever right!" she added. "Look at all the trouble we are in with the war. And at all that Nazi nonsense. I can't even listen to the *Mid-Summer Night's Dream* just because Mendelssohn was a Jew. I am supposed to ignore Tchaikovsky because he was an inferior Slav. Insane, that's what it is, insane."

She told me to go right ahead and tell that to Dr. Dietrich. Because her husband had died in Greece, she didn't care what happened to her. But my mother wouldn't let me hand in my report.

"He is using you as informers," she said.

And Mrs. Albrecht said the whole Nazi enterprise would never have gotten started if the Hitler family hadn't changed its name.

"They were called Schicklgruber, you know. Imagine saying 'Heil Schicklgruber!' Everybody would just have laughed."

I was a good little boy and obeyed my mother. I told Dr. Dietrich that I couldn't write a report because of a stomach ache. I offered to bring my Hitler stamps to school instead and to show them to everybody. He liked the idea. I also brought a picture of Günther Prien, the hero of Scapa Flow. And for good measure I brought another picture, this one of Adolf Galland, commander of the Luftwaffe fighter force. Like the Red Baron, he was an ace, having shot down 94 enemy aircraft in the Battle of France alone. The stack of news clippings under my bed was really handy.

Dr. Dietrich praised me for being so creative, but he didn't like at all what Fritz Hebbel had done. He had collected enemy leaflets and shown them to everyone. Since the war had started, one of them said, 37.8% of our soldiers, but only 2.5% of our Party leaders had been killed or captured. Dr. Dietrich made Fritz put his hands flat on the desk. He hit them for a long time with the Yellow Uncle.

He also made all of us stay after school to listen to the radio. First, there was music. Zarah Leander sang. "I Know That Sometimes a Miracle Will Happen." It was a song from her movie, *The Great Love*. Then Adolf Hitler made a long speech.

"The Jewish-Bolshevik arch enemy has launched a massive attack," he yelled. "He seeks to reduce Germany to ruins and to exterminate the German people. While old men and children are to be murdered, women and girls are to be debased as whores. The rest are to march to Siberia. But we shall suffocate their attack in a bloodbath!"

Fritz kept rubbing his fingers; the Führer continued:

"What our enemies are fighting for, they themselves, except for their Jews, don't know. What we are fighting for is clear to all of us: For the preservation of the German person, for our homeland, for the children and grandchildren of our people. Let the world know that this nation will never capitulate!"

Dr. Dietrich sat with his eyes closed. I sneaked a look at the leaflet in *my* pocket:

"The new Germany needs men, not skeletons. Therefore, capitulate!"

The Führer's voice grew hoarse:

"You must fight like Indians, and be brave like lions! You must be cunning! Shoot till the last bullet is spent, then fight to the last blow with the rifle butt! Every means by which you hold your position and destroy the Bolsheviks is right and holy. There is no turning back. Those who don't want to fight and seek to desert will be liquidated. Defeat every coward, smart aleck, and pessimist!"

The music came back. Dr. Dietrich opened his eyes. I crumpled up the leaflet inside my pocket.

Soldaten! In der Hitlerarmee ist Euch der unabwendbare
Untergang gewiß; die Rote Armee aber garantiert Euch in russi-
scher Gefangenschaft das Leben, die Sicherheit und die Rück-
kehr in die Heimat nach Kriegsende.

Ihr habt die Wahl:

LEBEN
oder sinnloser
TOD!

Dieses Flugblatt gilt als Passier-
schein für eine unbegrenzte Zahl
von deutschen Soldaten und Offi-
zieren, die sich den russischen
Truppen gefangengeben.

Эта листовка служит пропус-
ком для неограниченного ко-
личества немецких солдат и
офицеров при их сдаче в плен
Красной Армии.

akg-images, London, United Kingdom

A leaflet dropped by the Soviets in 1945

Soldiers! In Hitler's army your inevitable destruction
is certain; in Russian captivity, however, the Red Army
guarantees you life, safety, and return to your home
after the end of the war.
You have a choice:
LIFE OR SENSELESS DEATH

This leaflet serves as a passport for an unlimited
number of German soldiers and officers who surrender
to Russian troops.

24. PEOPLE'S STORM
[January – February 1945]

Let me tell you now about the last few months of the war. By the time we had made it to 1945, the whole world was on fire, but I was preoccupied with a much smaller war of my own. I so *hated* people who claimed to know God's opinion about everything, who had a direct pipeline to the Almighty, and who never missed a chance to tell others so! I am talking, of course, about good old Pastor Jahn. It must have been about the middle of January, as I was walking through the school corridor to get to my music class, when I ran into him. It so happened that there was nobody else around, and he used the occasion to have the last word in our discussion.

"You know, Hans," he hissed, with his eyes turning into ominous little slits, "a prayer of mine is about to be answered…" and faster than you can say One, Two, Three, he slapped me on the left ear and the right ear and the left one again. For a brief moment, I stood chin-to-chest with Pastor Jahn as his fingers dug into my shoulders and he shook me violently as if he were trying to shake off a poisonous snake. Then he slapped me one more time across the face—for good measure, as he put it—and walked off as if we hadn't even met. My nose was bleeding and I silently swore revenge.

Being with my music teacher, Miss Mahler, was an entirely different matter. She was nice to me. She was also very smart about political things, which is why my mother liked her, too. When they first met, Miss Mahler had said "Good Morning" rather than "Heil Hitler" to her. We both knew what she was doing.

On the day of my run-in with Pastor Jahn, for example, Miss Mahler went to the blackboard and wrote down the names of all the great musicians we were about to study that year:

Christoph Willibald Ritter von Gluck (1714–1787), Josef Haydn (1732–1809),

Wolfgang Amadeus Mozart (1756–1791), Ludwig van Beethoven (1770–1827),

Karl Maria von Weber (1786–1826), Karl Loewe (1796–1869),

Franz Schubert (1797-1828), Felix Mendelssohn-Bartholdy (1809–1847),

Robert Schumann (1810–1856), Guiseppe Verdi (1813–1901), Richard Wagner (1813–1883).

In my mind, one name stood out as if it had been written in red, and I instantly thought of my visit with Mrs. Thomas, who ran the grocery store. Mendelssohn was a Jew, and Dr. Dietrich would surely have turned red in the face if he had seen that name on the board. But there it was, nevertheless. However, for the time being, Miss Mahler was safe. Nobody else in class had noticed a thing and we were turning to Richard Wagner first.

"Richard Wagner," Miss Mahler said, "was born in Leipzig in 1813; he was buried in Bayreuth in 1883. At age 20, he already held his first job as a conductor; he spent the rest of his life writing many Romantic operas, often based on Germanic legends."

She mentioned Tannhäuser (1845), Lohengrin (1848), The Ring of the Nibelungen (1852 and later), and Parsifal (1872).

"The Ring of the Nibelungen," Miss Mahler said, "comes in four parts. The first of these is *Rheingold,* It tells the story of a Germanic god, Wotan, who makes a deal with giants to build him a great mansion in the sky, to be called Valhalla, where the souls of slain heroes are to reside. In return, he promises them Freia, who is the caretaker of the Garden of the Gods, which contains apples that give eternal youth…"

I only half listened to the story. My eyes drifted to the clouds sailing past the window—I saw pouch-like *cumulonimbus mammatus,* indicating the approach of a severe thunderstorm—and I looked in vain for a glimpse of the gods residing above them in the sky. My mind pictured airplanes diving out of these very clouds, spitting fire and destruction upon us who would not believe…

"The second part of the Nibelungen," I heard Miss Mahler say, "is called *Valkyrie.* It tells the story of a knight, called Siegmund, who must fight Hunding, his arch enemy. But Siegmund has fallen in love with Hunding's wife Sieglinde, who shows him the oak into which a stranger once put a sword. Siegmund succeeds in getting it out; it is Wotan's sword! Wotan watches all this from the sky and decides to let Siegmund win, but after Freia points out that Siegmund is an adulterer, he orders one of his handmaidens, Brunhilde, to give the victory to Hunding. She disobeys, and Siegmund wins. Wotan, now furious, kills Siegmund himself, but Brunhilde hides Sieglinde from the angry god. As punishment, Wotan places Brunhilde on a rock surrounded by an ocean of flames…."

I saw airplanes diving out of clouds, spitting flames from their wings, and I felt the heat from the sea of flames surrounding our house when it was still there. I felt dizzy and scared and I wished I had my Valerian drops.

"The third part of the Nibelungen," I heard Miss Mahler say, "is called *Siegfried,* who turns out to be the son of Siegmund and Sieglinde. Siegfried learns to be a blacksmith and remakes Wotan's sword. Siegfried uses it to kill the giant called Fafner, and when Siegfried touches the giant's blood, he can suddenly understand the language of animals. A kindly bird shows him the way to

Brunhilde, whom Siegfried frees after fighting Wotan himself."

And I saw airplanes dive out of clouds, spitting flames from their wings, and I felt the heat from the sea of flames surrounding our house, and I saw images of blood, the lieutenant's blood and Dieter's blood, and my heart pounded in my chest. But Miss Mahler was relentless.

"The fourth and last part of the Nibelungen," I heard Miss Mahler say, "is called the *Twilight of the Gods*. At this point in the story, we find Wotan deeply depressed about his loss to Siegfried. He cuts down the World Oak and stacks its wood around Valhalla to burn it down....In the end, Siegfried is killed, his body is burned on the banks of the Rhine, Brunhilde jumps onto the pyre, and the heavens turn a fiery red. The twilight of the gods has come, because the gods were too guilty and too weak."

And I saw airplanes dive out of clouds, spitting flames from their wings, and I felt the heat from the sea of flames surrounding our house, and I saw images of blood, the lieutenant's blood and Dieter's blood and I saw charred bodies piling up in the street and the sky a fiery red, as it always was when we emerged from the shelter after a raid....

"Hans," Miss Mahler said, "are you even listening?"

I looked around and, except for Miss Mahler, everyone was gone.

"As I said, you are a little behind the rest of the class so far as music is concerned," Miss Mahler said, "I think it would do you good to have some private lessons with Mr. Kalitz. I'll talk to your mother about it."

******

And so it was to be. Private lessons were arranged, and Mr. Kalitz, who was not in the military because he had a deformed leg, made me listen to the Nibelungen, and all sorts of other recordings, on the record player in his living room, every Thursday afternoon, right after school. I don't remember much about the music, but I do remember his walking stick which stood right next to the couch on which I was to sit. As was customary in those days, his walking stick was covered with all sorts of tiny metal plates that indicated the places he had visited in some earlier and happier days: Copenhagen, Paris, Ibiza, Malta, Rome. But Mr. Kalitz smoked cigarettes, and I hated the smell of them in his house and on his breath. And he annoyed me further by continually cleaning his ears with a tiny silver scoop attached to an ivory handle. So I was determined to sabotage the whole enterprise until one Thursday afternoon when, upon opening his front door, I heard the characteristic boom, boom, boom, BOOM of the BBC. He was mighty nervous when he realized what I had heard, but I told him I was an old friend of the BBC and he had nothing to fear from me.

That was the day we became best friends and these are some of the stories we heard:

1945

January 12	Marshal Konyev's First Ukrainian Front opens offensive along Vistula River
January 18	Russians troops take Warsaw, the first European capital to have fallen to Hitler's *Blitzkrieg*. As a result, Russians stand 433 kilometers from Berlin
January 23	Russian troops enter German territory in East Prussia
	Swedish radio confirms: Russian troops, finding Russian soldier dead in village street, liquidate whole population of village
	More members of the German resistance, linked to the July plot, are killed in Plötzensee prison, including Count Helmuth von Moltke, Eugen Bolz, and Erwin Planck, son of Nobel Prize winner Max Planck
January 30	The Strength-Through-Joy ship *Wilhelm Gustloff*, having departed the Baltic Sea port of Gdynia with over 5,000 East Prussian refugees, is sunk by a Russian submarine
	Russian troops reach Oder River
February 13	First of several Allied air raids on Dresden, which is totally destroyed
February 24	Russian troops seize Lower Silesia

To my surprise, some of the events just noted were more or less confirmed even by Radio Berlin. During the Vistula offensive, war correspondent Heinz Meyerlein was quoted as follows:

"The Russians are using their new Joseph Stalin super-tank on an ever-increasing scale. This most powerfully gunned and armored vehicle in the world, carrying, as it does, a 122 mm gun, is more than a match for our best tank, the Royal Tiger, and its 88 mm gun."

Likewise, on January 30, the 12th anniversary of Adolf Hitler's government, and, ironically, also the 2nd anniversary of the Stalingrad defeat, Dr. Goebbels admitted to recent military retreats, but concluded, nevertheless, by yelling "We shall win, because we must win!"

And in late February, the bombing of Dresden was confirmed by all German radio stations. An outraged speaker on Radio Germany noted "the wanton destruction of churches, hospitals, and cultural treasures in a city that had no strategic value, was undefended, and was crammed with Silesian refugees." Radio Berlin reported 15 square kilometers flattened and 50,000 dead. It even recounted the burning, by a special SS detachment, of 6,865 corpses on pyres in the *Altmarkt* [Old Marketplace].

******

It was about then that Dr. Dietrich canceled school and organized a rally in front of the Town Hall. A policeman blew a trumpet and Dr. Dietrich told everyone that it was time for all Ziesar citizens to help organize a *Volkssturm* [People's Storm] against the enemy. Ever since last October, he said, town after town had joined in; now it was our turn. Every male aged 12-16 or aged 45 and above and, therefore, currently outside the *regular* army, was to be trained for this new *civilian* army. Having just turned 12 the previous summer, I didn't like what I heard. My mother was standing next to me; she must have been reading my thoughts.

"They are not going to get my boy," she said, stroking my hair, but then there was that trumpet again.

"Under Heinrich Himmler, Supreme Leader of the SS and Minister of the Interior," Dr. Dietrich said, "the People's Storm is ideally suited to stop the enemy advance. Make no mistake about it, you kill the enemy or he kills you. Every hour, we get new reports of terrible happenings in the occupied areas. In East Prussia, Marshal Konyev's Cossacks use their sabers to hack down every living thing, even those who try to surrender. His tanks charge into columns of brave defenders, running them down and crushing them under their tracks. Vicious Mongols drench women and children with gasoline and set them on fire…and out west, savage Blacks machine-gun cripples in a hospital... That's why you *must* join the People's Storm and strike the enemy at the throat. You must defend the fatherland to the last drop of blood! Heil Hitler!"

There was that trumpet again. My mind drifted back to the BBC and its boom, boom, boom, BOOM signature. "Three short notes and one long note," Mr. Kalitz had said, "is the Morse code for V, which stands for *victory*. It's also the opening of Beethoven's Fifth Symphony." I liked learning things like that.

"Idiots," my mother said, "now they want to sacrifice teenagers and the elderly; they are not going to get you, Hansel, not as long as I'm alive."

She hugged me and we went home. But my mother couldn't foresee what would happen in school the next day. Dr. Dietrich canceled all regular classes and brought us all into the big auditorium, where he showed us two films, one about Soviet barbarism, the other about the People's Storm.

The first film told the story of Nemmersdorf, an East Prussian village that had been briefly occupied by the Russians on October 22, 1944. When German troops under General Friedrich Hossbach liberated the village a few days later, the announcer said, they could not believe their eyes, which is why they filmed it all: Not a single person in the village was alive; all had been murdered in the most bestial fashion. Some had been crushed by tanks; babies had had their heads bashed in; dozens of naked women had been nailed to barn doors, in cruciform positions, like Jesus on the cross! That should motivate all of us, Dr. Dietrich said, to defend the fatherland to the last drop of blood.

The second film featured Reich Youth Leader Artur Axman at the Berlin *Reichssportfeld* [Reich Sports Field]. He was training Hitler Youths in the use of the *Panzerfaust*, a rocket-propelled grenade, a single one of which could allegedly destroy a tank.

"The *Panzerfaust*," he said, "must be fired only at close range, preferably at the tank's turret."

We watched the formation of the first *Panzerjagd Division* [Tank Hunting Division], consisting of Hitler Youths on bicycles, each carrying two *Panzerfausts*, one on each side of their handlebars. And while the bicycle division rode off into the sunset, Artur Axman's voice talked of the heroism of Sparta, of performing tasks, even suicidal tasks, that would prove our unwavering loyalty to the Führer.

Then Dr. Dietrich gathered up all of us who were at least 12 years of age and marched us down to the castle. In the central yard, several policemen were waiting next to a series of harvest wagons, but the horses were missing. Dr. Dietrich said we would be outfitted presently and we would receive our first training later that afternoon. For that purpose, he arranged us in a long line, which reminded me of all the queuing I had done at stores in Berlin.

The first outfitting station was a wagon filled with uniforms of all shapes and sizes. Some of us received army jackets, but when we struggled to get our arms through sleeves made for grown-ups, the emphasis shifted to a rather chaotic array of head gear. There were only a few smaller-sized steel helmets for boys; the regular army helmets dropped over our ears and eyes. There were also a bunch of *Käppis* [side hats] and even a few World War I *Pickelhauben* [peaked caps]. I managed to get a *Pickelhaube* and, like everyone else, a fancy armband with the inscription "German People's Storm---Army."

The second wagon was filled with weapons and ammunition, again of many different types. There were some sabers from the War of 1870/71, some World War I service pistols, a whole bunch of 1940 French rifles with 4 bullets each, and all sorts of hunting rifles. Because I couldn't hold a rifle to my shoulder—it was too long for my short arms—the policeman gave me one of those hand grenades with wooden handles that were piled up behind him. But all that unexploded ordnance made me awfully nervous and I put the grenade back when he wasn't looking.

The third wagon contained several large boxes, each labeled *Volkshandgranate #45* [People's Hand Grenade #45]. Those grenades, we were told, would be used in our practical training presently. We were asked to carry one of the boxes into the open fields outside the castle yard, but it was far too heavy. That's why the policemen carried it themselves.

Once outside the yard, Captain Werther, who was the Chief of Police, took over. He taught us how to line up in rows of three, march to the sound of Left…Left…One, Two, Three, Four, Left…, then stop, and make an about-face for inspection. He cursed, cajoled, and threatened us when we didn't stand straight enough or when a jacket wasn't buttoned right or somebody's hair wasn't properly combed. Then he grasped a pole with a rolled-up flag from his deputy, planted the pole's butt firmly on ground, and shook the flag loose until its red field and white circle with the black swastika broke into the light. Then he drew a sword, held it up, where it gleamed in the sun, and made us take the oath.

"In the presence of this blood banner," we repeated after him, "which represents our Führer, I swear to devote all my energies and my strength to the savior of our country, Adolf Hitler. I am willing and ready to give up my life for him, so help me God."

The ceremony concluded with our singing *Die Fahne hoch, die Reihen fest geschlossen, SA marschiert, mit festem Schritt und Tritt…* [The flag held high, the formation tightly closed, SA marches, with firm step and stride…]

However, we weren't done yet. Captain Werther also gave us a piece of advice.

"When fighting the Russians," he said, "you must always be aware of one thing: The Russians never fight fairly; they always break the rules. They may lie on the ground, for example, pretending to be dead, but when you move over them, they leap up and shoot. Or they may wave white flags of surrender, but then fire on those who come to capture them. You must be ready for their Asiatic tricks!"

And finally, we were introduced to the People's Grenade, which turned out to be nothing but a lump of concrete surrounding an explosive charge and detonator. We were each asked to throw one as far as we could and watch it explode. Not all of us did well. Those who hesitated were called "little grandmothers" and those who didn't throw far enough were cursed in the name of all the Germanic gods looming above us in the sky….

******

Back in school, Dr. Dietrich concluded the day with a bit of *theoretical* training.

First, we each received a tiny booklet with useful Russian phrases. That's when I learned my first Russian words: Ruki vverch = Hands Up!

Second, we each received a piece of white cardboard, containing the following printed summary of the Geneva Convention:

A PRIMER ON PRISONER-OF-WAR RIGHTS

1) From the moment of surrender, German soldiers are considered prisoners of war and stand under the protection of the Geneva Convention.*

2) As soon as possible, prisoners of war are to be brought to collection points that are far enough from the danger zone to assure their personal safety.

3) They are to receive the same food, in quantity and quality, as members of the Allied armies and are to be treated, if sick or wounded, in the same medical facilities as Allied troops.

4) Medals and items of value are to be left in the possession of prisoners of war. Money can be confiscated, but only by officers at the collection points and in return for a receipt.

5) Sleeping facilities, room distribution, and similar matters in the prisoner of war camps are to be equal to those accorded Allied troops.

6) According to the Geneva Convention, prisoners of war may not be subjected to torture, nor be subjected to public curiosity. At the end of the war, they are to be sent home as soon as possible.

Note:

In order to avoid misunderstanding during the process of capture, the following is recommended: Lay down weapons, put helmet and belt on ground, hold hands high, and wave with handkerchief or this leaflet.

*Soldiers are defined as all armed persons who are wearing a uniform or some other identification that can be seen from afar.

For our peace of mind, a giant red note was printed diagonally across the above:

Also valid for the People's Storm

******

When I got home with my newly acquired armband and literature, my mother threw another one of her ever-more-frequent fits. She yelled and screamed a lot and forbade me in the strictest terms ever again to participate in any People's Storm activities. If they ask you to, come straight home, she said. Mrs. Albrecht agreed wholeheartedly.

"So that's what it has come to," she said, "now they are ready to sacrifice children in a last-ditch defense. And, you know, it wouldn't even work. Mr. Kalitz says the *Panzerfaust* can't even penetrate the armor of the Russian tanks; God knows how he knows. He also says Russian sharpshooters would sit in the trees and pick off People's Storm fighters long before they got anywhere near the tanks."

"What a pleasant image," my mother said sarcastically.

I didn't tell her about the Nemmersdorf film. The thought of it kept me awake most of the night. I kept counting my pulse and my heart was racing.

******

On the next day, school was back to normal, but I had another run-in with Pastor Jahn. It all happened in the afternoon when a special train arrived, filled with women and children from East Prussia. Captain Werther and some of his policemen met them at the station with a whole bunch of horse-drawn wagons, and, having determined that they were all Lutherans, the captain had a brilliant idea.

"You can all live at the Superintendent's house," he said. "There are lots and lots of furnished rooms ready and waiting for you."

And off they went to Cloister Street Number 3, where Aunt Rachel, no doubt, let out a loud cry that traveled all the way to the Heavenly Father himself. But that came later. Still at the railroad station, Pastor Jahn took it upon himself to bless the assembled crowd, thanking God, our Heavenly Father, for having saved the refugees from the Red Beast and having brought them to a place of safety and peace.

When he was finished, I asked the Pastor, quite humbly, whether I could ask a question that had been bothering me. Without waiting for an answer, I said:

"You said in class 'there is no gender in heaven.' Why then do you always refer to the Heavenly *Father*, as you just did, and say *He* and *Him* and such? Are you saying God is a *man*, contradicting here what you taught us in class? Or is this like the ice-water-steam thing, with God being a man in one place, a woman in another, and something neuter in still another?"

Pastor Jahn snarled, jerked the reins of his horses, and his wagon took off down the dusty road toward the village and the church.

Toward the end
of the war, those once
considered too young
or too old for the
military were mobilized
and armed:
**For Freedom and Life.
People's Storm.**

The armband says:
**German People's
Storm—Army.**

Langewiesche-Brandt, Ebenhausen near München, Germany

25. WEREWOLVES
[March 1945]

A couple of weeks after the East Prussians invaded Aunt Rachel's cloister-house—she compared them to an angry swarm of ants crawling over *everything*—the rest of the village lost its serenity as well. I remember the sudden end to our relative peacefulness and the dawn of a new era of frantic activity and, ultimately, violence and death. It all started on a Saturday morning in March, the day we were planning to celebrate Helmut's third birthday.

Suddenly, there was noise in the street. My mother, Helmut, and I ran to our windows above the butcher shop and came upon an amazing scene. As far as our eyes could see, our street was filling up with wagons, slowly, ever so slowly, making their way from east to west. There were no cars or trucks, just wagons drawn by teams of horses and an occasional pair of large brown oxen. More often than not, six or even eight horses were hitched together; sometimes, several wagons were hitched together as well. Some of the wagons were covered, with tarpaulins and bed sheets and even Persian rugs, but we could still see people looking out the back, lying on tall piles of straw and hay. Other wagons were flat and open, and we could see couches and chairs and boxes on them piled three meters high. Presently, a wagon passed with kitchen utensils hanging from its sides. The frying pans made quite a racket because of the cobblestones.

Some wagons were full of animals behind wire mesh. We saw chickens and ducks, turkeys and geese, goats and sheep, pigeons and pigs. Cats sat on top of cages and poked their claws through the wire, scaring the pigeons. And cows! There were hundreds of cows, tied to each other and to the wagons, mooing and ringing bells, screaming and dripping milk, getting caught behind trees along the street and leaving piles of green shit.

And there were people, of course, hundreds of people, walking and tottering besides the wagons and behind them, pushing baby carriages filled with belongings, carrying bundles of clothes tied to poles that sat on shoulders like rifles in a parade.

I thought of Noah's ark as each wagon crawled, imperceptibly crawled, past our windows, day and night, in sun and rain. Mesmerized, we stared at the activity in the street, trying to comprehend what it all meant, and, just like ours, hundreds of other eyes watched from behind lacy curtains and followed the movement of the endless caravan. If anything happened to interrupt its forward motion, unseen people would shout: "No room here" and "No food here, go on, go on!" But that was sometimes impossible.

I remember watching one of the wagons, this one drawn by a pair of weary horses and led by exhausted women and children walking beside them—walking slowly, one step at a time, going where? Their wagon, overloaded like all the rest, creaked and groaned, its steel-rimmed wheels pounded against the cobblestones, and I saw horseshoes striking stone and making sparks. Suddenly, the axle broke. I saw the wagon teeter and spill household objects, jars of food, and even the huddled shapes of two older women, their clothes in tatters. The whole procession came to a halt.

We ran into the street, my mother holding on to Helmut, and I, as usual, forgetting to wear socks and shoes. Mr. Albrecht was there already and quickly determined that there was no hope.

"That wagon cannot be fixed," he said to a woman with a scarf, "but we can find you another one at the castle. We'll help you move your things. In the meantime, nobody is going anywhere, I'm afraid. Your wagon's blocking the street."

Captain Werther appeared out of nowhere. He was worried about the same thing. He didn't like the idea of having hundreds of women and children and their grandparents and their animals camping out in the middle of Breite Weg, but there was precious little he could do about it then. He liked the idea of donating a wagon from the castle, and he quickly put the whole police department to work on the project.

In the meantime, everyone was settling down on the sidewalks all over our village, temporarily abandoning the covered wagons and baby carriages and hand carts and bicycles in the middle of the street. Through the open door of the pharmacy next door, I heard the radio play a song. Zarah Leander again. *Davon geht die Welt nicht unter* [That won't make the world go down], she sang. How ironic!

Mrs. Albrecht promised to bring some food to those outside her shop; and I saw my mother talking to the woman with the scarf and her two little girls. As luck would have it, the lady came from Schweidnitz, the very place in Silesia where one set of my grandparents had grown up before they came to Berlin and gave birth to my mother. I heard them talk about the Silesian town where my mother had gone on vacation decades ago, visiting all sorts of aunts, uncles, and cousins of hers. And I heard the lady with the scarf talk of her two-month trek, of Shturmovik fighters, with red stars painted on their sides, appearing out of nowhere, their cannons reaching out to kill and kill, only to fly off, turn, come back, and kill again. I heard them talk of bullets flying into fields, if they were lucky; but into men, women, children and animals, if they were not, leaving behind screams and splintered wood and thrashing bodies of men and beasts, dying side by side. I heard them talk of disemboweled horses, left right there where life ran out or, perhaps, rolled into the nearest ditch and barely covered with a bit of soil. I listened to her story and thought of Dieter, but I felt nothing, nothing at all.

My eyes wandered down the street, where two foals were muzzling up against their mothers, and I caught the smell of horse dung, just as I always had outside the pub back home. And I noticed how thin the horses were, I could see all their ribs, and I also saw the bloodstains where they stood with their feet worn raw from unshod hooves. Mr. Albrecht saw it, too; he called the blacksmith to have a look. Mr. Albrecht also got a pail and took care of a cow that was mooing in agony from swollen udders, because those who should have milked her had somehow disappeared.

"Perhaps the cow's owners had gone down the road to church," I thought, "it being Sunday and all." Still, the cow wanted to be milked; it didn't know it was Sunday and it didn't have to go to church anyway.

My mind was in a daze. I pictured the scene at the church down the street where people just now would be leaving their seats, aisle by aisle, go to the front, kneel on the steps of the altar, open their mouth to catch a wafer, and take a sip from the silver goblet—"the chalice of salvation," as Pastor Jahn had called it. And in-between sips, I pictured him cleaning the rim of the goblet with a white handkerchief and I thought how unsanitary it all was and that I should point it out to Pastor Jahn to make him mad. A dog barked, all those images disappeared, and I was back in the street. But, as I said, I felt nothing, nothing at all, not even when the blacksmith came and took care of the horse and jokingly offered to nail a horseshoe to my naked foot.

I saw my mother fill a thermos with hot milk for children, stuff rucksacks with food for their mothers, place feedbags full of oats around horses' necks, water them at a nearby trough. I fed an apple to a foal. I heard little children whimper and I wondered whether their mothers were sleeping, lying unconscious, or already dead?

******

As in a dream, I wandered off to Mr. Kalitz to get an update on the news. To be well informed, clearly, was getting to be a matter of survival—that much I knew—and the news we received from the BBC was not good:

1945

March 3	Western Allies take Cologne
March 8	U.S. forces cross the Rhine at Remagen
March 24	Russians under Marshal Georgi Zhukov break through Oder defenses, smash their way beyond Küstrin, stand 52 kilometers from Berlin
March 30	Russians take Danzig, capture 10,000 prisoners, 45 submarines
	Royal Air Force Lancasters and Halifaxes, along with U.S. Flying Fortresses and Liberators, are bombing Berlin for 32nd night in a row

On the way home, I ran into Aunt Rachel. She told me I could go to her cellar and take all the apples I wanted. The East Prussians were stealing her blind as it was. And one family, she said, had infested her house with bedbugs. She'd have to call the exterminator. I should tell my mother we were lucky to have moved out.

When I got to Aunt Rachel's house, I ran into Martin and his sister Simone. They were living in the mahogany room and were the cause of the bedbug scare. I knew Martin from school; he had been placed in my class, but his sister was much too young and still at home. I liked Martin. Like me, he was interested in everything and he always had good information. That day was no exception. He had been studying French in East Prussia—they called it "the language of Frederick the Great"—and when I ran into him, he had just looked through his dictionary to find the French word for bed bug. He wrote it down for me; *punaise* it said, but Martin said that *punaise* could also be a thumb tack. I loved to be educated like that.

I also loved the political posters Martin had collected over the years. He was just like me! One of them was over two years old and had been posted in Tarnow, a city in southeastern Poland. His daddy had sent it to him and I made a copy of it, which I still have today. What a chilling reminder it was of what was happening in lots of places at the time and what had probably happened to Mrs. Nussbaum, my mother's friend in Berlin:

ANNOUNCEMENT!

In order to carry out the expulsion of Jews as ordered by the SS and the Krakow police, the following is announced:

- The expulsion of Jews begins on September 10, 1942.

- Every Pole who by his actions in any way endangers this expulsion, makes it more difficult, or helps others to do so, will be punished most severely.

- Every Pole who harbors or hides a Jew during or after the expulsion will be shot.

- All entry permits to the Jewish residential area are invalid as of the date of this announcement. Whoever enters the ghetto nevertheless will be punished most severely and may well be shot.

- Whoever, directly or indirectly, buys possessions of Jews, receives them as gifts, or acquires them in other ways, will be punished most severely. Every Pole who is in possession of items belonging to Jews is required to report such possession at once to the security police in Tarnow; otherwise he can count on the most severe punishment for plundering.

- During the transport of Jews from the assembly point to the railroad station it is forbidden to set foot on the following areas: Lemberg Street, Holz Square, Bernadiner Street, Old Market, Narutowicza Street, Kommandantur Street, Sport Square at the Railroad Station. The inhabitants of the aforesaid streets and squares are ordered to lock all doors and windows when the group in question is approaching and are not to observe the march in any way. Offences against these orders will be punished.

Tarnow, September 9, 1942
Dr. Pernutz, District Captain

And there was another poster of more recent origin. It came from Martin's home town and urged East Prussians to join the People's Storm. Martin said I could take it home and read it there.

******

The flow of refugees never stopped. Day in and day out, the scenes were the same, but life had to go on. We still had school. My battle with Pastor Jahn continued as well. I remember the day I asked him about the deluge thing.

"From where did Noah get all the animals?" I asked, looking as innocent as I possibly could. "So many of them live in different lands, even on different continents. How could he catch them all? Did he travel a lot?"

"Did he take bed bugs, too?" I added.

Pastor Jahn was trying his best to ignore me.

"How does one catch a squirrel?" I asked.

"Climb a tree and act like a nut!" I said, not waiting for an answer, and the whole class burst out in laughter.

Predictably, Pastor Jahn came after me with the Yellow Uncle, but I was saved by the bell. Dr. Dietrich was calling a special meeting of the *People's Storm*, right then and there, in the big auditorium.

******

"Our subject today," Dr. Dietrich said, "is *Werewolves*. Many of us will soon be called upon to join a movement codenamed *Der Werwolf*. It is similar to the *People's Storm*, yet differs from it in significant ways. It is similar in purpose, being set up for one thing only: to fight our enemies. The movement is different in the sense that its work is to be carried out *behind enemy lines*, which requires the utmost secrecy. The film will explain."

Down came the window shades and the big white screen, and the projector was rolled into place. "The film you are about to see," a voice said in the dark, "is based on a novel by Hermann Löns, which tells the story of the Thirty Years' War from 1618-1648. Although the film deals with the conflicts between Catholics and Protestants in a time long ago, the essence of its story speaks directly to us: *By setting up a secret resistance movement, a people can continue to fight an enemy even after an apparent defeat* and *that* may well become our task as well."

"By becoming werewolves and dedicating yourselves to duty and self-denial," Dr. Dietrich said after we had seen the film, "you can prove your loyalty to your Führer and your country. And in the process, you will learn to exhibit the character traits of that great man whose portrait hangs on the wall to your left, Frederick the Great. You will learn to be tough on the outside, but, like that great Prussian King, a werewolf can be soft on the inside. It is no accident that Frederick the Great, the great warrior, also played the flute and wrote verses and befriended Voltaire, the great philosopher of the Age of Enlightenment."

Having thus enlightened us, Dr. Dietrich turned to practical matters. His secretary rolled in an exhibit of werewolf equipment, which each of us was to receive when the time was ripe. As it turned out, a werewolf's gear included five items:

- a silencer pistol
- a raincoat lined with explosive
- cans of oxtail soup packed with plastic explosives
- a few sheets of edible rice paper to send messages
- suicide pills "to escape the strain of interrogation and the inducement to commit treason"

However, Dr. Dietrich explained, once received—and the time wasn't ripe yet—all of these items were to buried in a secret spot and we were to go about our business as if nothing had happened. Not even our parents could know. Further practical training was to follow on the next day.

*****

On that day, as promised, all the werewolves received a shovel and were marched to the edge of our village. There was a faint drone of bombers way up in the sky, but nobody seemed to notice them.

"At every road leading into this village," Dr. Dietrich explained, "we are going to dig a big hole, large enough to swallow a tank. The enemy's main strength at the moment is tanks. If we stop the tanks, we stop the enemy."

Everyone began to dig, but I didn't understand. Did tanks have to drive on the road? Nobody else seemed to ask that question.

The digging was tiring, because we kept running into rocks and the roots of trees near the road. We stopped digging when the big men came with wagonloads of logs, which they pulled though narrow gates they had built on the sides of the road, stacking one log on top of the other and thereby building a wall. But Captain Werther didn't like it when he saw us malingering.

"Are you tired and hungry, little grandmothers?" he asked. "Get to work! I'll tell you when you are tired and hungry!"

It was just about then that a truckload of soldiers from the POW camp came by. Ironically, they bypassed the tank trap by driving on the grass. An officer jumped out and inspected the work-in-progress. Then he had some kind of argument with Dr. Dietrich and Captain Werther.

"No one ever consults army commanders about the placements of these things," I heard him say. "In fact, in the entire war, I have never seen a tank trap impede a tank attack."

That made sense to me, and when no one was looking, I sneaked home. I sat on my bed and, before my mother could throw it away, I carefully read the long poster Martin had given me. My eyes kept returning to one section, which frightened me:

Men of the East Prussian People's Storm!

In this province, from now on, every village will become a citadel and every city a fortress.

You, men of the People's Storm, have dug the trenches and have built the tank barriers.

There, where you have built, you will also fight with your weapon, and each one of you knows the place at which he will stand and fight with his machine gun, with his anti-tank grenade.

Forward!

No one retreats here

Here we fight for our homeland, for Prussia!

Here we fight for Germany and our National Socialist Revolution!

Long live the Führer!

Your District Leader

Erich Koch

I didn't want to fight, but that, it seemed, was precisely what Dr. Dietrich was preparing us to do. Unfortunately, I couldn't very well ask my mother about the whole thing. I knew she would instantly burn up the poster, but I needed it for further study. So I rolled it up, put a rubber band around it, and stashed it under the bed. I also looked for my Valerian drops, but my mother had hidden them.

akg-images, London, United Kingdom

Refugee column near the end of World War II

26. THUNDER
[April 1945]

In the week following our werewolf work, my mother found the East Prussian poster I had brought home and it made her livid.

"That guy is ranting and raving, just like Adolf," she said angrily, crumpling up the poster and tossing it on the floor. "He's positively insane! Don't give it another thought, Hansel. They can dig all the trenches they want, but I will not let them drag us into any fighting."

"Could I have some Valerian drops?" I asked.

Just then, Helmut started crying and Radio Germany was issuing another urgent appeal. This time, a werewolf was talking, asking everyone to join the group and to do so *now*.

"Every Bolshevik, every Englishman, every American on our soil must be a target for our movement," the werewolf said. "And any German, whatever his profession or class, who puts himself at the service of the enemy and collaborates with him, will feel the effect of our avenging hand…"

Then they broadcast a live concert by the Berlin Philharmonic, organized by Albert Speer, to prove to the world that, even on April 12, 1945, everyone in Berlin was alive and well. Thus it came to be that far away, in a small room over Ziesar's butcher shop, we listened to Beethoven's Violin Concerto, Bruckner's 8th Symphony, and the finale of Wagner's Twilight of the Gods. What we didn't know, but learned many months later, was the fact that Hitler Youths, armed with baskets of cyanide capsules, later stood at the concert hall's exit doors and offered their wares to the members of the audience as they left.

Meanwhile, as Wagner's music poured out of our radio, I looked out of the window and noticed that our street was empty. For several days now, the flow of refugees had ceased, but unbeknownst to us, something else was just about to take its place.

On the very next morning, when Helmut and I raced each other to the windows after we woke up, we found our street jam-packed once again, this time with columns of military vehicles, most of them in various stages of serious disrepair, and jointly stretching, once again, from one end of the street to the other, as far as our eyes could see. We saw trucks filled with soldiers and weaponry, their engines now stalling, then revving, their headlights covered with black electric tape, except for narrow slits, to make for safer beams at night; we saw battered tanks lurching and bumping forward on the cobblestones, pulling cannons behind them; we saw covered wagons with big red crosses on their sides, all pulled by teams of horses; we saw fancy Mercedes convertibles displaying officers in charge; and, finally, we saw dozens upon dozens of flat-bed wagons, pulled by tractors here or oxen there, even by a lone elephant, all of them loaded and overloaded with rows of wounded soldiers, lying on thick beds of hay and straw—soldiers without arms or legs, with bloody stumps of knee, with chests or heads encased in white turned red to match the crosses on the side.

"An elephant! An elephant!" Helmut cried excitedly.

I heard thunder in the east.

******

My mother made me watch out for Helmut; I watched her from above, as she ran into the street to look for my father. A soldier screamed. My mother called on me to bring him wine to ease the pain; I didn't want to go. I didn't want to see the blood, but she said "Come!" The caravan moved on, I ran, the bottle slipped, broke on the cobblestones; a soldier screamed.

My mother ran to catch the group. One-twenty-one, the eastern front, my father's company! She had to know.

"Sir, can you hear? Arthur Keller. Did you know him?" my mother asked.

"No, ma'm, never did."

"Where are you coming from? Where have you been?"

"Battle of Cottbus," someone said, "couldn't hold the Neisse line, but the One-twenty-one was there."

My mother ran to catch another group. One-twenty-one, the eastern front, my father's company!

"Sir, my dear sir, did you know Arthur, do you know what's happened to him?"

"God, ma'm, oh God, I do. Last saw him at Cottbus. 'Trudchen,' I heard him cry, and he was gone."

And my mother fainted in the street. A cow stepped over her, left by the refugees. The soldiers' caravan moved on.

I heard thunder in the east.

******

Mrs. Albrecht put my mother on the couch of her living room and fed her peppermint tea. She also gave milk, bread and liverwurst to Helmut and me. And she told my mother not to despair.

"It's pandemonium out there," she said. "These men are shell-shocked, half unconscious. They don't know what they did or didn't see. But we could go and talk to those they left behind in the inn down the street. It's a field hospital now, you know."

And so it was. After my mother felt better, we got Mr. Albrecht to donate a few liverwursts for the hospital and also to watch Helmut, while Mrs. Albrecht, my mother, and I made a trip down the street. The *Prince of Prussia* was unrecognizable. A couple of ambulances were parked outside and a huge Red Cross had been painted on the front door. The lobby was filled with women who had brought water and food and mounds of fresh bandages torn from sheets. The man from the Black Eagle pharmacy was there, too, stocking a cabinet with aspirin, bandages, salves, and similar things. And a Red Cross worker was unloading boxes filled with Front Fighter Packages. I read the label. Each package contained one *Kommisbrot* [a rock-hard army loaf of bread], ¼ liter of schnapps, a small cake, selected sweets, and a bar of chocolate.

But our attention was quickly drawn to the rest of the inn. Every room and every corridor was filled with wounded soldiers, most of them lying on blankets spread out on the floor. We saw men with hollow cheeks, unshaven and unwashed, greasy and covered with sweat, some of them squatting next to piles of bloody pads of gauze, surrounded by squadrons of flies circling above them, walking on their faces and hands and feet and, finally, landing on their bandages and feeding on the clotted blood seeping through. We saw drawn faces lost deep in weariness, perhaps past all feeling, some mute and oblivious to others, some staring at us or groaning and wailing and imploring, some talking to themselves, others calling out the names of those who might help if they were only there. We saw men writhing in pain or retching or wandering through the corridors, all dazed, and unbelieving that this is what had happened to the three great armies of the east.

I felt someone's eyes on me and saw a man, still bloody and dressed in his rancid wool uniform, his hands reaching out for me, gripping. I shrank back in horror, but I heard him ask for my mother.

"You were looking for Arthur," he said to her in a hoarse voice. "I'm Leo Krell; I know him, saw you in the street. I can tell you about Cottbus."

My mother held his canteen, while he took a drink. Her hands were trembling; my heart was pounding. We were waiting for the bad news.

"It was one of the worst battles ever," he said. "The Russians had crossed the Neisse; we were trapped in that tall pine forest to the west. So they decided to have fun with us and play the *Stalinorgel* [Stalin's organ]; oh how we hated that thing! It's a new type of artillery, spewing out shells at the fastest pace you'd ever seen. They shriek and whistle and whoosh through the air and sound like an organ playing in church. But the worst of it is, they sent their shells to explode in the *tops* of the trees, making that deafening roar and then filling the air with deadly fragments of pine. It was bedlam on the ground."

He coughed and coughed, and he coughed up blood, and my mother gave him another drink.

"Well, you see," he continued, "Arthur was there and, at one moment, he was fine. Then came a shell, erupted right in front of us, making a bright orange flash and spewing dirt and rocks and iron fragments all around. And suddenly, there was all that smoke, making my eyes sting and choking the breath out of me, and I ran through the smoke and Arthur was *still* there on the other side. And that's the last I saw of him."

"So he could still be alive?" my mother asked.

"Certainly could," Leo Krell said.

My mother promised to come back in the morning, with lots of food, but when we did, they told us that Soldier Krell had died during the night. Perhaps, that was all for the good. We had just listened to a speech by Heinrich Himmler on the morning news. He promised "severe punishment for those who give food to retreating troops."

"The German soldier is obligated to stand and fight to the death," he had said. "Only traitors retreat."

And Himmler had issued a new decree for those who disobeyed his order to stand fast, no matter what. "Death and Punishment for Dereliction of Duty" it was called.

******

They were going to bury Leo Krell and two other soldiers right next to the church. Rather than go to school, I decided to watch Pastor Jahn in action. There were five women at the cemetery and two soldiers and the grave digger when I got there. Pastor Jahn didn't seem to notice me, or anyone else for that matter, and he was already half-way through his sermon.

"The dead are gone," I heard him say, "and gone with them are their faces and voices and their minds, and all the images of the years of their short lives. Gone is the knowledge of whether they had wives or children, whether they had white handkerchiefs or not, carried pocket knives, good luck charms or Luther's catechism, whether others liked them or hated them….

But not all is lost. We can pray for their souls."

I heard ravens cursing and squirrels chirping and carrying on in the trees above the open graves. I heard the tinkling of sheep bells in a nearby field and the lowing of cows. And I heard thunder in the east as the assembly prayed in unison:

"I believe in God the Father, Almighty Creator of Heaven and Earth, and I believe in Jesum Christum, his only Son, our Lord, who was conceived by the Holy Ghost, born by the Virgin Mary, suffered under Pontio Pilato, was crucified, dead and buried, descended into Hell, on the third day was resurrected from the dead, ascended into Heaven, where he sitteth at the right hand of God, the Almighty Father, from whence he shall come to judge the quick and the dead. And I believe in the Holy Ghost, the Holy Christian Church, the Communion of Saints, the forgiveness of sins, the resurrection of the flesh, and an eternal life. Amen."

The ravens were still cursing as the grave digger flung the dirt into the open graves. I thought of the promised resurrection of the flesh, but my mind gave me images of beetles and maggots doing their work, leaving nothing but belt buckles and bones and buttons of uniforms, carrying tiny inscriptions, "God With Us."

Just then, right on schedule, the church bells pealed above us, sending a large flock of pigeons aloft into sky, their wings resonating like the voice of God. And I heard thunder in the east.

And right there, at the entry to the cemetery, I found another bunch of leaflets of the type the Russians had been dropping every night. "Berlin Encircled!" one of them said. It talked of the overwhelming power of Soviet forces and the utter foolishness of exhausted German troops and untrained members of the People's Storm to resist them. Another leaflet, signed by the Supreme Command of the Red Army, offered "Special Rewards for German Officers and Soldiers" who surrendered to the Red Army now. These included 1) extra food, 2) housing in a highly desirable climate, 3) choice of work, 4) rapid mail delivery to relatives in Germany, and 5) accelerated return to Germany or, if desired, to any other country at the end of the war.

******

In the days that followed, my mother wouldn't let me go to school. She was determined to keep me out of the clutches of Dr. Dietrich and his harebrained schemes, which was fine with me. That way I missed the deployment of anti-aircraft and anti-tank cannons at the eastern edge of our village, another brilliant plan by someone who could not imagine the Russians coming from the west. That way I also had time to visit Mr. Kalitz, who was equally reluctant to take up arms in the last-ditch defense of his country. Jointly, we pieced together the latest news, as broadcast by the BBC. For us, the most significant stories were these:

The Americans stood at the Elbe near Magdeburg, some 50 kilometers to our southwest. The Russians were encircling Berlin and had taken Brandenburg, a mere 26 kilometers to our northeast, which explained the thunder I had heard for days. There were *cannons* in the east!

******

Each day, we made a list of newsworthy items to take to my mother; one of them read like this:

1945

April 11	U.S. troops reach the Elbe at Magdeburg
April 13	American President, Franklin D. Roosevelt, is dead
	Russian troops take Vienna
	Russian forces cross Oder River on wide front, begin Battle for Berlin
	German troops expected to use weapons of despair in defense of their capital, most likely Sarin and Tabun nerve gas

Radio Berlin, meanwhile, provided additional news. The death of President Roosevelt was reported as a "sign" that victory would be ours. The "heroic resistance of encircled German troops in East Prussia" was seen as another such sign. And on April 17, Heinrich Himmler solemnly announced:

"No German town will be declared an open city. Every village and every town will be defended with all possible means. Any German who offends against this self-evident duty to the nation will lose his life as well as his honor."

On the occasion of the Führer's birthday, on April 20, Reich Minister Goebbels declared:

"The Führer is in us and we are in him. The Führer is in each of us and each of us is within him."

He promised that the Führer would soon unleash a massive counter attack with new wonder weapons, tied to V3 and V4 rockets. That was also the day on which Dr. Dietrich made a speech on the steps of the Town Hall. He said there was good news from Berlin. A super secret wonder weapon of incredible power was now being readied. It would make the V2 rockets look like toys. In a matter of days, the new weapon would be in use and would reverse the tide of the war. Adolf Hitler was the only one who could and would save us from Bolshevism.

"Germans *will* conquer the world! Sieg Heil!" he said.

By then, Mr. Kalitz and I had collected further bits of news:

April 20	On Hitler's birthday, U.S. forces take Nuremberg, the shrine of National Socialism; first Russian troops reach outskirts of Berlin
April 25	Marshal Georgi Zhukov, commander of the 1st White Russian Front, and Marshal Ivan Konyev, commander of the 1st Ukrainian Front, complete the encirclement of Berlin

******

Before long, the Werewolf Station at Königswusterhausen was broadcasting an appeal to werewolves of Berlin and Brandenburg to rise against the enemy and engage in partisan action. My mother turned off the radio, but she couldn't turn off the noise in the street. We ran to the windows and witnessed the unfolding of another spectacle yet.

"My God, *Kettenhunde* [Chain Hounds] all over the place," my mother said.

Helmut jumped out of bed to have a look, too. They were right across the street now, about a dozen of them, wearing black boots, black uniforms, black helmets, the ones with skulls and crossbones. Like dog collars, big silver medallions hung on their chests on long, silver chains— symbols of absolute power over life and death. They carried brushes and buckets full of white paint. For a moment, they stopped in front of Furtwängler's tobacco store. Then they painted a sentence across the walls of three houses:

NOT ANOTHER FOOT OF SOIL TO OUR ENEMIES!

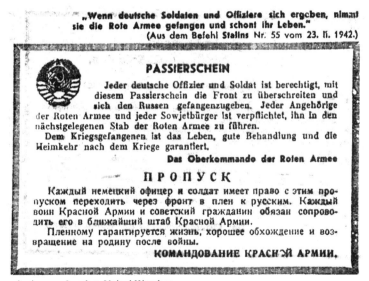

akg-images, London, United Kingdom

"When German soldiers and officers surrender, the Red Army takes them prisoner and spares their lives."
(From Stalin's Order Nr. 55 of November 23, 1942)

Safe Passage Certificate

Every German officer and soldier is entitled, with the help of this certificate, to cross the front line and surrender to the Russians. Every member of the Red Army and every Soviet citizen is obligated to deliver him to the nearest command of the Red Army. The prisoner of war is guaranteed life, good treatment, and return home after the war.

Supreme Command of the Red Army

27. GALLOWS
[April 1945]

One morning in April, there was a lot of commotion at the Town Hall, just a few houses down the street from us. My mother said I could go and investigate, and I got there just in time. A crowd had gathered in the street and the Chief of Police was standing next to the Thousand-Year Oak, talking to one of the Chain Hounds who was wearing the Knight's Cross with Oak Leaves and Swords, which made me think he was the man in charge. I must have been right; he climbed to the top step and made a speech.

He said gallows would be set up in front of the Town Hall that night. Henceforth, his SS men would execute any and all traitors right then and there. He trusted, he said, that the population would fully cooperate, and he reminded everyone to turn in enemy leaflets and to remember the *Sippenhaft Laws* [kinship responsibility laws], which made close relatives of traitors into accessories who were equally guilty.

"Death to all traitors! Heil Hitler!" he said.

Captain Werther made a speech, too, explaining the measures about to be taken.

"In the coming days," he said, "instant death sentences will be carried out against members of the armed forces and, if necessary, their closest relatives, for various acts of desertion and treachery. Such acts include the obvious, such as running away from the field of battle, malingering in the hinterland, creating self-inflicted wounds in order to be shipped to a hospital, and putting on civilian clothes."

"But," Captain Werther continued, "we will be watching also for more subtle signs that particular soldiers are planning to preserve their pitiful lives at the expense of the German people—signs such as possessing or spreading around enemy leaflets or carrying white handkerchiefs, which can be used to signal surrender."

Captain Werther also told us what had happened to Dr. Weiss after he ran off to the west.

"Black savages strung him on a tree upside down till his head burst," he said.

That scared me and I so craved my Valerian drops! I ran home to my mother, but she said Captain Werther, like Dr. Dietrich, was a fanatical liar; nobody could possibly know where Dr. Weiss had gone and what had happened to him. She also gave me one Valerian drop.

Being thus reassured, I went back down to find out what else the Chain Hounds had done with all the buckets of white paint. I made a list of all the slogans they had painted on the walls of houses on our street. Some of their slogans were really long and spanned four or five houses; others were much shorter:

"Those who are afraid of an honest death in battle deserve the mean death of cowards."

"Protect our women and children from the Red Beasts!"

"Traitors take care, the Werewolf is watching!"

"We will never surrender!"

"We believe in Victory!"

******

During the next week, I helped my mother get ready for what we all knew would surely come. Before all else, I had to get food; then I would ferret out the latest news. Mr. Albrecht lent me his bicycle so I could check out the dairy and the wind mill; both of them stood a kilometer out of town on the road to Paplitz. I had made the trip before, bringing home milk and butter from one place and a sack of wheat flour from the other. But that had been three months ago, and things had certainly changed. The road was now littered with abandoned things: Broken wagons without horses, wrecked army trucks in camouflage paint, perambulators and hand carts without wheels, torn suitcases, empty ammunition boxes, forsaken weapons, cast-off helmets, pitiful piles of crockery and toys.… And I came upon the carcass of a horse, smelling sickly and vile. Strips of meat had been hacked from its flanks, by then thick with maggots; thousands of flies rose up in black swarms to greet me. I felt ill, like throwing up, and wished I had my Valerian drops.

Still, I continued on my mission. On my way back, with a canister of cottage cheese, a jug full of whey and, alas, no flour at all, I distracted myself by counting the wooden crosses on the side of the road. They had been fashioned from nearby trees, birches usually, often listing just a name, sometimes rank and years of birth and death, and sometimes nothing at all.

Things got much worse when I pedaled onto Breite Weg. A Chain Hound stood in the middle of the road, legs astride, holding a pistol. A soldier in a gray-green uniform lay in front of him. The Chain Hound jammed the muzzle against the man's forehead, and I saw the man rise to his knees, then to his feet, the pistol following, his eyes closed, waiting, I presumed, for the last sound he would ever hear. But then the Chain Hound put away the pistol and took the lapels of the man's coat in both of his hands, pulling the man's head into his collar and making it disappear like that of a turtle I had once seen at the zoo. I didn't wait to watch and hurried home.

******

The next morning, we found three soldiers hanging from the gallows in front of the Town Hall. Each of them had a different sign around his neck, written in large black letters:

"Whoever fights *can* die. Whoever betrays his fatherland *must* die. *I had to die*!" one sign said.

"Here I hang because I did not believe in the Führer" said the next one.

"I was a coward, but died just the same!" said the last one.

And in the glass case, right next to the Town Hall door, the Chain Hounds had posted their evidence of one soldier's treachery, a Safe Conduct Certificate, signed by General Eisenhower.

******

It was time to go on my second mission and collect the news, which I tried to do on the very next day. But Mr. Kalitz wouldn't cooperate, not with the Chain Hounds in town and soldiers swinging on the gallows for treachery. So, my mother and I had to rely on the Goebbels Snout, but that was easier said than done.

On April 25, Reich Minister Goebbels broadcast a message to all women and girls.

"Take up the weapons of our wounded and fallen soldiers and fight!" he yelled. "Defend your freedom, your honor, and your life! Build a wall against the Mongol hordes!"

Then Radio Germany fell silent, never to be heard from again. Something terrible, we were sure, had happened in Berlin. We thought of Aunt Martel and my grandmother, but there was nothing we could do. My mother cried and I kept playing with the dials. Radio Hamburg was still on the air, reporting stories that made it into my notebook like this:

1945

April 26	General Dwight D. Eisenhower apparently halts Western Allied forces at the Elbe, refusing to aid the Red Army in the Battle for Berlin. This Anglo-American/Russian rift is a good sign for Germany!
April 28	Reich Commissar for the Netherlands, Artur von Seyss-Inquart, orders all German troops to stop fighting in Holland
	The Duce, Benito Mussolini, killed by Italian partisans! After being shot, strung up by his heels on Milan's main square, the Piazzale Loreto, Radio Stockholm reports
April 29	General Heinrich von Vietinghoff, Commander-in-Chief of German forces in North Italy, surrenders unconditionally

---

There was more! In the evening of May 1, Radio Hamburg repeatedly warned its listeners of an important announcement about to be made. My mother, Helmut, and I joined the Albrechts in their living room, which is why I noted down the time. At 21:40 hours, the station began to play Wagner's *Twilight of the Gods*. And then it came:

"*Achtung! Achtung!* Our beloved Führer, Adolf Hitler, has fallen on the field of honor at the head of his troops…."

The Führer's successor, the station said, would be Grand Admiral Karl Dönitz, who would, in turn, give an important speech on the next day.

"So Hitler Youth Quax made it after all," Mr. Albrecht said with a grin and, except for Helmut, we all knew what he meant. We had all seen the propaganda movies, featuring *Quax, the Crash Pilot*, the overeager Nazi youth. The equally devoted Grand Admiral Dönitz, the once so popular head of Germany's U-boat fleet, had often been compared to Quax.

On May 2, again on Radio Hamburg, Grand Admiral Karl Dönitz confirmed the Führer's death. He pledged that the war would go on to save us from the Russians, but German troops would henceforth fight the Western Allies only if they helped the Russians. In that spirit, he said, he had ordered German forces to evacuate Norway and Denmark.

******

Later that week, with Adolf Hitler dead, the Chain Hounds gone, and Dr. Weiss having walked back into town quite unharmed, I found Mr. Kalitz much more cooperative. As a result, we got a final bit of news from the BBC, which I also recorded in my little book:

1945

May 2   U.S. forces capture Munich and then Braunau, Hitler's birthplace

British forces bypass Hamburg, take Lübeck on the Baltic Sea

Russian forces hoist the hammer-and-sickle flag over the Reichstag in Berlin;

General Helmuth Weidling, commandant of Berlin, surrenders; estimated losses in the Battle of Berlin: 300,000 Soviets, 1 million Germans

May 3   Grand Admiral Karl Dönitz proposes to make separate deal with Western Allies; is rebuffed by Field Marshal Bernard Montgomery

May 4   German forces in the Northwest surrender in Lüneburg; document signed by Admiral Hans Georg von Friedeburg and Field Marshal Bernard Montgomery

An American leaflet which, if discovered on a German soldier by the SS, could easily cost the soldier's life:

Safe Passage Certificate

The German soldier who presents this safe passage certificate is using it as a sign of his honest desire to surrender. He is to be disarmed. He is to be well treated. He has the right to receive food and, if necessary, medical attention. He is to be removed from the danger zone as soon as possible.

Dwight D. Eisenhower

Supreme Commander

Allied Expeditionary Force

The English translation on the reverse side serves as instruction for the Allied outposts

28. MONGOL DANCE

[May 1945]

With Brandenburg, and then Berlin, in Russian hands to our east and the Americans on the Elbe to our west, we all knew that it was a matter of days, perhaps hours, before we would be occupied by one side or the other. Everyone hoped that the Americans would get to us first, given the horror stories we had heard about the Russians, but that wasn't likely, if Radio Hamburg was to be believed. For some unknown reason, the Americans wouldn't cross the Elbe, a mere 50 kilometers away. Accordingly, everyone's mind turned to making last-minute preparations for the worst.

Mr. Albrecht dug a big hole in the backyard and got ready to bury all his liquor bottles, lest the Russians found them and went on a drunken rampage. Mrs. Albrecht made a bonfire nearby, ever so reluctantly feeding it with pictures of her son Werner, all of them showing him in Army uniform with swastikas on his lapels. She was soon joined by Mrs. Ebner, Mrs. Holland, and Mrs. Gronostalski, our neighbors from Cologne. Among other things, they contributed a picture of the Führer, an SA uniform, and lots of family pictures of various brothers, fiancés, husbands, sons, and uncles, all in some kind of uniform. Watching them thus cover their tracks made me think of all the Hitler pictures in my own book of the 1936 Olympic Games. I went up to get it and then remembered my Hitler stamps, too. My mother came down with me to watch the show. But I didn't want to lose my stamps; nor did I want to give up the book with all its three-dimensional effects. Rather than burning it, I stashed it next to Mr. Albrecht's liquor hoard and let him bury it.

Just then we saw a truck appear through clouds of dust, coming up the side road from the fields. It stopped, it moved, it came to our house! We saw red crosses on the side. A soldier asked for my mother.

"I know, I know," she sobbed. "Just go and let me be."

Mrs. Albrecht talked to him, and then let out a piercing shout:

"Trudchen come here, he's alive!"

My mother stared at them in disbelief and made the soldier tell the story: a piece of shrapnel in his head at Cottbus, surgery in the field, transfer to Brandenburg, then Hanover.

"He's fine, I swear, will be like new; he sends his love. The English have him now."

And my mother jumped across the yard, embraced the messenger, let go a flood of tears and kisses, cries and laughter.

"Good luck to all of you," the soldier said. "We've got to run. North to Havelberg; Schwerin, if we are lucky; it's the only way out of here now."

The soldier turned and saw the sign next to the cellar door. "LSR" it said, which stood for "*Luft Schutz Raum*" or "air raid shelter."

"LSR has a new meaning now," he said, with a grin: "*Lernt Schnell Russisch!*" [Learn Russian Fast!], and off they sped, the low-hanging branches swatting their truck as it raced out of sight.

******

The flow of refugees had ceased. The German Army had disappeared. The Chain Hounds were gone, too, but the Chief of Police was still there. In fact, Captain Werther argued with a group of women in front of the police station.

"A bunch of traitors, that's what you are," he yelled. "There's going to be no white flag on the church tower as long as I am in charge!"

Dr. Dietrich was there, too.

"Every male in a house where a white flag appears will be shot," he said.

"And there is going to be no defeatist evacuation of this village," he added.

A man swayed from the gallows near the Town Hall. A black plane roared down the center of the street, no higher than the trees, and I saw its red star! And then there was silence; silence to the east and to the south; silence to the west and to the north; silence everywhere.

******

Somehow, on that fateful Monday afternoon of May 7, 1945, we all went into the cellar at the same time: My mother, Helmut, and I, and the Albrechts, and the three families from Cologne—the Ebners, the Hollands, and the Gronostalskis—except for Mr. Albrecht, women and children all.

I didn't like it. I thought of Berlin and looked with disdain at the ceiling, lacking, as it did, even the most rudimentary type of support. Should they decide to shoot artillery at us, we could easily be buried again, I knew. But I felt nothing; no pounding of the heart, no dizziness, no choking at the throat. I felt calmer than I had in years.

"If the Russians just knew us," I thought, "they wouldn't want to kill us. We might even become friends."

Still, sometimes and ever so briefly, my mind kept drifting into places I had forbidden it to go. It wandered on the edge of dreams, allowing vague images to pass across it, images of blood and fire, of blackened ruins and charred bodies, of pitiful refugee columns and soldiers moaning in pain.

But then a clock struck three and all of it was gone.

I climbed a chair and waited at the cellar window, merely a hole in the cement wall without glass, and I stared into the street. It was so quiet; the village seemed paralyzed. I could hear the clacking of the storks' bills on top of the castle and the flapping noises made by the large white flag at the tower of the church. Someone had put it there anyway!

I thought of the warning issued by the Brandenburg Werewolf earlier that day: "All that matters is perseverance and a remorseless will to achieve victory! We warn you! Villages that betray us and show the white flag will experience total destruction!" Others around me must surely have had similar thoughts. The tension in that cellar was unbelievable, as if we were all standing in the middle of a newly frozen pond, waiting for the ice to break and drown us all. And then I saw him: A solitary rider in the center of Breite Weg, followed by a cloud of dust much larger than a single horse could make. His horse was white, its gait was slow. He sat up straight and proud, his chest covered with medals. He rode past the bakery, the shoe store, the grocery store; he moved past the pharmacy, past us, and on towards the gallows at the Town Hall, just out of my view.

And a phalanx of chariots came onto Breite Weg out of the dust, three abreast, and reached from wall to wall across the street. I saw little horses, pulling giant wheels, and single riders crouched on seats of straw between the wheels. I heard the heavy breathing of the little beasts, the clatter of their hoofs, the rumbling of the wheels.

I thought of the newsreels from Paris Mr. Eisler had shown and noticed the contrast between the scene unfolding here and that other scene, not so many years ago, of the German Army, goose-stepping along the Champs Elysées.

I heard voices then; the single rider had returned; I saw his khaki uniform; I saw his face: a Mongol Khan! He stopped and pointed to the house across the street. The sun made sparkles on his crescent sword.

"Mongols, my God, Mongols," Mrs. Albrecht wailed, "they're going to burn us alive."

"Shut up," Mrs. Gronostalski said.

Then there were voices again and someone banged on our front door. I saw Mr. Furtwängler and Mrs. Furtwängler and their boys coming from their tobacco store across the street.

"Open up, open up," they yelled. "Hurry, hurry!"

Mr. Albrecht took the iron pipe he was clutching and went up to let them in. He locked the front door after them.

"They are taking our house," Mr. Furtwängler said. "They just pointed those guns at us and waved us out the door. But the fellow on the white horse, he has a sword."

"Mongols, my God, Mongols," Mrs. Albrecht wailed.

"I told you to shut up," Mrs. Gronostalski said.

That's when my mother decided to take us back up to our room.

******

From behind our curtains, we saw waves of chariots pass our house that afternoon, pulled by tiny horses with wooden yokes around their necks, nodding their heads and snorting, pawing at the road whenever they came to a stop, then passing on.

Later, we learned the names of those ubiquitous wagons filled with straw and pulled by those shaggy little ponies. *Panje wagons*, they called them. Later, we also learned the names of other vehicles that moved past our house: the *Studebaker* trucks filled with soldiers in brown uniforms, the *Dodges* towing light guns, the *Chevrolets* with mortars in back, and the *Deere* farm tractors hauling howitzers. And we also saw the tank troops in their padded black helmets, guiding their famous T-34's.

That night, of course, nobody slept. And one of the tanks moved around outside, making a racket. Again and again, it came out of the side street, churning up the earth and pushing a huge pile of wooden beams in front of it, tearing up the cobblestones in its wake. A pyre of wood grew in the middle of the street, right in front of our house, shaped like a pyramid, three meters high. The wood looked like the railroad ties we had planted in the fields to keep the tanks from getting into town, and Mrs. Albrecht carried on something awful downstairs. We could hear every word upstairs.

"They're going to burn us alive," she yelled.

"Shut up your goddamn mouth," Mr. Albrecht said.

Outside, the Mongols poured gasoline on the railroad ties. We could smell the pungent odor through our open windows. A lot of soldiers appeared and formed a circle. The chariots and horses made a circle, too. We saw them fire their pistols and rifles and submachine guns into the air. And then something exploded, and a fire burned in the middle of the street. I held on to Helmut, and thought of the stories the Chain Hounds had told. My mother stood close behind us. Soon, we felt the heat of the fire, even though it was in the middle of the road and the road was wide and our curtains were mostly drawn. None of us dared breathe.

The fire reached for the sky.

And we heard a voice, a single, beautiful voice, nearly imperceptible at first, but intense; softly, growing louder; slowly at first, but moving faster, and faster. "Kalinka, Kalinka, Kalinka moya," and a hundred voices joining the first, bodies joining arms, and a hundred faces burning with fire.

We heard feet jump in the fiery night, and saw a circle of men and swords whirl around the flames. And a whirlwind filled the street. Then silence.

The fire reached for the sky. Again, that single, beautiful voice; soft, growing louder; slow, moving faster. "Kalinka, Kalinka, Kalinka moya," and a hundred swords sparkled in the night.

When the fire died down, they threw branches on it and a new shower of sparks swirled skyward, making the fire roar again and drive away the shadows of the night. And then, too, we could read the message across the street:

NOT ANOTHER FOOT OF SOIL TO OUR ENEMIES!

Keinen Fussbreit Boden mehr unsern Feinden!

Langewiesche-Brandt, Ebenhausen near München, Germany

The Nazi view of the Red Army:
Not another Foot of Soil to Our Enemies!

29. RAMPAGE

[May 1945]

Everyone was relieved that the Mongols preferred to burn railroad ties rather than people. By morning the day after their arrival, even Mrs. Albrecht had calmed down. She kept saying how cute all those "ponies" were out there in the street. And in the light of day, Helmut and I noted something else that was cute: Many of the panje wagons were decorated with carpets and many of their Mongol inhabitants were sleeping on feather beds hidden in the midst of all that straw! Moreover, down to the left, near the grocery store—we could hardly believe our eyes—we spotted *camels* in front of some of the wagons parked there. Equally interesting, a bunch of Mongols were busily roasting an entire pig on a spit, right in the middle of the street! But my mother wouldn't let us go down to investigate.

"You are *not* to leave this house!" she said firmly.

"But we need water and I have to go to the toilet," I said. "May I go to the backyard?"

"The backyard only," my mother said, "and only if Mr. Albrecht is there."

******

Before long, the Mongols figured out that Mr. Albrecht had a butcher shop; the big pig's head hanging over the door, and just below our windows, made it pretty obvious. Mr. Albrecht had his hands full from then on. They brought over some of the pigs from a farm down the street, and gestured wildly. They wanted sausages, long strings of sausages. Then they brought over a huge brown ox and, later, a goat. I watched Mr. Albrecht tie up the pigs. He pulled them up to a hook on the ceiling, hind legs first, and then cut their throats. He gathered the blood in buckets to make blood sausage later. He numbed the ox with a single blow of the sledgehammer, then picked up a metal cylinder and fired a shot into the ox's head. He also made big funny eyes at the Mongols who were standing around to watch. He held the cylinder to his own head, but didn't pull the trigger. Everyone laughed. He went up to the Mongol captain, who was watering his horse, and held the cylinder to *his* head. The captain pretended to be dead and fell to the ground. Everyone laughed some more.

And everyone just *died* laughing when I decided to try out the only Russian words I knew—the ones I had learned during my People's Storm training.

"Ruki vverch! [Hands Up!]," I said to the captain, and he gladly obliged.

Just then, Mrs. Albrecht came running into the back yard, gesturing almost hysterically.

"There are savages, there are savages out there!" she screamed.

Mr. Albrecht calmly rolled up the skin of the ox, heavily sprinkled with salt, lit the coals at the bottom of the smoking chamber, and then followed her into the street. Everyone else went along, too, still laughing. I stopped at the front door, as my mother had commanded, but I could still see what was going on. A tank stood in front of the pharmacy next door. The tank was decorated with red banners and flowers and three black soldiers sat on top of it. They were laughing, too. They watched a fourth soldier, also black, trying to catch a chicken in the middle of the street. He wasn't succeeding. I ran upstairs to tell Helmut to look out the window. Like me, he had never seen black people before, either. That's when we also saw the new sign above the Furtwänglers' tobacco shop.

"Komendatura" it said.

And when we looked down the street, right or left, we saw red flags hanging from lots of windows. Each flag had a circle in the middle, made of a darker red than the surrounding area. That was the spot where the white circle with the swastika had been.

"I don't believe it," my mother said. "I guess it's 'Heil Stalin' now."

******

Just then, there was an incredible bang and another and another still, and the earth shook. We saw blinding flashes, even though the sun stood high in the sky. The air filled with rockets exploding and bombs whistling. Showers of sparks rained down, and the noise grew louder and came faster. A house down the street began to burn, and all the Mongol soldiers got on their chariots and drove away. The tank made a terrible noise as well, and I thought of Mt. Vesuvius burying the people of Pompeii. I had seen it all in my grandmother's Liebig books.

A man came running from the railroad tracks. He said a munitions train had blown up.

"Must have been the sparks from the locomotive," he said.

But just then Dr. Dietrich raced by on a bicycle. He wasn't wearing his SA uniform and his face was red. His face was white the next morning when we were all marched to the Town Hall to see him hanging from the gallows, along with the Chief of Police. The two werewolves, it turned out, had used a *Panzerfaust* on a munitions train.

By morning, tanks and trucks ringed the village, and the Mongols with their cute ponies and camels were definitely gone. Cossack cavalry men, sitting on regular horses with swords strapped to their saddles, had taken up positions every hundred meters along the street, as far as we could see. And White-Russian soldiers, half of them women, were just then pouring out of trucks parked in the center of Breite Weg. With submachine guns slung across their chests, they went into every house, and they looked into every room. One soldier came up to our place. On entering, he fired a short burst onto the ceiling, bringing down a shower of plaster and one of the flypaper things. Helmut had been sleeping in his crib and started to cry; my mother covered her mouth with her hands. I stood by the window, very quietly, doing nothing. The soldier looked around, opened the wall closet, and stabbed into it with his sword. My mother's housecoat was slashed. Another soldier came in and took my mother's wedding ring. He scared her with a knife when she couldn't get it off fast enough.

"Davai! Davai!" he yelled.

He also took the porcelain fish which my mother used as a mold when she made pudding.

Other soldiers went through the backyard and the Albrechts' garden and put their swords into the ground. In no time at all, they found the big chest that was buried there. I guess it was pretty obvious with the freshly turned earth. I watched them open the lid. They laughed when they saw Mr. Albrecht's wine bottles, but they were angry about all the other things. They dangled the air raid helmets and war medals in front of Mr. Albrecht's nose.

"Fashist! Fashist!" they yelled.

They discovered my Hitler stamps, too, and threw them on the ground. Then they leafed through my book about the Olympic Games of 1936. Each picture was printed twice, and when one looked at it through a special set of glasses, as I have said before, one could see everything in three dimensions, but the Russians didn't figure it out. Still, Adolf Hitler was visible in almost every scene, three-dimensional or not, and the Russian soldiers didn't like it at all.

"Gitler, Gitler!" they said and trampled the book underfoot.

That's when a group of former POWs came into the yard. I could tell, because they were filthy and bearded and still had the R on the back of their jackets. They also wore shabby uniforms that were stained and ripped, and their boots were falling to pieces. One of the men was particularly scary. He had bloodshot eyes and held a bayonet in his hand, but without the rifle. He went through Mr. Albrecht's apartment to find himself a new wardrobe. He also took a bunch of cans from Mrs. Albrecht's kitchen. He opened one of them with the bayonet; I ran away and hid upstairs.

******

Later, a company of soldiers with fixed bayonets marched past our house. They were singing. With the accent on the last syllable of each word, their song sounded exactly like "Liverwurst! Liverwurst!" I never figured out what it meant, not even in later years when I spoke Russian. Meanwhile, down the street, at the shoe store, a group of women soldiers had discovered a cache of silk stockings and high-heeled shoes. Before long, they were walking on high heels among the cobblestones, their boots under one arm, their submachine guns under the other. Some of their male comrades, meanwhile, were trying to ride their newly plundered bicycles, wobbling dangerously from one side of the street to the other. People watched them from behind their curtains and laughed. But they didn't laugh for long.

******

Mrs. Holland came back from the baker's, just four houses down the street from us, and told everyone that soldiers were holding Gisela Senf in the barn.

"Mr. Senf was lying in the yard behind the bakery shop," she said, her voice quivering and almost giving out. "Like dead, but he was alive. He said he went berserk when he saw them holding the muzzle of a pistol in Gisela's mouth to ensure her compliance. They must have knocked him out."

Mrs. Ebner came back from the pharmacy next door and told everyone how Erna Diehl had been raped by dozens of soldiers, one after the other, and her mother had been raped as well when she tried to interfere.

"Imagine," she said, with tears streaming down her face, "a seventeen year old child!"

Mrs. Gronostalski came back from across the street, where she had just gotten a new job as interpreter—none of us had known before that she spoke Russian fluently—and her news wasn't any better.

"A woman just brought in her daughter to the commandant," she said. "Black bruises on her face and neck, her eyes swollen shut, cuts on her hands, she is a mess. They've been raping her all night, wouldn't even give her a break to breast-feed her baby!"

"And the commandant, calmly smoking his makhorka, greeted them with total indifference, almost amusement," she continued, "and you should see what he says to the *Russian* girls!"

"Russian girls?" Mrs. Albrecht asked.

"Oh yeah," Mrs. Gronostalski said, "the liberated ones from the POW camp. They have been raping them, too, even in sight of the officers. And you know what he says, the Commandant? 'You are here' he says, 'it can't have done you any harm' he says. The trouble is, they think these girls have collaborated with the Nazis; otherwise, they would have fought to the death or joined the partisans! He even has a sign above his desk, the Commandant has. 'Be ruthless to all turncoats and traitors to the motherland,' it says."

There was that big silence in the room, and one could hear the birds in the backyard. But I hadn't understood anything that had just been told.

"What's *rape*?" I whispered to my mother.

She promised she would explain that very night, and then my mother and Mrs. Albrecht and all the others whispered a lot as well, just as my mother and Mrs. Meyer and Mrs. Nussbaum had in Berlin, and then Mr. Albrecht got the big key and locked up all the doors.

By nightfall, red light illuminated the skyline, just as it had in Berlin. It was eerie, as the fires set off by the explosions reflected off low-hanging clouds. Something else was eerie, too. By then, all the houses on the other side of the street, on both sides of the Komendatura, were occupied by Russian soldiers and we were mighty scared.

All the women in our house met in Mrs. Albrecht's living room, while I had to watch Helmut upstairs. They did a lot of redecorating in a hurry, because Helmut and I didn't recognize the place later when we went downstairs. The couch was gone and so were the overstuffed chairs and all the animal pictures. In their place was an altar, covered with a white cloth and lots of candles burning. A large, wooden cross, with Jesus hanging from it, stood on the altar and pictures of Mary, the Mother of God, hung on the wall. Rows of folding chairs faced the cross, and a house organ stood in the corner. The smell of incense was in the air. The Albrechts, it seemed, had become Catholic!

I couldn't understand it, but before I could ask, Helmut came running to tell us about the Italians on the sidewalk. Mr. Albrecht let them in, along with a few Belgians and Frenchmen who had been freed from the POW camp just south of the village and all of whom had somehow managed to fashion and bring along copies of their national flags. Having studied them in school, I instantly recognized the vertical blue-white-red of France, the vertical black-yellow-red of Belgium, and the vertical green-white-red of Italy. The Italians gave my mother a big hug and opened a giant dairy can that was full of soup: potatoes, milk, and pieces of meat. There was more than enough for all of us.

Later that night, when drunk Russian soldiers battered down the front door and stormed in with their bayonets pointing at us, they came upon a remarkable sight: A congregation of Frenchmen and Belgians, of Italians and Germans—bareheaded men holding on to their tricolor flags and scarf-covered women hiding their faces before the Heavenly Father—all singing Martin Luther's "A Mighty Fortress is Our God." It was the only hymn Mrs. Albrecht could play.

We couldn't believe what happened next: The Russian visitors took off their hats, bowed to the crucifix, and left!

That night, after Helmut was asleep, my mother kept her promise and talked with me—mostly about love and a little bit about sex and the violence that is called *rape*. Frankly, I didn't understand most of it; there was too much talk about birds and bees and none of this made any sense at all. But we hugged, which felt good and safe and we fell asleep in the chair by the window, now facing the Komendatura.

******

The next morning, Mr. Kalitz stopped at the Albrecht house. He had been at the baker's and had found the old Mr. Senf with a knife in his heart. He had also found Gisela, the baker's daughter. She had hanged herself in the very barn she hadn't been allowed to leave. That's when Mr. Albrecht, Mr. Kalitz, and all the women in the house met in the new chapel for a council meeting. I don't know what was said, because I had to watch Helmut, but I do remember later asking Mrs. Gronostalski to teach me the Russian word for rape.

"Iznasi'lovaniye," she said, looking rather puzzled.

"You know," she added, "you should learn the rest of the language; it may well come in handy one of these days. I can teach you, if you like, especially now that the school is closed."

I liked the idea. Before the day was gone, Mrs. Gronostalski had given me a sheet with the Russian alphabet as well as a poster she had picked up at the Commandant's office. I couldn't read a word, of course, but she said we could use the poster as our textbook.

"It's a copy of the first order issued by the Commandant of Berlin," she said.

ПРИКАЗ

НАЧАЛЬНИКА ГАРНИЗОНА ГОРОДА БЕРЛИН

27 " апреля 1945 года.   № 1.   _город Берлин._

СЕГО ЧИСЛА Я НАЗНАЧЕН НАЧАЛЬНИКОМ ГАРНИЗОНА И КОМЕНДАНТОМ ГОРОДА БЕРЛИН.

ВСЯ АДМИНИСТРАТИВНАЯ И ПОЛИТИЧЕСКАЯ ВЛАСТЬ ПО УПОЛНОМОЧИЮ КОМАНДОВАНИЯ КРАСНОЙ АРМИИ ПЕРЕХОДИТ В МОИ РУКИ.

В КАЖДОМ РАЙОНЕ ГОРОДА ПО РАНЕЕ СУЩЕСТВОВАВШЕМУ АДМИНИСТРАТИВНОМУ ДЕЛЕНИЮ НАЗНАЧАЮТСЯ РАЙОННЫЕ И УЧАСТКОВЫЕ ВОЕННЫЕ КОМЕНДАТУРЫ.

ПРИКАЗЫВАЮ:

1. НАСЕЛЕНИЮ ГОРОДА СОБЛЮДАТЬ ПОЛНЫЙ ПОРЯДОК И ОСТАВАТЬСЯ НА СВОИХ МЕСТАХ.

2. НАЦИОНАЛ-СОЦИАЛИСТИЧЕСКУЮ НЕМЕЦКУЮ РАБОЧУЮ ПАРТИЮ И ВСЕ ПОДЧИНЕННЫЕ ЕЙ ОРГАНИЗАЦИИ («ГИТЛЕР-ЮГЕНД», ФРАУЕНШАФТ, «ШТУРМЕНТЕНБУНД» и проч.) РАСПУСТИТЬ И ДЕЯТЕЛЬНОСТЬ ИХ ВОСПРЕТИТЬ.

РУКОВОДЯЩЕМУ СОСТАВУ ВСЕХ УЧРЕЖДЕНИЙ НСДАП, ГЕСТАПО, ЖАНДАРМЕРИИ, ОХРАННЫХ ОТРЯДОВ, ТЮРЕМ И ВСЕХ ДРУГИХ ГОСУДАРСТВЕННЫХ УЧРЕЖДЕНИЙ В ТЕЧЕНИЕ 48 ЧАСОВ С МОМЕНТА ОПУБЛИКОВАНИЯ НАСТОЯЩЕГО ПРИКАЗА ЯВИТЬСЯ В РАЙОННЫЕ И УЧАСТКОВЫЕ ВОЕННЫЕ КОМЕНДАТУРЫ ДЛЯ РЕГИСТРАЦИИ.

В ТЕЧЕНИЕ 72-х ЧАСОВ НА РЕГИСТРАЦИЮ ОБЯЗАНЫ ТАКЖЕ ЯВИТЬСЯ ВСЕ ВОЕННОСЛУЖАЩИЕ НЕМЕЦКОЙ АРМИИ, ВОЙСК «СС» И «СА», ОСТАВШИЕСЯ В ГОРОДЕ БЕРЛИНЕ.

НЕ ЯВИВШИЕСЯ В СРОК, А ТАКЖЕ ВИНОВНЫЕ В УКРЫВАТЕЛЬСТВЕ ИХ БУДУТ ПРИВЛЕЧЕНЫ К СТРОГОЙ ОТВЕТСТВЕННОСТИ ПО ЗАКОНУ ВОЕННОГО ВРЕМЕНИ.

3. ДОЛЖНОСТНЫМ ЛИЦАМ РАЙОННЫХ УПРАВЛЕНИЙ ЯВИТЬСЯ КО МНЕ ДЛЯ ДОКЛАДА О СОСТОЯНИИ ИХ УЧРЕЖДЕНИЙ И ПОЛУЧЕНИЯ УКАЗАНИЯ О ДАЛЬНЕЙШЕЙ ДЕЯТЕЛЬНОСТИ ЭТИХ УЧРЕЖДЕНИЙ.

4. ВСЕ КОММУНАЛЬНЫЕ ПРЕДПРИЯТИЯ, КАК ТО: ЭЛЕКТРОСТАНЦИИ, ВОДОПРОВОД, КАНАЛИЗАЦИЯ, ГОРОДСКОЙ ТРАНСПОРТ (МЕТРО, ТРАМВАИ, ТРОЛЛЕЙБУС);

ВСЕ ЛЕЧЕБНЫЕ УЧРЕЖДЕНИЯ;

ВСЕ ПРОДОВОЛЬСТВЕННЫЕ МАГАЗИНЫ И ХЛЕБОПЕКАРНИ ДОЛЖНЫ ВОЗОБНОВИТЬ СВОЮ РАБОТУ ПО ОБСЛУЖИВАНИЮ НУЖД НАСЕЛЕНИЯ.

РАБОЧИМ И СЛУЖАЩИМ ПЕРЕЧИСЛЕННЫХ УЧРЕЖДЕНИЙ ОСТАВАТЬСЯ НА СВОИХ МЕСТАХ И ПРОДОЛЖАТЬ ИСПОЛНЕНИЕ СВОИХ ОБЯЗАННОСТЕЙ.

5. ДОЛЖНОСТНЫМ ЛИЦАМ ГОСУДАРСТВЕННЫХ ПРОДУКТОВЫХ СКЛАДОВ, А ТАКЖЕ ЧАСТНЫМ ВЛАДЕЛЬЦАМ В ТЕЧЕНИЕ 24 ЧАСОВ С МОМЕНТА ОПУБЛИКОВАНИЯ НАСТОЯЩЕГО ПРИКАЗА ЗАРЕГИСТРИРОВАТЬ У ВОЕННЫХ КОМЕНДАНТОВ РАЙОНОВ ВСЕ ИМЕЮЩИЕСЯ ЗАПАСЫ ПРОДОВОЛЬСТВИЯ И РАСХОДОВАТЬ ИХ ТОЛЬКО С РАЗРЕШЕНИЯ РАЙОННЫХ ВОЕННЫХ КОМЕНДАНТОВ.

ВПРЕДЬ ДО ОСОБЫХ УКАЗАНИЙ ВЫДАЧУ ПРОДОВОЛЬСТВИЯ ИЗ ПРОДУКТОВЫХ МАГАЗИНОВ ПРОИЗВОДИТЬ ПО РАНЕЕ СУЩЕСТВУЮЩИМ НОРМАМ И ДОКУМЕНТАМ. ПРОДОВОЛЬСТВИЕ ОТПУСКАТЬ НЕ БОЛЕЕ, КАК НА 5—7 ДНЕЙ. ЗА НЕЗАКОННЫЙ ОТПУСК ПРОДОВОЛЬСТВИЯ СВЕРХ УСТАНОВЛЕННЫХ НОРМ ИЛИ ЗА ВЫДАЧУ НА ЛИЦ, ОТСУТСТВУЮЩИХ В ГОРОДЕ — ВИНОВНАЯ В ЭТОМ АДМИНИСТРАЦИЯ БУДЕТ ПРИВЛЕЧЕНА К СТРОГОЙ ОТВЕТСТВЕННОСТИ.

6. ВЛАДЕЛЬЦАМ И УПРАВЛЯЮЩИМ БАНКОВ ВРЕМЕННО ВСЯКИЕ ФИНАНСОВЫЕ ОПЕРАЦИИ ПРЕКРАТИТЬ. СЕЙФЫ НЕМЕДЛЕННО ОПЕЧАТАТЬ И ЯВИТЬСЯ В ВОЕННЫЕ КОМЕНДАТУРЫ С ДОКЛАДОМ О СОСТОЯНИИ БАНКОВСКОГО ХОЗЯЙСТВА.

ВСЕМ ЧИНОВНИКАМ БАНКОВ КАТЕГОРИЧЕСКИ ЗАПРЕЩАЕТСЯ ПРОИЗВОДИТЬ КАКИЕ БЫ ТО НИ БЫЛО ИЗЪЯТИЯ ЦЕННОСТЕЙ. ВИНОВНЫЕ В НАРУШЕНИИ БУДУТ СТРОГО НАКАЗАНЫ ПО ЗАКОНУ ВОЕННОГО ВРЕМЕНИ.

НАРЯДУ С ИМЕЮЩИМИСЯ В ХОЖДЕНИИ ИМПЕРСКИМИ ДЕНЕЖНЫМИ ЗНАКАМИ ОБЯЗАТЕЛЬНЫ В ОБРАЩЕНИИ ОККУПАЦИОННЫЕ МАРКИ СОЮЗНОГО ВОЕННОГО КОМАНДОВАНИЯ.

7. ВСЕ ЛИЦА, ИМЕЮЩИЕ ОГНЕСТРЕЛЬНОЕ И ХОЛОДНОЕ ОРУЖИЕ, БОЕПРИПАСЫ, ВЗРЫВЧАТЫЕ ВЕЩЕСТВА, РАДИОПРИЕМНИКИ И РАДИОПЕРЕДАТЧИКИ, ФОТОАППАРАТЫ, АВТОМАШИНЫ, МОТОЦИКЛЫ И ГОРЮЧЕ-СМАЗОЧНЫХ МАТЕРИАЛЫ, ОБЯЗАНЫ В ТЕЧЕНИЕ 72 ЧАСОВ С МОМЕНТА ОПУБЛИКОВАНИЯ НАСТОЯЩЕГО ПРИКАЗА ВСЕ ПЕРЕЧИСЛЕННОЕ СДАТЬ В РАЙОННЫЕ ВОЕННЫЕ КОМЕНДАТУРЫ.

ЗА НЕСДАЧУ В СРОК ВЫШЕПЕРЕЧИСЛЕННЫХ ВЕЩЕЙ ВИНОВНЫЕ БУДУТ СТРОГО НАКАЗАНЫ ПО ЗАКОНУ ВОЕННОГО ВРЕМЕНИ.

ВЛАДЕЛЬЦЫ ТИПОГРАФИЙ, ПИШУЩИХ МАШИНОК И ДРУГИХ МНОЖИТЕЛЬНЫХ АППАРАТОВ ОБЯЗАНЫ ЗАРЕГИСТРИРОВАТЬСЯ У ВОЕННЫХ КОМЕНДАНТОВ РАЙОНОВ И УЧАСТКОВ. КАТЕГОРИЧЕСКИ ЗАПРЕЩАЕТСЯ ПЕЧАТАТЬ, РАЗМНОЖАТЬ И РАСКЛЕИВАТЬ ИЛИ РАСПРОСТРАНЯТЬ ПО ГОРОДУ КАКИЕ БЫ ТО НИ БЫЛО ДОКУМЕНТЫ БЕЗ РАЗРЕШЕНИЯ ВОЕННЫХ КОМЕНДАНТОВ.

ВСЕ ТИПОГРАФИИ ОПЕЧАТЫВАЮТСЯ И ДОПУСК В НИХ ПРОИЗВОДИТСЯ ТОЛЬКО С РАЗРЕШЕНИЯ ВОЕННОГО КОМЕНДАНТА.

8. НАСЕЛЕНИЮ ГОРОДА ЗАПРЕЩАЕТСЯ:

А) ВЫХОДИТЬ ИЗ ДОМОВ И ПОЯВЛЯТЬСЯ НА УЛИЦАХ И ВО ДВОРАХ, А ТАКЖЕ НАХОДИТЬСЯ И ВЫПОЛНЯТЬ КАКУЮ-ЛИБО РАБОТУ В НЕЖИЛЫХ ПОМЕЩЕНИЯХ С 22.00 до 6.00 УТРА ПО БЕРЛИНСКОМУ ВРЕМЕНИ;

Б) ОСВЕЩАТЬ ПОМЕЩЕНИЯ С НЕЗАМАСКИРОВАННЫМИ ОКНАМИ;

В) ПРИНИМАТЬ В СОСТАВ СВОЕЙ СЕМЬИ, А ТАКЖЕ НА ЖИТЕЛЬСТВО И НОЧЛЕГ КОГО БЫ ТО НИ БЫЛО, В ТОМ ЧИСЛЕ И ВОЕННОСЛУЖАЩИХ КРАСНОЙ АРМИИ И СОЮЗНЫХ ВОЙСК БЕЗ РАЗРЕШЕНИЯ ВОЕННЫХ КОМЕНДАНТОВ;

Г) ДОПУСКАТЬ САМОВОЛЬНОЕ РАСТАСКИВАНИЕ БРОШЕННОГО УЧРЕЖДЕНИЯМИ И ЧАСТНЫМИ ЛИЦАМИ ИМУЩЕСТВА И ПРОДОВОЛЬСТВИЯ. НАСЕЛЕНИЕ, НАРУШАЮЩЕЕ УКАЗАННЫЕ ТРЕБОВАНИЯ, БУДЕТ ПРИВЛЕКАТЬСЯ К СТРОГОЙ ОТВЕТСТВЕННОСТИ ПО ЗАКОНУ ВОЕННОГО ВРЕМЕНИ.

9. РАБОТУ УВЕСЕЛИТЕЛЬНЫХ УЧРЕЖДЕНИЙ (КАК ТО: КИНО, ТЕАТРОВ, ЦИРКОВ, СТАДИОНОВ), ОТПРАВЛЕНИЕ РЕЛИГИОЗНЫХ ОБРЯДОВ В КИРХАХ, РАБОТУ РЕСТОРАНОВ И СТОЛОВЫХ РАЗРЕШАЕТСЯ ПРОИЗВОДИТЬ ДО 21.00 ЧАСА ПО БЕРЛИНСКОМУ ВРЕМЕНИ.

ЗА ИСПОЛЬЗОВАНИЕ ОБЩЕСТВЕННЫХ УЧРЕЖДЕНИЙ ВО ВРАЖДЕБНЫХ КРАСНОЙ АРМИИ ЦЕЛЯХ, ДЛЯ НАРУШЕНИЯ ПОРЯДКА И СПОКОЙСТВИЯ В ГОРОДЕ — АДМИНИСТРАЦИЯ ЭТИХ УЧРЕЖДЕНИЙ БУДЕТ ПРИВЛЕЧЕНА К СТРОГОЙ ОТВЕТСТВЕННОСТИ ПО ЗАКОНАМ ВОЕННОГО ВРЕМЕНИ.

10. НАСЕЛЕНИЕ ГОРОДА ПРЕДУПРЕЖДАЕТСЯ, ЧТО ОНО НЕСЕТ ОТВЕТСТВЕННОСТЬ ПО ЗАКОНАМ ВОЕННОГО ВРЕМЕНИ ЗА ВРАЖДЕБНОЕ ОТНОШЕНИЕ К ВОЕННОСЛУЖАЩИМ КРАСНОЙ АРМИИ И СОЮЗНЫХ ЕЙ ВОЙСК.

В СЛУЧАЕ ПОКУШЕНИЯ НА ВОЕННОСЛУЖАЩИХ КРАСНОЙ АРМИИ И СОЮЗНЫХ ЕЙ ВОЙСК, ИЛИ СОВЕРШЕНИЯ ДРУГИХ ДИВЕРСИОННЫХ ДЕЙСТВИЙ ПО ОТНОШЕНИЮ К ЛИЧНОМУ СОСТАВУ, БОЕВОЙ ТЕХНИКЕ ИЛИ ИМУЩЕСТВУ ВОЙСКОВЫХ ЧАСТЕЙ КРАСНОЙ АРМИИ И СОЮЗНЫХ ЕЙ ВОЙСК, ВИНОВНЫЕ БУДУТ ПРЕДАНЫ ВОЕННО-ПОЛЕВОМУ СУДУ.

11. ЧАСТИ КРАСНОЙ АРМИИ И ОТДЕЛЬНЫЕ ВОЕННОСЛУЖАЩИЕ, ПРИБЫВШИЕ В ГОРОД БЕРЛИН, ОБЯЗАНЫ РАСКВАРТИРОВЫВАТЬСЯ ТОЛЬКО В МЕСТАХ, УКАЗАННЫХ ВОЕННЫМИ КОМЕНДАНТАМИ РАЙОНОВ И УЧАСТКОВ.

ВОЕННОСЛУЖАЩИМ КРАСНОЙ АРМИИ ЗАПРЕЩАЕТСЯ ПРОИЗВОДИТЬ САМОВОЛЬНО БЕЗ РАЗРЕШЕНИЯ ВОЕННЫХ КОМЕНДАНТОВ ВЫСЕЛЕНИЕ И ПЕРЕСЕЛЕНИЕ ЖИТЕЛЕЙ, ИЗЪЯТИЕ ИМУЩЕСТВА, ЦЕННОСТЕЙ И ПРОИЗВОДСТВО ОБЫСКОВ У ЖИТЕЛЕЙ ГОРОДА.

Начальник Гарнизона и Военный Комендант города Берлин
Командующий Н-ской армии генерал-полковник Н. БЕРЗАРИН.

Начальник штаба Гарнизона генерал-майор КУЩЕВ.

Langewiesche-Brandt, Ebenhausen near München, Germany

Order
of the Chief of Occupation of the City of Berlin

April 27, 1945   Nr. 1   City of Berlin

Today I have been named Chief of Occupation and City Commandant of Berlin.

All administrative and political power is transferred into my hands in accordance with an authorization by the Command of the Red Army.

Military area and district commandants are appointed in all city districts according to the previously existing administrative divisions.

I command:

1. The inhabitants of the city are to keep complete order and remain at their residences.

2. The National Socialist German Workers Party and all organizations under it (Hitler Youth, N.S. Women's Corps, N.S. Student Corps, etc.) are to be dissolved. Their activities are hereby outlawed.

The entire leading personnel of the National Socialist German Workers Party, secret state police, regular police, and security force, and of prisons and all other government bureaus is to report for purposes of registration to the military area and district commandants within 48 hours after the posting of this order. Within 72 hours, all members of the German Army, of the SS and of the SA who are remaining in the city of Berlin are to report also for purposes of registration.

Whoever does not report by the deadline, or is guilty of hiding such persons, will be held strictly accountable according to the laws of war.

3. The officers and employees of district administrative offices are to report to me for purposes of reporting on the condition of their offices and of receiving orders concerning the further activities of these offices.

4. All communal enterprises, such as power stations and water works, canal authorities, mass transit (subway, elevated trains, trolleys, and buses), all hospitals, all food stores and bakeries are to resume their work again for purposes of serving the population. Workers and employees of the aforementioned enterprises are to remain at their places of work and to fulfill their duties once again.

5. Employees of government food storage facilities, as well as private owners of stores of food, are to report for purposes of registration all existing stores of food to the military district commandants within 24 hours after the posting of this order, and they are to dispense such stores only with permission of military district commandants.

Until special orders are given, the distribution of food in food stores is to occur according to previously existing norms and food coupons. Food is not to be distributed for more than 5–7 days.

Those officials who are guilty of dispensing food over and above existing norms, or who dispense food for coupons belonging to persons not any more in the city, will be held strictly accountable.

6. Owners of banks and directors of banks are to cease and desist from all financial transactions temporarily. All safes are to be sealed immediately. They are to report at once to the military commandants about the conditions of the banks.

It is categorically forbidden to all bank officials to take away anything of value. Whoever is guilty of disobeying this order will be punished most severely according to the laws of war.

The occupation scrip of the Allied Military Government is put into circulation as legal tender along with the national means of payments currently circulating.

7. All persons who own firearms and swords, ammunition, explosives, radio receivers or transmitters, cameras, automobiles, motorcycles, gasoline and oil are to deliver the aforementioned to the military district commandants within 72 hours after the posting of this order.

Those guilty of not delivering all of the above-mentioned objects by said deadline will be punished severely according to the laws of war.

The owners of printing shops, typewriters, and other means of duplication are ordered to report to the military area and district commandants for purposes of registration. It is categorically forbidden to print, duplicate, post, or put in circulation in the city any documents without the permission of the military commandants.

All printing shops will be sealed. Entry will be granted only after permission of the military commandants.

8. The population of the city **is forbidden**

a) to leave their houses between 22:00 and 08:00 hours in the morning Berlin time, to appear in streets or yards, to be present in uninhabited rooms and to do any type of work therein.

b) to light rooms without shades.

c) to take into the family, without permission of the military commandants, any persons, including members of the Red Army and of Allied Troops, for purposes of living there or staying overnight.

d) to appropriate arbitrarily the property and food left behind by officials or private persons.

Residents who violate the above-mentioned prohibitions will be held strictly accountable according to the laws of war.

9. The operation of entertainment enterprises (cinemas, theaters, circus, stadium), religious services and the operation of restaurants and inns, are permitted until 21:00 hours Berlin time.

For any use of public enterprises for purposes hostile to the Red Army, for disturbing order and peace in the city—the officials in charge of these enterprises will be held strictly accountable according to the laws of war.

10. The population of the city is warned that it is held accountable according to the laws of war for any hostile behavior towards members of the Red Army and Allied Troops.

In case of attempts on the lives of members of the Red Army or Allied Troops or the commission of other crimes against persons and war materiel of the units of the Red Army or Allied Troops, the guilty will be handed over to a military tribunal.

11. Units of the Red Army and individual members thereof who arrive in Berlin are under obligation to reside only in residences provided by the military area and district commandants.

The arbitrary eviction or movement of inhabitants, the expropriation of goods and values, and the searching of houses of city residents is forbidden to the members of the Red Army without permission of the military commandants.

Chief of Occupation and
City Commandant of Berlin
Commander in Chief, Nth Army,
Brigadier General N. Bersarin
Chief of Staff of Occupation,
Major General Kushchov

30. PAYING TRIBUTE

[June 1945]

About a month after the Russians got to Ziesar, they put up a huge bulletin board in front of the Town Hall. We could tell that there was something going on because of the crowd under the Thousand Year Oak, which we could see right from our windows above the butcher shop. My mother sent me to investigate, having decided, along with all the other women in our house, never to leave the house herself, if at all possible. The Russians continued to drag women off the street (the Commandant having dismissed Mrs. Gronostalski's complaints as "bourgeois humanism"), but they tended to be kind to children, especially boys.

Outside the Town Hall, I discovered two posters, both behind glass. The first one contained excerpts, translated into German, from *Pravda*, the Russian newspaper. I later learned from Mrs. Gronostalski that *Pravda* meant *Truth*. Without judging the truth of what was printed, I penciled copious notes onto my miniature writing pad, which I still carried along whenever I went out. Although the news was about a month old, it was still news to us:

1945	
April 25	Soviet and U.S. troops link up at Torgau on the Elbe
May 7	At 2:41 A.M. local time, in a little red schoolhouse in Reims, France, then General Dwight D. Eisenhower's Headquarters, Germany surrenders unconditionally, thereby ending the bloodiest conflict in history exactly 5 years, 8 months, and 6 days after it began
	Relevant documents are signed by General Alfred Jodl, German Army Chief of Staff, on orders of Grand Admiral Karl Dönitz, and by Lt. General Walter Bedell Smith, Chief of Staff of the Allied Armies; German Foreign Minister Lutz Schwerin von Krosigk breaks the news to the Germans
May 8	German forces surrender Prague
May 9	The final surrender of German forces in the east takes place at Karlshorst, a Berlin suburb. Relevant documents are signed by Field

Marshal General Wilhelm Keitel, Supreme Commander of the Army, by
General Hans-Jürgen Stumpff, representing the Air Force, and by Admiral
Hans Georg von Friedeburg, Supreme Commander of the Navy

The second poster, also in German, was of more immediate concern:

ORDER NR. 1, CHIEF OF OCCUPATION, VILLAGE OF ZIESAR

All persons who have in their possession firearms or swords, ammunition or explosives, radio receivers or transmitters, cameras or typewriters, automobiles or motorcycles, and gasoline or oil, are hereby ordered to deliver the above-mentioned items at military headquarters within 72 hours after the posting of this order.

Failure to deliver all of the above-mentioned items within the above-mentioned time limit will subject the guilty to the harshest penalties of war.

Furthermore, and also within said 72 hours, all inhabitants of this village, and all others present within it, who are aged 10 to 65, are to appear at said military headquarters for purposes of registration and work assignment.

Those who do not report within said time limit, or who are guilty of hiding such persons, will be held accountable according to the rules of war.

June 10, 1945
Lazar Mayants, Major

Later that morning, we left Helmut with Mrs. Holland, the guardian angel of the chapel. He was only three and she was almost seventy; therefore, they didn't have to do a thing. The rest of us—my mother and I and the Albrechts and all the other women and children from Cologne—marched across the street to the Komendatura to register, but the woman, in order to look as unattractive as possible, all wore winter coats and scarves, even though it was June.

Mr. Albrecht also took a bunch of sabers along. He said his father had used them in the War of 1870-71. My mother took our radio, although it had been dead for over a month, and I took our *Agfa* camera, even though it had run out of film long ago. A soldier tossed the radio out the window of the Furtwängler house, right onto the back of a truck; then he tossed the camera onto the back of another. We didn't think either one survived the impact. Then he took my mother's wristwatch away and he took mine as well. Mine had been a gift from Aunt Martel, which made me sad.

"Uri! Uri!" the soldier had said, rather impatiently.

We figured that was his way of saying *Uhr*, the German word for *watch*. Actually, he already wore seven of them, all on his left arm. I counted when he reached up to give us the pamphlets from the upper shelf. Then he sent us into the next room. There the commandant sat in an overstuffed chair, working a giant abacus, six feet square. He dictated something to Mrs. Gronostalski, who introduced him as Major Mayants (the stress being on the second syllable) and then helped him register us. She told my mother and all the other women to be at the electric power plant the next morning at eight. Mr. Albrecht was to remain at the butcher shop, and I was to go to the Town Hall, also at eight.

That afternoon, other soldiers once again searched all the houses, apparently looking for the forbidden items noted in the Major's Order Nr. 1. With submachine guns slung across their chests, they looked into every nook and cranny of every house, pulling out drawers and flinging them aside, smashing china and clocks and mirrors as they went about their business, eviscerating pillows and mattresses with their bayonets and, in some cases, stirring up a snow storm of feathers from open windows, and, finally, stuffing all sorts of booty down the fronts of their jackets, including door handles and faucets, light bulbs and watches. Rumor had it that the ignorant Slavs were counting on getting water and electric light by just screwing faucets into walls and light bulbs into ceilings when they got home to the Ukraine or somewhere, but I wasn't so sure that this explanation was correct.

That afternoon, too, carpenters came and put up new street signs. They were in Russian though, and I quickly put to work Mrs. Gronostalski's alphabet sheet. That's how I discovered that Russian was easy. We now lived on Ulitsa Josef Stalin, although the *ulitsa* part didn't make sense until I learned that it meant *street*.

The carpenters also put up a picture of Stalin on the front of the commandant's house. They whitewashed the words the Chain Hounds had painted on the walls. Later, they painted another sentence, this time in red, a quotation from Stalin, Mrs. Gronostalski said:

THE HITLERS COME AND GO, BUT THE GERMAN PEOPLE IS FOREVER

Other men built wooden arches every 100 meters or so along the main street and also at all the street corners. Mrs. Gronostalski called them "arches of triumph." They were so tall that all the traffic could go under them, sort of miniatures of Berlin's Brandenburg Gate. They were also painted red. The Russians hung pictures of Marx and Engels on all the arches, and also of Lenin and Stalin and, in some cases, of Russian soldiers with babies in their arms. The soldiers painted lots of Russian words, too, but they didn't make sense to me, even after I turned their letters into Roman ones. I first figured *Slava* had something to do with the Slavs, but then Mrs. Gronostalski told me it meant *Glory* or *Hail*, as in "Hail to the Soviet Soldier," which proved that Russian was more difficult than I had thought.

******

The next day, my mother and all the other women were mobilized into a "labor brigade." They were marched into the power plant and told to take it apart and load it onto freight cars waiting in the yard. My mother said they were sure nobody would ever be able to put it all together again in Russia, without proper blueprints and engineers, but they still had to do it. People kept dropping the parts and losing the nuts and bolts. Even when they were careful, their work came to naught. More often than not, the iron parts were too heavy for the crates the Russians provided, so their bottoms fell out when anyone tried to lift them. One of the generators sat near the railroad tracks for years, right next to an old Pak [*Panzerabwehrkanone* = tank defense cannon], both rusting in the weather.

Other women were told to take apart one half of the double railroad tracks, which was also to be shipped to Russia. "Rabota, rabota!" [Work, work!] the Russians yelled. They also managed to hook up a radio to a loudspeaker, which is how we learned that Radio Berlin was back on the air. They played Beethoven and told endless stories about concentration camps. Millions had been murdered and cremated, they said, and detailed records had been kept about every single one of the victims.

Mrs. Dietrich didn't believe a word of it. She said that the Russians were probably implementing the Morgenthau Plan and were looking for any excuse to justify it.

"The Jews in the Kremlin sing the same tune as the Jew Morgenthau in America," she said. "They want to strip Germany of her industrial capacity and turn her into a nation of peasants."

"Maybe that would be for the best," Mrs. Albrecht said.

"But why blame the Jews for everything? It would make much more sense to blame the Catholics," she added, "Hitler was one."

******

As for me, I was sent off to the forest with an axe almost my size. All the boys and men were to find and cut trees that were at least 15 centimeters across and load them onto railroad cars as well. "Excellent supports for mine shafts," Mr. Kalitz said; he had been made our foreman.

He showed me how to fell a tree. I did it with just thirty strokes, but he said I would do much better than that in a few weeks. He did it in six strokes, but then we still had to cut off all the branches. None of us, of course, had any chain saw in those days, but I never felt that I was suffering from all the physical labor. Despite the pine pitch on my fingers and the splinters and skinned knees, and lots of mosquito bites, I had fun! I spent most of my life outside that summer and nothing would bring me inside except when I was on fire or bleeding and, therefore, convinced that I would die an agonizing death momentarily.

Each noon, Russian soldiers came with a mobile field kitchen and large kettles of soup. The soup had lots of meat in it and milk and potatoes, too. I had never tasted such good food in my life! I also learned a new word. The food was cooked in a *Gulaschkanone* [goulash cannon], a cast-iron stove with a super-long smokestack, which made the whole arrangement look like a cannon.

One evening, I inflated my rubber ball and played ball with the Komendatura guards in the middle of the street. They also showed me new money that was blue and had big numbers on it. They wanted to buy my inflatable ball, but I said I would have to think it over.

"Thinkitover, thinkitover," they said and laughed.

We cut wood for several weeks, and, finally, I could do a tree in ten strokes. Mr. Kalitz said I could be proud. Once he said I could take the afternoon off and go swimming in the old gravel pit. Russian soldiers were swimming there, too, and they were naked, which, incidentally, made them look a lot less dangerous. One of them showed me lots of blue money and pointed to my bathing suit. I guessed that he wanted to buy it, and I might have sold it, for we needed a radio. But I didn't know how to take off my trunks without being naked myself. They all laughed.

When I got home, I was glad I hadn't made the deal. There were radios for sale in the hardware store as well, for new money only, but what had I been thinking? By then, the electricity had gone out all over town! Still, each night, my mother and I managed to play rummy despite the lack of electric light. I had made black candles with wax that Mr. Kalitz had given me, and my mother was very proud of me. She was proud for other reasons as well. Thus, I had also made myself a pair of wooden shoes, with a single leather thong across the top, like the clogs I had seen in pictures of people working in Holland's tulip fields. And I had found an old iron in a barn that could be filled with glowing charcoal so that my mother could do her ironing.

I did one thing, though, that my mother didn't like. I had been looking at pamphlets the Russians had given away, which I had been hiding under my bed. The pamphlets were full of skeletons, piled high, and gas ovens and barbed wire fences.

"Four million men, women, and children," one of the pamphlets said, "were killed in the

German extermination camp Oswiecim, also known as Auschwitz, in Poland. They were killed by gassing, shooting, starvation, poisoning, and torture. The Soviet Army liberated Auschwitz on January 27, 1945."

My mother didn't want me to get my nightmares back, and she also didn't want Helmut to find such pictures in our place. She threw them all away, but that did little good. The Russians announced that the entire population aged 10 and above was to appear at the school auditorium during any evening next week to see a new film about Auschwitz. Attendance would be taken. When we went, we saw even more horror than the pamphlets had shown. My mother kept covering my eyes with her hand, but I still saw enough.

After the film, we were offered more pamphlets about the same general subject. To my surprise, my mother took one of them. She must have been thinking of my father; I realized it when I saw the title: *The Concentration Camps of the Reich Capital.*

The next day, when my mother was downstairs with Mrs. Albrecht, I took a look at the pamphlet. It featured *Ravensbrück*, a special camp for women, located some 80 km north of Berlin, and *Sachsenhausen*, where my father had been, located in the town of Oranienburg, some 30 km north of the capital. I read of Ravensbrück's "Nacht und Nebel" [night and fog] prisoners, accused of high treason and, therefore, destined to disappear without a trace. "Return not desired," their papers would say and that meant a death sentence, to be carried out through hunger or exposure or medical experiments or even outright shooting, while "trying to escape."

And with even greater interest, I read of Sachsenhausen, created in the summer of 1936, right after Heinrich Himmler became Reich Leader of the SS. At first, the pamphlet said, it was a camp mainly for German political opponents of the regime, Communist and Social Democrat. Officially, the camp was designed "to help these misdirected citizens to turn around politically and recover the work ethic." In time, the camp also took in "biologically and racially inferior" prisoners, ranging from Jews and Slavs to Sinti and Roma Gypsies, homosexuals, and "asocial elements," such as professional criminals. Later still, room had to be made for "special prisoners," such as the heads of state of annexed or occupied countries, like the Austrian Chancellor Kurt Schuschnigg, and all sorts of prominent individuals, such as Stalin's oldest son or Martin Niemöller, the leader of the Confessional Church, or the conspirators of the 20th of July plot.

During the war, the pamphlet said, the camp also housed forced laborers from all the occupied countries and (mostly Polish and Soviet) POWs. The prisoners of war were employed in places such as Oranienburg's Heinkel airplane plant or Berlin's Siemens electrical equipment factories. Others were less lucky, being put to work right at the camp, perhaps on the *Schuhprüfstrecke* [shoe testing range], where prisoners had to walk for days and weeks with shoes having different types of non-leather soles to test the usefulness of artificial materials for army boots. Others still had to work in the *Klinkerwerk* [brick works], where prisoners produced bricks for Albert Speer's grand post-war construction projects in Berlin.

Altogether, the pamphlet said, the camp took in 200,000 prisoners between 1936 and 1945. Of these, 30,000 died from hunger, exhaustion, sickness, cold, mistreatment, executions, medical experiments, or mass killings. In the fall 1941, for example, some 12,000 Soviet POWs were shot by an experimental "bullet-in-the-neck machine." And in the spring of 1942, some 250 Jews were used to test an experimental "gas-them-on-the bus" project that ultimately inspired the infamous gas chamber and crematorium. On February 1, 1945, in anticipation of the Battle of Berlin, a mass killing of British and Soviet officers occurred, and on April 21, 1945, the remaining prisoners were marched out of the camp in freezing weather in the northwesterly direction of Schwerin or they were shot, if they couldn't march.

Moreover, the pamphlet said, since 1938, Sachsenhausen had been the administrative SS headquarters of *all* German concentration camps. Himmler loved the place; he called it "the most modern, up-to-date, and most expandable concentration camp of all."

The camp was liberated, I learned, by the Red Army on April 22, 1945, during the encirclement of Berlin.

akg-images, London, United Kingdom

The gate of the Sachsenhausen concentration camp, like that at Auschwitz, announced:
"Arbeit Macht Frei" [Work Makes You Free].
The camp was set up "scientifically," in the shape of a giant equal-sided triangle. This is a picture of its main roll-call area, a bare exposed stretch of ground, baking hot in summer, lashed by icy winds in winter, where thousands died.

31. TYPHUS
[July 1945]

By the summer of 1945, if they had survived the Russian onslaught, many people began to hear from their relatives. We were no exception. I remember one of those days. Helmut and I were looking in the mirror that hung behind the door and that hadn't been smashed by the Russians because they couldn't see it when the door was open. We were making faces, but my mother told us to stop it.

"If you get startled by a sudden noise, your face could freeze like that," she said. "Do you want to look like that for the rest of your lives?"

"But there's not going to be a sudden noise," I said. "And I wouldn't mind looking like this."

Then I spotted the mailman across the street. I hadn't seen him for several months, not since March anyway. My mother said I could run out and see what was happening, and he *did* have mail for us, mail from Aunt Martel in Berlin. But the news wasn't good. My mother opened the envelope ever so slowly, as if it contained something that might bite her, and then let out a cry. She covered her face with her hands, as she always did when something bad happened.

"Oma died," she sobbed, "last April, and we didn't even know."

She let me read the letter. My grandmother had died just before the Russians got there, Aunt Martel said; the doctors thought it was stomach cancer, but what do they know? And then their house was blown to bits at the last minute as well; it was just a sooty heap now, but Aunt Martel was still living there, in the cellar. Aunt Martel said she had to wear a heavy winter coat whenever she went out, even in July. For one thing, if she left anything in the cellar, it would be stolen by the time she returned. More importantly, if she looked too feminine walking down the street…you know the Russians, she said.

She also said that all the ruins were plastered with pieces of paper, like these:

"Winter boots, felt-lined. Excellent condition. Will trade for children's shoes."

"Any information: Anna Reese? Previously at Glogauer Strasse 33."

"Your future revealed! Madame Lamberti. Personalized star charts. 20 Marks."

"War widow, 2 children. Attractive. Excellent cook. Seeking husband. Must have apartment."

When I had finished reading the letter, my mother was still sobbing and I was suddenly seized by a terrible thought: Might my grandmother's death have been *my* fault? I recalled the last birthday party we all had had at her place, with exactly thirteen people sitting around the big table in my grandmother's living room and Aunt Lotte taking a pin with a big red head from her sewing kit and sticking it into the tablecloth.

"That way, we have *fourteen* heads," she had said, "and we're safe."

I had known of the superstition. When there were thirteen heads around a table, one of them wouldn't survive another year. But I had also disdained such obviously false notions; so I had removed the red pin when nobody was looking, just to prove everybody wrong. Now I was sorry, very sorry. In fact, I felt so guilty that I decided to escape my mother's looks and hang out in the backyard.

******

Downstairs, to my surprise, the Albrechts were celebrating. They were having wine and bread and a barbecue grille filled with sausages, because their son Werner had just come back from Italy. He had been quarantined at Brandenburg, they said, because of all sorts of diseases going around, including cholera, diphtheria, dysentery, scarlet fever, and even typhus.

"He came home on the last train," Mr. Albrecht said. "The Russians sealed off the railroad station this morning. They won't allow trains to unload any more passengers."

"It's the Russians' own fault," Mrs. Albrecht added. "Just look at the unsanitary conditions under which they prepare food and the way they slaughter livestock on straw by dirty roadsides! Have they never heard of germs?"

"Lots of people haven't," I thought, picturing Pastor Jahn doing the communion thing and having everyone drink from the same chalice. I decided to let that go for the moment, but to check out what the Russians were doing. So I ambled over to the Town Hall. There *was* news; as usual, it was over a month old:

1945

June 5 As a matter of international law, Germany has ceased to exist. The victorious powers have divided the former Germany into four occupation zones, to be governed by an Allied Control Council, the first members of which are General Eisenhower, General Montgomery, and Marshal Zhukov.

Soviet Zone: Brandenburg, Mecklenburg, Saxony, Saxony-Anhalt, Thuringia

U.S. Zone: Bavaria, Hesse, Württemberg-Baden, Bremen

British Zone: Lower Saxony, Nordrhein-Westphalia, Schleswig-Holstein, Hamburg

French Zone: Baden, Rheinland-Palatinate, Württemberg-Hohenzollern

---

The bulletin board also contained a Health Warning from Dr. med. Werner Weiss. In order to avoid infectious diseases, such as dysentery and typhus, he urged everyone to add chlorine tablets to drinking water or, if unavailable, to bring water to a rolling boil for 1 minute before drinking. Likewise, he urged us only to eat foods that have been thoroughly cooked and that are still hot and steaming. Avoid raw vegetables and fruits that cannot be peeled, he said, and note that some vegetables, like lettuce, are easily contaminated and very hard to wash well. When you eat raw fruit or vegetables that can be peeled, wash your hands and peel the food yourself. Do not eat the peelings. In a nutshell, **boil it, cook it, peel it, or forget it!** And wash your hands often, with plenty of soap, he concluded. But I knew we didn't have any soap.

While reading the warning, I also ran into Aunt Rachel. She had gotten mail as well, she said. Uncle Eddy would be home soon. He had returned from France, but was quarantined at Brandenburg. Aunt Rachel looked so different from just a few months ago. She was emaciated and coughing a lot. She said Dr. Weiss had told her she might have tuberculosis or even lung cancer. She was supposed to fend it off by drinking lots of red wine with raw eggs blended into it. That seemed strange to me, but by the time I got home, I forgot to tell my mother because of the commotion in the hallway.

"Don't you ever let me catch you at that again!" Mrs. Albrecht yelled at Mrs. Ebner. "Now we all have to sit in the dark for another week. Hypocrites, that's what you are, a goddamn bunch of Catholic hypocrites! You kneel in front of that cross all night and then steal everybody's electricity in the morning!"

"Calm down, calm down," Mrs. Holland said, "what's the matter with the two of you? Had a bad night's sleep?"

"Found her frying eggs on the hotplate, that's what the matter is," Mrs. Albrecht replied. "For all I know she's ironing her boys' shirts as well when she's hiding behind that door all day!"

"I guess you have a point there," Mrs. Holland said. "We must post a sign-up sheet. With 20 kilowatt hours per week and five families, we have four thousand watts per family. Anyone who wants to run that 500 watt hotplate can use up her share in eight hours and then sit in the dark. And anyone who wants to run a 50 watt bulb can have eighty hours of light instead. It's really very simple."

"It's not as simple as that," Mrs. Ebner said, glaring at Mrs. Albrecht. "How do we know *she* won't cheat? You know she thinks she owns the place. Wouldn't even let the boys get some pears off the tree. She watches the gooseberries like a hawk, and for all I know she's the one who made off with the vitamin pills from the kitchen last week!"

That's when Mr. Albrecht and Mrs. Gronostalski joined the fight, and I decided it was time to make my move. I put on my long-sleeved shirt and slipped down to the backyard. Passing the barbecue grille, I went straight to the smoking chamber, and how I hated the way its door creaked! I pulled out the longest liverwurst I could reach, slid it up my right arm, and was back in our room before anyone could count to one hundred. For a moment at least, my mother and Helmut were very happy. We hadn't eaten a thing in two days, except dry bread, dandelions, and thistle spinach.

******

That afternoon, Mr. Kalitz came by. He helped finish building my little wagon, and we tried it out. We pulled it to the forest, cut down a fat tree and sawed up the trunk to fit the wagon. Back home, we sawed some more, using the sawing-jack. We did it together; he stood on one side, I on the other. Then I took the axe and split each block five ways so the pieces would fit into our iron stove. Mr. Kalitz laid the foundation of the wood pyramid, right next to the big dung pile Mr. Albrecht was building for his garden.

"When it's finished, it'll hold enough wood for the whole winter," Mr. Kalitz said about the pyramid, "and every piece will be dry. And if you need kindling, just go the forest and get a wagonload of pinecones; they work like a charm."

But Mrs. Albrecht was still in a bad mood, despite the fact that her son was back. She complained to my mother about letting a young boy do such hard work.

"Child abuse," she said. "That's what it is, pure child abuse."

She didn't know a thing. As Mr. Kalitz had said, I was strong as an ox. And I was my mother's man. In fact, to prove the point, I went out to the wheat field and got her a huge armful of red poppies and blue cornflowers. They grew everywhere and the farmers considered them useless weeds. What did they know? My mother was very happy.

******

Later that day, I went to the store to buy more flypaper. The golden strips on our ceiling were covered with black flies because we didn't have any screens and the butcher shop below us attracted thousands of flies. I took a long time going to the store and I lingered in front of its window for almost an hour, pretending to study the pitiful wares on display. I also studied the poster that explained why electricity had to be rationed. It had something to do with Germany being split in half and all the coal being far away in the Ruhr. That didn't make much sense to me, given that most of our generators were rusting at the railroad station. But actually, I didn't care. I spent most of my time looking at the house across the street. I hoped for a glimpse of Helga.

When I got back, they were still fighting in the hallway, but not about electricity. This time, my mother and Helmut were there, too. My mother said we should be given a second room because my father would come back soon.

"Everyone else has two rooms," my mother said to Mrs. Albrecht, "and the one across the corridor from ours would be ideal."

"Impossible," Mrs. Albrecht said, "where am I to put my son? And my good porcelain? Out in the barn?"

"Porcelain? Why don't you shove it up your ass?" Mrs. Ebner said.

That's when Mrs. Albrecht slammed her door and turned on her 1000 watt fan.

******

In the following days, I managed to get bread from the bakery, now run by Mr. Senf's oldest son, and more sausages from the backyard. Mr. Albrecht couldn't sell them anyway; they all belonged to the Russians who kept bringing in animals for slaughter, regularly as clockwork. Otherwise, I spent my time putting the finishing touches on a board game that I was creating for our evening entertainment. Having acquired a pair of dice, a leather cup in which to shake them, and some playing tokens, I had created the game like this:

First, I pasted together pieces of white cardboard to create a panel, 80 centimeters wide and 40 centimeters tall, onto which I copied the world's continents and oceans from my world atlas book. Then I added all sorts of stopping points, starting with Berlin as #1 and ending with Berlin as #50 as well. A world traveler, I figured, might move to Paris, London, Madrid, Rome, Athens, Istanbul, Warsaw, Moscow, and Baku, and I linked these places with big fat lines. From there, my imaginary traveler moved to Ankara, Baghdad, the Central Sahara, Guinea, the Congo, Benguela, Cape Town, Madagascar, Teheran, and Bombay. And on and on my traveler went, to Darjeeling, then Lhasa, Peking, Tokyo, Sumatra, Central Australia, the Solomon Islands, Hollywood, the Central USA, and Central Canada. A further lap around the globe linked Greenland, New York, Panama, Rio de Janeiro, the Amazon River Valley, Cape Horn, the Central Pacific, Alaska, the North Pole, and Siberia's Nizhne Kolymsk. Finally, my globetrotter would visit Krasnoyarsk, the Ural Mountains, Leningrad, Lapland, Spitsbergen, Iceland, the North Sea, Hammerfest, Stockholm and return to Berlin.

For days, I had been working on the project, adding little drawings of the Eiffel Tower next to Paris, of bull fighters next to Madrid, of St. Peter's cathedral next to Rome, of Greek temples next to Athens, of Islamic minarets next to Istanbul and Baghdad, and so on around the world. Before long, my board was covered with Eskimos and igloos, whales, seals, and penguins; skyscrapers, the Statue of Liberty; Alaskan gold diggers and loggers; Red Indians and wigwams; Indian fakirs, snake charmers, and elephants, the snowy rocks of Mount Everest; the Great Wall of China; tigers roaming tropical islands inhabited by head-hunting cannibals; Pacific natives rowing from island to island; Cossacks defending their fortress in Krasnoyarsk; Spitsbergen icebergs breaking into the Arctic Ocean, and Hammerfest, Europe's northernmost town, bathed in uninterrupted daylight for months on end. With all of this, I got a lot of inspiration and help from Mr. Kalitz and the giant picture dictionary in his living room.

On that particular day, only a few drawings were left: Baku oil fields; worshippers milling around Mecca's Kaaba; safaris between Saharan oases led by camels; lions, zebras, and giraffes roaming the Serengeti Plain; and shipwrecks in the stormy seas off Cape Horn. Any traveler, my rules said, would move forward depending on the toss of the dice, but could also be pushed back or be stuck in a particular spot, depending on the types of events my drawings illustrated.

I remember it now: It was dark outside and it was hot when my mother and I were playing my game for the first time. Mosquitoes kept buzzing my head, and then our candles, and I had reached Tokyo, #24. That was a lucky break; it gave me a direct plane ride to Hollywood, #28. That's when I heard voices in front of the house. For a moment, I thought it must be time to go to chapel again, but there weren't any Russians out there. Looking out the windows, we just saw a man and a woman in the street, holding an umbrella and an aluminum pot.

"Trudchen," they were saying, "Trudchen," but not very loud. They were almost whispering.

"My God," my mother said, leaning out of the window to get a better look. "It's Liesel and Herbert out there!"

They looked like two ghosts in the candlelight. They were so thin, and I thought of the concentration camp pamphlets the Russians had handed out. Our visitors had ragged clothes, too, and their naked feet were covered with blisters and sores. Uncle Herbert didn't say a word. Aunt Liesel raised her hands toward my mother.

"Your sister has come, asking for mercy," she said with her usual dramatic flair and then she collapsed, right there in our room above the butcher shop.

"Walked all the way from Berlin," Uncle Herbert explained, in a tired but rather matter-of-fact voice. "Followed the ruts made by tanks to stay clear of land mines."

"They raped her seventeen times," he added, without the slightest show of emotion.

******

My mother gave him a withering look, but said nothing. She made a fire in the iron stove to heat some water. She took a sponge and washed Aunt Liesel's feet. I knew we didn't have soap. I thought of Crossen and my father and how useful iodine might be. I remembered Uncle Herbert's icy coldness back in Berlin and of the terror he promoted there. I pictured him being taken to the KGB office across the street, the Russian equivalent of the Gestapo, and I wondered what my mother would do next. I found out almost instantly.

Someone banged on the front door.

"Personnel check, personnel check," Mrs. Gronostalski shouted.

We saw the Russian soldiers down the street and knew what was coming. My mother looked at me, pointing a finger first at Uncle Herbert and then at the backyard. I grabbed Uncle Herbert's hand, we ran down the back stairs, and I showed him to the barn. But he wouldn't go in.

"I know what they do," he said. "They set barns on fire and shoot at anyone who comes out. Or they send in the dogs to find you under the hay."

There was no time left. I pointed to the latrine and raised the side door. The stench was overpowering. And Uncle Herbert, the *Greifer*, crawled into a mountainous hell of shit and piss, newspaper and big black flies.

By the time the Russians came to our room, I was asleep on top of a big brown blanket. I could feel Aunt Liesel's hips.

******

I don't remember much of the coming weeks. I felt weak with a headache and all my joints and muscles ached. And I was so hot. My mother said I had a fever of 40 degrees Celsius for weeks and was delirious. Also, my eyes were bloodshot, I had a furry white tongue and dark red spots on my body that turned purple, she said. I only know that I was sweating and my heart was racing and that I had the bed all to myself. Mrs. Holland said my mother should cover me with cat furs, and she even brought some. But Dr. Weiss's nurse told my mother to forget about the cat furs and keep me cool. That she did, with her fancy Chinese fan and by sponging me a lot. I don't know who was right. When I was well enough to talk to them, typhus had killed Mrs. Holland and the nurse, too.

But I later did read the pamphlet my mother had picked up at Dr. Weiss's office.

"Typhoid fever," it said, "is a life-threatening illness caused by the bacterium *Salmonella Typhi*, which lives only in humans. Persons with typhoid fever carry the bacteria in their bloodstream and intestinal tract. In addition, a small number of persons, called carriers, recover from typhoid fever but continue to carry the bacteria. Both ill persons and carriers shed *S. Typhi* in their stool."

"You can get typhoid fever," the pamphlet said, "if you eat food or drink beverages that have been handled by a person who is shedding *S. Typhi* or if sewage contaminated with *S. Typhi* bacteria gets into the water you use for drinking or washing food. Therefore, typhoid fever is more common in areas where hand washing is less frequent and water is likely to be contaminated with sewage. Once *S. Typhi* bacteria are eaten or drunk, they multiply and spread into the bloodstream. The body reacts with fever and other signs and symptoms."

My mother also told me that Dr. Weiss had told her of a new medicine, called *antibiotic*. It was used in England and America to treat diseases like typhus. Persons given antibiotics usually begin to feel better within 2 to 3 days, and deaths rarely occur. But we didn't have such medicine. In the end, in Ziesar, about 1 in 5 patients who contracted typhus died.

******

But there was one good consequence: Inside the village at least, there were considerably fewer rapes! That happened because Mrs. Gronostalski taught everyone the Russian word for typhus and lots of people pasted a warning sign on their front doors, saying **TIF**, using Cyrillic letters, of course. **ТИФ** scared off the Russians. In addition, many women, like my mother and Aunt Liesel, dotted their faces with rose-colored spots, imitating the typhoid rash.

32. JUTTA

[August 1945]

While I was still in the middle of my typhoid delirium, I pictured my Uncle Herbert being caught by Captain Lysenko, the KGB man across the street. I knew him well; he was one of the soldiers who played ball with me. I had always taken him to be a dedicated Nazi hunter, given the anti-fascist posters with which he had decorated his office. He had given me one of them—copied by the thousands from a famous Russian artist, he had said. It promised "death to the fascist reptile."

A Soviet propaganda poster
Death to the Fascist Reptile!

Captain Lysenko also spoke fluent German, unlike any other Russian I had ever met, which had made it possible for me to find out all sorts of interesting things. For one thing, I had learned that KGB stood for Komitet Gosudarstvennoi Bezopasnosti or State Security Committee.

More importantly, I had been told how Russian intelligence officers were trained to unmask a liar. They closely watched the people they interrogated: Were they fidgeting, sliding their chair back and forth, cracking their knuckles, crossing their arms in front of their chest, touching their knees beneath the table, checking their watch, bring their hands to their face? All these were sure signs of a liar at work, I had been told. Clearly, Uncle Herbert didn't have a chance. He was always scratching his nose or wiping something from the corners of his eyes.

Yet things worked out differently. As I learned later, my mother had gotten Mrs. Gronostalski's help in bypassing the KGB and registering Uncle Herbert and Aunt Liesel as "refugees from Silesia." And the new man in the Town Hall had found them a room in a farm house on Emil Beer Strasse at the edge of town. For her sister's sake, my mother had decided not to turn in her brother-in-law.

Also, while my mind was still in a feverish haze, Mrs. Albrecht had relented and had given us the second upstairs room across the hall. That's where my mother had kept Helmut so he wouldn't catch anything from me or anyone else. I do recall one thing, however, a visit from Uncle Eddy. He appeared out of nowhere, it seemed, shaking the whole staircase as he made his way up to our room, and standing over me like a giant. My feverish eyes remembered him from Berlin and saw him just like that, complete with his green-gray uniform, the Knight's Cross on his chest, field glasses slung across his right shoulder, saber to the left, hanging on his belt, along with canteen and pistol, and eyes glittering with evangelical fire. I can still see him now, putting his right hand on my shoulder and invoking the name of the Father Almighty, asking him to pass on his healing power through him to me, just as it had passed from Jesus, his beloved Son, to Peter, the Rock on which the Church was built, and from there on to all the servants of God from generation to generation, right to Martin Luther and beyond, whenever they, in turn, were ordained to serve their Lord. It must have worked. Instead of dying an agonizing death, as I had expected, I was up and about within days. Naturally, I ran to the Town Hall to check up on the news and, as usual, it was nearly a month old.

1945

July 5	Allied Control Council: U. S., British, and French troops to take part in the occupation of Berlin
July 17 – August 2	Harry Truman, Joseph Stalin, and Winston Churchill (soon replaced by Clement Attlee) convene a conference at Potsdam on the future of Germany and Japan.

As to **Germany**, decisions are made on

demilitarization

denazification

trials of war criminals

new democratic parties and freedom of speech

reparations

the importation of food

territorial changes (noted below)

1) The Königsberg area of East Prussia is to be ceded to the Soviet Union

2) Polish territories east of the Curzon Line, covering 180,000 square kilometers, are to be ceded to the Soviet Union

> 3)   German territories east of the Oder-Neisse Line, covering
>   104,000 square kilometers, are to be administered by Poland;
>   an estimated 14 million Germans are to be expelled from
>   these areas, as well as from Hungary and Czechoslovakia
>
> As to **Japan**, the Allies demand unconditional surrender

As I wrote it all down on my notepad, I saw Werner Albrecht sitting on the Town Hall steps with Jutta Zweig. Most of the time, Werner was now helping his father in the butcher shop. He looked just like the elder Mr. Albrecht, but he weighed a lot less and was, of course, much younger. I knew he was 28; Mrs. Albrecht had said so on the day he came back from Italy.

"Just a week after his birthday," she had said, "he's back, he's home again!"

I knew Jutta Zweig, too; she was the daughter of Aunt Rachel's housekeeper and had helped in the garden at harvest time. Jutta was only 20 and she was so pretty, with her long chestnut-colored hair and the white dress filled with red polka dots. Looking at her touched some mysterious chamber in my heart, which I could not ignore. I felt jealous when I saw Werner Albrecht hugging her and kissing her, right there on the Town Hall steps in the middle of the day, a mere 200 meters diagonally across from the place where the commandant had made a new home for himself. But I didn't know at the time what a big surprise was waiting for me later that day.

******

That evening, as I had done before, I defied the curfew and climbed the hayloft at the baker's. As long as there was electric light, I could see through the high windows into the oven room and, if I was patient enough, I could run off with a freshly baked loaf of bread. The entire room, floors and walls included, was covered with light yellow tiles and it was spanking clean. A long table stood in front of the huge oven and Mr. Senf's son Fred mixed the dough on top of it, just as his father had before he was killed by the Russians. Like Werner Albrecht, Fred was in his twenties as well, and he, too, had recently come back from the war. I knew his routine. He would cut off a pound of dough or so from the big pile, roll it on the table, let it rise for a while, shape it into a loaf, make three decorative cuts on top, brush the top with water to make a shiny surface, and load it into the oven with the help of a long-handled wooden board. Later, he would retrieve the loaves from the oven in the same way he had first inserted them and load the finished loaves onto a cart, ready to be rolled into the shop. But this time, there was more.

I saw Fred take off his white coat. Then he spread a blanket on top of the tiles above the oven and lit a cigarette. And suddenly, Jutta was there. She wore a yellow dress and a big straw hat. I couldn't hear what they said and I couldn't breathe. He didn't move, but she smiled. She tossed her hat onto the cart with the loaves, and her dress slid to the floor. She was naked, and I had never seen a girl before, not like that, but he didn't move.

I saw her lift her arms above her head, and she smiled. I wanted to touch her breasts. But he stood up, and they kissed, and she was hidden behind him. Then I saw him undress and he lifted her up to the roof of the oven; it was five times the size of a bed. They sat on the blanket and rocked like a chair, but I couldn't hear what they said. He put his hands on her breasts and his head in-between them. She smiled.....

******

I hardly slept that night and it wasn't the typhus. In the morning, I left early and went to the house of Jutta. I sat on the stone across from her door and waited. I worked on a sentence I would say once she came. When she did, I forgot it.

"Hans, it's you," she said, "did you like the mushrooms my Mama brought you?"

No words would come. I stared, and she said: "I'll tell you what. I'm going for blueberries next week with the neighborhood kids, want to come?"

I stared at her hair and the curves of her breasts, and I wondered how soft she was.

"Of course, you want to," she said, and I nodded and turned, and I bumped into the pharmacist coming through the door. I heard them laughing as I ran.

******

I walked to the swamp that day and made a flute out of reeds. I played my flute in the shade that day and had feelings I didn't understand. I walked around in the fields that day and knocked at the house of Jutta.

She opened the door and looked surprised; once again, I forgot the planned sentence. She smiled: "Have you come to play your flute? Come in and sit."

"Oh no," I said, "it's just…it's just about the mushrooms."

"Mushrooms?" She smiled. "Of course."

I saw her chestnut hair, white dress, red polka dots. I looked at her bare feet, and had feelings I didn't understand.

"They say you collect them," I said. "Could you take me when you go?"

"Sure," she said, "be here at six."

******

In the morning, I took the basket and looked at the fog. Then I sneaked down the street and knocked at her door.

"Listen!" she said. "Listen to the birds! That one's a thrush."

And we walked through the field of cornflowers and poppies and rye, and the sun came up.

"Today is the perfect time for chanterelles," she said. "They look like trumpets, yellow and orange and are delicious to eat. They are fragrant, too, but I'll show you some others as well."

"That one is a toadstool," she said, "not a good idea at all. But it's pretty, isn't it? Look at the red roof and the white polka dots."

"Just the opposite of your dress," I said. "It's white with red dots," and I looked at the curves of her breasts and wondered how soft she was.

The ground was soft with moss and the pines were tall. My feet were wet from the dew on the grass and the slightest nudge of some overhanging branch brought down a shower of raindrops on both of us. There had been thunderstorms last night.

"I love this place in the morning," she said, "and wow! There are hundreds of them!"

I didn't see a thing, but she showed me the bumps in the moss that were hiding the mushrooms.

"You just have to read the signs," she said. "They always leave a subtle trail."

She showed me green mushrooms, too, and dark brown ones with thick white stems. I found beige ones with yellow bottoms that turned blue when I touched them.

"That reminds me," she said, "do you know the test? Tell your Mama to put a peeled onion in the pot when she boils the mushrooms. If the onion doesn't turn blue, you can safely eat the mushrooms."

On the way home, we sat in the meadow carpeted with clover and I brought her a bunch of red poppies. She read a poem to me from a little blue book, by Schiller, and she sang a sad song. Later, we crossed the big highway to get back to the village. A column of Russian troops was going west, with tanks, trucks, and motorcycles. And suddenly, the motorcycles followed us on the dirt road in a big cloud of dust and they surrounded us. I saw their slit eyes when the Mongols pointed their guns at us, and they motioned me to lie down on the grass next to the road, on my back, arms spread out, like Jesus on the cross. They pointed a pistol at Jutta. Three of them dragged her out of sight, but I could hear them yell and her cry. One soldier decided to rest the barrel of his rifle at the center of my forehead. I saw him grin, I felt the cold metal, and I froze.

Time stood still. I closed my eyes to escape that dreadful grin; I felt a colony of ants meandering across my feet. I heard crows fretting and shrieking in the branches of pine trees above, complaining about us who had disturbed their lives.

I almost prayed, but caught myself in time. There was no use in praying for anything at all. And I clearly heard the cuckoo clock ticking in my head—ticking away the last seconds of my life. If I lived at all, I was sure, I would be insane.

I felt so numb, but then I noticed the silence after the motorcycles had roared away. Ever so slowly my feelings returned, like the morning light after a long night, when the darkness grows transparent, just a bit, when shapes emerge from among the shadows and then take on color, when silence yields to the twittering of birds, when suddenly the world is back again, fresh and new. I was surprised to be there.

I went to look for Jutta. She was kneeling next to a tree, sobbing softly. I touched her, and I kissed her on the forehead. We held one another and cried.

We took a shortcut across the fields to the castle, but that was a mistake as well. In a thicket of blackberry bushes, almost hidden among the brambles, we made a gruesome find. We discovered a skull, still attached to a collection of bones and rags and buttons and a rusted rifle, all of which was once a man in uniform. I decided never to go outside the village again.

******

The next day, from our window above the butcher shop, I spied Jutta walking down the street, each arm linked with a Russian. They sat down in front of the Komendatura and someone played an accordion. The Russkaya. Jutta was giggling, and I couldn't understand. Nothing in this world made any sense.

I also saw Werner Albrecht crossing the street, but I didn't know then that I would never see him again. The next morning, they found him in the alley next to the butcher shop. Like old Mr. Senf, the baker, not so long ago, he had a knife in his heart.

******

My mother said we should be grateful for being alive after all the terrible things that had happened around us in the past years. And soon my father would be back and all would be well again! She took us to church that Sunday to hear Uncle Eddy's first sermon after his return. I didn't like the idea. Being in the church gave me a headache and made me feel dizzy. I insisted on sitting way in the back, near the open door so I could escape if I had to.

"Oh thou Almighty God, merciful Father!" Uncle Eddy said. "I am but a poor, miserable, and sinful man, and I confess before thee all my sins and misdeeds through which I have ever angered you and for which I have well deserved your eternal punishment. But for all these sins and misdeeds I am truly sorry, and I repent them thoroughly, and I implore you in your bottomless mercy and because of the holy, innocent, and bitter suffering and death of your beloved son, Jesu Christi, that you may be merciful and accepting of me, poor and sinful wretch of a man that I am."

I felt sick. My mother said I could stand outside the church door for a bit. When I dared return, Uncle Eddy was preaching from a pulpit high above the congregation. I counted the angels decorating the underside of the pulpit, all carved in wood. Some of them were blowing trumpets.

Then I tried to occupy my mind by translating Uncle Eddy's words into Pig Latin, moving the first letter of each word from the front to the back and adding an "a." Thus, "poor and sinful wretch of a man" turned into "oorpa ndaa infulsa retchwa foa aa anma." But I couldn't keep up with the sermon; Uncle Eddy's voice kept interrupting my thoughts.

"Be not wise in your own conceits," Uncle Eddy said. "Thus we read in Romans, Chapter 12: Recompense to no man evil for evil. Provide things honest in the sight of all men. If it be possible, as much as lieth in you, live peaceably with all men. Dearly beloved, avenge not yourselves, but rather give place unto wrath, for it is written: Vengeance is mine; I will repay, saith the Lord. Therefore if thine enemy hunger, feed him; if he thirst, give him drink: for in so doing thou shalt heap coals of fire on his head. Be not overcome of evil, but overcome evil with good."

Then the organ played and everyone joined to sing a hymn:

> "Now thank we all our God,
> With heart, and hands, and voices,
> Who wondrous things hath done,
> In whom the world rejoices...."

33. CHAIN REACTIONS

[September 1945]

They buried Werner Albrecht on the last day of World War II. To be sure, at the time, I didn't know about the war in the Pacific having ended, but I did find out some two weeks later when they put up another installment of news on the Town Hall bulletin board. I wrote it all down on my trusty notepad so I could show it to my mother.

1945

August 6   Hitler's V-3 has become a reality! A new kind of weapon, called the *atomic bomb*, was dropped on Japan today by an American B-29 Superfortress, the Enola Gay. The power of the bomb was equivalent to 20,000 tons of TNT that would normally be carried by 2,000 B-29s. The blast wiped out Hiroshima, population 318,000, and created a blinding flash many times a brilliant as the midday sun. A massive cloud boiled up to over 13,000 meters. On the ground, the bomb vaporized even steel towers, and a heavy pressure wave, accompanied by a tremendous sustained roar, knocked down people over 8 kilometers away.

August 9   A second atomic bomb dropped on Nagasaki, population 253,000

The Soviet Union declares war on Japan, occupies Manchuria

August 15   Japan surrenders, on Emperor Hirohito's order

The secret of *radar*—short for radio detection and ranging—is announced: The new technology sees through the heaviest fog and the blackest night and was responsible for Allied successes in fighting German planes and submarines.

September 2   Japan signs rigid surrender terms, on the famed superdreadnought Missouri, in Tokyo Bay. Present are General Douglas MacArthur and Foreign Minister Mamoru Shigemitsu, signing for the government, and General Yoshijiro Umezu, signing for the Imperial General Staff.

War Minister Korechila Anami commits suicide, citing his responsibility for the first defeat in 2,600 years of Japanese history

That was interesting news, indeed, and, as I said, I wrote it all down in the middle of September, which happened to be the day on which we all went back to school for the first time in over five months.

So far as our school was concerned, things had certainly changed! Dr. Dietrich, of course, was gone, having been hanged at the Town Hall way back in May after his foolish werewolf attack. And most of the other teachers we once knew were gone as well. Miss Mahler was still there and she had become principal. Pastor Jahn was still there, but he was to teach Geography. All the other teachers were new, having been imported from Russia, one and all. Unlike other teachers we had ever met, the new ones didn't have university degrees and were supposed to be "learning by doing," which is why they were called Newteachers, which itself was a new word that Miss Mahler introduced as a deliberate merger of adjective and noun.

We met in the big auditorium to learn other things as well. For one thing, Miss Mahler said, there was going to be no more corporal punishment. It was a disgusting Nazi habit and the Russians forbade it. In addition, we were all going to repeat the grade we left way back last spring, having lost so much time since. For me that meant starting the 7th grade for the third time, having once done so in January 1944 in Berlin and then again in September of 1944 in Ziesar.

There was a new line-up of subjects. Religion, for example, was out; Russian was in. As for me, my subjects were these:

German, Russian, English, Latin.

Current Affairs, History, Geography.

Mathematics, Biology, Chemistry, Physics.

Drawing, Music, Sports.

In addition, Miss Mahler said, we would also be graded on Cooperation, Penmanship, and Orderliness in Textbooks and Notebooks.

We were given a whole stack of textbooks. Some were old; others were donated by the Academy of Sciences of the USSR and published by the State Publishing Agency in Moscow. It was easy to spot the old books. They still had an eagle with spread wings on the front cover, along with claws resting on a swastika, although a feeble attempt had been made, with the help of black ink, to cross out these old rubber stamps. One of my books had been wrapped into an old newspaper to hide the swastika on the cover, but apparently nobody had bothered to look at what the paper said. But I did. I found a page from the November 16, 1941 edition of *Das Reich*, with an article by Dr. Goebbels, entitled *The Jews Are Guilty*. "The Jews," it said, "will be annihilated, according to their own Law: an eye for an eye, a tooth for a tooth."

******

My first class that day was Geography, and I was happy that Pastor Jahn wasn't allowed to hit me anymore. Just in case he did, I relished the thought of turning him in to Miss Mahler or even the Russians. I also figured that he had too much time on his hands, now that Uncle Eddy, the Superintendent of the Church, was back and had taken over the preaching. What I hadn't figured on was that Pastor Jahn would be doing his own preaching in a different way.

Before all else, he had us draw a map centered on the Middle East, but reaching from Italy in the west to India in the east and Arabia in the south. In the following weeks, he had us fill in the detail, like the Sea of Galilee, also known as Lake Tiberias, lying 214 meters below sea level, and being fed and drained by the Jordan River.

"That's where our Lord Jesus found Matthew, the despised customs officer," Pastor Jahn said, "and made him one of his disciples. Later, somewhere between 62 and 66 A.D., Matthew wrote one of our gospels, in Hebrew."

Likewise, we located Jerusalem, Antioch, and Rome, where Markus, originally called John, Pastor Jahn said, traveled and wrote his gospel, this one in Greek. And then there was Lukas, a physician, who wrote a gospel, too, who left Antioch, Syria, to teach in Macedonia, Dalmatia, Galatia, and Italy.

Having found and labeled those places, we learned about John, a fisherman and the youngest disciple, also a gospel writer, who preached in Jerusalem and then Ephesus, Asia Minor. And there was Peter, another fisherman, infamous for denying Jesus in a moment of weakness, but famous also for great faith and courage later on, teaching everywhere from Jerusalem to Babylon and Rome, where he was crucified, hanging—at his own request—on a cross upside down.

"He didn't think he was worthy of dying in exactly the same way as his Lord and Master," Pastor Jahn said.

In the same sneaky fashion, he taught us about Jakobus the Elder, fisherman and brother of John, "one of the first witnesses to the resurrection" and also the first martyr, killed by sword in 42 A.D. And we learned of Thomas, who was slain by Brahmins in India, and of Bartholomew, killed in Armenia, and of Simon, who preached in Mesopotamia, Persia, Egypt, and Libya, and of Judas, who betrayed Jesus and died by the sword in Phoenicia, and, finally, of Paul, the carpet weaver and overeager Pharisee, who persecuted Christians in the name of Mosaic Law, only to meet Jesus on the road to Damascus, then travel to Arabia, Cyprus, Galatia, Macedonia, live in Corinth and Ephesus and, finally, in Nero's Rome, where he died a martyr's death.

"Just think of it," Pastor Jahn said, "the appearance of Jesus on earth started a *chain reaction* that spread from a handful of disciples to some 70 apostles and through them to all the countries on your maps and, ultimately, around the globe."

I know he said more, but I wasn't paying attention at the time. I had been leafing through the new art book we had received for our drawing class and I came across a beautiful reproduction of Renoir's *Blond Bather*, 1881. She reminded me of Jutta and I decided to cut out the page and keep it no matter what.

******

Our second class that day was History, taught by Newteacher Hirsch. He decided to review the story of Adolf Hitler, beginning, as he put it, with "the grotesque 1923 Munich beer cellar putsch" right to the end of the war. He described Hitler's "interminable speechifying, his wild gesticulations and foaming at the mouth, his shifty staring eyes and his monstrous, bloodthirsty fantasies." He pictured Hitler as "a deranged, repulsive hoodlum representing the cesspool of humanity." I had heard all this before, way back in Berlin, when examining Mr. Joseph's newspapers and coming across a Communist Party ad.

Mr. Hirsch talked of Hitler's ruthless rise to power and the early indications of what he was about: ending the freedom of the press, arranging the boycott of Jewish stores, kicking Jews out of Germany's civil service, setting up concentration camps for political opponents, burning books, mocking organized religion (as by replacing Christmas with winter solstice ceremonies), banning labor unions, neutralizing or banning political opposition parties (Stahlhelm, Social Democrats, Communists).

Mr. Hirsch also told us about the 1935 Nuremberg Laws:

1) the *Reich Citizenship Law* that introduced the distinction between Aryans, called *Reichsstaatsbürger* (full-fledged Citizens of the National Socialist Commonwealth) and Jews, called *Staatsangehörige* (mere State Residents)

2) the *Law to Protect German Blood and Honor* that outlawed intermarriage and strongly discouraged other relations between Aryans and Jews

Mr. Hirsch reviewed the role of the SA [*Sturmabteilung*], known as storm troopers or brownshirts (he called them "a bunch of thugs") and told us about June 30, 1934, the Night of the Long Knives, when Hitler, "in a fit of paranoia," summoned SA leaders to Bad Wiessee, Bavaria, only to have 200 of them killed, including Ernst Röhm, the top man.

Mr. Hirsch similarly reviewed the role of the SS [*Schutzstaffel*], known as blackshirts; once merely a handful of Hitler's personal guards, later expanded into "an army of precision killers" that ran the concentration camps. "Yet," said Mr. Hirsch, "the public succumbed with hypnotic trance to the glamour of depravity. Something of a *chain reaction* was set loose, and the world witnessed an ecstasy of evil." Table A, he said, says it all:

Table A: The Consequences of the Fascist War

Country	Military Deaths	Civilian Deaths
Soviet Union	7,500,000	15,000,000
Germany	2,800,000	500,000
Japan	1,500,000	333,333
United Kingdom	397,762	65,000
United States	292,000	—
France	210,600	108,000
Italy	77,000	40,000
All Combined*	**15,000,000**	**34,000,000**
* Includes other countries and the murder of 6 million Jews in concentration camps		

******

Mr. Hirsch also gave us a homework assignment, an essay on Horst Wessel, the infamous SA man who was responsible for the song we always had to sing during the Hitler years. I was lucky; Mr. Kalitz knew all about him.

"He was the son of a Lutheran pastor," he said, "became a storm trooper early on, in 1930, loved to be in those bloody street battles in Berlin, fighting Communists. Then he fell in love with a prostitute and moved in with her. Their landlady tried to eject them for living in sin, or at least to pay double rent. They refused. She sought help from the Communists who were glad to oblige and shot him dead. Among his possessions, someone found a poem—*The Flag Held High*—and when Goebbels got hold of that, he had it set to music and made up a story about Wessel, making him a martyr. The rest, as they say, is history."

Mr. Kalitz helped me a lot that year and history became one of my favorite subjects—unlike another one that I should tell you about. Our final class, on the first day of school after the war, involved Current Affairs. It was taught by Newteacher Wolf who was also slated to teach us Russian. His concern was the dropping of atomic bombs, and he managed to scare us to death in no time at all.

"It is one thing," he said, "to drop a couple of bombs on Japan, but if anyone ever drops a whole bunch of them, maybe a dozen or so (nobody knows for sure), a critical mass of split atoms builds up and a dangerous *chain reaction* occurs. As a result, water begins to evaporate and that process, once started, can snuff out life all over the earth!"

That statement got my full attention; I even put aside my beautiful Renoir girl.

"What is it that would evaporate?" I asked. "Water in brooks and rivers? The whole Pacific Ocean?"

"There comes a point," he said, "if they drop even one more atomic bomb, a chain reaction will be set into motion and every single drop of water on earth will evaporate. That will be the end of life as we know it."

"Even the water in wells underground?" I asked.

"Even the water under the ground," he said.

"But once all that water is in the air," I protested, "won't the air be saturated and it'll all rain right back to the ground?"

"More about that next time," he said. "Time's up for today."

On the way home from school, I was worried. I kept thinking of Mr. Wolf's chain reaction. What about land-locked lakes, I thought, or the snow and ice on the North and South poles? And I kept thinking of the inevitable flood of rain. I even thought someone might have had the Bomb at Noah's time and caused the deluge.

******

By the time I got to the Town Hall, I could see all the jeeps in front of our house. A lot of Russian MPs milled about; and I wished they'd handle their damn submachine guns more carefully. Someone could get killed. Mrs. Albrecht wailed, as usual.

"Why do they do this to us? Why do they do this to us?" she moaned.

The Russians, I learned, had dug up their son's grave and were taking him away.

Upstairs, the news was only slightly better. There was a letter from my father and another one from Aunt Martel. My father was writing from Brandenburg. He had been released by the British, but rearrested by the Russians during quarantine. Unlike Werner Albrecht, who had been in Italy, or Uncle Eddy, who had spent the war in France, the Russians were investigating carefully anyone who had been at the eastern front. It might take months, my father said. My mother was crying.

Aunt Martel was still living in the cellar, but she was now in the American sector of Berlin. No more Russians to contend with. She sent a picture of her street to prove the point.

akg-images, London, United Kingdom

A Berlin street scene after the 1945 division into four sectors of occupation.

34. BREAD WINNERS

[October 1945 – February 1946]

In the fall of 1945, at just about the time we all went back to school, we learned what it meant to be hungry. That seems odd, given that we were living in the countryside and it was harvest time, but it makes sense once you think about it. For one thing, many farmers hadn't plowed or seeded their fields in the spring because of the chaos that accompanied the last months of the war. Many farmers had been too busy dealing with refugees, building tank traps, and attending werewolf meetings. In addition, fields that had been prepared were often devastated by the retreating and conquering armies that flowed across them like a deluge. Finally, and more recently, crops that had made it to harvest time were often confiscated by the Russians. As a result, food stores had emptied out and soon there was nothing left to sell. The baker didn't have flour to bake anything. The grocery store had exactly three items when I last checked; I bought them all: some chunks of suet, a bag of flour crawling with maggots, and a single can of salt herrings.

Theoretically, and despite the daily foraging by the Russians, *farmers* had lots of things to eat, given their private gardens filled with fruits and vegetables and their barnyards full of chickens and geese and cows and pigs. And they had sheep, too, so many sheep! Indeed, Helmut and I had made a habit of watching the village shepherd and his trusty little border collie, walking from farm to farm every morning at sunrise, gathering up three sheep at one gate, twelve at the next, seven more across the street, and so on, and finally moving an army of hundreds of wooly beasts down School Street to the meadows for the day. What fascinated us even more was their return trip at dusk. Somehow, that little dog saw to it that precisely the right sheep were deposited at their respective homes. They all looked alike to us; how did the little black-and-white creature manage to do it?

But I am rambling here. The point is that we were rapidly running out of things to eat and my mother couldn't very well go out to look for food at the farms because of what the Russians did to women. I offered to become the bread winner, and I soon discovered numerous ways of doing my job.

******

Often after school, I sat on the steps to the butcher's shop. That was all right, I was in nobody's way, for that store was empty as well. Mr. Albrecht rarely sold anything these days, except cow udders and lungs which the Russians didn't like. Once he even sold horse meat; we always snapped up whatever we could. Horse meat was weird; even when cooked, it *smelled* like a horse.

As I said, I sat on the steps and soon I was surrounded by farmers' kids, which meant it was time to hold my daily auction. I hid my postage stamps in a little book and crouched on my knees. My customers gathered around me, with eggs in their hands. Helmut leaned out the window above us. I put a first stamp on the step, a huge, yellow one from Finland, and said: "Anyone?" Twelve greedy eyes stared at the stamp, but there were no takers. I placed a second stamp next to the yellow one, making sure no one could see the others in my book. "Anyone?" Klaus said: "A deal," and two stamps changed hands for an egg. At the end of my auction, I said: "Same place, same time tomorrow," and Helmut turned to our mother and yelled: "He's got six."

******

Later in the afternoons, I went outside the village, pulling my wagon. I liked to stay on the roads, because they were lined with apple trees, plum trees, and bushes of elderberry. The trees on different roads belonged to different farmers and the habit of planting them along all the roads rather than in an orchard, I was told, had been introduced way back in Napoleon's time when he had swept across Germany on his way to Russia. Usually, to avoid detection, I went a kilometer out of town, filled up the wagon with fruit, and covered it with something innocuous, like a layer of chestnuts or pinecones or some brush and straw. But this was dangerous. Sometimes, farmers chased me with big dogs. At another time, former Polish POWs, who were still hanging around the area, caught up with me. They looked at all German boys as embryo SS and checked in my armpit for the tell-tale SS tattoo. Then they made me stick up my arms and searched my pockets. They found my little gold coin with the red ladybug on top that Dieter had given me for good luck, way back in Berlin. They hurled it into the gravel pit. They also found my collapsible knife and held it to my throat. They took it with them when they left.

I decided to stay off the roads. I went into the fields with a hoe and dug for potatoes and carrots after the harvest; the farmers always missed a lot, and they didn't mind. I also walked through the wheat fields when the farmers were done; they said it was alright to glean. But I didn't like gathering the wheat, because my wooden clogs kept falling off—I didn't know how to attach the makeshift straps—and the stubbles cut my feet. Luckily, my mother and Aunt Liesel did the threshing when I got home.

Once I brought home a lot of fish. It was a Sunday and I had taken the half-shell of a large bomb I had found and gone canoeing in it down the brook that flowed between the cloister and the castle. A group of Russian soldiers sat at the point where the brook flowed into the castle pond. They had their guns ready and shot the last stork just when it sailed over the top of the pine trees. That was sad; I had so liked the stork. I actually cried, which was weird because of all the bad things that had happened to me when I hadn't felt a thing. The soldiers wanted my watch, but I didn't have one.

"Uri, Uri," they said.

Then they tossed hand grenades into the pond and made me gather up the dead fish with my canoe. They let me have a dozen.

"Karasho, kamerad! Karasho!" they said. I already knew what it meant. "Good, comrade! Good!"

There was a surprise for me when I got home. My mother had made false liverwurst, a mixture of grits and marjoram. Aunt Liesel had baked a cake with false coffee grounds, topped with marmalade made of red beets. She had also made tea from apple peels. More importantly, she had found all kinds of new postage stamps for me at the post office. Some of them were old Hitler stamps, but the words "Destroyer of Germany" were printed across Hitler's face. The new stamps showed houses under construction and farmers plowing at sunrise.

******

Just before winter came, I went into the forest to gather up the beechnuts that the squirrels hadn't gotten first. At the Town Hall, one could exchange 50 pounds of them for a certificate promising 1 pound of margarine. It took me days to get it, but I did and that was my Christmas present for my mother. She was very happy.

I also picked up wagonloads of elderberries, which my mother pressed to make juice. I remember us once drinking a whole pitcher full of the juice; it looked just like red wine and was delicious. The rest of that meal was not so great. I had stored the potatoes and carrots in the cellar under a pile of straw, just as Mr. Albrecht had told me, but the frost got to them anyway. That gave the potatoes a sickeningly sweet taste after being boiled, while the frozen carrots turned to mush after they thawed. But we ate it all. In those days, even Helmut ate every last drop of the soups my mother made; we didn't have to bribe him with visions of flowers or fairytale characters waiting at the bottom of an empty bowl.

Helmut and I also ate all the vitamin pills that my mother had gotten from the pharmacy next door. We thought they were candy and we both got very sick and red in the face.

One night in early December, Mr. Kalitz came and told us about an American truck that had gone off the Autobahn and burned. I went with him to investigate and we found it loaded with big wheels of charcoal. Mr. Kalitz took a knife, cut the edges away, and turned up a treasure of soft, melted cheese. We filled my wagon to carry home all we could of the charcoal-cheese. True enough, in a few days, the maggots appeared, but my mother said the cheese was just turning into meat. We ate all of it, for we didn't like the stomach ache from eating dried dandelions and frozen turnips. Still, we dreamed a lot of better days and sometimes we shared our thoughts. My mother had visions of candles and soap and hot water, she said, and of milk and meat, which made me sneak out and steal another sausage from the smoking chamber downstairs. As for me, I was clamoring for things one could only dream about in those days, like bananas and oranges and chocolate hussars....Just in case, I decided to send a Christmas wish list to Aunt Martel in Berlin; decades later, I found it among her affairs:

Dear Aunt Martel:

How are you? I am fine. Here are the things I would most like for Christmas:

1 loaf of white bread

1 eraser

1 pencil

notepads

any book

cookies

anything edible!!!! Exceptions: None

Aunt Liesel wonders whether you could find her six candles.

Sorry I can't write any more. Helmut wants to lick the envelope shut and refuses to wait any longer.

Your Hans

*****

It was a cold winter that year. A week before Christmas, I looked down into the back yard, which we could do from the window in our second room, and saw Mr. Albrecht swearing by the pump. He stood on a sheet of ice. Even though the pump was packed in a thick coat of straw, it wouldn't yield any water. I was glad I had filled up our pails the day before. Even in school, the ink in our desks had been solid for a week. Sometimes at school my hands and feet were so cold that my fingers and toes got really white and then blue and numb. Putting my hands in my pockets and stamping my feet didn't always help. Then I had to run home to thaw out in a pot of warm water, which made my fingers and toes turn red. Dr. Weiss said I had Raynaud's disease rather than frostbite, but who knows? I still have the symptoms today.

The day our pump died was also the day Aunt Martel appeared for a surprise visit. She was on one of the trains that arrived once a week filled with city folk looking for food. There was a sign at the railroad station warning "black market transactions strictly forbidden," but nobody paid any attention to that. Hordes of people with rucksacks and suitcases would emerge from the train and walk from farm to farm, offering to trade city possessions for food of any kind. I saw people trading dishes and dolls and clothing and even Christmas tree ornaments for eggs, flour, and potatoes, only to disappear on the next train, loaded down like mules.

"Before long," Mr. Kalitz said, "even the cows in the barn will live on Oriental carpets."

In any case, Aunt Martel emerged from one of those crowded trains, having come straight from Berlin, and that's why Aunt Martel, Aunt Liesel, and Uncle Herbert joined my mother, Helmut, and me for Christmas dinner that year. It turned out to be a strange gathering, indeed. For one thing, the food was less than presentable. There was flour soup, made with water, but filled with chunks of sausage I had stolen from the Russians downstairs. We also had lots of potatoes, frozen one and all, and then plenty of turnip mush. Actually, it wasn't so bad; what happened next was another matter.

Uncle Herbert was puffing on his pipe, smoking dried rose petals, as was common in those days, when Aunt Martel asked him whether he was sorry yet. Showing total indifference to the question, he changed the subject to the pamphlets the Russians kept distributing around town.

"Those concentration camps," he said, "I am certain they never existed," Uncle Herbert said. "Except for Siberia, of course," he added, "which is where the Russians must have taken all those disgusting pictures."

That's when my mother took the pitcher of cold water from the table and emptied all of it over Uncle Herbert's head.

The rest of the day didn't go much better. After Aunt Liesel and Uncle Herbert had left, we all went to hear Uncle Eddy's Christmas sermon, which turned out to be a mistake. Despite the fact that it was Christmas, his subject was the Seventh Commandment, Thou Shalt Not Steal.

"What does that mean?" Uncle Eddy thundered from the pulpit. And he answered his own question:

"We shall so fear and love God that we don't abscond with our neighbor's money or possessions, nor acquire them in exchange for worthless goods or by engaging in unfair trades, but we should always take care of, improve, and protect our neighbor's possessions and livelihood."

"There's been a lot of thievery in this village lately," Uncle Eddy continued, "and it has to stop. Hunger is no excuse! You must have faith in the Lord, for it is written: 'Ask and you shall receive.' Pray to the Lord and God, our merciful Father, will provide."

My mother didn't like the sermon. She had a big fight with Uncle Eddy afterwards. He said he couldn't invite us to the cloister because Aunt Rachel was ill and, more importantly, those East Prussians had stolen everything they owned. And my mother said something about Uncle Eddy being hypocritical as well as insane, which *he* didn't like. But I was happy enough. Aunt Martel had brought me pencils and notepads and wonderful pictures of postwar Berlin. And she had also brought me a little suitcase full of old money from the 1920's, the days of the hyperinflation, when it cost thousands and later millions of marks just to buy a loaf of bread. In those days, Aunt Martel said, one had to spend one's pay on the way home from work because prices would double by the next day. In any case, I loved the idea of having that old money with all those zeros on each bill. I just knew it would enable me to engage in all sorts of wonderful, unfair trades with the farmer boys. But I didn't always trade my wares for food. Once I traded a paper bill from the 1920's for a drawing of Ziesar way back in 1710. I still have it today.

******

In early 1946, we had an even bigger surprise than Aunt Martel's visit: My father came home! Suddenly and unannounced, there he was. I found him in my mother's arms when I came home from school and it felt strange, just as it had some years ago at the railroad station in Berlin. I saw a tall, thin man in an army uniform, but all the insignia were missing. Despite the time of year, he was tanned, suggesting that he had spent a lot of time outside. I also noticed a big scar on his forehead. And I saw his belt buckle. It still said "God With Us."

"Hansel," he said, "how big you are!"

But it felt awkward to hug him. It took quite some time for that feeling to subside. It helped that we did some projects together.

First, my father agreed to play the organ in church and that turned out to be fun. The giant pipe organ was played from a spot way above the congregation and my father, it turned out, was a master at it. He could play both the regular keyboard with his hands and a second one with his feet at the same time, but in order to do it, he needed help. The giant instrument needed the support of a pair of bellows, which were hidden in the church tower behind the pipes. I was just the right man to do the job and, as an added bonus, it kept me from sitting among the congregation down below. All I had to do was jump on a giant lever, grasp a wooden bar above my head with my hands, and push my body down towards the floor. That would fill the bellows with air and then, as it slowly escaped, I was automatically pushed up again towards the ceiling, where I could repeat the procedure.

Indeed, there was another bonus still: Using a long rope, I could ring the church bells before the service and also afterwards, which I did with great fervor and joy, each time sending hundreds of pigeons into the air. And during the sermon, when the organ had to be quiet, my father and I practiced translating Uncle Edie's sermon into op-language, which was created by taking any sentence and inserting the syllable op in front of every vowel. Thus "In the name of the Father and the Son and the Holy Ghost" turned into "Opin thope nopamope opof thope Fopathoper opand thope Sopon opand thope Hopolopy Ghopost." That was a lot of fun and I beat my father every time when we tried to see who could finish first.

We had a second fun project, too. This one involved getting firewood from the forest. I selected two of the sharpest axes from Mr. Albrecht's barn and loaded them into my wagon. My father said I could climb into the wagon, too, and he pulled me all the way, pretending to be a horse. At the forest, I challenged him to a race, all the way to the big oak and back. He won.

He challenged me to climb a tree. He was in the top of it before I could even figure out how to begin. But cutting down a 15 centimeter tree was the biggest contest of them all. I took eleven strokes, and my father said I could be proud. He did it in five strokes. He was very strong. He let me feel his muscles.

My father was smart, too, not with the op-language, but when it came to being a bread winner. One day, he took me to the big highway, and we gathered up a large bag of cigarette stubs. A stream of Americans drove to Berlin and back on the Autobahn, and they never finished their cigarettes.

At home, we opened the stubs and had a big pile of American tobacco on the table. Sometimes, we could even identify the brand from the cigarette butts. *Lucky Strike*, it might say, or *Camel, Pall Mall, Chesterfield, Old Gold*, and *Philip Morris*. My father got a cigarette roller out of his bag and a pile of neat thin paper. We rolled a lot of cigarettes that day, and they all looked like new.

But my parents didn't smoke. The next day, we went on a long trip with our wagon. First we went to the dairy, taking the straight route across the fields. The dairyman gave us lots of cottage cheese, a can of milk, and even a chunk of butter—all for ten cigarettes. Then we went to the miller, the one in the next village, who always wanted Aunt Liesel to take off her bra. He traded ten pounds of flour for twenty cigarettes. He also gave us some yeast. But when we got home, the flour had maggots in it.

We also stopped at lots of farms in the miller's village, and my father asked for potatoes. Each farmer gave him a dozen or so, and our wagon was filled to the top when we got home.

We went back to the highway often, and we didn't tell anyone about the source of our cigarette wealth. Years later, I learned that cigarettes had become a regular currency all over Germany in those days. There was even a new word for people like us who kept the system afloat: *Kippensammler* [cigarette butt collectors] they were called. Even Mr. Albrecht was ready to trade. He was always willing to supply sausages for a smoke, but he only gave us the ones he made from old horses. I still had to sneak down at night to get the liverwurst.

We also had fun looking at the pictures Aunt Martel had brought from Berlin. I liked best the one of the *Tiergarten*, Berlin's Central Park, which she and I had often visited in the past. There used to be lots of giant old trees, surrounded by thousands of fragrant, flowering bushes in the summer, and all sorts of marble statues along its winding paths. I think I told you about that once before. But the picture showed none of that. The *Tiergarten*, I learned, had been the scene of one of the fiercest battles in the last days of the war. Almost every single tree, bush, and statue had been destroyed, leaving behind, miraculously, only the central monument, the tall Column of Victory that celebrated Germany's triumph over France in 1871. The picture Aunt Martel had taken that summer showed a farmer plowing the park, in the very center of Berlin, in order to wrest a bit of food from the ground, while the Goddess of Victory looked on.

akg-images, London, United Kingdom

The Column of Victory in Berlin's *Tiergarten,* a Central Park used for agriculture following World War II

35. HOOLIGANISM
[April – June 1946]

In the spring of 1946, Lieutenant Trapeznikov replaced Major Mayants as Ziesar's commandant. Mrs. Gronostalski said he was a devoted Communist and deeply shocked by what he called "antisocial activities" in our village—by Russians and Germans alike. There would be a lot of changes, she predicted.

"He is determined to win the hearts and minds of everyone for Communism," Mrs. Gronostalski said. "As a first step, he has issued strict orders to the garrison that any further violence would be treated as a capital crime. He would not hesitate, he said, personally to shoot rapists on the spot; they are a blemish on the Motherland; they stand in the way of people embracing a new way of life, based on Marxism, Leninism, and Stalinism."

"As for the rest of us," she continued, "he is going to make sure, he says, that 'everyone does honest work and the results are shared equally by all.' There's even a new sign on the wall behind his desk: 'He who does not work, neither shall he eat!' it says."

Everyone in the Albrecht house was relieved to hear the news, if it was to be believed, at least the part about rapes. And there was more good news as well. Mrs. Gronostalski thought she could get my father a job with the commandant, as chief of statistics. All they had to do was walk across the street and set it up. Mrs. Gronostalski said I could come along and try out my Russian.

"Ya lyublyu russkiy yasik, yasik nashevo velikovo sosyeda na vostokye," I said.

"Ya nye znayu mnogo slov," I quickly added.

These were sentences we had just learned in school.

"I love the Russian language, the language of our great neighbor to the east," said the first one. "I don't know many words," said the second.

The commandant laughed, and my father did get the job, along with an office in the Town Hall.

******

There were two things my father had to do. His first task involved copying the commandant's list of the village population and dividing it into farm families and non-farm families. He then was to distribute ration coupons for various food items to the latter group, while also policing the bakery, butcher shop, and grocery store, which ultimately had to account for any loss of inventory by handing back the spent coupons. Black market transactions with the help of cigarettes were strictly forbidden.

My father's second task was much more involved. Once a week, he was to prepare a giant table for the commandant, listing, in a first column, the names of all the farmers and, in numerous subsequent columns, the sizes of each farmer's fields; the degree to which they were plowed, seeded, planted, or harvested; the extent to which they were devoted to growing barley, oats, rye, wheat, potatoes, sugar beets, asparagus, or just plain grass; and, last but not least, the numbers of chickens and geese, cows and pigs, horses and tractors currently owned, along with the number of eggs collected, the liters of milk produced, the pounds of silage fed to pigs, and so on, almost without end.

As page after page was glued together, some of the tables turned out to be 5 meters long, almost three times my father's height, but that was alright. The commandant *liked* large tables. To produce them, my father walked from farm to farm every day and filled the table grid with numbers. Mrs. Gronostalski wrote in the column headings in Russian when he was done. I got into the act as well. Aunt Martel had brought me an animal-and-plant stencil kit for Christmas. It allowed me to trace 250 different figures and then fill in the result with colored markers. The commandant liked my visual aids, especially my rendering of the fatted pig. He gave me a reward: a Russian officer's hat made with fine, light-brown leather on the outside and sheep's wool on the inside and also on the outside rim. It also had white wooly ear flaps that one could let hang or button to the top. And in front, there was large shiny metal star, colored red, with a golden hammer and sickle on it and surrounded with golden ears of wheat.

Despite the fact that it was summer, I wore the hat when I accompanied my father on his daily rounds to the farms. But the farmers were not happy with either of us. They thought the commandant was just trying to make them work harder and for less, and they were probably right. Everyone knew that farmers were supposed to feed their families and then deliver *all* the rest of their output to the Russians. And the commandant was obviously watching their every move, having recently outlawed "black butchering," the practice of secretly slaughtering some unregistered animal in the middle of the night and then disposing of it on the black market.

******

I don't remember how it happened, but that was also the time at which my parents got into the Big Fight. Maybe it was the constant griping by all the farmers that got my father down. Maybe it was my mother talking to my father about Leo Krell and how he had died and thus reminding him, as if he needed reminding, of the Hitler years and the war, and my father saying that he had never known any Leo Krell but that, perhaps, it had been a friend of his who tried to escape the penal regiment by taking on a false identity in the last agonizing moments of the war. Maybe it was a sudden flood of bad memories coming back to both of them; just seeing Uncle Herbert in town could have done it. But one thing is for sure. Day after day, my father had been coming back from the commandant filled with potato schnapps, barely able to walk, and quickly passing out on the bed. Or on the floor. When it came to drinking, the Russians were a real inspiration.

My mother was not about to let that pass. She had been robbed of her husband once and she would not be robbed again. Because of him, she had journeyed into hell, had endured years of fear, hunger, and violence. Now he had returned, and he was not the same. That's when my mother told my father to quit drinking right then and there or she and the children would be gone. She meant it, he knew it, and apparently he did.

******

Back in school that spring, we had to do a lot of memorizing, especially in English and Physics. Memorizing English, taught by Miss Mahler, was simple enough. There was Milton, *On His Blindness*, and I performed beautifully, in front of the whole class. *When I consider how my light is spent...* The memorizing that Mr. Clausen, our physics teacher, required of us, on the other hand, was impossible, which, ultimately, caused all the trouble that spring. The subject was Measures and Weights and it all started innocently enough.

"With respect to length," Mr. Clausen said, "the most important unit of measurement is the *meter*. It equals one ten millionth part of the shortest curved distance from pole to equator."

"As we all know," Mr. Clausen continued, "1,000 meters make 1 kilometer, a unit we all employ every day. But you should also know and memorize some of the most common non-metric measures: the Prussian mile of 7,532 m; the English mile of 1,609.34 m; the world nautical mile of 1,852.01 m; and the Russian mile, or versta', of 1,066.78 m."

In the same fashion, Mr. Clausen reviewed for us area measures, such as the *square meter* ("1 million of which equal 1 square kilometer and, thus, 100 hectares," he said) and volume measures, such as the *cubic meter* ("equal to 1,000 liters," he said), and measures of weight, such as the *gram* ("with 1,000 grams equaling 1 kilogram and 1,000 kg, in turn, equaling 1 ton," he said). But then he got carried away, *dictating* definitions, such as these:

- **horsepower** = the power needed to lift 75 kilograms to a height of 1 meter in 1 second
- **ohm** = a unit of electrical resistance equal to that of a conductor in which a current of 1 ampère is produced by a potential of 1 volt across its terminals
- **ampère** = a unit of electric current, equal to the steady current that (when flowing

in straight parallel wires of infinite length and negligible cross section, separated
by a distance of 1 meter in free space) produces a force between the wires of 2 times
10^{-7} newtons per meter of length
- **volt** = a unit of electrical potential, equal to the difference of electric potential between
two points on a conducting wire carrying a constant current of 1 ampère when the power
dissipated between the points is 1 watt
- **watt** = a unit of power equal to 1 joule per second
- **joule** = a unit of electrical energy equal to the work done when a current of 1 ampère is
passed through a resistance of 1 ohm for 1 second

Understanding nothing, I could not imagine myself memorizing these definitions by the next
class. Stalling for time, I said:

"You use the terms ampère and volt in the definition of ohm and then define both. But you fail
to define a newton, which is used in the definition of ampère."

Mr. Clausen looked at me with disdain.

"A newton," he said, rather reluctantly, "is the unit of force required to accelerate a mass of 1
kilogram by 1 meter per second per second."

Not knowing the difference between speed and acceleration, that answer really bothered me.

"You mean, perhaps, 'per second' and not 'per second per second,' as you put it just now?"
I asked.

"I mean precisely 'per second per second'" Mr. Clausen said decisively and in a louder voice
than before and his hand reached for the Yellow Uncle. Apparently, he hadn't gotten the message.

"No corporal punishment," Miss Mahler had said.

But that's what we got before the class was over. The Yellow Uncle was visited upon many of
us. There had been too many dumb questions, Mr. Clausen said, and somehow he never managed
to answer any of them. And, as I said, that's what started it all.

******

When I got to school the next day, some of the farmer boys were already holding a caucus.
They were going to teach Mr. Clausen a lesson and I agreed to help. By the time he walked into
class, he found us counting aloud in unison:

"One, two, three, four, five ..."

"Quiet!" he yelled, and swish went the Yellow Uncle.

"Eight, nine, ten, eleven, twelve ..."

"What *is* this?" he shouted. "Have you gone mad?"

"Sixteen, seventeen, eighteen ..."

"Stop it, you hear! I am a learned man; you cannot do this to me. Stop it, do you hear!"

"Twenty-seven, twenty-eight ..."

Three of the bigger boys got up and opened the window. They picked up Mr. Clausen, shoved him out the window head first, but held on to his feet. We were, after all, on the second floor.

"Hurrah," shouted the crowd, and "Hey, teach," someone said, "repeat after me, and do it fast: 'How much wood would a woodchuck chuck if a woodchuck could chuck wood? It would chuck all the wood that a woodchuck could chuck if a woodchuck could chuck wood.' Go!"

Mr. Clausen complied in a hurry, and everyone gave him a hand.

"Yeah," someone said, "and now try this; five times fast: 'Sweet Sue sells sea shells at the sea shore.' Go!"

Mr. Clausen tried again, and they pulled him in. He was very red in the face and ran out of the room. Soon Miss Mahler came. As I told you, she was the new principal. And she called us a bunch of hooligans and promised that we would pay for our misdeeds in the summer.

"You seem to have a lot of excess energy," she said, "and I promise you that it will be put to good use. This summer, each of you will work, from daybreak to sunset, and, if necessary, the summer after that as well. Each one of you will learn the meaning of order and discipline."

She also told us about building a new society of *Communism*, in which all people would be brothers and sisters and would give their best for the well-being of all. And she warned us about new tyrants who had arisen in the West, a group of evil men out to destroy "the emerging communities of brotherhood in the East."

"They are dangling over us the sword of Damocles," she said. "Their atomic bomb could snuff out life all over the earth in an instant. That's where your energies should go: Building brotherhood at home and fighting the tyrannical monsters of the West!"

Wow! Where did that come from? I wondered what had happened to the sweet Miss Mahler I had known. Was she drunk, perhaps? I had seen her drink from that vodka bottle in her office more than once and she never seemed to drink anything else. Perhaps, I thought, she was worried about her breath, just in case Mr. Wolf was moved to give her a kiss.

******

On the way home, I walked past the Town Hall and looked at the news. Although it had just been posted, it was five months old:

November 1945

An International Military Tribunal has convened in Nuremberg to initiate the trial against 21 former political leaders and generals of the Nazi regime, including, among others, Göring, von Ribbentrop, Keitel, Kaltenbrunner, Rosenberg, Frank, Jodl, von Papen, Sauckel, and von Schirach

Like the misdeeds of the Nazi leaders, ours was not forgotten by the time summer came. Miss Mahler turned out to be a woman of her word.

"It is time to avenge your crime and to teach you the meaning of socialist morality," she said. The day school let out, we were given our assignments for the rest of the summer.

First, we were taken to the potato fields and shown the bugs that American planes were dumping every night while flying to Berlin.

"The monopoly capitalists are trying to starve us into submission," Miss Mahler said, "but the people shall prevail."

We crawled through endless kilometers of potato fields, each one of us with a row of plants between the knees, squashing the evil bugs with little stones. The sun was merciless. By noon, the sand got terribly hot, and I thought of slaves in cotton fields. But, if the truth is to be told, I also made sure to have a row next to Helga. That way I could get ahead of her by a meter or two and turn around often to smile. And I could look inside her blouse and see her little breasts.

******

Whenever we had finished with the potato bugs, and it was a repetitive job that had to be redone at least once a month, we dug the gardens. The commandant had come up with a new slogan that appeared all over town:

"Junkerland in Bauernhand," it said. "The gentry's land into the peasants' hands."

Under the new program, the commandant expropriated all the farmers' land in excess of 100 hectares and divided it into 5-hectare-plots to be given to non-farm families who wanted to farm. Many of the East Prussian and Silesian refugees took him up on his offer. They were called Newfarmers—like Newteachers, that was another new word fusing adjective and noun. But, and that is the main point here, additional smaller plots of land were available to all other families for gardening and that's where our second assignment came in.

We were marched onto a piece of pasture land and told to dig it up with little spades. The plows and horses were needed for more important things, and we had the excess energy. But the girls couldn't do the job, the grass was too thick. They were sent off to gather Queen Anne's lace and chamomile for the local pharmacist and beech nuts for the margarine factory in Brandenburg. Some of them had to gather acorns to be fed to pigs.

My parents got one of the garden plots and we all worked it, on weekends mainly. We planted potatoes, tomatoes, cucumbers, cabbage, kohlrabi, onions, and carrots. We also planted climbing green beans after building a structure made of tall poles. But we weren't very lucky. There was no water nearby and when the rains failed to come, all the plants died. On the few occasions when everything flourished, everything was stolen over night just before harvest time. I tried to plant tomatoes a second time, but they were still green on the vine when the first frost killed them.

******

So far as our school assignments were concerned, there was a third one as well. Despite the blisters on our backs, the calluses on our hands, and the wounds on our knees from all the crawling on the potato fields, we were sent to take care of the sugar beets. We crawled over endless rows with tiny plants that had to be thinned just right, and with big fat plants that had to be weeded and watered with buckets from the brook. And we were supervised by none other than Mr. Clausen himself, who stood at the end of the rows, berated us for our dirty fingernails, and cheered us on by calling us "anti-social parasites."

"Those who don't work, don't eat," he said. "So work."

Strange as it may sound, Uncle Eddy said the same thing during his Sunday sermon that my father and I secretly watched from my hideout on the organ bellows.

"For it is written in 2 Thessalonians, chapter 3," Uncle Eddy said. "Finally, brethren, pray for us that we may be delivered from unreasonable and wicked men: for all men have not faith. Now we command you, brethren, in the name of our Lord Jesus Christ that ye withdraw yourselves from every brother that walketh disorderly, and not after the tradition which he received of us. For yourselves know how ye ought to follow us: for we behaved not ourselves disorderly among you; Neither did we eat any man's bread for nought; but wrought with labour and travail night and day, that we might not be chargeable to any of you: Not because we have not power, but to make ourselves an example unto you to follow us. For even when we were with you, this we commanded you, that *if any would not work, neither should he eat*. For we hear that there are some which walk among you disorderly, working not at all, but are busybodies. The grace of our Lord Jesus Christ be with you all. Amen."

My father said Uncle Eddy was crazy and, rather than listening, we decided to study the new poster that the commandant had asked my father to put up at the Town Hall. In the background, the poster showed images of two socialist folk heroes, August Bebel (1840-1913) and Karl Liebknecht (1871-1919). Bebel, my father said, helped found the Social Democratic Workers Party in 1869, which later became the SPD. And in the waning days of World War I, just two hours after Philipp Scheidemann had proclaimed the German Republic from the balcony of the Reichstag, Liebknecht, standing on the balcony of the Emperor's Palace in Berlin, proclaimed the Free Socialist Republic. And on the last day of 1918, he helped found the Communist Party of Germany, KPD. Shortly thereafter, Liebknecht was kidnapped by soldiers and shot to death in the *Tiergarten*, my father said.

In the foreground, the poster showed what was happening now. The new leaders of Germany's Communists and Social Democrats, Wilhelm Pieck on the left and Otto Grotewohl on the right, both freshly imported from Moscow, were shaking hands on a deal that merged their parties into the Socialist Unity Party of Germany, SED. They were asking voters to choose them over the newly formed Christian Democratic Union, CDU, and Liberal Democratic Party, LPD.

"But without me," my father said. "No more politics for me."

"But then what return did you get from the things of which you are now ashamed?" Uncle Eddy thundered below us. "The end of those things is death. But now that you have been set free from sin and have become slaves of God, the return you get is sanctification and its end, eternal life. For the wages of sin is death, but the free gift of God is eternal life in Christo Jesu our Lord. Amen."

Langewiesche-Brandt, Ebenhausen near München, Germany

Unity of the Workers' Movement –
Unity of Germany!
Vote SED
[Socialist Unity Party of Germany]

36. METAMORPHOSIS
[September – October 1946]

Mrs. Gronostalski had been right about Lieutenant Trapeznikov. He was determined to shake things up in our village and to bring about a big *metamorfoza*, as he liked to say. He did, for Russians and Germans alike. To everyone's relief, the violence disappeared almost overnight. And there were outward changes that were fairly obvious, like all the fresh red paint appearing on the triumphal arches in the streets. More important things happened *behind* the scenes.

I remember the day in September of 1946, right after school had started and I was finally in the 8th grade, when I got my new *Igelit* shoes at the grocery store. For one thing, they are hard to forget, because they were weird shoes made from a new material, called *plastic*. They were dark brown and shiny and had no seams of any kind, nor did they have any eyes for shoelaces. They looked like they had been *cast* to fit my feet perfectly, more like a pair of tight-fitting, but rigid socks than shoes. It was equally weird that I had to get my new shoes at the grocery store, because the shoe store had disappeared and become the House of German-Soviet Friendship. The sign over the door said so, in Russian as well as German, and the inside had all been spruced up with loads of red fabric and bookcases filled with new books and, of course, large portraits of Marx, Lenin, and Stalin.

In any case, just after I had bought my new shoes, I noticed Aunt Liesel and Uncle Herbert walking down the street in my direction. I hadn't seen them for months, and they sure looked different. Both of them were all dressed up in new clothes and not so thin anymore. However, Uncle Herbert was still smoking a pipe with his own brand of "tobacco" made of dried rose petals; I could smell it. But my eyes were riveted on the red armband he was wearing, not unlike the swastika armband I had seen him wear in Berlin, but the swastika was missing, of course. He saw me staring at the armband and then at the button in his lapel. There was a hammer and sickle on it and its rim was red. The button with the brown rim and the swastika was gone.

"Well, you can be the first to know," Uncle Herbert said, "I'll be the new mayor, starting tomorrow. I've been going to school in Burg, have joined the SED, and am looking forward to a lot of important work around here. We'll be living above the police station, right next to the Town Hall."

I said nothing, but he must have seen the shocked expression on my face.

"There'll be a new police force soon; we'll call it the People's Police," he explained.

"You can tell your parents," he added rather formally.

I was still speechless and watched them walk down the street—past the pharmacy and butcher shop on the right, past the Komendatura on the left, crossing over to the Thousand Year Oak, past the Town Hall, and into the old police station next door, as if they owned the place.

******

"Opportunist, that damn opportunist," my mother said, "I suppose when the time comes, he'll wear a green armband, too."

My mother was instantly worried about my father's job, but Mrs. Gronostalski said that my father would continue working directly for the commandant. No problem there. She was right once again. In the coming weeks, Uncle Herbert pretty much ignored us—perhaps, we knew too much, and he didn't want to upset the applecart, or he was just too busy to do otherwise. But he didn't put on a green armband; my mother was wrong on that account.

First, Uncle Herbert got all the farmers together in the school auditorium, the old farmers and the Newfarmers alike, and told them about *land reform* and *collectives*. I went to listen.

"Wouldn't it be much better," Uncle Herbert asked, "to put all the land in the village together into one giant farm and then jointly farming it for the good of all?"

"Instead of each of you wasting half the day moving among different fields—plowing a little field south of the village at sunrise, then sowing winter wheat on another little patch north of town later that morning, then harvesting cucumbers east of town in the early afternoon, and finally making hay in a little pasture out west," he said, "think of how more *efficient* it would be for all the properties to be combined, for all the fields to be giant, for every one of you just doing one thing on any given day!"

"In addition," he said, "such a rational division of labor on a collective farm would make possible the use of new equipment, like tractors and harvesters. In contrast, the use of such machines on numerous, tiny, dispersed patches of land simply makes no sense."

"And at harvest time," he added, "you can just *share* the crops produced, as you share them now within your families."

The farmers didn't buy his ideas. They grumbled a lot about sharing the land and the tools and the work and said they would end up sharing their crops by loading them onto railroad cars going to Russia. The Newfarmers, having just received their own land, were particularly mad at Uncle Herbert. Newfarmer Birkenfeld called him an asshole.

******

Second, Uncle Herbert got all the store people together—there weren't many of them left, just Mr. Albrecht, the butcher, Mr. Senf, the baker, Mr. Adler, the pharmacist, and Mr. Kalitz, who was now running the grocery store—and he told them about "the immorality of trading for profit." He urged them to join the HO, the new *Handelsorganisation*, a nationwide consumer stores organization that would be owned and run "by the people." To explain his point, he held up a giant green cabbage.

"Look at this cabbage," he said. "Last month, farmers who sold cabbages like this one got precisely 10 pfennigs for it. But you," he pointed to Mr. Kalitz, "were charging 30 pfennigs a head and do you know what a buyer had to pay for it in Berlin?"

Uncle Herbert answered his own question:

"Berliners had to pay 90 pfennigs, fully *nine* times what a farmer got for it! There is no excuse for such rip-offs. Once the people own all the stores, what the farmer gets and what the consumer pays will be more or less the same. There will be no more Jewish traders and insurers and other such exploiters in-between!"

Except for me, nobody seemed to notice the slip about the Jews. The store people, perhaps, were too upset about the handwriting on the wall. Mr. Albrecht was hopping mad. He said he wasn't about to lose his butcher shop, no matter what the reason. Mr. Adler asked whether Uncle Herbert had ever owned a store. Had he ever heard of paying a mortgage or an electric bill or all the other bills for its maintenance, which *requires* a markup over the price at which goods are bought? And Mr. Kalitz, who had gone to college in the 1920s, said Uncle Herbert was an idiot.

"I've read Karl Marx, too," he said. "and all that talk about cabbage growers being *productive* workers, and store owners being *unproductive* workers and, thus, a bunch of exploiters, is a lot of bull. In the real world, the process of production is not confined to physical manufacture or the growing of a crop only. A cabbage in Ziesar in September is not the same thing as a cabbage in Berlin at Christmastime."

"Those who transport that cabbage through space and time," Mr. Kalitz added, "are just as productive as those who grow it in the first place. Unless you've been living on the moon, you know that it takes horses and wagons or trucks or railroad cars and *real human effort* to move those cabbages to Berlin. You call that unproductive labor?"

"And given that Berliners want cabbages not just in September when we harvest them here, but also at Christmas and Easter and all kinds of other times of the year," Mr. Kalitz continued, "you surely must admit that we need warehouses and retail stores to make that possible? And Mr. Adler is right; all these cost money to build and maintain!”

“Yeah! Yeah!” the crowd shouted.

“And we need even the ‘unproductive’ labor of your despised insurers,” Mr. Kalitz added. “What if half the cabbages spoil or are stolen on their long journey from Ziesar’s fields at harvest time to Berlin’s dining room tables at Christmastime? For that reason alone, the ultimate seller must collect twice as much *per head* of cabbage as what the grower got for it. The difference just pays for the other head that disappeared and was never sold, but for which the grower got 10 pfennigs, nevertheless!”

Except for Uncle Herbert, of course, everyone gave Mr. Kalitz a standing ovation. On that night at least, Uncle Herbert got nowhere.

******

Third and finally, Uncle Herbert got real busy with the denazification campaign. Any former member of the National Socialist German Workers Party could show up at the Town Hall and apply for denazification. The commandant had set the rules; Uncle Herbert administered them. There were two ways in which one could wash away one’s Nazi past and then be eligible to become a respected member of what the commandant called “the new society of Communism.”

Some people could claim that they had only been *Schein-Nazis* [facade Nazis], which meant they had only given the (false) *appearance* of being a Nazi in order to have an easier life. They had been brown on the outside only; they hadn’t really believed in the Nazi cause. They had done nothing and known nothing. Mrs. Dietrich of all people, the sister of Hitler’s erstwhile District Leader of Magdeburg and the wife of Ziesar’s last mayor, who had been hanged for werewolf activities, claimed to be one of them. Uncle Herbert quickly denazified her and, in no time at all, she showed up in our school as my new teacher of math.

Theoretically, there was a second way to get the coveted *Persilschein* [Persil Certificate], named after the laundry detergent *Persil*, that washed away the sins of someone’s Nazi past. Like the *Persil* ad of old, one might become “pure as the driven snow” by producing a letter from someone who had been helped or treated kindly at a time when it was dangerous to do so. Letters of thanks from Jewish survivors, who had been kept out of the camps or had been secretly hidden and fed, or who had merely been treated kindly when walking on the forbidden sidewalk, rather than in the muddy street, these were particularly prized. But no one in Ziesar came up with anything like that.

I know all this because I saw the commandant's rules when I checked out Aunt Liesel's and Uncle Herbert's apartment after school one day. They had lots of new furniture by then, which no one else could afford or even find. They had all sorts of new books, too. Many of them looked alike, except that they had different numbers on them and different colors. The Lenin ones were blue and went from one to twenty. The Stalin books were red and went from one to thirty, but number 17 was missing. I saw a volume of poetry by Maxim Gorkii and various writings by Karl Marx, nicely shelved in chronological order: *The Economic and Philosophical Manuscripts*, 1844; *The Communist Manifesto*, 1848; *Theories of Surplus Value*, 1861-1863, and *Capital*, volumes 1-3, "written in 1867-1880, and edited by Friedrich Engels in 1883-1894." Uncle Herbert was always reading, Aunt Liesel said. It seems he was turning himself into a good Communist. For a moment I wondered: Might he have been one of those "beefsteak Nazis," brown on the outside but red in the middle, finally trading in the raised arm for the clenched fist? No, I dismissed the thought. My mother was right; a damned opportunist, that's what he was.

*****

Meanwhile, now that law and order had returned, the commandant was eager to transform the rest of us as well. My parents and all the other adults had to sign up for "political awareness courses" that were offered in the school auditorium every Wednesday night. And we 8th-graders, most of us in our last year of school and slated soon to join the world of hard-working proletarians, were fed a heavy diet of Marxism-Leninism-Stalinism in every class we took. Mr. Hirsch, our History teacher, focused on Karl Marx and his teachings. Mr. Wolf, our Current Affairs teacher, reviewed the work of Lenin and Stalin. And all the other teachers, no matter what their subjects, still managed to link them to the new doctrines of the day.

"**Karl Marx (1818-1883)**," Mr. Hirsch wrote on the blackboard.

"He was born in the West German city of Trier," Mr. Hirsch said, "and he descended from a long line of rabbis, which explains why he has been called 'the last of the Hebrew prophets.' In fact, however, in order to attend a good school, and ultimately the universities of Bonn, Berlin, and Jena, Marx was baptized into the Christian faith when he was six."

"Marx's own teachings," Mr. Hirsch told us, "have their roots in the *dialectical approach* of Georg Wilhelm Friedrich Hegel, his philosophy professor at the University of Berlin."

Mr. Hirsch gave us a week to research the subject and write an essay. Mine, which paraphrased a pamphlet I found in the House of German-Soviet Friendship, received a grade of 1, which was the best. I still have a copy; it read like this:

The Dialectical Approach

By Hans Keller

The **dialectical approach** is a way of looking at the world that rejects the uncritical acceptance of *outward appearances*. Instead, it helps us gain true understanding of the *essence* of all the things we observe by focusing our attention on their *inner contradictions*, which, in turn, foreshadow *metamorphosis* or *inevitable change* in what we observe right now.

As an example, consider a tadpole swimming in a pond. An uncritical observer focuses on its outward appearance and describes it—perhaps, in great detail. And the thing so described is real, not a delusion. Yet still, the description is misleading because the tadpole is not a fixed thing! To understand its essence, we must recognize those inner contradictions—not in the sense of logical impossibilities, but in the sense of inner pressures and stresses, inner tension, inherent conflicts, opposing forces—that are bound to produce change, development, evolution, metamorphosis, revolution—call it what you like.

In our tadpole case, there is a hidden dynamic process at work that brings quantitative change (a bigger tadpole) and then qualitative change (a tadpole changing into a frog). The tadpole, thus, is but a transitory stage of a larger unfolding reality. In the same way, a person trained in the dialectical approach sees the fly in the maggot, the butterfly in the caterpillar, the oak in the acorn, and the apple, or even the new apple tree, in the apple blossom.

Mr. Hirsch said that my rendering was simply marvelous, and he posted it on the bulletin board in the hallway. He also used it as a springboard to explain Karl Marx.

"Karl Marx," he said, "didn't study tadpoles or acorns, but the social arrangements of people. For that purpose, he reviewed the popular descriptions of *economic systems*—of the social arrangements by which millions of people in every country cooperate in the production, distribution, and consumption of thousands of different goods. Unfortunately, Karl Marx found those descriptions inadequate, because the economists of his day—he called them 'vulgar economists' to draw attention to their shortsightedness—were focusing on the tadpole, that is, on outward appearances only. They failed to see the inner essence of these social arrangements."

Mr. Hirsch offered to enlighten us, and he did.

"When you focus on the outward appearance of an economy only," Mr. Hirsch continued, "things are simple enough. Just as we need certain ingredients to bake a cake—a baker, an oven, fuel, and, of course, flour, butter, milk, and so on—so we need a combination of *three kinds of resources* to make every single good that we produce.

First, and most obviously, we need *human resources* or *labor*; that is, the physical and mental effort of people. There can be no bread without the baker.

Second, we need *natural resources*; that is, the gifts of nature no human being has made. Think of land and all the plants and animals upon it, of the minerals and fuels underground, and even of the oceans teeming with life. There can be no bread without the land on which the bakery stands and on which the wheat is grown.

Third, we need *capital resources*; that is, the tools, widely defined, that people have made in the past. Here you must picture in your minds not just hammers and spades, but also factory buildings and blast furnaces, barns and warehouses, highways and railroads, horse-drawn carriages and trucks, milling machines and piles of raw materials in yard. There can be no bread without brick ovens and sacks filled with flour."

"The vulgar economists of Marx's day," Mr. Hirsch continued, "were content with describing the resources different countries had and the ways in which they used them to make goods and apportion them among people. But they failed to see the *essence* of the arrangement. Not so Karl Marx."

"He recognized a crucial fact: Most natural and capital resources in his day were *owned* by a tiny minority of the population, which he called the *capitalist class* or *bourgeoisie*. In contrast, the majority of people owned their own bodies only and they had to sell their labor in order to live. Marx called this majority the *working class* or *proletariat*."

"And Marx called this type of economic system *Capitalism*," Mr. Hirsch told us, "and he recognized an inner tension within it, which he called the *class struggle*. That struggle pitted the working class *against* the bourgeoisie. Inevitably, they struggled over the *economic surplus*, the difference between the value of goods produced and the amount needed to maintain the human, natural, and capital resources that helped produce those goods. To the extent that the greedy bourgeoisie kept the economic surplus, Marx said, it *exploited* the proletariat. This exploitation angered the workers and sooner or later, Marx predicted, they would expropriate the bourgeois exploiters and seize political power. Then a new era of *Communism* would be ushered in, as is happening in Ziesar, right here and now."

Well, that was quite a mouthful and explains, of course, why my mind had gone somewhere else long before Mr. Hirsch had finished. *There can be no bread without the baker* were the last words on my notepad that day and they took me straight back to the night over a year ago when I had spied on Fred Senf and Jutta Zweig making love among the newly baked loaves at the bakery shop. And that image, in turn, made me dream of Helga who was sitting right there, two rows in front of me, and who just might be persuaded to join me at the new movie house the Russians had opened on Castle Street. It certainly was worth a try. But Mr. Hirsch interrupted my reverie.

"Under Communism," he said triumphantly and with a loud voice, "the bourgeoisie is gone and the workers themselves own all the natural and capital resources in common. That makes them the masters of the productive process rather than its slaves."

"West Germany," Mr. Hirsch added, "is still a country of Capitalism, but, having studied Marx, we know its future!"

He pointed to the new slogan on our wall, a 1848 quotation from Karl Marx, he said, which nicely summarized Marx's grand vision of historic evolution:

"Let the ruling classes tremble. . . . The proletarians have nothing to lose but their chains. They have a world to win. WORKING MEN OF ALL COUNTRIES, UNITE!"

******

Mr. Wolf, our Current Affairs teacher, continued the story on the very next day.

"Vladimir I. Lenin (1870–1924)," he wrote on the blackboard, right below the spot where Mr. Hirsch had written the name of Karl Marx. It had never been erased.

"Vladimir Ilyich Ulyanov, which was his original name," Mr. Wolf said. "He was born in Simbirsk, Russia. His father was a councilor of state and later became a nobleman, but his brother was hanged for complicity in an attempt on the life of Czar Alexander III. That led Lenin to study Marx, in addition to his law books at the University of Kazan. Lenin was deeply influenced by G.V. Plekhanov, who organized the first Russian Marxist group. By 1895, in St. Petersburg, Lenin founded the League of Struggle for the Liberation of the Working Class."

Too much screeching of chalk at the blackboard. I stuffed cotton balls into my ears—one of the few things for sale at the pharmacy—and thereby erased most of the annoying sound. And I stared at Helga. I loved her black hair. And I dreamed about her breasts. I imagined them to look like the Renoir girl in my pocket.

"But," Mr. Wolf continued much more quietly, "Lenin did more than spread Marx's ideas. He developed them further in a 1902 tract, entitled Shto dyelat? [What is to be done?] Workers, left to themselves, Lenin feared, only develop a *trade-union consciousness*; they become aware of the need to fight employers for better wages and working conditions, and that is it. They do not develop a *communist consciousness*; they do not recognize their possible role in abolishing *the entire capitalist wage system.* That realization is reached, Lenin argued, by intellectuals, who are trained to view the broad sweep of history and who must, therefore, raise the consciousness of the working class above the day-to-day bread-and-butter issues."

"And I couldn't care less," I said to myself.

"Such is done best," Mr. Wolf quoted Lenin, "by forming a highly centralized and secretive Party, a professional vanguard of highly disciplined and dedicated revolutionaries, who lead the workers to Communism."

"Indeed," concluded Mr. Wolf, "at a stormy Congress of the Russian Social Democratic Labor Party, which was held in London in 1903, these ideas of Lenin were discussed. The majority of delegates, the *Bolsheviks*, supported Lenin; a minority, the *Mensheviks*, opposed him. By 1917, when Lenin returned to Russia to lead the October revolution, his ideas had won out. The rest is history."

"This Communism stuff is really painful," I thought, "almost as bad as Uncle Eddy's sermons."

But there was to be no relief. Within days, Mr. Wolf turned to another one of our new gods. **"Joseph V. Stalin (1879–   ),"** he wrote on the blackboard.

"Yossif Vissarionovich Dzhugashvili was his original name," Mr. Wolf said. "He was born in Gori, Georgia. Like Lenin, he was repeatedly arrested, jailed, and exiled, but always escaped. By 1912, as a member of the Central Committee of the Bolshevik Party, he put out first issue of *Pravda*, the major Soviet newspaper of today. And *Pravda* means what?"

"The Truth," we answered in unison.

"Excellent," Mr. Wolf said. "Before the year is up, we'll read an entire issue of it. All it takes is a lot of hard, honest work, which precisely what Comrade Stalin would expect of you."

Mr. Wolf held up a copy of *Pravda* and pointed to a line at the top of the front page.

"Rabochii vsech stran, soyedinyaetyez!" it said. "Workers of all countries, unite!"

"Sooner or later," Mr. Wolf continued, "just as a tadpole turns into a frog, the hidden inner forces of Capitalism will lead to Communism, a classless society in which all resources are owned and used in common. This change in property relationships will, in turn, Comrade Stalin predicts, produce a dramatic change in the *outlook* of people. A new type of Selfless Person will emerge, who contributes freely to the welfare of all and who gladly follows Marx's command:

From each according to his ability, to each according to his need."

******

Mr. Wolf also said it was time to put Stalin's ideas into practice. Accordingly, he arranged for all the 8th graders to stay out of school for two weeks and join the sugar beet campaign. In the first week, every morning at sunrise, we were assigned to various farms to help with the sugar beet harvest. By afternoon, teams of horses pulled big wagons full of beets into the village and we dumped them in the farmers' yards.

In the second week, we scrubbed the beets with brushes and cut them up and loaded them into big copper kettles half full of water. The kettles reminded me of the one in our attic in Berlin where my mother had washed our clothes. Apparently the raw material campaign had never made it to here. Just like the village church bells, these kettles hadn't been melted down. We stayed up all night stoking the wood fire and stirring the beets with large wooden ladles. After endless hours, the beets became a sauce, which turned golden and then brown. And then the sauce thickened and the brown mush changed to black with a lighter crust, while our eyes turned red from lack of sleep.

Finally, in the end, our tired feet, hundreds of little bare feet, carried earthen vessels filled with black syrup, and metal boxes brimming with brown sugar, into house after house throughout the village. That was our first practical experience with *Communism*, and our work made Mr. Wolf very happy.

Indeed, I seem to have learned Mr. Wolf's lesson very well, because later that fall I twice *volunteered* to help other people, which was proof positive that the spirit of Communism had found a home in my heart. The first occasion involved Mr. Kalitz who had been ordered to plow a field, but had trouble doing so on account of his bum leg. Following my suggestion, he hooked up a team of oxen to a plow and guided them, while I managed the plow handles behind them and did the harder part of the work. After that, I even volunteered to help Uncle Eddy ready the church for the Harvest Thanksgiving Service. I loaded up the altar with piles of potatoes and apples, with asparagus, melons, and sugar beets, and also with carrots, celery, and bundles of wheat. It was a pretty sight, but that day ended badly, nevertheless. Just when we were finished, my father came in and landed an uppercut on Uncle Eddy's chin, almost knocking him to the ground, right there in front of the altar! I suppose Uncle Eddy had had it coming for a long time, but it still was a big surprise to me, this being the first and only time I had ever seen my father do anything like that. I soon found out why.

Earlier in the day, a car had gotten out of control and run into a tree near the Town Hall where my father was working. He had run out and found the driver unconscious, leaning over the steering wheel. Just then Uncle Eddy had come along and made a spectacle of himself by laughing loudly. Instead of helping the injured driver, Uncle Eddy had pointed to a couple of little statues dangling from the rear view mirror, one of St. Anthony, the other of Maria, the Mother of God.

"Just look," Uncle Eddy had laughed, "how their false gods protect the Catholics!"

That would have been enough to set my father off, but there was another thing. Later on, little Helmut had seen Uncle Eddy walk along the opposite side of our street and had called out to him, "Uncle Eddy! Uncle Eddy!" and Uncle Eddy, the proud Superintendent of the Lutheran Church, had raced across the street and boxed Helmut's ears mercilessly for making such a spectacle of him. I suppose this must have reminded my father of that fateful day in 1940 Berlin when Uncle Eddy had made him do pushups on the sidewalk because of a similar infraction.

"Don't you ever lay a hand on my children again," my father said after he had knocked Uncle Eddy to the ground.

✶✶✶✶✶✶

On the day school started again, I saw Uncle Herbert in front of the Town Hall. He tore down all the black market signs from the bulletin board:

"For Sale: One Rug for a Radio." And "Wanted: Razor Blades, have Eggs."

Then he posted a newspaper story inside the glass case; I copied all of it:

October 1, 1946

After more than a year, the Nuremberg trial of top Nazi leaders concluded today.

It took 403 sessions and 16,000 pages of transcripts to reach these verdicts:

Death by hanging:

- Hermann Göring (most influential Nazi leader, next to Hitler)
- Joachim von Ribbentrop (Foreign Minister, active in the deportation of Jews from France and Italy to extermination camps)
- Ernst Kaltenbrunner (Chief of the Reich Security Office and Gestapo)
- Alfred Rosenberg (chief racial ideologist, editor of the *People's Observer*)
- Hans Frank (Minister and Reich Commissioner for Justice, Governor of Occupied Poland)
- Wilhelm Frick (Minister of the Interior, author of Nazi racial laws)
- Julius Streicher (Editor-in-Chief of the anti-Semitic paper, *Der Stürmer*)
- Fritz Sauckel (Plenipotentiary General for the Allocation of Labor; imported 5 million slave laborers from France and Eastern Europe)
- Artur Seyss-Inquart (Austrian Chancellor, managed annexation, later Reich Commissioner of the Occupied Netherlands)
- Field Marshal General Wilhelm Keitel (Military Chief of Staff)
- General Alfred Jodl (Chief of the Operations Section of the German Army, imported forced labor from Denmark, Belgium, Holland and France)

- Martin Bormann, in absentia (Hitler's Deputy in charge of Party affairs, arranged expulsion of millions of Jews to Polish death camps, as well as the utilization of Ukrainian slave labor)

Life in prison:

- Rudolf Hess (once Hitler's Deputy)
- Walther Funk (once Hitler's Press Chief, later Minister of Economics, later President of the Reichsbank
- Grand Admiral Erich Raeder (Commander-in-Chief of the Navy)

20 years:

- Baldur von Schirach (Hitler Youth Leader)
- Albert Speer (Reich Minister for Armaments and Munitions)

15 years:

- Baron Constantin von Neurath (Foreign Minister, later Governor of Occupied Bohemia and Moravia)

10 years:

- Grand Admiral Karl Dönitz (Commander-in-Chief of the Navy and later successor to the Führer)

Acquitted:

- Hjalmar Schacht (Banker)
- Franz von Papen (Chancellor June-November 1932, then Hitler's Vice Chancellor and diplomat)
- Hans Fritzsche (Radio Broadcaster)

Note: Additional trials for crimes against humanity will be held later against diplomats, doctors, leaders of the economy, scientists, and other generals.

Uncle Herbert also pinned a new poster to the Thousand-Year Oak. It had a picture of Adolf Hitler on it, but Hitler's face was turning onto a skull. There were only two words on the poster. "Nuremberg, Guilty!" it said.

Langewiesche-Brandt, Ebenhausen near München, Germany

37. MISGIVINGS

[November 1946 – June 1947]

During my last year of school in Ziesar, things happened that made me suspicious of the New Marxist Society that Lieutenant Trapeznikov was so eager to build. Mostly, these were events at school, but a letter from Aunt Martel at graduation time confirmed my qualms. It started in 1946, just before Christmas vacation, when Mrs. Dietrich reappeared in her new role as our teacher of math.

"Our subject this week," she said, "is the mathematics of interest. It is a lot of fun and you can master it in no time, because you have already studied percentages and exponents, both of which come in handy here."

"Picture a country in which people lend and borrow money at an annual interest rate of 5%," Mrs. Dietrich continued. "In such a place, someone who lent out 100 Marks for 1 year would expect to receive a reward of 5% of 100 Marks, or 5 Marks, in a year, collecting a total of 105 Marks. That's simple enough. But things get more complicated once we consider longer periods of time. For example, if that person then lent out the 105 Marks for another year, the money would grow by 5% of 105 Marks, or 5.25 Marks, in the second year, reaching a total of 110.25 Marks."

"This process of turning present Marks into a larger amount of future Marks with the help of an interest rate is called *compounding*," Mrs. Dietrich continued, "and it is easily summarized by a simple formula."

She put the formula on the board, along with her example:

Compounding

If we denote

- the present time by 0 and, therefore, the present value of money by PV_0,
- the annual interest rate by i (such that 5% is written out as 5/100 or .05), and
- the future time by t and, therefore, the future value of money by FV_t, then

$$FV_t = PV_0 (1 + i)^t$$

Example:

Given an annual interest rate of 5%, 100 Marks in year 0 turn into what in 2 years?

$FV_2 = 100 (1 + .05)^2 = 100 (1.05)^2 = 100 (1.1025) = 110.25$

Mrs. Dietrich asked us to figure out what we would get back in 5 years, if we put 100 Marks into a savings account now.

"127.63 Marks," I said, after working with the formula.

"Excellent," Mrs. Dietrich said. "But now answer this: If you lived in our hypothetical 5% interest country and someone who owed you money had promised to pay you 127.63 Marks in 5 years, how much money might you just as well accept now as full payment of that debt?"

"100 Marks," Helga said before I could.

"Because one could put 100 Marks into a savings account and still get 127.63 Marks in 5 years," I quickly added.

"Precisely," said Mrs. Dietrich, "and that brings us to the second part of our lesson."

"The reverse process of using the interest rate to turn future Marks into a smaller, but equivalent amount of present Marks is called *discounting*," Mrs. Dietrich said, and she put this second formula on the board, along with our second example:

Discounting

$$PV_0 = \frac{FV_t}{(1 + i)^t}$$

Example:

Given an annual interest rate of 5%, 127.63 Marks to be received in 5 years are worth what now?

$$PV_0 = \frac{127.63}{(1 + .05)^5} = \frac{127.63}{(1.05)^5} = \frac{127.63}{1.2763} = 100$$

"However," said Mrs. Dietrich, "the pure mathematics of interest, although fun, should not blind us to the most important lesson to be learned here today: Like the earning of profit, the charging of interest is a *deeply immoral act*! Great men—from Moses to Aristotle, from Mohammed to Thomas Aquinas—have recognized this fact over the centuries. So have, more recently, Marx, Lenin, and Stalin. The taking of interest, they have pointed out, occurs routinely under Capitalism; it is but another way by which the bourgeoisie exploits the proletariat. But soon, under Communism, where all resources will be owned jointly by the working class, the very concept of interest will disappear."

I didn't know at the time how much trouble Comrade Dietrich's little lesson in morality would bring me in years to come. And that some people would actually end up in concentration camps for their unwillingness to accept the Marxian view of interest!

******

Ever since Mr. Kalitz had had that wonderful fight with Uncle Herbert in the school auditorium, I had taken to hanging out with him at the grocery store after school. I liked talking with him a lot better than taking the piano lessons long ago, in which I had invariably failed. The day of Mrs. Dietrich's lesson on interest was no exception. Having heard my story, Mr. Kalitz said he had just what I needed. He sent me to the attic to retrieve his old college textbooks from a big green box and he quickly selected two of them: Eugen von Böhm-Bawerk, *Karl Marx and the Close of his System*, 1898, and, by the same author, *Capital and Interest*, 4th edition, 1921.

"Now there you'll meet some common sense," Mr. Kalitz said.

"Böhm-Bawerk was a famous Austrian economist and once even Austria's Minister of Finance," he explained. "He'll tell you what Karl Marx and your Uncle Herbert have in common. They're both idiots."

I spent a fascinating afternoon with Mr. Kalitz. He said he had majored in economics at Berlin's Humboldt University in the 1920s and he had just loved Böhm-Bawerk. With respect to interest, he said, it arose in *all* societies and for a good reason: It was *not* a phenomenon of the class struggle between the haves and the have-nots, as Marxists claimed, but a phenomenon of *barter across time*. I should read the books and write an essay on the subject for Mrs. Dietrich, he said.

I did and got us both into big trouble. But I kept my essay to this day. It went like this:

Thoughts About Interest

By Hans Keller

The phenomenon of **interest** occurs in all societies and reflects two facts unrelated to the class struggle and very much related to the inevitable passage of **time.**

First, there is **time preference**: Given the uncertainties of life—people are mortal and never know when they will die—consumers everywhere, when given the choice, prefer goods now to identical goods in the future. Therefore, people can be persuaded to save current income, lend it to someone else, and, by this very act, unnecessarily *forgo* current consumption goods, only by the promise of a future return that *exceeds* their current sacrifice. In short, impatient, mortal consumers, who hate abstinence and waiting, may, nevertheless, lend out part of the money they now have—as long as they get it back in the future with a sufficiently large *interest premium* that enables them to acquire an amount of future consumption goods in excess of the amount currently sacrificed.

Second, there is **time productivity**: It is a technical fact that producers everywhere can permanently raise output by employing indirect, time-consuming methods of production. If they cut the production of consumption goods now, producers can use the resources so released to make capital goods, and they can then employ these capital goods to produce a permanently larger flow of consumption goods in the future. This technological fact enables producers to pay the interest premium that impatient consumers demand before they are willing to give up their claim on current consumption goods.

The famous Austrian economist Böhm-Bawerk told a story like this:

Think of Robinson Crusoe, all alone on his apparently deserted island, surrounded by nothing but natural resources and possessing no capital resources of any kind. With his bare hands, and perhaps a stick, he might catch 8 small fishes a day. Over time, his daily food production might equal 8...8...8..., and so on, forever. Now let him go hungry for a day and *sacrifice* the 8 fishes he might have caught. He could use his time to make a net and build a canoe. Starting the next day, being the new and proud owner of *capital*, he could paddle to the middle of a lake or venture onto the ocean on a calm day and catch 16 fishes a day or 8 in half the time. And he could spend the rest of the time repairing net and canoe, making them last forever. So food production could equal the series 8...0...16...16...16... and so on, forever. The 8-fish sacrifice on a single day would have yielded an 8-fish *increase* in output on all future days, a return of 100% interest per day!

Shortly after I had handed my essay to Mrs. Dietrich, for the kind of extra credit she always solicited, all hell broke out. I was summoned to the principal's office and Miss Mahler said my essay was an insult to the new Marxist society we were building. She demanded I hand in my Böhm-Bawerk books.

"They should be burned," she said and she also wanted to know where I had gotten such trash. I didn't tell her and she said that I had seriously compromised my chances of going to high school.

Unfortunately, Mr. Kalitz's name was found in the books and my Uncle Herbert, the mayor, had no trouble making the connection. The People's Police searched Mr. Kalitz's house. He wasn't home at the time, but they knew how to get in. From the looks of it, they busted open the door with their boots; the wood was ripped from all the hinges. And later that week, Mr. Kalitz had to bring his ID papers to the Mayor's office. Uncle Herbert put a red rubber stamp on the front page.

"Enemy of the People," it said.

******

"So it's starting again; it's starting all over again," my father said. "They are burning books, and the Gestapo has been replaced by the People's Police."

My parents told me to stay away from Mr. Kalitz, but I lied when I said I would. He was just too interesting and we went back a long time, all the way to the days of the war when we had listened to the BBC. But my father said *he* would help me with my history essay for Mr. Hirsch; so I let him.

Mr. Hirsch had said that Marxism was now conquering the world because of the historic inevitability thing, Capitalism collapsing from its inner tensions and Communism taking its place. He had put a long list of countries on the blackboard to prove his point: Poland, Rumania, Bulgaria, Yugoslavia, Hungary, Czechoslovakia, and Eastern Germany—all these, he said, were ready to embrace the New Society. And others would surely follow: Western Germany, Italy, France— everywhere Communist Parties were flourishing. He wanted us to *explain* these trends.

But I shouldn't have asked my father. My father said it was a psychological thing. The Communists were focusing their attention on the poorest workers everywhere. And they explained the harshness of their lives not by natural circumstances—such as lack of education, lack of training, lack of health, lack of fertile land and fancy tools to work with. Nor did they explain it by the workers' personal failings—such as their own stupidity or laziness, perhaps. The explained the workers' miserable lives rather by their *exploitation* by greedy capitalists. As the Communists put it, the workers are poor not because they produce so little, but because they produce a lot and the bourgeois capitalists routinely steal most of their output!

"Now," my father said, and one could just hear the old SPD man coming back to life, "contrast this analysis with Marx's vague vision of a better future: Although he provides no detail, he holds before the poor workers the promise of a *classless* society (no more thieving capitalists), a society run by joyful workers (no more being bossed around by harsh commands or coaxed to work by some minimum wage). Marx promises a society where workers—the proud owners of *all* resources— produce a lot and gladly share their riches (no more hunger and misery)."

"That's a powerful story," my father concluded. "How could one *not* join the Communist Party?"

He said so mockingly and he sounded just like Mr. Kalitz. That's when my mother joined in, which was a first on matters like this and, therefore, a big surprise.

"Do you know what a Rorschach test is?" she asked.

And when I said no, she told me about the inkblots and different people interpreting them differently and psychologists analyzing these interpretations in order to look into people's minds.

"Well," she said, "when Marxists paint that vague picture of an ideal future, they are handing people a Rorschach inkblot into which they can then project their fondest dreams. And when they compare these dreams with all-too-real defects of actual societies, how can they possibly reject *that* future?"

"But no," she said, "you can't write any of this."

And I didn't, but my reservations about the New Society had just grown stronger still.

******

By the spring of 1947, I had a run-in with Mr. Wolf as well. He had dictated a few sentences in German about "Communism—the final stage of historical evolution" and he wanted us to translate all that into Russian.

"But Mr. Hirsch has taught us never to be fooled by outward appearances," I said, being the all-too-smart little troublemaker I had become. "We are always supposed to look for inner tensions that foreshadow further developments. Therefore, shouldn't we also look for inner tensions in Communism? From such tensions, perhaps, we could predict the disappearance of Communism and its replacement by something else."

"Just as we can predict the demise of the tadpole and the emergence of the frog," I added.

Mr. Wolf was not happy. He said I was disrupting the class and that there were no inner tensions in Communism—*by definition*!

I should have let it go, but I didn't.

"You can't *define* away the truth," I said—what a teenager I had become—and then I asked about all the farmers in Ziesar being hopping mad now that the land reform had expropriated them and had created the giant Ziesar Collective Farm, where nobody owned anything and everybody worked like a Marxian wage slave.

"Isn't that a kind of inner tension?" I asked.

That really made Mr. Wolf angry! He said I was a known rabble-rouser and I would be dealt with in due course. Within days, I was assigned to work with the carpenter after school to drain my excess energy. The carpenter was putting up a giant portrait of Karl Marx, because our school had just been renamed from People's School Ziesar to Karl Marx School Ziesar. In addition, I had to write an essay on the *life* of Karl Marx, to be handed in at the principal's office within two weeks.

That's why I had another consultation with Mr. Kalitz who, in my view at least, knew everything. He did not disappoint me.

******

"Marx's father was actually a prosperous lawyer," Mr. Kalitz said. "He had refused to become a rabbi and thus broken a long family tradition. Karl loved him, they say, but hated his Dutch mother who would not support her son's lifelong tendency to live off others. My God, for years, that guy lived off his parents, then his in-laws, and then his friend and collaborator, Friedrich Engels. Ironically, the Engels family owned textile factories in Germany and England, but Marx wasn't bothered by taking all their exploitation money."

I was taking notes furiously.

"Also, we should note that Marx led a wild student life," Mr. Kalitz said, "carousing and drinking and engaging in fist fights and duels and sinking heavily into debt. I think that's why he had to leave the university at Bonn and then Berlin, but, finally, he got a philosophy degree at Jena, a well-known diploma mill."

That diploma mill part required some explanation, and I just loved it.

"Then what?" Mr. Kalitz asked himself. "Oh yeah, he was a newspaper editor for a while, which got him into trouble with the Prussian authorities. So he emigrated to France, Belgium, and England, where he settled down in the British Museum, reading and writing for years. He's buried in London, too. Saw his grave once."

"And one more thing," Mr. Kalitz added. "They have told you, no doubt, about all the religious fervor that made the workers put out the Communist Manifesto of 1848? Well, in fact, it was not written by workers at all, but by Karl Marx and a tiny group of radical intellectuals, all under the age of 30 at the time and all of them the offspring of privilege, calling themselves the proletariat."

"And here's a joke for you," Mr. Kalitz said. "When you're 20 and not a Communist, you have no heart. When you're 30 and still a Communist, you have no brain."

I just loved that man!

"My God," he added, "just look at what's happening on Ziesar's new collective farm! Do you think anybody, and I mean anybody, will ever again spend all weekend lovingly washing and waxing those new tractors or repairing and painting the barns? When they were privately owned, that's exactly what happened. Now that nobody owns them, they'll fall into disrepair in no time. Just watch and see!"

This time around, I used my head. I put none of this into my essay. Instead, I paraphrased an essay on the life of Karl Marx from a pamphlet at the House of German-Soviet Friendship. Miss Mahler was real happy and gave me a gold star.

******

I should get to the letter I mentioned earlier. In June of 1947, just before graduation time, we received a letter from Aunt Martel and it shocked us all. She was working then for the tax department of West Berlin; that part was fine. But her friend Eva, now living in East Berlin, had a new job in Oranienburg and had told her that the Sachsenhausen concentration camp was back in business!

There were tens of thousands of prisoners, she had told her. Some of the new prisoners were German officers transferred from Western Allied camps, others were former Nazi officials. There were also Nazi collaborators, like film and theater directors and SS doctors. But many of the prisoners, and this was the shocking thing, were alleged anti-Communists, who had confessed under torture. Still others were alleged werewolves, who had been denounced by someone for "acts against the Soviet occupation forces." In addition, and perhaps even more surprising, there were thousands of *Russian* inmates. They included former POWs who had been classified as Nazi collaborators, because they hadn't fought to the death, and large numbers of regular soldiers who had contacted venereal diseases in Germany.

"There we go again," my father said. "Now they do it in the name of Marx."

"What are venereal diseases?" I asked.

My mother told me to ask my father and my father told me to ask my mother.

38. THE INTELLIGENTSIA
[August 1947 – March 1948]

In the summer of 1947, the teachers of Ziesar's Karl Marx School had a faculty meeting. There had been thirty graduates and, as was customary at the time, 10 percent of them were to be selected to go on to high school and then the university. The rest would spend four years in various apprenticeships, work for two more years as journeymen, and emerge, by age 20 or so, as Masters in their fields—as fully qualified bakers, blacksmiths, butchers, carpenters, electricians, farmers, plumbers, and the like. Temporarily, I was assigned to work with the village carpenter, but that faculty meeting would determine the rest of my life.

My parents wanted me to go on to high school—as the crow flies, the nearest one was 33 kilometers away in Burg near Magdeburg—but my chances of selection seemed slim. For one thing, only three of us could go; for another, the commandant had made it clear that children of workers and peasants were to be preferred. Would my father at least qualify as a worker?

Beyond that, I was convinced that many teachers hated me. I thought of Pastor Jahn, the new Geography teacher, and how often I had annoyed him till he was red in the face. I remembered asking him whether Hitler and Stalin had been appointed by God (Romans 13: There is no government authority except from God, and wherever governmental authority exists it has been instituted by God).....asking him how Noah got all those animals to go into the ark.....asking him how to link up the "three gods," Father, Son, and Holy Ghost, with his ice-water-steam analogy.....and asking him whether we might examine the usefulness of prayer by finding out how many loved ones in our village had been prayed for or not at all and how many members of each group had survived the war....He had called me an "impudent brat" and "a rotten city kid," and even "a Satanic child." He had beaten me up when he could. Why would he vote for me now?

And I thought similarly of Newteacher Wolf, whom I had pounded with questions about the chain reaction evaporating the Pacific and our groundwater alike and then all of it raining right back, and, more recently, about Communism having inner tensions and, therefore, *not* being the last stage of history.

And then there was, of course, that flap about interest and the Böhm-Bawerk books, which had gotten me into trouble with Math teacher Mrs. Dietrich and principal Miss Mahler, and, last but not least, there was the hooliganism thing with Physics teacher Clausen, who had been furious with me for questioning that "1 meter per second per second" thing and had called me an "anti-social parasite" for helping to hang him out of the window. Things didn't look good.

What I didn't know was that my mother had been talking to Aunt Liesel behind my back and that Uncle Herbert, the new SED mayor, had the final say in the selection process. So one day, as I was checking out his ever-growing collection of books, he came over from the Town Hall and told me that Helga Vogt and I would be among those going to high school in the fall. I was flabbergasted.

"Your rank in class couldn't have been topped," he said.

He must have seen the look of amazement on my face.

"It takes worker or peasant blood," I said.

"Or it takes pull," he grinned, "and I have a lot of that."

I was still staring in disbelief.

"You saved my life that night," he said, quite unexpectedly.

Considering the way I did it, putting him in the latrine, it was mighty decent of him to think so.

******

Later that summer, the whole village population got new ID booklets, each complete with a photograph and a fingerprint. We were supposed to carry them at all times, but they were good only for a 10 kilometer radius from home. Anyone who wanted to venture out farther, in order to visit an aunt in Brandenburg, perhaps, had to get a special permit from the People's Police and also had to register upon arrival at the destination. Helga and I, therefore, got a special stamp on page 3, authorizing us to travel back and forth by train between Ziesar and Burg. We also got a rubber stamp on the front page, which classified us as "Intelligentsia." Other people were classified as either "Workers" or "Peasants." That's how I discovered that my father was a worker after all.

"So the classless society still has classes," he said to my mother. "I can count three of them."

"Hush," my mother said, "don't get into any trouble now."

******

And thus, one morning at 6 A.M., enveloped in a cloud of black smoke, Helga and I rode off in the Iron Horse for the trip to Burg. I made sure to sit next to her, and we compared the provisions our mothers had managed to put together for us. My rucksack was filled with two jars of string beans, and my mother had packed a lot of potatoes around them. I also had two loaves of bread and a jar of red currant jam, but they were crammed into my leather satchel, along with Caesar's *De Bello Gallico* and a brand-new text, published by a Berlin/Leipzig Workers' Cooperative and entitled *Textbook of Physics for High Schools, Part I, containing 309 illustrations.* Helga had turnips and carrots and a big bundle of *Suppengrün* [soup greens], a common item then found in grocery stores, consisting of a bunch of vegetable stalks—celery, kohlrabi, parsley, red beets, and such—that were held together with a rubber band and were said to be perfect ingredients for a delicious soup. She also had a loaf of soggy rye bread, a hundred or so sheets of piano music, and our old Russian book. I suggested we have our meals together and benefit from the variety. I figured she knew that I wasn't really thinking of food; and she didn't say no. Then I took her Russian book and read the first page aloud.

"I love the Russian language, the language of our great neighbor to the east," it said.

The Russian soldiers in our compartment laughed, just as the commandant had when I tried the sentence on him some time ago.

At the railroad station in Burg, we could still read the slogans the Chain Hounds had painted. They had painted them in white, but someone had carefully covered each letter with tar. We could read the messages just as well in black.

WHEELS MUST ROLL FOR VICTORY, one sentence said.

THE FÜHRER IS ALWAYS RIGHT, said another.

RIFLES TO THE PEOPLE, said the third.

******

My new Monday-through-Friday home was a room in the Fischers' second-floor apartment, located on a little side street not very far from my new school. Just as the rest of the apartment, my room was super clean. It had light, newly polished oak floors and light birch wood furniture to match: a twin bed with a single blanket, a desk, a wash basin with an oval mirror, and a water pitcher.

"Worthy of a monk," I thought, and that's when I noted the picture of Wartburg Castle hanging on the wall, the place where Martin Luther translated the Bible and threw an ink bottle at the devil. It seemed to be everywhere.

There were two windows in my room, without curtains, shades or screens, looking down onto the cobblestone street. The sun was shining when I first got there, and the room looked bright, friendly, and peaceful. Across the street was a bottling company which I was to visit often during my high school years; they spent all day filling heavy glass bottles with my favorite green woodruff drink. But I didn't know that at first. What I did see was the slogan on their white-washed wall, carefully painted over, but legible, nevertheless.

NATIONAL SOCIALIST ORDER OR BOLSHEVIK CHAOS, it said.

Actually, there was someone else destined to live in my room, but I didn't learn about that till three months later when Mr. Fischer came home from his tour.

Mrs. Fischer loved all the food I had brought and showed me pictures of her husband. He was a huge man, very much like Mr. Albrecht, but he was made of muscles instead of fat. I could tell because he was almost naked in all the pictures. Believe it or not, he was wrestling with a circus bear and doing all kinds of amazing stunts!

******

The Hans and Sophie Scholl High School, a large building made of dark red bricks, looked just like my school in Berlin. Even my classroom was identical, except that a picture of Ernst Thälmann had replaced that of Frederick the Great. I had never heard of the man, but that omission was soon remedied in our Modern History class. Ernst Thälmann, we learned, was a famous Communist, born in Hamburg in 1886. As a young man, he joined the Transport Workers' Union and the SPD [Social Democratic Party of Germany]. Later, during the Weimar Republic, he became the leader of the newly formed KPD [Communist Party of Germany], a member of the Reichstag, and even the Party's presidential candidate in 1932, when he garnered 13.2 percent of the vote as compared to Hitler's 30.1 percent. In 1933, he was dragged to Gestapo headquarters at Berlin's Prinz Albrecht Strasse and terribly tortured. In the end, he was held in solitary confinement at the Buchenwald concentration camp, where he was executed in 1944.

Dr. Hertling, our History teacher, also explained the name of our school. Hans and Sophie Scholl had been university students and members of a secret anti-Hitler group, called the White Rose. In February 1943, following student demonstrations against Hitler in Munich, they were arrested and instantly beheaded. But Dr. Hertling didn't usually tell such gruesome stories. In fact, he was a sweet old man with white hair, who taught not only History, but also German, English, Latin, and Geography. Being Head Teacher, he also graded us on Behavior, Cooperativeness, Industry, and Penmanship.

We had only three other teachers, despite the fact that we spent 3 hours each per week on 13 subjects. In addition to Dr. Hertling, we had Dr. Kahlenberg (Biology, Chemistry, Physics, and Mathematics), Dr. Schablin (Art and Music), and Newteacher Mr. Klaus (Russian and Sports).

******

Dr. Hertling, I soon discovered, was not only kind, but also incredibly smart. He certainly deserved the "intelligentsia" label. Consider how he taught the subject of Geography.

"In your schooling so far," he said, "you have all studied Geography with the help of maps drawn on two-dimensional pieces of paper. That was good enough for learning the names and locations of all the countries of the world and of their major cities and rivers and mountain ranges and such. But, as you well know, the earth is *not* a flat plane. It is a globe, and this fact requires us to rethink much of what you have learned so far."

Then Dr. Hertling placed a large globe on the table and, turning to the blackboard, seemed to turn into a teacher of math.

"You are all familiar with the facts," he said, "that the sum of angles in a right triangle comes to 180 degrees and that all kinds of computations about specific angles within such a triangle, and about the lengths of specific sides of such a triangle, can be made with the help of certain trigonometry rules about sines and cosines and such."

As a reminder, he wrote this on the board as he spoke.

Concerning a right triangle on a plane:

1) Choose any acute angle (i.e., any angle of less than 90 degrees) in such a triangle. Then the ratio of the length of the side opposite to this acute angle to the length of the hypotenuse is called the **sine.**

2) Choose any acute angle (i.e., any angle of less than 90 degrees) in such a triangle. Then the ratio of the length of the side adjacent to this acute angle to the length of the hypotenuse is called the **cosine.**

"Well, guess what?" Dr. Hertling continued, as he turned around to face his globe and us at the same time. "Once you leave behind the blackboard-like *plane* and turn to the more realistic *globe*, all those rules change!"

"Once you consider spherical triangles, such as triangles drawn on this globe, for instance," he said, "all of their sides are *curves* rather than straight lines, and the sum of angles in such triangles can lie anywhere between a minimum of 180 degrees and a maximum of 540 degrees!" That certainly was a surprise, at least to me!

"And the difference between the sum of the angles of a spherical triangle and the sum of the angles of a plane triangle is called *spherical excess*," Dr. Hertling added.

I was amazed. That day, we reviewed all sorts of rules for sines and cosines in triangles drawn on a plane and learned about new and different rules, called *Napier's Rules*, which applied to sines and cosines in triangles found on a globe.

"John Napier," Dr. Hertling said, "was a Scottish mathematician, who lived from 1550 to 1617. He invented logarithms as well as the rules of spherical trigonometry, which we shall apply now to the globe called Earth."

And so we did, after Dr. Hertling put this graph on the board:

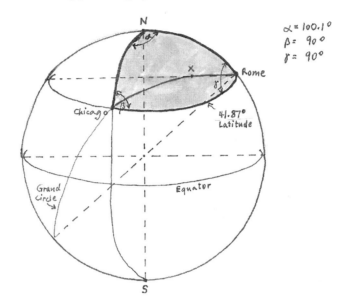

"Consider Chicago and Rome," he said. "They are located on a globe with a radius of 6,370 kilometers. Both cities lie on the same latitude of 41.87 degrees north of the equator. Their longitudes differ by $\alpha = 100.1$ degrees. Now focus on the shaded spherical triangle that is formed by the longitude lines going through Chicago and Rome, respectively, and the latitude line between the two. Notice how much we already know about this triangle:

- We know that $\alpha = 100.1$ degrees, the difference between the two longitudes.
- We know that $\beta = 90$ degrees; it is, after all, the angle between Chicago's longitude line (pointing due North towards the North Pole at N) and its latitude line (pointing due East towards Rome).
- We know that $\gamma = 90$ degrees; it is the angle between Rome's longitude line (pointing due North towards the North Pole at N) and its latitude line (pointing due West towards Chicago).

- We also know the distance between Rome and the North Pole (and the identical distance between Chicago and the North Pole); it is 90 degrees (the North Pole to Equator angle) minus the Rome/Chicago latitude of 41.87 degrees. Thus it is 48.13 degrees.

And here are some questions:

a) What is the distance between the two cities, if one travels along their common line of latitude?

b) What is the shortest distance between the two cities along the *grand circle* going through point X?

c) What is the take-off course flown by an airplane that wants to fly the grand circle from Rome to Chicago?

d) Where on this grand circle will the airplane reach the northernmost point?"

Using Napier's Rules, we found the answers in no time:

- a = 8,287 km
- b = 7,745 km
- c = 308.55 degrees, or Northwest, if we call East 90 degrees, South 180 degrees, West 270 degrees, and North 360 degrees
- d = at point X, at latitude 54.39 degrees north of the equator, comparable to the latitude of the Baltic seaport of Kiel

Before our first month was up, Dr. Hertling helped us compute dozens of similar problems. One involved a trip in the southern hemisphere, between Cape Town and Sydney, both of them located on the same 33.9 degrees of latitude *south* of the equator, but separated by 8.8483 degrees of longitude. Other problems involved Berlin (latitude 52.41° north; longitude 13.11° east), Hong Kong (latitude 22.30° north; longitude 114.17° east); Moscow (latitude 55.76° north; longitude 37.57° east); New York (latitude 40.76° north; longitude 73.97° west), Paris (latitude 48.84° north; longitude 2.34° east); Stockholm (latitude 59.34° north; longitude 18.06° east); and Vienna (latitude 48.23° north; longitude 16.34° east).

I figured that an airplane flying the grand circle between Hong Kong and Paris would fly a distance of 9,628 kilometers and would, in the absence of wind, need a northwesterly take-off heading of 322.26 degrees, while landing on a southwesterly heading of 239.35 degrees. And I kept dreaming of being a pilot one day.

******

Dr. Kahlenberg's Physics class was equally fascinating. Once again, I figured right away that he was very, very smart; not because of the many subjects he taught, but because of the way he taught them. Our new textbook was filled with pictures of Russian geniuses who had invented and discovered *everything*, from the microscope to the phonograph and steam engine, from electromagnetism to Jovian moons and the frequencies of sound. But Dr. Kahlenberg kept telling us about the stupid capitalists who had attributed these feats to men like Jansen, Edison and Watt, or even Maxwell, Galileo, and Hertz. But he always had a twinkle in his eye.

"But one thing is true," he said, just in case someone had missed that twinkle, "the first successful transmission of information via electric waves occurred in 1895 and was made by the Russian physicist Alexander Popov. His Italian colleague, Guglielmo Marconi, repeated the experiment two years later and over a longer distance."

Dr. Kahlenberg's teaching of astronomy was even more intriguing. He called it Outer Space Science and his teaching also involved a large globe, but this one was all black and was called the *celestial sphere*. We were to imagine us earthlings near the very center of this globe, at some point of observation, called X, with the zenith, Z, directly above us and the nadir, Z', directly below us, diametrically opposite the zenith. By projecting the earth axis onto point P, the position of Polaris, also known as the North Star (and always sitting at the end of the handle of the Little Dipper), we were to imagine the *World Axis*, PP'. And, at a right angle to that axis, we were to picture the *Heavenly Equator* (on which the three prominent stars of Orion were sitting).

"The celestial sphere rotates around the world axis," Dr. Kahlenberg said after he had finished painting the picture of it all on the blackboard.

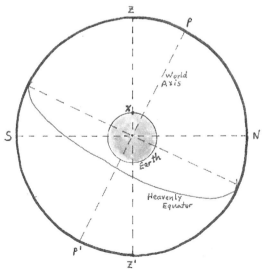

Before long, we learned about the paths of various celestial objects, their culmination ("the highest point they reach above an observer's horizon"), their declination ("the angular distance to the object, measured north or south from the heavenly equator"), their eccentricity ("the deviation of the object's path from a perfect circle"), and so much more. In the end, we knew about star days and sun days ("the time between two successive culminations) and even the computation of Central European Time!

"When and where does the sun rise and set in Berlin on October 25?" was one of my homework assignments.

"It rises at 6:54:37 Central European Time in a southeasterly direction of 109.95 degrees. It sets at 16:46:37 CET in a southwesterly direction of 250.05 degrees," was my answer.

Helga had a different assignment: "On which days of the year does the sun rise in Göttingen in a direction of 111.66 degrees and at what times does it rise?"

We figured out the answers together: "The days were February 2 and October 29. The respective times were 7:43:32 CET and 7:13:2 CET."

Then we went to the movies. Astronomy and movies went together perfectly, for the movies were shown in the planetarium, and we could look through the telescope afterwards. We loved the fairy tale movies the Russians showed, and we loved to look at the moon. She let me hold her hand.

******

But I had other extra-curricular activities as well. On the last day of November, the day on which the United Nations voted to partition Palestine between Arabs and Jews, Mr. Fischer appeared, having finished his circus tour, and he was delighted at having me for a "son." On many a Saturday morning, before Helga and I took the train back to Ziesar, Mr. Fischer took me out to the forest to catch rabbits. Because guns were not allowed, he used a pink ferret as a substitute. When Mr. Fischer found a warren, and somehow he always did, he covered all of the exits with nets and sent in the ferret. Sometimes, we would get a dozen fat rabbits in ten minutes. The ferret always sucked their blood, but we ate a lot of rabbit meat. Unlike in later years, when I had rabbits as pets and struggled with the thought that animals, just like people, surely had *souls*—an idea that my Uncle Eddy vehemently denied—I didn't feel any sympathy with their plight. Perhaps we had been too hungry too often, which made our sudden rabbit wealth seem like a special gift at Christmas time, not unlike the fatted geese we all used to eat way back in Berlin.

But there was one drawback. Mrs. Fischer made Mr. Fischer put the ferret in *my* room at night, and it ran back and forth a lot, making a racket with its claws on the bare floor. I often wondered whether it would suck my blood while I slept and I didn't sleep well at all.

Mr. Fischer also brought home a lot of other things. He went on several trips to West Germany and crossed the Iron Curtain at night in a manner he wouldn't discuss. Once—I remember the day in late January of 1948 because the radio was full of stories about Mohandas K. Gandhi having been killed by a Hindu—Mr. Fischer came back with mountains of cigarettes, coffee, and oranges. On another trip, he got dozens of bicycle inner tubes—an extremely rare and precious commodity at the time—and a suitcase full of herrings. I went to Burg's Russian quarter to pick him up whenever he came back from one of these outings, which was strange considering how afraid everybody still was of the Russians, but it was the proper way to do things around there. Mr. Fischer couldn't very well walk out of the front of the railroad station with all the German policemen milling about and showing off their newly acquired rifles and bayonets.

It worked like this: Mr. Fischer left the train at the edge of town when it stopped there because of the highway. That was a perfect spot for us to meet because the Russians lived there and the German People's Police had no business being there. I always took two bikes to meet Mr. Fischer. He said I was the sneakiest person on earth, and I could be proud of it. But he still wouldn't tell me how he ever got to West Germany and then back to Burg with all that loot.

In addition to the rabbits, we ate a lot of herrings that year, but we also did a lot of trading. Most of it was barter because the *Reichsmark* was considered worthless and the blue Russian money was hard to find. But there were rumors about an imminent currency reform that would introduce a new *Deutsche Mark*. In the meantime, cigarettes and inner tubes were the best currency. Both were worth their weight in gold, and we easily bartered them for milk, butter, cheese, and good bread. Palmolive soap wasn't a bad currency either. Still, I was worried a lot, not only about the ferret in my room, but also about the stories I had heard about the new *Volksschädlinge*, those "evil men who hurt the People" by their black marketeering. Such "criminals" often seemed to disappear without a trace. I wondered whether I would be one of them, being sent to *Sachsenhausen* perhaps, but I didn't dare ask my parents.

The Black Market
means
DEATH
of the New Currency

Stamp out the black market!

Black marketers are parasites
on working people!

Langewiesche-Brandt, Ebenhausen near München, Germany

39. A SPARK IN THE HEART
[April – August 1948]

In the spring of 1948, Mrs. Fischer took a typing job at the Town Hall and Mr. Fischer left Burg to go back on tour with the circus. Thus, I was always alone in the apartment right after school—except for the ferret, of course, which I quickly put in the new cage Mrs. Fischer had bought. One day, I used the opportunity to check out the Fischers' living room bookcase, and I got a big surprise.

I am not talking about all the books on the top shelf: Friedrich Gottlieb Klopstock, Gotthold Ephraim Lessing, Christoph Martin Wieland, Johann Gottfried Herder, and of course, Germany's idols, Wolfgang von Goethe and Friedrich von Schiller. Nor am I talking about the middle shelf, which also looked like it had been set up for our German literature class: Friedrich Hölderlin, Novalis ("pen name of Friedrich von Hardenberg," the cover said), Joseph von Eichendorff, Heinrich von Kleist, Eduard Mörike, and Ludwig Uhland. It was the lower shelf that caught my interest—at first with its odd collection of books and then with the special book hidden behind all the others. In the front, in plain sight, stood Wilhelm Raabe, Theodor Fontane, Stefan George, The New Garden Book I ("with special emphasis on ground covers, shrubs, and vines"), The New Garden Book II ("with special emphasis on soils, fertilizers, diseases, and pests"), and Dr. Oetker's Basic Cookbook ("guaranteed success with your most favorite meals"). And behind them all, carefully wrapped in an unmarked white cover, I found a 510-page tome, entitled *Love Without Fear.* Now those pages, along with no fewer than 55 illustrations of sexual positions, I simply had to study in detail, which I did, every afternoon between 3:39 when I got home and 5:14 when Mrs. Fischer arrived. But while the theme of the book was the joys of sex and the peace one would experience by avoiding pregnancy, the book nevertheless managed to fill me with dread! Unlike my parents, it told me everything one could possibly want to know about venereal diseases, photos included, and I was so sorry I had asked! In fact, I was so upset that I abandoned my fantasies of inviting Helga to my room and letting the ferret out to make her jump into my bed. I took her on a carriage ride instead. Once spring had come, one could buy a half-hour horse-and-buggy ride for as little as 1 mark in front of the railroad station. The horses had bells, and the evening was beautiful. The moon wasn't out, but the stars seemed close enough to touch. Helga let me put my arm around her and hold her hand. I wondered whether I might kiss her one day.

******

They promised us a class trip to the Baltic once we had finished our first year of high school. As it turned out, Helga and everyone else did go that July, but I stayed behind in Ziesar working in the fields. I should have seen it coming, but I didn't.

It started at about the time when Newteacher Mr. Klaus was made principal. They said it had something to do with his being Czech and having spent the war years in Moscow. Be that as it may, I remember us spending a lot of time in his class reading *Izvestiya* and *Pravda*, the Russian newspapers, and learning Russian words and grammar in the process. But Mr. Klaus wanted us to learn more than that and he carefully selected articles dealing with economic and political differences between West and East.

"In the Soyedinyonniye Shtati Ameriki [United States of America]," we learned, "natural and capital resources are privately owned and their services, just like those of people, are traded for money in markets, as are the products they help produce. Under the watchword 'free enterprise,' these private resource owners produce whatever they happen to like, without regard to the fact that the economy, like the human body, is an intricate, interdependent system that requires the careful *coordination* of the activities of millions of people."

"But no one does the coordinating," the newspaper said, "and the result is a mess, chaos, the eternal cycle of boom and bust, bringing with it inflation here, unemployment there, and poverty and injustice everywhere."

"How different things are in the Soyuz Sovietskich Sotsialistichiskich Respublik [Union of Soviet Socialist Republics]! "In the Communist society," we were informed, "natural and capital resources are owned by the People as a Whole and are allocated by a Central Planning Board in accordance with a carefully coordinated plan. Instead of the Blind Forces of the Market, Reason and Science are in charge. No business cycles there!"

We read similar articles about the *political* systems—articles that contrasted USA-style free speech and majority voting ("leading to constant controversy and ever-changing governments") with the one-party Dictatorship of Proletariat ("implying orderly and effective governance"). No wonder, we were told, that American and Russian foreign ministers, first meeting in Moscow, then in Paris, couldn't agree on anything, not even on such simple matters as the release of German POWs or the Soviet Union's just demands for reparations from Germany.

It was during one of these classes that Mr. Klaus wrote **CCCP** on the blackboard and called on me to write out the corresponding Russian words. Given that C stands for S in the Russian alphabet, and P stands for R, I knew the answer: SSSR = Soyuz Sovietskich Sotsialistichiskich Respublik [Union of Soviet Socialist Republics], but I made the mistake of *pronouncing* CCCP as Cee Cee

Cee Pee rather than Ess Ess Ess Ar. Somehow that made Mr. Klaus very, very angry. He called me a durak durakom [utter idiot] and that's what I remained to him from then on.

Unfortunately, Mr. Klaus also taught Sports, my least favorite subject. I was genetically unable ever to catch a ball, which is why my class mates never failed to choose me *last* for playing on their teams. In addition, no one had ever taught me the rules of various games, such as soccer or tennis, which made me look even more stupid. These facts did not escape Mr. Klaus. He was determined to straighten me out by torturing me whenever he could, and I came to dread our gym class, because I could never climb the ropes as everyone else could, and he always called me a "little old grandmother." I also feared swimming in the big outdoor pool, mainly because it was full of water rats, but Mr. Klaus didn't care. In fact, he took great delight in my obvious discomfort. "Durak durakom," he kept saying. I was tempted to answer him with the worst swear words I had ever heard in my life (and that all of us had learned from our Russian friends), but I didn't dare.

******

My classes with Dr. Schablin, on the other hand, were another matter. Under the general rubric of Art, she introduced us to Graphic Design that spring, and she encouraged us to write essays on subject matters of our choice and to illustrate our arguments with appropriate graphs. Under the guidance of Mr. Kalitz, whom I still saw on the weekends, I decided to write on "The Interest Rate and the Wealth of Nations." That was fine with Dr. Schablin, but it was another reason why I got into such trouble with Mr. Klaus later on. Consider what I wrote:

Just as Robinson Crusoe could forgo 8 fishes for a day and divert his labor from catching fish with his bare hands to building a canoe and making a net (which would enable him to catch not 8, but 16 fishes on all future days and thus earn a 100% *interest return* per day), so every society can make similar choices. Every society can always divert *some* human, natural, and capital resources away from the production of consumption goods (an act called *saving*) and use these resources to build new capital goods (an act called *investing*). Over time, a society that saves and invests can accumulate more and more capital goods (similar to that canoe and net) and its annual production of all sorts of goods can grow (similar to Crusoe's fish production). In such a wealthier society, everyone can be better off.

I illustrated my point with the following graph and explanation:

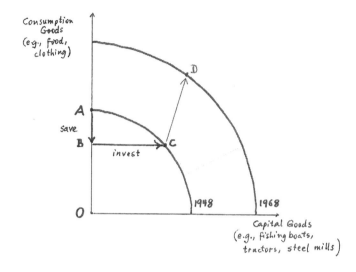

Dr. Schablin was very happy with my "marvelous example of graphic design," as she put it, and she placed my illustrated essay on the school bulletin board. She gave me a grade of 1, the best. In fact, of course, Mr. Kalitz deserved the praise, but I didn't say anything about that. And worse still, while I should have stopped right then and there, I gave it one more try. Egged on by Mr. Kalitz back home, I came up with a sequel in no time.

Unfortunately, except for its conclusion, my second essay has been lost, but I remember the general idea. I decided to compare the likely consequences if a communist country, such as the USSR, and a capitalist country, such as the USA, were to forego equal amounts of consumption goods (Crusoe's fishes again) in order to produce capital goods (like Crusoe's boat and net). Who would manage to raise future productive capacity the most, I asked, and boldly concluded that legions of self-interested capitalist entrepreneurs, always seeking the most productive uses of their funds, would easily beat communist central planners. The latter, I said, being less than omniscient, might forego the construction of boring barns and silos in favor of a much more spectacular-looking project, like a steel plant. But those very barns and silos that they failed to produce might have prevented the destruction by weather and wild animals of crops otherwise stored in the open or might have prevented the death of animals otherwise exposed to winter storms. And the export of crops and animals so saved might have yielded funds to import twice as much steel as the new steel plant could produce! Profit-seeking capitalists would quickly figure this out.

"What is the end result?" I asked, and this was my conclusion:

Consider two countries, A and B, initially with an identical output of 100 monetary units. Let A's output grow at a slow 2.5% per year, because central planners, sitting in the nation's capital city, lack the detailed knowledge for selecting the most productive investment projects. Let B's output grow at 5% per year, because investment decisions are made by private entrepreneurs who are intimately familiar with the circumstances of their businesses and are, therefore, more likely to know which investments will raise output the most. Then, after a mere 25 years, the output of B will be almost double that of A. After 50 years, the output of B will be 3.3 times that of A, and after a century, B's output will be 11.1 times that of A. Given the same population growth, country A is headed for poverty; country B is on its way to great prosperity.

Country	Annual Output Growth Rate	Initial Output	Output After 25 Years	Output After 50 Years	Output After 100 Years
A	2.5%	100	185.39	343.71	1,181.37
B	5.0%	100	338.64	1,146.74	13,150.13
B/A ratio		1	1.8	3.3	11.1

For emphasis, I graphed the diverging national outputs in a diagram and, again, Dr. Schablin posted my essay as a perfect example of the meshing of text with graphical art. But, as I said, I should have known better. It was just too obvious that A stood for USSR and B for the USA.

******

In the middle of May, on the day David Ben-Gurion proclaimed the new state of Israel and, thus, established the first Hebrew nation in 2000 years, Mr. Klaus called me to his office and asked me to explain my "anti-Communist propaganda" and my "obsession with the interest rate." He said I clearly had not understood the teachings of Karl Marx on the subject.

"Interest is the result of exploitation of the poor by the rich," he said. "There simply is no room for that concept under Communism."

He strongly urged me to join the FDJ [Free German Youth] and take the Communist youth organization's Marxism-Leninism-Stalinism course on Wednesday nights. In fact, he said, I was one of the few holdouts; almost everyone else in school had joined long ago.

"If you really want to go to the Baltic this summer," he added ominously, "you better join up now. My secretary has the application form. Pick one up on your way out."

Perhaps I should have, but his blackmail annoyed me. I walked past Miss Lisius and never asked her for the form. And that explains what happened during our last week of school, which was the week in June when the Russians cut all the rail and highway routes to West Berlin. I remember the day—it was my father's birthday, June 24, 1948—when Mr. Klaus called the entire school, students and teachers alike, into the large auditorium to talk about the blockade of West Berlin, a place that had become "a cancer in our midst," he said. And then, to my utter surprise, he called on *me* to join him at the front and he asked me to defend myself. I alone, he said, hadn't joined the Free German Youth, and that was a blot on the school's record.

Before I knew it, there was a lot of organized booing and shouting, and then Mr. Klaus said the time had come for my self-criticism. I looked at the audience, a sea of noise, I trembled, my heart was beating in my throat. And all those voices swelled together to make an overwhelming sound and I thought of running out the door. Luckily, my eyes fell on Maxim Gorkii and Joseph Stalin, life-size portraits hanging on the wall next to the stage, and I read the quotations underneath:

"One must always say a firm Yes or No."

And the other: "Into the heart, into the center of the heart, one must throw the spark."

These words! They took on life; I found my voice.

"I just don't like being pressured," I said simply. And then I talked about my father. I talked of so much greater pressure brought to bear some years ago when his life and lives of wife and son were hanging in the balance. I talked of Sachsenhausen.....of cruel guards with skulls and crossbones on black uniforms...of my father being offered his freedom for joining them....of his spending years in minefields as punishment for firmly saying "No!"

And I talked of the Russian song that Mr. Klaus had taught us all: "From Moscow to the black-earth fields of the Ukraine; from the Caucasus to the Northern Sea of ice....there is no place on earth where man can breathe more freely!"

"Is this the freedom we are being told about?" I asked.

There were no more boos, Mr. Klaus dismissed the crowd, and Dr. Hertling, smiling broadly, shook my hand as I left.

******

That summer, on the very day that America defied Russia by opening an airlift to West Berlin,

Helga and the rest of my class took the train to Stralsund and drove onto the island of Rügen, where, I was told, they vacationed on the beach underneath white cliffs of chalk. As for me, I paid for my recalcitrance, as Mr. Klaus had put it, and went to work on Ziesar's collective farm. That turned out to be not so bad at all.

I learned all sorts of things, such as milking a cow and plowing a field with a couple of oxen, this time all by myself, without Mr. Kalitz helping me. And I had plenty of time to read another questionable book; this one on *The Collectivization of Soviet Agriculture, 1928-1937*, which Aunt Martel had sent from West Berlin. The story was fascinating. I found out that Russia's peasants had responded to the program with great hostility, just as Ziesar's farmers had. In fact, the Russians had been much more rebellious—destroying buildings, machinery, and inventories of food and seeds, and engaging in the wholesale slaughter of the newly confiscated livestock. As a result, during the first five years of collectivization in the USSR, the numbers of cattle declined from 60.1 to 33.5 million, those of hogs from 22 to 9.9 million, those of sheep and goats from 107 to 37.3 million, and those of horses from 32.1 to 17.3 million. And ever since, the book said, Soviet collective farm output has lagged considerably behind any comparable figure in Western Europe and America.

I promised my parents not to breathe a word of this to anybody once I was back in school. In fact, to reassure them, I wrote a politically harmless essay for Dr. Schablin's art class during the summer. It dealt with a beautiful painting that was slowly emerging from behind a white wall in the chapel attached to Ziesar's castle. Entitled *The Paradise*, the painting had been created around the year 1500 and pictured the Almighty Father, or maybe Jesus, amongst vermilion (vivid red and orange) flower arrangements. To please the Bishop of Brandenburg, the scene had been painted with genuine cinnabar, a heavy mercuric sulfide, $Hg\,S$, and principal ore of mercury. At the time, I learned, cinnabar had been more expensive even than gold! Still, during Luther's Reformation, overeager Puritans had covered the whole thing with white paint, but that paint had been peeling off since the 1860s, ever so slowly revealing the underlying scene. In conclusion, I noted that vermilion was also known as *Chinese red*. Might it not be true, I asked, that China's Reds under Mao Zedong will similarly emerge from obscurity as winners in China's civil war? My mother told me to keep politics out of it, as I had promised her, and to strike out the last sentence.

"Ins Herz, mitten ins Herz muss man den Funken werfen."

Into the heart, into the center of the heart, one must throw the spark.

"Man muss immer ein festes Ja oder Nein sagen."

One must always say a firm Yes or No.

Gorkii und Stalin, 1932

40. ESCAPE

[September 1948 – August 1951]

In the fall of 1948, during my second high school year, Mr. Fischer offered to take me along to West Germany on one of his smuggling trips. I didn't dare tell my parents, who would have had a stroke at the idea of my crossing what Churchill had called the Iron Curtain. I simply sent a note to the school about having caught a terrible cold and figured I would be back before the weekend. Mr. Fischer took care of the rest. He had his *Quellen* [sources of supply], as he liked to put it. In this case, he was referring not to his suppliers out west, but first and foremost to his friends at the People's Police who gave us both a permit to travel to Mr. Fischer's circus, allegedly roaming about somewhere in the Harz Mountains.

"You've been like a son to me this past year," Mr. Fischer said. "It's time for you to see the world."

Permits in hand, we took the train to Wernigerode, a town near the border, and, looking out the train window, I suddenly recognized the Slavic origins of the names we saw. To a Russian, who calls a town *gorod*, Wernigerode sounds like Werner's town, just like Leningrad is Lenin's town and Stalingrad Stalin's town. Even back home where my parents were, Ziesar sounded suspiciously like za ozero, the Russian words for "by the lake," Lakeside perhaps.

We boarded a tourist bus into the Harz Mountains, pretending we were going to climb the Brocken, at 1,140 meters the tallest peak in the region. They stopped us twice, but our papers must have looked fine. I had never seen mountains before, and they were beautiful, filled with tall fir trees, moss and ferns, and brooks of pure water, cascading over streets of stone. Mr. Fischer kept on walking, right up the Brocken, and the fir trees gave way to scrubby pine.

By evening, the mountain top appeared from behind a cloud, and both turned pink and then purple. In one direction, we had a gorgeous view of *altocumulus stratiformis*, the small heaps of clouds arranged in layers up high, which turned into glorious colors at sunset. We went into a shack, and an old man appeared. He embraced Mr. Fischer and was introduced as an old circus pal of his. He looked just like Rübezahl, the good-natured ghost of Silesia's mountains—tall, with a white beard and long, flowing hair. I thought he must have been 100 years old at least, perhaps 200. I also thought of Berlin and all the Rübezahl books I had read on the balcony. That night, we crossed the border, about half a kilometer from the shack. Rübezahl had told us all about the dogs and the changing of the guards. We avoided them all. It seemed easy, but in retrospect I wonder: Didn't they have mines, as they certainly did in later years, or were we just lucky?

******

West Germany was a big surprise. We took the train from Braunschweig to Hamburg, where Mr. Fischer had "business." The train was clean, fast, and there wasn't any black smoke. Nor were there any police checkpoints. Most of the ruins in the cities were gone. There were still empty lots, but also plenty of parks, filled with newly planted trees and fountains and flower beds. There were new houses everywhere, finished or under construction, "with the aid of the Marshall Plan" the signs said, and people wore wonderful clothes. In contrast, my legs prickled from the rough cloth of my pants, and my feet sweat inside my plastic shoes.

"Come over from the Soviet Zone?" a man said next to me; it was that obvious.

And the stores! I spent hours looking at the stores, while Mr. Fischer was hanging out with all sorts of buddies of his. They sold everything in the stores, even things we could only dream about back home—coconuts, oranges, and pineapples, soap and real sponges taken from the sea, newfangled ball point pens I had never heard about, and books; so many books about so many things.

******

We had no trouble getting back to Rübezahl. It was dark at the time, but my mind was filled with the neon lights of Hamburg. The next day, we were off on the train and I wondered how we could pass all the controls on the way to Burg. I had lots of time for worry, too, because the train stood forever in the Magdeburg station waiting for the Berlin express going west. By then, all the railroad lines in the Soviet Zone had single tracks. The Russians had taken the other tracks as reparations. While we waited, I read the big sign painted on a nearby wall. I had seen it during the Nazi days even in Berlin, but the Communists were using it all the same.

GEMEINNUTZ GEHT VOR EIGENNUTZ [Community Welfare Comes Before Self-Interest], the sign said.

Naturally, that made me think of all the black market posters, the sacks of sugar inside the legs of my pants, and about the cocoa, coffee, and cigarettes that hung from my waist. But I needn't have worried. Mr. Fischer knew what he was doing. Presently, a man in farmers' overalls walked up to us and Mr. Fischer gave him a package, just as the Saxons came onto the platform—policemen with bright, green uniforms and the familiar Saxon drawl.

"Inspayction, inspayction," one of them said, but for some unknown reason, they never entered our compartment.

Mr. Fischer was all smiles. He kept trying to teach me Skat, a card game everybody played, but that I never managed to understand. By the time we got to Burg, we were home free. The chief guard at the station knew Mr. Fischer and he received a package as well. In addition, there was a big commotion in front of the station house and everybody was too busy watching it. Apparently, the man running the greenhouses next to the station had been walking across the square with two pails covered with straw. An overeager policeman had stopped him and asked what he was carrying.

"Cow shit, just cow shit," the man had said.

"Don't you fuck with me," the policeman had answered and had parted the straw to reach to the bottom of the pail. The gardener hadn't been lying! And that's when we arrived on the scene. I thought the gardener would get shot on the spot. Instead, the Saxon let out a piercing yell, the German equivalent of the Russians' favorite phrase:

"Fuck your mother in the mouth!" he said.

Everyone laughed.

******

Perhaps we had been lucky going to West Germany when we did. Such excursions became next to impossible by the spring of 1949 when the political division of Germany was more or less solidified by the creation of the Federal Republic of Germany in the West and the German Democratic Republic in the East. I read about it in the *Tagesspiegel* [Daily Mirror], a West Berlin newspaper for which Aunt Martel had entered a gift subscription. At the time, the paper was still arriving in my mail with just a day's delay. Reading the paper, I learned all about the founding of NATO and the determination of its 12 members to protect West Germany and West Berlin from any Soviet aggression. I learned about Israel becoming the 59th member of the United Nations and later about the ending of the Soviet blockade of Berlin after 328 days and 277,264 airlift flights. And then the western news came to an abrupt end. A curt notice from the post office informed me that enemy propaganda would henceforth be destroyed prior to delivery. In the new German Democratic Republic, I never saw the *Tagesspiegel* again.

All along, there was plenty of news, of course, in *Neues Deutschland* [New Germany], an alternative paper coming to our school from the other side of Berlin. It was filled with stories about the Molotov Plan, giving rise to the East European Council for Mutual Economic Aid that countered the wicked Marshall Plan concocted by American monopoly capitalists. And we learned about Andrei Vishinsky, the new Soviet Foreign Minister, who assured us that American and British plans for an atomic war would be thwarted by the new atomic bomb then in the possession of the USSR. That was also the time when a giant new flag came to adorn our school—the flag of our new classless society, featuring close cooperation among farm workers (symbolized by ears of wheat), industrial workers (symbolized by a hammer), and the intelligentsia (symbolized by a compass). In fact, earlier that summer, leaving my compass and math books behind, I had learned all about that cooperation, while working, once again, on Ziesar's collective farm. This time, my schooling in honest work put me into the white-asparagus fields, where I crawled on my knees along rows that were precisely measured to be 1 kilometer long and that featured mounds of white sand along each row such that the crosscut of each, as my instruction sheet put it, "resembled an equal-sided triangle with 30-centimeter sides." As the asparagus grew into the sand from the black earth below, it remained white, and when its tip peeked through the triangle's top, I reached down with a knife and harvested another spear.

******

In the fall of 1949, just after the big ado about the great new alliance between Stalin's Russia and Mao Zedong's China, my third high school year was interrupted briefly by the news of Aunt Rachel's death. She had been suffering for a long time, allegedly from lung cancer, although she had never smoked a single cigarette in her life. Clearly, all that red-wine-plus-raw-eggs medicine had failed. Uncle Eddy insisted on running the service for his wife and we all had to attend. That was the first time Helmut wore a little suit, but he didn't know how to put on the tie. I tried to help my little brother, but couldn't do it while facing him. I had to drag him to the mirror and make him stand in front of me. While standing behind him and facing the mirror, I knotted his first tie.

As usual, Uncle Eddy's sermon made little sense to me. But he handed out copies of it later, which I kept.

"We are saying farewell today to our beloved wife and sister Rachel," Uncle Eddy said. "But grieve ye not, for she who lived a life of selfless devotion has merely died to the flesh. Just as surely, she has been raised to the spirit by the grace of our Lord, Jesus Christ.

What shall we say then? Are *we* to continue in sin that grace may abound for us as well? By no means! But how can we who died to sin still live in it? Do you not know that all of us who have been baptized into Christ Jesus were baptized into his death? We were buried therefore with him by baptism into death, so that as Christ was raised from the dead by the glory of the Father, we too might walk in newness of life. For if we have been united with him in a death like his, we shall certainly be united with him in a resurrection like his. We know that our old self was crucified with him so that the sinful body might be destroyed, and we might no longer be enslaved to sin. For he who has died is freed from sin. But if we have died with Christ, we believe that we shall also live with him. For we know that Christ being raised from the dead will never die again; death no longer has dominion over him. The death he died he died to sin, once for all, but the life he lives he lives to God. So you also must consider yourselves dead to sin and alive to God in Christ Jesus. Let not sin therefore reign in your mortal bodies, to make you obey their passions. Do not yield your bodies to sin as instruments of wickedness, but yield yourselves to God as men who have been brought from death to life, and your bodies to God as instruments of righteousness. For sin will have no dominion over you, since you are not under law but under grace.

What then? Are we to sin because we are not under law but under grace? By no means! Do you not know that if you yield yourselves to any one as obedient slaves, you are slaves of the one whom you obey, either of sin, which leads to death, or of obedience, which leads to righteousness? But thanks be to God, that you who were once slaves of sin have become obedient from the heart to the standard of teaching to which you were committed, and, having been set free from sin, have become slaves of righteousness.

I am speaking in human terms, because of your natural limitations. For just as you once yielded your bodies to impurity and to greater and greater iniquity, so now yield yourselves to righteousness for sanctification. In the name of the Father and the Son and the Holy Ghost. Amen."

What any of this had to do with Aunt Rachel's death I haven't figured out to this day.

****

Later that school year, in the first half of 1950, I believe, all of our classes dealt with the theme of death as well, although there was no mention of the Father and the Son and the Holy Ghost, and the death we were contemplating was our own. Mr. Klaus had clearly coordinated what was being taught, regardless of whether the subject was Russian, Physics, Geography, or anything else. It started in our Russian class with our reading of a lengthy article in *Pravda*, which reiterated the "obvious fact" that the United States was planning an atomic war to obliterate the Communist world. The "proof" given involved President Truman's February 1 decision to produce "a hydrogen super-bomb, the world's mightiest weapon yet."

Dr. Kahlenberg's physics class took it from there.

"While the old 1945 uranium-plutonium bomb *splits* atoms," he said, "the new hydrogen bomb *fuses* atoms, which will give it a power that can be 1,000 times greater."

But we learned more than that!

"Actually," Dr. Kahlenberg said, "hydrogen, of atomic mass 1, cannot be made into a bomb. The new weapon should be called the *triton bomb*, because its basic element is tritium, a hydrogen isotope of atomic mass 3. And a triton, in turn, is the nucleus of tritium, composed of one proton and two neutrons."

We were so glad to know.

Before long, even Dr. Hertling got involved, despite the fact that he was clearly not a Communist. We reviewed the geography of the Far East and learned that President Truman—the world's Chief Terrorist, he always said with a wink—was sending military aid to Formosa and Korea, thereby setting the stage for the first use of the new triton bomb.

The general theme of imminent destruction continued to dominate all of our classes, even in the fall of 1950 when we returned for our last high school year. Ostensibly, Dr. Schablin's class was dealing with Chinese and Japanese art, but got invariably sidetracked into scary stories of U.S. forces landing behind Communist lines at Inchon, Korea, and the later showdown at the Yalu River, which was seen to foreshadow a Third World War, fought with atomic weapons, and the end of us all.

******

As it turned out, no one dropped a triton bomb on us, but I had an experience that was only slightly less dreadful. After an endless series of colds, our school doctor said that I must have my tonsils removed and he sent me to the local hospital for the procedure, an event that will forever remain etched in my mind. The hospital doctor did not believe in general anesthesia and assured me the whole thing would be over in no time. While I lay on my back, a nurse pried open my mouth and the doctor attacked my throat with a shot of Novocain, using the longest needle I had ever seen. It must have been 20 centimeters long; easily. Then they hung a glass jar above my head, connected it to a black rubber hose that made sucking noises, and went to work on my throat. The pain was unbelievable as the doctor used some kind of miniature saw on me—I so wished I could have turned off that awful sound—and I watched the jar above my head fill up with blood. I thought I would surely die. A triton bomb would have been a relief.

******

Somehow, I survived. I didn't bleed to death, nor die from infection. I was lucky. It felt so good to be still alive and, a couple of weeks later, I rewarded myself by asking Helga for a date. We went dancing at our special place, and it was all our own. An unlikely place it was, too: the House of German-Soviet Friendship. People stayed away from it usually, but they needn't have. The Russian officers were very nice; we often played chess with them, and I sometimes pitted my brain against their abacus. They always won.

They had a marvelous room with soft lighting, fancy furniture, and the best radio in town. Also, they went away when we told them to. We could sit on the couch and Helga and I could kiss. And we could dance to the tunes of RIAS, the Radio In the American Sector of Berlin, which was ironic, given the place we were in.

We also listened to the news a lot, but Helga thought that the RIAS people told a lot of lies and that it was downright treasonous to pay attention to them. Listening to western broadcasts, she said, was a kind of "moralische Selbstverstümmelung" [moral self-mutilation]. It was bound to destroy the listener's morale and, if the enemy lies were spread, that of others as well.

This assessment of hers bothered me a lot; it sounded just like the official Party line and no wonder; she had joined the FDJ [Free German Youth] and I still had not. Having been such an avid BBC listener during the war, I didn't like Party lines, but I didn't say anything.

For the most part, during that last year of school, Helga and I avoided the subject of politics and focused on more immediate tasks, such as hugging and kissing in all sorts of hidden spots and, when necessary, preparing for our final exams in April and May. Each of us finalists—and there were only thirteen left—had been given one major project to complete before receiving the coveted *Certificate of Ripeness*. Believe it or not, that was what our high school diploma was officially called. Helga was to demonstrate her maturity with a major piano performance, which was scheduled before the entire school on April 20, 1951. I remember the date because it was also Hitler's birthday. As for me, I was to demonstrate my adulthood by showing to the assembled teaching staff "the sense in which differential calculus was the exact opposite of integral calculus" and doing the whole thing in Russian! Other class mates got other assignments still—there was one for each, drawn by lot, with three months to prepare and three hours to demonstrate. I kept a list:

- A Summary of the History of English Literature, in English
- An Outline of the History of the British Commonwealth, in English
- The History of Art: Egypt, Greece, and Rome (4000 B.C. to 500 AD), in English
- The History of Art: Gothic, Renaissance, Baroque, and Rococo (1250-1760 AD), in German
- Electricity and Magnetism, in German
- Acoustics and Optics, in German
- The Science of Meteorology, in German
- Basic Laws of Chemistry, in German
- A History of the German Language, in German
- A Summary of Carolus Linnaeus, *Systema Naturae,* from protozoa to vertebrata, in Latin
- A Summary of Caesar's *De Bello Gallico*, in Latin

At just about the time we all gave our performances, Mr. Klaus announced that the danger of atomic war had slightly decreased. President Truman, he said, had relieved the war-mongering General of the Army, Douglas MacArthur, of all his posts. He had replaced him with the more rational Lt. General Matthew B. Ridgway. As a result, a U.S attack on China, via North Korea, was less likely, as was an attack by Generalissimo Chiang Kai-Shek, via the Formosa Straight. For the moment, we could all sleep more easily, he said.

That day, Helga received her notice of admission to the Conservatory in East Berlin and we promised each other to meet there in the fall. As it turned out, that was easier than we first thought, because my parents had made plans of their own, which were to bring us back to Berlin as well. For months, I learned, my parents had been shipping packages of our belongings—including my crucial collections of notes about everything—to Aunt Martel in West Berlin, and their plan called for us to follow the packages there right after my graduation.

******

There was no way for an entire family to get permits to travel to Berlin, not even to the Soviet-occupied eastern sector, given that anybody, once inside the city, could easily escape the German Democratic Republic by walking across the street into West Berlin. We decided to split up. I would go on my own; my parents and Helmut would go separately. Furthermore, to avoid suspicion, we would take no luggage, except a rucksack to carry some food, and we would circumvent the ever present police checks by staying away from buses and trains and simply *walking* to Berlin. On the map, as the crow flies, the distance was 80 kilometers; even doubling it, to account for the zigzag shape of country roads in the real world, would not make the trip an insurmountable task.

Mr. Fischer helped plan my own escape. First, he got me an official permit to travel to his nonexistent brother in Genthin, which I did by train. Then I was on my own, but not without Mr. Fischer's maps. All I had to do, he said, was walk along the Elbe-Havel Canal to Plaue, where the westbound Havel River flowed through a lake and turned north towards Rathenow. Moving east along the banks of the Havel, I would pass Brandenburg, and then, staying north of Werder and Potsdam, I would come upon Sakrow, where they had all kinds of excursion boats traveling on the river. Given that the border was right in the middle of the river, it would be easy to end up on Peacock Island in West Berlin, Mr. Fischer said. All I had to do was swim a short distance or stay behind when one of those boats stopped at that Havel island, where Frederick the Great had built a summer palace and had seen to it that hundreds of peacocks would forever run free.

That's exactly how things worked out. Carrying a rucksack full of bread and using an umbrella as a walking stick, I moved along the edge of pine forests near the canal and then the river, passing through giant ferns and scaring rabbits as I went. They scared me as well; I must have been more nervous than I was ready to admit. Every sound, no matter how natural, made me think of the People's Police.

To avoid suspicion, I also carried a metal specimen box of the type we had used in botany class. If I ran into someone, I could always argue that I was collecting samples of plants for a project in school. On one occasion, when I was actually picking up a bit of moss, I ran into a fox that locked eyes with me and froze in place for the longest time. I told him I was his friend, but he bolted when I spoke.

Because the moon was full and I didn't want to be seen, I walked quite a bit at night and spent much of the daytime not moving at all, lying instead among the ferns, watching the sun rays pass through the hazy sky and the trees above, and listening to droning insects all around. Avoiding detection, however, was easier said than done. Once I was trying to sleep at the edge of a meadow, under the swooping boughs of a weeping willow, and all the cows ambled over to my spot and stared down at me. Under ordinary circumstances, that would have been fun, but not that day. The last thing I needed was some enterprising farmer coming by to check out what was going on. At another time, a group of ravens discovered me and made an endless racket whenever I took a step. I don't know why they always had to be bickering so much.

The weather gave me trouble as well. Most of those August days were oppressively hot and humid, and I found relief by swimming in the Havel, which I always kept in sight. But I had not anticipated thunderstorms, which came in the late afternoons and scared me to death with all that lightning. My umbrella notwithstanding, they also turned my clothes into a damp mess, which never managed to dry. All the while, I was looking for beech trees and oaks, thinking of the old nursery rhyme my mother had read to me. According to her story, one was to seek out beech trees to survive a lightning storm, while oak trees attracted lightning and meant certain death!

Die Buchen sollst Du suchen; den Eichen sollst Du weichen!

But all worked out in the end. I never ran into the People's Police and I knew I wouldn't once I had swum across the Havel and met the peacocks of Frederick the Great under a grove of poplar trees. I lay on the ground to dry out a bit and remember how their leaves were fluttering, showing off the paler green of their undersides. From there, I made my way through familiar parts of town towards Aunt Martel's place, but I noticed how all sorts of names had changed. The Kronprinzenallee had become Clayallee, after the American military governor and airlift hero. The old Augusta-Viktoria Platz had become Breitscheidplatz, after the SPD leader murdered in

Buchenwald. Later that day, in the center of West Berlin, oddly enough, I did run into a company of Russians. They were marching through the Brandenburg Gate, or what was left of it, playing trumpets as they came, right towards me. But they were not invading the west; nor were they out to catch an escaped citizen of the German Democratic Republic. They were just going to lay a wreath at the new Soviet War Memorial that stood just a hundred meters or so inside West Berlin.

akg-images, London, United Kingdom

Soviet company marching through Berlin's Brandenburg Gate

41. A NEW LIFE

[August 1951 – February 1952]

As I made my way through West Berlin on that hazy summer day in 1951, having just escaped from the East, I was suddenly struck by the finality of the step I had taken. There was no turning back, just as on that day seven years earlier when a bomb had wiped out our house in Berlin. In a way, I realized, I had already lived two lives; a third one was about to begin. My Aunt Martel was elated to see me sitting in front of her door when she came home from work. My parents and Helmut didn't arrive till three days later, which gave us time to get acquainted again. Before all else, we threw away my dirty, wet clothes and I had a wonderful hot bath. That in itself, like my being there, was quite a miracle; Aunt Martel's new apartment, unlike our old one or my grandmother's for that matter, came equipped with hot water! In addition, all the rooms had central steam heat; radiators had taken the place of the old tile ovens everyone used to have. And the kitchen had a gas stove with a little blue pilot light centered among four burners. One could start any one of them with a simple click. Come winter, there would be no need here for lugging firewood and brown coal briquettes up from the street and then struggling to get a fire going. How times had changed!

On that first evening, I told Aunt Martel all about my trip. I remember her being shocked about my swimming in the Elbe-Havel Canal, amidst oil drums, dead fish, and all sorts of green slime. She was worried about my health and made me aware, long before it was fashionable, of what industrial effluents could do to people and the flora and fauna of this world. While we talked, she found me new clothes in the packages my mother had been sending for months. In return, I gave her the only present I could at the time, my black umbrella walking stick with the shiny handle that looked like ivory. Aunt Martel liked the pictures of Paris that were printed on the umbrella top—the Eiffel Tower, the Arc de Triomphe, and a cathedral, the name of which we didn't know.

Aunt Martel also served me one of my favorite meals, mashed potatoes and a delicious sauce of chanterelles. There was *Rote Grütze* pudding and vanilla sauce as well; she had remembered! I was so happy by the time I was ready to fall asleep—to fall asleep in Berlin, it occurred to me, for the first time in seven years! This time no sirens would blare.

******

Clank, clank, clank.
Mr. Joseph was banging on the ceiling pipes. Then silence and darkness...

"Don't stop! Don't ever stop!" Mrs. Schmidt cried out to Mr. Joseph. "Let someone else do it for a while. Just when we stop, they listen and decide it isn't worth it to dig."

Clank, clank, clank.

The light flickered on and off. I rubbed my eyes and tried to get rid of all the dust. Then I saw what it was. It was the little blue pilot light on the stove, and I suddenly realized what it meant! Why hadn't I thought of it before? There were gas pipes hanging on the ceiling of this cellar and Mr. Joseph was banging on them! If he wasn't careful, there would be a leak, and everyone in the cellar would be blown to bits in a giant explosion not unlike the one at the Gas Works near Wildenbruch Park. I tried to warn Mr. Joseph, but no sound would come out of my mouth. I was choking on all that plaster dust.

Clank, clank, clank.

And then something went boom, Boom, BOOM, and the earth shook and I heard the loudest noise I had ever heard in my life.

I woke up with a start. My heart was racing and I felt so hot.

******

Aunt Martel said it was just a bad dream and easy to explain if I looked outside. The sun had just come up and its rays were trapped in a huge cloud of dust across the street.

"They're taking down the ruins on the other side," Aunt Martel said. "A different one each morning and by evening it's all gone. Sorry, I should have warned you. We are all used to it by now. 'Controlled implosions,' they call them."

By then some of the dust had settled and I could see the remaining skeleton houses down the street, with the familiar bare walls and black holes where doors and windows had once been. I also saw rows of pockmark bullet holes in all the walls—a reminder of what had happened here while I was gone. And I remembered my grandmother's street, which had been similarly filled with ruins —minus the bullet holes—at the time of her 1944 birthday party when I had removed Aunt Lotte's pin with the big red head from the tablecloth. I still felt guilty about that.

"Where did they bury Oma?" I asked. "I think I'll take some flowers while you are at work."

"At Rachel's Cemetery in Neukölln," Aunt Martel said, "but that's a sad story. She isn't there anymore."

"Not there anymore?" I asked. "Where is she?"

"Nowhere," Aunt Martel answered, and she started to sob.

"During the air lift," Aunt Martel said. "It happened during the air lift. They needed a lighted approach corridor to the Tempelhof runway and the cemetery was in the way. They bulldozed a long stretch of land, ruins and houses and graves alike. They sent a compensation check."

******

That morning, I went to the cemetery to check things out. One couldn't miss the long stretch of paired steel towers, each painted red and topped with a big light, each standing in a block of hardened cement where graves had once been, and all of them, jointly, descending underneath an invisible glideslope towards the threshold of Tempelhof's longest runway. I sat underneath one of the towers where my grandmother's grave *might* have been and put down the little bunch of flowers I had bought down the street.

My mind went to the day they buried Leo Krell in the cemetery next to the Ziesar church and I could almost hear ravens cursing and squirrels chirping and carrying on in the trees above his open grave. I also thought of the day the Russian MPs had come with their submachine guns and had dug up Werner Albrecht's grave and had taken him away. A lightning bolt flashed through my head, right there in the middle of the day.

I saw the old woman fall from the window across the street. People screamed. I heard a thud. She didn't move. She wore a long, white nightgown, and I saw her white hair turn slowly red and then her gown. My mother grabbed me and took me home. I was scared and it felt as if my heart wanted to come out of my throat. And I saw red fire trucks hose down red cobblestones....

The street car screeched outside the old cemetery gate and I was back, feeling very, very strange. My heart was racing and my head hurt. I took my pulse. One hundred fifty-nine. I wished I had some Valerian drops.

I walked to Aunt Martel's place to go to bed and fell asleep almost at once. The walk from Genthin, I thought, must have been more exhausting than I had been willing to admit.

"Why don't you find a nice cozy spot in the cemetery where things aren't so hectic?" the street car conductor yelled at the old woman. "Then you can feed the cemetery plants—from below!" All the people laughed and laughed and the laughter wouldn't stop. I climbed over the ruins to escape the sound that was mocking me with echoes from all the skeleton walls. And suddenly the sound came from below the ground, from all the corpses that were decomposing under mounds of debris because the rescuers hadn't come in time. And I ran faster to escape their smell and I came upon the carcass of a horse, smelling sickly and vile. Strips of meat had been hacked from its flanks and thousands of flies rose up in black swarms to greet me. But armies of beetles and maggots stayed behind doing their work, leaving nothing but belt buckles and bones and buttons of uniforms,

carrying tiny inscriptions, "God With Us."

I woke up out of breath and felt ill, like throwing up. I could still hear waves of laughter, which was scary indeed, but I didn't say anything to anybody.

******

When the rest of the family arrived, Aunt Martel's apartment got pretty crowded, but my parents were out a lot, looking for jobs and a place to live. At first, nothing seemed to work and my father spent hours each day near the ticket counter of the subway station, pretending to be short just a quarter or a dime and, with feigned embarrassment, pleading with other travelers to help him out. That way, he got enough money to pay for our food.

Eventually, my mother found a bookkeeper's job at Zille's, a coffee import firm, and my father ended up on an assembly line at Quandt's, a precision optical equipment manufacturer. I managed to join Quandt as well, but in the payroll office. There we spent all day working new and noisy electric calculating machines. Every computation was done twice; first by one person, then checked by another. I had a special job processing a large pile of legal documents, mostly court orders garnishing the wages of men who had failed to make alimony payments or provide child support or pay off their loans on time. Because all payments were made in cash, I would simply take money out of one envelope and put it in another, while inserting appropriate legal notices in each. In the midst of my work, I had fun reading copies of all the court papers—the complaints, the rebuttals, the lawyers' arguments, the judges' rulings, and more.

In my less busy moments, I rummaged through the personnel files of other people and learned all the secrets of my coworkers in the payroll office. I also came upon a fascinating room. It was filled with the files of thousands of foreign workers—mostly French, Belgian, and Dutch—who had worked at Quandt during the war. Every single file provided a detailed accounting of someone's life over the course of several years, enough to write a novel, and some of the stories were amazing and horrifying at the same time: There was the mother who had been forced to leave her one-year old child behind in France and who pleaded to be allowed a visit back home. "Request denied," said the red rubber stamp, complete with eagle and swastika. There was the old man whose daughter was about to be married in Belgium and who begged to be allowed to be there, even for a single day. "Request denied," said the rubber stamp. There was the woman who was freezing in the dormitory, asking for another blanket, and the man who had toothaches and was asking for a dentist, and there were others who merely wanted permission to go to the cellar during the air raids. "Request denied."

Someone like me, I thought, should take this material and spend a year writing a book. But I made a big mistake, which I regret to this day. I took my idea to the firm's director—a Ph.D. in Business Administration, his office sign said—and Dr. Ebert listened to me with great interest. But before the week was up, on the day the trucks came to pick up a thousand boxes filled with camera lenses destined for Persia, Dr. Ebert's men came down from the top floor and shredded the whole roomful of precious wartime files.

******

Thanks to the Marshall Plan, we got an apartment in a brand-new building at the edge of Tempelhof airport. From our 4th floor balcony, we could look down on the runways as well as the cascading set of approach-path towers that stood where my grandmother's cemetery had once been. As in Aunt Martel's case, hot water came out of our faucets and I should have been happy for that reason alone. In addition, I had just been accepted at the Free University of Berlin, where I was set to study economics and law. But despite all the good fortune, I had trouble falling asleep. For one thing, once it got dark, there were strobe lights flashing red along the edge of our roof, just above our balcony windows. For another, there was a lot of unusual noise from all the airplanes that glided past our roof at irregular intervals. Some of the planes were almost silent, except for a whooshing sound and the clanking of flaps being extended just before touchdown. Others made thundering noises as wheels came down just a few meters above our heads. Others still made sudden and startling engine sounds as pilots added power to keep their planes from descending below the glideslope and, therefore, smashing into our roof or landing short of the runway threshold....

The pottery was smashing against the Wagners' apartment door, but it sounded like the grenades exploding in the pond. I tried to get away from the Russians, but there was pounding on our door. I heard voices of strange men and yelling and the shuffling of feet. Something crashed on the floor in the next room and my mother cried out. I wanted to get up and look, but I was trapped. The braces had been locked for the night. Someone pointed a bright light at my face. Then the front door slammed shut and I heard an army of heavy boots make their way down the stairs. Then the noise started all over again, but my mother held on to my shoulder with her hand, while Helmut sat on her lap. We heard cracks like thunder, and the earth shook. We heard a shower of broken windows landing on the pavement above. Again, there was that nerve-wracking hum of engines overhead and then, suddenly, dozens of lights flashed all around us.

"My God," the woman said, "they are going to parachute right into us!"

Parachutes, each sparkling with a thousand lights, it seemed, hung overhead, motionless. The train stood in a landscape as bright as day.

"Christmas trees, just Christmas trees," the lieutenant said.

I woke up with a start and felt so hot. I was breathing much too fast. I took my pulse while watching the fluorescent dial on my night table clock. One hundred sixty-two.

In retrospect, it is easy to say that I should have talked to someone about all those dreams and flashbacks of mine, but in those days I was too afraid that others may think I was crazy. And maybe I was. Consider the fact that I did talk with my good old teddy bear! I have no idea how Aunt Martel had gotten a hold of him and how she had kept him all those years, but there he was. I remember being taken aback, because by then Teddy had no eyes and the whole body, really, had turned into a mere pile of tattered rags. But at 19 years of age I took him anyway and kept him with me at night. We talked a lot. That seemed better than listening to the radio and silly songs like Bully Buhlan's "I still have a suitcase in Berlin." It had become a great hit, which made no sense to me.

******

At about the same time, I enrolled at the Free University of Berlin. England's King George VI had just died and his daughter Elizabeth, then age 25, had become Queen. I remember listening to the burial ceremonies on our radio after coming home from my first semester classes and being shocked by the way the English were pronouncing Latin phrases. They acted as if Latin were part of the English language and even the Archbishop of Canterbury seemed ignorant of the way Caesar actually spoke the language. Truly shocking, I thought.

As I said, I set out to study economics and law, a prerequisite for joining the Foreign Service, which I had decided to do. I intended to become a diplomat and help banish war from the earth forever! I was very serious about my plans, but my law professor made fun of me and said that I might just manage to become Ambassador to Liechtenstein. For one thing, he said, I didn't speak enough languages, which caused me to enroll in Spanish and French. For another, he said, I wasn't a Count or Baron or Duke and my name didn't even have a "von" in it, but by long-standing tradition, all of Germany's good Foreign Service jobs went to members of the former nobility, despite the fact that all those titles had been officially abolished decades ago.

But I was determined to give it a try and immersed myself in Spanish and French, along with Roman Law and Adam Smith, Frédéric Bastiat, and John Maynard Keynes. Even my extra-curricular activities came to serve my new goal. At the Student Union, a new building financed by the Ford Foundation, I joined the Esperanto Club, where I listened to a lecture given by a man calling himself an *Esperantist*.

Esperanto, I learned, is a language designed to facilitate communication among people of different lands and cultures. It was created by Dr. L.L. Zamenhof (1859–1917) and first published in 1887 under the pseudonym 'Dr. Esperanto', meaning 'one who hopes.' Unlike national languages, Esperanto allows communication on an equal footing between people, with neither having the usual cultural advantage accruing to a native speaker. No more trying to communicate "uphill" for one side.

"Esperanto," our speaker said, "is also considerably easier to learn than national languages, because its design is far simpler and more regular than such languages. Esperanto is phonetic: every word is pronounced exactly as it is spelled. There are no 'silent' letters or exceptions. Even more than its vocabulary, it is Esperanto's grammar and rules which makes it exceptionally easy. Unnecessary complications have been eliminated: there is no grammatical gender, the word order is relatively free, etc. The rules have also been simplified as much as possible: there is only one verb conjugation, all plurals are formed the same way, a prefix can be added to any word to change it to its opposite (good/bad, rich/poor, right/wrong), and so on. Thus, after perhaps 30 minutes' study, one can conjugate any verb in any tense."

Having once struggled with Latin, English, and Russian, I was fascinated. I took home with me *The Sixteen Rules of Esperanto* and knew them in no time. I quickly learned the vocabulary as well, which was not surprising, given the fact that about 75 % of Esperanto's words come from Latin and Romance languages (especially French), about 20 % come from Germanic languages (German and English), and the remaining 5% come from Slavic languages (Russian and Polish) and from Greek (mostly scientific terms).

"For a native German speaker," my introductory book said, "we may estimate that Esperanto is about five times as easy to learn as English, French or Spanish, ten times as easy to learn as Russian, twenty times as easy to learn as Arabic or Chinese, and infinitely easier to learn than Japanese. Many people find that they speak Esperanto better after a few months' study than a language they learned at school for several years."

Although I was prepared to quarrel with the numbers in the previous paragraph (how could one possibly come up with them?), I did find the language as easy as advertised. Within a couple of months, I could read Brecht, Gibran, Shakespeare, and Dante in Esperanto! Once I fell asleep using Esperanto to ponder Dante's fires of hell.

Outside, the Mongols poured gasoline on the railroad ties. We could smell the pungent odor through our open windows. A lot of soldiers appeared and formed a circle. The chariots and horses made a circle, too. We saw them fire their pistols and rifles and submachine guns into the air. And then something exploded, and a giant fire burned in the middle of the street. Soon, we felt the heat of the fire, even though the road was wide and our curtains were mostly drawn. None of us seemed to breathe. The fire reached for the sky and soon the sky shone brilliant red, like sunset in hazy summer. A hot wind came up; to the east, beyond the gardens, we could see the silhouettes of houses in flames. Down the street, sparks shot up above the roofs and rained onto the sidewalks below. Smoke billowed through all the window frames and the pub at our corner wasn't there. There was a smell, like tar burning. I wondered whether that was the smell of phosphorus.

"Contact with phosphorus, you'll have it one of these nights," Mr. Eisler said, "and the only thing that will save you from terrible burns is having a sponge ready and a pail full of water nearby. Or you might drape your heads in wet towels as you sit in your shelters. Always remember: Phosphorus hates water."

Quickly, I got up and parted the curtains in front of the balcony door. Flames mirrored in the big factory windows across the street. I opened the doors, climbed onto the bench, and looked down. A stream of dark figures flowed along the center of the street, with hundreds of torches held high and an eerie sound of drums. Pauline stood next to me on the balcony. And the cats, those Struwwelpeter cats, lifted their paws and implored her not to light the matches.

"Father has forbidden it," they cried, "meow meoh, meow meoh."

Then her dress caught on fire and the apron, then a hand, the hair, the entire child!

I woke up with a start and felt so hot. I took my pulse. One hundred sixty-two.

Otto Moravec, Vienna, Austria

A scene from the *Struwwelpeter* book

42. HYPOCHONDRIA
[March – October 1952]

Going on twenty years of age, I wasn't entirely naïve. I could see what was happening with the nightmares and all. I had heard people talk about this sort of thing, and I wasn't that much different from everyone else. We had all lived through the war. Having just come back to Berlin, it was not really surprising that my mind would become preoccupied with images of war. It was only natural and the solution was obvious, at least to me: I had to take the bull by the horns, so to speak, and *confront* the ghosts trapped in my mind!

Accordingly, I decided to forget about classes for a few days and visit the old places of my youth. I took the subway in the other direction and emerged on a street all too familiar. The heaps of rubble were gone. So were the black facades along the canal. Someone had planted new acacia trees. I walked to the empty lot where our house had been and sat down in the middle of the yard that wasn't there anymore. The old oak tree was gone, too, along with the goldenchain trees, the garbage bins, and the tall concrete wall. In my mind, I pictured the air-raid shelter door at the bottom of the side-house, also gone, and I thought I heard a flock of sea gulls, circling our balcony somewhere in the sky. I smelled the dust, just as I had those many years ago, and I remembered Dieter as he had been, frozen at the same size as on the day the Hitler Youths decided to torture us. And then a lightning bolt flashed through my head.

I could actually see the concrete wall, right there in front of my eyes, and all those beer bottle shards glistening in the sun along its top, daring me to escape. I felt the trunk of the oak against my back and also the pain in my arms and legs, spread out, as they were, and tied together with the rope on the far side of the tree. And I saw them pull out their pocket knives and, standing six feet away, hurl them at the tree as close to my body as they could. To the right of my head, under my arm pit, between my legs, the knives came—and missed. And I felt my heart in my throat, missing a beat now and then, and fluttering like a bird caught in a trap. And as if I were watching a movie, I saw Mrs. Nussbaum talking to my mother on the sidewalk where her store window lay in a thousand pieces. I saw myself stepping over huge slivers of glass, each one like a sword, threatening to cut me in half if I fell. I saw the lace curtains coming out of the broken windows, like ghosts waving their arms. And the ghosts looked at me with their fiery eyes and their eyes turned into those of the Mongol Khan whose crescent sword sparkled in the sun. I tried to get up and run, but my legs were still tied to the tree, and I saw bayonets stabbing our pillows and mattresses and then my mother's clothes. I tried to speak, but my voice was gone. They were holding a knife to my throat after they found my little gold coin with the red ladybug on top that Dieter had given me for good luck, way back in Berlin.

It seemed that no more than a few seconds had passed, but suddenly I felt so hot and my pulse was racing. I felt dizzy, too, as I stood up, and a scary blackness filled me, moving from the back of my head into my eyes and down through my chest to my arms and legs. I felt wobbly as I walked back to the street, but I was *not* going to count my pulse.

******

I took the back road along the gardens to look for my old school. At the corner I came across a movie theater that had never been there before. They were advertising Maria Schell, starring in *Elizabeth I.* The school, miraculously, was intact, but it seemed to have shrunk. At first, the building seemed abandoned, but the doors were open and there were carpenters and painters working on the second floor. They were listening to a radio; someone was singing *When the red sun sinks into the sea at Capri.* I found our classroom. The iron bars were still in front of all the windows, but the picture of Frederick the Great was gone. I sat in seat number Five. I had to sit because just then my heart skipped a beat and I felt scared about that. I remembered the day my name changed to Twenty, then Thirty, and Fifty-two. I could almost feel the sting of the Yellow Uncle, as I turned the handle of the teacher's closet to look for the cane, but the closet was locked.

I remembered another day when the closet had been filled with gas masks, and we had each gotten one of our own, and Mr. Eisler had warned us of British terrorists who were ready to attack us with incendiary bombs and poison gas. I could still hear his voice:

"Picture yourselves *trapped* in a smoke-filled room or in an air raid shelter, with, say, mustard gas leaking in. Before long, the percentage of oxygen declines and once it's gone below 15, you are dead!"

I remembered how I had watched the firemen later that day on our street as they pumped air into the cellar of the collapsed house next to the burnt-out church and how the bells had rung when the tower fell.

"A sign of God," Mr. Joseph had said.

And I remembered how we had feared the day on which we, too, would be trapped underneath, sitting in the dark, wondering about the rescue workers on the outside getting too tired to go on, wishing that time could stop before there was nothing left to breathe. Was I still breathing? I had to pinch myself to prove that I was. A workman came by and asked what I was doing.

"Just leaving," I said, and my heart jumped.

******

Quite automatically, I took the way home towards the canal, as Dieter and I had done, home towards our house that wasn't there anymore.

"Nothing to fear now," I thought. "No more Hitler Youths threatening to drown us in the canal, lest we hand over our favorite toys. No more dead bodies floating under the bridge and scaring us with the thought that we might be next, drowning in a cellar trap one night when the whistle bomb hits and the water pipes burst."

And there it was, the Elsensteg! I paused in the middle of the footbridge across the canal and glanced along the watery road to the east. New trees had been planted and brand-new houses had replaced the burned-out shells of long ago. I had the feeling of time having stood still, as if a film of my life had been rewound to an earlier age. A swarm of sea gulls came from underneath the bridge and circled before my eyes just as they had on that fateful day. And a lightning bolt flashed inside my head, my hands gripped the railing, and my feet refused to move.

I saw the seven angels which stood before God; and to them were given seven trumpets. The first angel sounded, and there followed hail and fire mingled with blood, and they were cast upon the earth; and the third part of trees was burnt up, and all green grass was burnt up. Red-and-yellow tongues flickered along the plane's wings; bullets stitched their way across the bridge. One plane, a burst of thunder, a single cry on Dieter's lips. I saw his head, half gone, half turned into a bloody mess. I saw the flutter of his hand, his body jerk, snow turning red. There was no solid ground beneath my feet, I could not breathe, my mind was numb, my body turned to stone. I couldn't move; my words, they wouldn't come.

A second streak of lightning flashed inside my head, I thought I'd fall like a bolt-struck tree. I shut my eyes, I opened them; I heard gulls fly overhead in rage.

******

And so I gave up. I had been wrong. I had been foolish to take the bull by the horns. I had been stupid to visit the old places and reminisce. I should go out and be with *people*, I figured. My thoughts went to Helga. I knew where she was. We had written to each other, but still hadn't met since my return to Berlin. My mother had been terrified at the thought of my crossing the border to visit Helga in East Berlin. Helga, on the other hand, had let me know that the Conservatory people were very strict; she had to practice her music twelve hours a day without letup. She couldn't be distracted by selfish things, she had said.

I decided to give it another try. To my surprise, Helga accepted my invitation to go to the theater and agreed to come over from East Berlin. We hugged and kissed at the S-Bahn [city railway] station and, suddenly, all was well with the world.

I had tickets for the Schiller Theater to see *Wilhelm Tell*. The show turned out to be a splendorous affair. The building was new. We liked the marble columns, the chandeliers, the soft red seats, and the atmosphere of so many people dressed up in lovely clothes. I wore a brand-new suit myself, a dark blue one, and a bow tie. Helga was beautiful. She wore a glittering evening gown of emerald green. Her black hair was cut in bangs across her forehead. It was long and straight on the sides and in back. She reminded me of Cleopatra.

"I love you," I said when I handed her the corsage.

"I have missed you, too," she smiled and took my hand.

We looked at the pictures of Switzerland in the lobby and read the words of the Rütli oath that was taken when the country was founded.

"We shall be a united nation of brothers," it said.

We sat in the very center of the audience. The lights dimmed, a hushed silence, the curtain rose. The stage setting was magnificent. The snow-capped mountains looked so real…Hermann Gessler, the tyrant, placed the apple on top of the little boy's head and told Tell to shoot the apple from his son's head with his cross-bow.

"What is the matter with me?" I thought.

My heart beat fast and strong inside my throat.

"Just a story, just make-believe," I said to myself. But my mind drifted to another time, the day the Chain Hounds had come into town and I had run into one of them in the middle of the street, standing legs astride, just like Gessler on the stage, and holding a pistol.

I could see him now, jamming the muzzle against the soldier's forehead, and I saw the man rise to his knees, then to his feet, the pistol following, his eyes closed, waiting, I presumed, for the last sound he would ever hear.

Suddenly, I felt the barrel of that rifle at the center of my forehead. I felt the cold metal and I saw him grin and stare at me, without mercy, with those fiery eyes of hate. I felt my heart in the middle of my throat, beating away the last seconds of my life…

With an eye on my wristwatch, I counted my pulse. One-hundred forty-two. But I hadn't been cautious enough. Helga looked at me, worried. On stage, Gessler had reached the narrow mountain pass. There was no way for him now to escape Tell's second arrow. The tyrant rode past the wall of Alpine rock; it looked so real.

"Are you all right?" Helga whispered.

"Of course," I said and noticed the bow tie in my lap. I opened another button of my shirt; I was so hot, and my heart skipped a beat. There were lightning and thunder on the stage. Hailstones were bouncing off the rocks, sounding like machine-gun fire.

Just like the night at the Baltic when the straw house burned down in no time at all; and the bombs made a lot of thunderous noises, too, like the grenades in the pond, and the pottery smashing against the Wagners' door.

I looked at Helga and pressed her hand.

"I must get out of here," I said. "Now!"

We sat on a marble bench outside, and her hand caressed my hair. I felt hot and dizzy. My pulse raced and I felt a dull pain in the center of my chest.

"I'm so sorry to have ruined our date," I said, but Helga told me not to give it a second thought. She herself had once been buried alive, in Brandenburg, she knew what was going on.

We took a taxi to the emergency room. The electrocardiogram showed nothing wrong with my heart and, by then, my pulse was normal. But a doctor didn't like the pain I felt. He gave me a shot of Novocain, with a giant needle, right into the center of my chest.

"To calm you down," he said.

******

My parents said that the ER doctor had been an idiot and could have killed me with the Novocain shot. I thought so, too, and decided henceforth to stay away from hospital emergency rooms and, maybe, from doctors in general. Luckily, I was still alive and not all was lost. Helga was willing to come over for another date.

By then it was June and time for the famous Industrial Fair, an annual event held underneath the broadcasting tower, a rather poor imitation of the Eiffel Tower in Paris. We took the elevator to the very top, watched the sunset create a spectacular display of pink *altocumulus undulates* clouds that looked like ripples on water, and had dinner at the tower restaurant way above the ground. I spent almost every pfennig I owned.

Once it was dark, we toured the exhibits in the brightly lit halls. One of them, in the automotive section, was particularly memorable. It featured a white convertible, under glass. The seats were made from real leopard skins, and the inside trim of the car was made of genuine silver and gold.

"Specially manufactured for his Majesty, the Emperor of Abyssinia," a sign said.

There were so many people milling about, I began to feel trapped in the crowd, but I didn't tell Helga about that. Besides, she didn't mind going outside. We enjoyed the fountains and flower beds, but we looked in vain for the moon and the stars. By then the sky looked pitch-black, but powerful searchlights had been turned on to mark the spot of the exhibit. The crisscross pattern in the sky made me think of all the other nights when I had seen the same sight.

Just before the sky filled up with Christmas trees and blackness gave way to brilliant red, when people whispered a lot and prayed and cried.

But those days were gone! I forced myself to study the election posters along the walls of the exhibition halls. One of them showed a road in perspective, just as we had drawn it in art class, with more distant objects getting ever smaller, leading to a single point in the far horizon. That's where a Russian bear stood with big eyes and a hammer and sickle on his hat.

"All the Roads of Marxism Lead to Moscow!" the poster said. "Therefore CDU"

It must have been a way for the Christian Democratic Union to slam the Social Democrats who were always advocating a *non-Soviet* type of Marxism.

Ironically, we came upon a booth that was filled with bears, but they weren't Russian bears. These bears were holding little copies of the Berlin flag, which also features a bear, because Berlin was founded in a forest filled with bears and the very name of the city means "little bear." Now it turned out that one could get a gun at the bear booth and shoot at a target for a fee. If one hit the bull's eye, one won a bear. I gave it a try and, to my everlasting surprise, won a bear for Helga.

Unfortunately, the shot I fired did something else. As the sound exploded in my ears, I felt myself transported to the day Captain Werther had made me throw the People's Grenade. A wave of dizziness came over me and I had a hard time pretending otherwise. But I didn't let anybody know, at least not until the next day when I went to see Dr. Haase, our new family doctor, and told her about my frequent bouts with dizziness. She said it must be my eyes and prescribed thick reading glasses to rest my eye muscles. In days to come, those glasses made me even dizzier. I threw them out.

******

A month later, Helga came again and this time I took her to the *Kurfürstendamm*, West Berlin's most famous avenue, where we saw a film starring Gary Cooper, called *High Noon*. Then we went to the Maison de France, a West Berlin equivalent of the House of German-Soviet Friendship in which we had spent so much time back in Burg. I had been taking French conversation classes at the place, but this time I took Helga to buy her a gift. I had it all planned ahead of time and we just happened to run into the perfume counter by Balmain, where we tried out *Vent Vert*, a fragrance to die for. Helga liked it a lot, just as I had, and I put a few drops on the back of her neck. I died a thousand deaths all evening long!

We went window shopping along the Kurfürstendamm, pressing our hips together as we walked under the neon lights. We looked at the displays in the shop windows and at the reflection of ourselves, embracing.

"A lovely couple," Helga said.

"I love you," I replied.

We turned the corner, and something took my breath away. I knew what it was, too. I knew right away. There was a little park with benches, lanterns, rows of forget-me-nots and pansies. And there was that dizziness again, my legs felt wobbly, I felt like throwing up. I asked Helga to sit down with me.

"I'm so sorry. Hold me for a second, just hold me," I said.

My vision blurred, my stomach ached, I couldn't breathe. But I was *not* going to give in!

"I remember this place," I said. "One night, my aunt and I came out of the theater over there. There had been an air raid. And when we came out, the street was filled with firemen and SS and Hitler Youths, all of them busily hauling corpses to the middle of the street, stacking them up, two, three, and four layers at a time, right there where the pansies are."

"Many of them were charred beyond recognition," I recalled, "some reduced to half their normal size like Egyptian mummies I had seen; others looked almost untouched, having been overcome, perhaps, by carbon monoxide in some closed cellar nearby, but rapidly stiffening even then and beckoning us for help with claw-like hands…. And around the corner, just next to the U-Bahn sign, a figure lay. I remember it now, all doubled up, in a pool of a liquid that was still feeding little bluish phosphorous flames. I saw a wedding ring glimmer on a charred hand."

Helga held me, and I cried. I hadn't cried, it seemed, for many years….

The next day, I went back to Dr. Haase.

"I keep having these spells of dizziness and my heart races and I have stomach pains and sometimes I feel like throwing up," I said.

Dr. Haase was annoyed that I hadn't been wearing the glasses she prescribed. Then she put a rubber tube down my throat and looked at my stomach with the fluoroscope. Then she rolled her eyes and sighed.

"There is nothing wrong with you," she said. "You're a hypochondriac. Get over it!"

******

On the next weekend, when her roommates went on a concert tour, I decided to see Helga in East Berlin. My mother was hysterical at the thought, having just read about the new 858-mile East

German barricades along the West German border, complete with barbed-wire fences, automatic shooting devices, land mines, and watch towers. I told her that didn't apply to Berlin; still, she pictured me being arrested by the People's Police and having to spend the rest of my life in the salt mines. She had a point there; they were always sending "criminals" to the Kaiseroda-Merkers salt mine in Thuringia.

"But what the hell," I thought. "I don't care. It'll be worth it."

But that's not what I *said*. I said I would be perfectly safe. I had, after all, West Berlin ID papers and nobody would know that I was a refugee from the DDR [German Democratic Republic]. My father said I shouldn't take along any western money; they always arrested westerners for currency violations and some of those arrested were getting 20 years in the slammer just because they had a pocketful of Westmarks. I promised I would take care of the problem and officially exchange a few Westmarks for an equal number of Eastmarks on the other side of the border. I knew that the East German exchange rate of 1:1 was a rip-off; one could get 10 Eastmarks for a single Westmark in the west.

Having thus calmed down my parents, at least a little bit, I took the trolley to the east. It went all the way, but the crew changed at the border. As promised, I walked ten meters into the DDR and exchanged my money at the absurd rate. In the meantime, the western crew sanitized the trolley car of all the election posters inside. One of them read: "Stalin Demands: Down With Adenauer! Now Especially: Vote Christian Democratic!"

The new driver was in a hurry. He kept stomping his feet on the bell whenever people or other traffic got in his way. I thought of boots stomping on marbles and of cemetery plants. My pulse went much too fast. I looked out the window and was amazed at the contrast to West Berlin. Although all the streets and sidewalks had been cleared, most of the old ruins were still there and, unlike in the west, it was a rare event to come across a new construction site. Nor were there newly planted trees or parks and flower beds at street corners. And although evening was upon us, there certainly were no neon lights! All in all, the place looked drab; even the new store signs were hard to read, already ruined by peeling paint.

I kept looking at the street signs; so many of them had changed and, quite predictably, they reflected the arrival of the new Communist society. The Horst-Wessel-Platz had become Rosa-Luxemburg-Platz, the Wilhelm Strasse was Otto-Grotewohl-Strasse, and the Dorotheen Strasse had turned into the Clara-Zetkin-Strasse. The Wilhelm-Platz was now Ernst-Thälmann-Platz, the Lothringer Strasse was called Wilhelm-Pieck-Strasse, and the Frankfurter Allee had turned into Stalin Allee. The grand old center of royal and imperial power, the Schloss Platz, was now Marx-

Engels-Platz, and even the name of our high school in Burg was there: the Karl-Friedrich-Strasse had become Geschwister-Scholl-Strasse.

Helga's place, in an old building that hadn't been bombed, was brightly lit; I could see the outline of her long legs through her dress when she opened the apartment door. Wow!

She sat in my lap and gave me a kiss for each one of the roses I had brought. Then she made me sit at the table and be patient. She served a delicious meal: dumplings, red cabbage, and veal; Hungarian wine and frozen plums from Bulgaria.

"I'm sorry," I said and pulled down the window shades. "I'm irrational, and I know it," I said. She knew about my compulsion to turn off the lights or pull the shades and gave me a hug.

The Chain Hounds stood in the street at night and fired their rifles into windows that showed the slightest sign of light. And planes swooped down from nowhere like storks, and their guns roared and broke the windows of the train, and the lieutenant never said a word, but Dieter did, and the sea gulls screeched.

Helga pulled me to her bed and made me lie down.

"My favorite hypochondriac, that's who you are," she said and smiled.

She turned off most of the lights and sat down at the piano. She played softly, beautifully. She was a master now. I felt so good, lying there in semi-darkness.

When Helga had finished, I stood behind her, pulled her up from the chair, turned her around towards me. I caught the smell of *Vent Vert* as I kissed her hands, her elbows, her neck, and it drove me wild.

"Can I sleep with you tonight?" I asked.

There was a long silence.

"We better not," she said, "we better not."

My arms circled her waist and I whispered her name, over and over again. My hands passed through her hair and held the back of her head. I kissed her eyes, her lips.

"You are my counterpart in life," I said, finally.

I brought my hands down to her breasts and couldn't breathe.

"No one has ever," she said.

"What are you afraid of?" I asked, kissing her neck.

"No one has ever," she said.

"You can sleep with me," she whispered, "but just *sleep* with me, nothing else."

I lay down with her and we whispered a lot and I kissed almost every inch of her and buried my head between her breasts and slept in perfect peace….

We woke up early and decided to dance. Radio East Berlin was of no help. They were talking of the Five-Year-Plan. We tuned in AFN, the American Forces Network, from the other side of town. Glenn Miller. Frank Sinatra. That was better.

******

That fall, we had many dates on the eastern side of the city. Once we went to Treptow Park, which I remembered as a happy place where my parents had taken me when I was a little boy in the 1930s. But it was a happy place no more. The whole area had become a Soviet War Memorial, featuring a 38 foot statue of a Russian soldier standing atop a pedestal made from marble reclaimed from Hitler's Chancellery. The soldier held a sword in one hand, while cradling a rescued child in the other. Helga and I agreed that holding onto a raped woman would have been more appropriate. Nor did we like the rows of granite blocks that had replaced the once beautiful lawns and that were inscribed with uplifting advice from Joseph Stalin.

Another date was much more fun. We spent a whole day at the Müggelsee, a large lake at the edge of East Berlin. We lay in the grass and remembered things, like the day the engineer let us ride in the locomotive with him, all the way from Ziesar to Burg. We carved a heart into an oak and wrote our names inside it. I made a flute out of reeds, just as I had in Ziesar years ago. I plucked the petals of a flower; she loves me, she loves me not, she loves me. We sang for each other that day, in a row boat among the water lilies. We lay in each other's arms and fed ducks and swans. I made a wreath of flowers and placed it on Helga's head; she made one for me. I read poems to her, while she dreamed in the sun. She described the sunset to me, while I dreamed in her lap.

"You will never go away, will you?" I asked.

"Of course not, silly," she said.

******

That evening, there were fireworks everywhere. We had almost forgotten; they were celebrating the third anniversary of the DDR. We watched from Helga's balcony and it was eerie. As the fireworks reflected off low-hanging clouds, the skyline slowly turned red and my mind took me back to earlier nights that I was so determined to forget.

I kept seeing fiery faces leering at me from amongst the lace curtains. I saw a ghost lurking behind the tile oven that stood in the corner of the room. I could hear the tinny music in the street. Panic rose within me, choking me. And a paralyzing thought flashed through my mind: What if they use the flamethrower to kill the maggots and the rats and the flies, as they often did before digging out the dead, when we aren't dead yet?

Clank, clank, clank.

Helga knew what was happening and she had just the cure. We both had that special sense of humor and she could always make us laugh, even at ourselves. That evening was no exception. Helga was funny. She had found a little book at the library, she said, entitled *Hypochondria*. We should read it together, she said, and all bad memories would disappear.

"The study of hypochondria," the booklet said, "goes back at least to the 4th century B.C., when the Greeks used the term to describe symptoms like indigestion and melancholy that were reported by men and were believed to be traceable to the hypochondrium, the region under the rib cage. If women showed similar symptoms, they were referred to as *hysteria,* and traced to a misalignment of the uterus. Treatments included bloodletting with leeches, inducing patients to vomit, and making them sweat."

We both laughed about that, especially the sweating part, given that I was always complaining about being too hot.

"In medieval times," the booklet continued, "similar symptoms were contributed to witchcraft and treated with potions and incantations."

"I need a potion," I said, and Helga got me a drop of *Vent Vert*.

"By the 17th century," the booklet said, "an English doctor, named Thomas Sydenham (1624-1689), who had previously studied Saint Vitus' dance, a nervous disorder affecting children and pregnant women, made a new list of the symptoms of hypochondria. According to him, they included digestive trouble, convulsions, shortness of breath, and heart palpitations. He thought they arose from the brain and were set off by emotions, such as fear and grief."

"Yes, yes," I said laughing. "Right on! It's all in my head; I shall never take my pulse again."

Helga gave me a kiss and said I could sleep with her again that night.

"Just sleeping," she said.

"And kissing all over," I answered.

"By the 18th century," our booklet said, "a Scottish doctor, named George Cheyne (1671-1743), came along. He wrote an essay entitled *English Malady, or a Treatise on Nervous Diseases of all Kinds, as Spleen, Vapours, Lowness of Spirits, Hypochondriacal and Hysterical Distempers.* He described hypochondria as "the English malady" because he found the English particularly prone to persisting in fears that they had a serious disease even after doctors had reassured them that they were healthy. He noted that the disease occurred mainly in people of high intelligence and thought it was caused by moist air, variable weather, heavy food, and sedentary living."

That made us both laugh some more.

"Yes," I said, "it's the intelligence mixed with the moist air and my sedentary living. They should send me back to the sugar beet fields!"

The Hypochondriac
Honoré-Victorin Daumier, 1841

43. REVOLUTION
[November 1952 – November 1953]

During my second year at the Free University, the Cold War heated up. When visiting Helga in East Berlin, I followed my old habit of reading the poster columns at the street corners. On her side of town, they were filled with stories about the warmonger Eisenhower who, in November of 1952, had won the American presidency in a landslide and was reported to have lost no time stirring things up. I remember two stories in particular, both being endlessly discussed in early 1953. First, there was the matter of the U.S. 7th Fleet having been withdrawn from the Formosa Strait, which presumably freed Chiang Kai-shek to raid the mainland and, thus, make trouble for Mao Zedong, "our great ally in the Far East." Second, there was the matter of the treacherous Pole who had flown a Russian MIG-15 to Denmark and, thus, given the western powers a first look at an undamaged copy of that type of plane. If one were to believe the East German press, that act alone might touch off World War III.

I thought all the fuss was absurd and even hilarious, but Helga didn't agree. At the time, her piano concerts were appearing on the East Berlin radio and, for some reason I couldn't understand, she took her employer's propaganda quite seriously. Before long, the Cold War infected us as well. We argued a lot about politics and I made things worse by sharing with her the draft of my first book, entitled *Soviet Reparations Policy in East Germany, 1945-1953*. I also showed her two of articles of mine that were slated to appear in *Kyklos*, the International Review for Social Sciences, and dealt with the same subject.

Helga read the summary of my forthcoming book:

Chapter 1. The Legal Basis. The subject of German reparations was first discussed at the Yalta Conference, in February 1945. The Allies were determined not to repeat the errors of 1919. The Versailles Treaty which had demanded the impossible—namely, that Germany make huge cash payments *in dollars*—had precipitated Germany's hyperinflation, massive redistributions of wealth, and the rise of Hitler. At Yalta instead, Roosevelt, Churchill, and Stalin agreed to exact future reparations *in kind only* and to do so with the goal of destroying Germany's war potential. For this purpose, Stalin demanded 1) the removal of capital resources—factories, equipment, inventories of finished goods and raw materials, and the like—over the course of two years, 2) annual deliveries from current production, over the course of twenty years, and 3) the use of German labor, without specifying details as to where and when. Roosevelt and Churchill wanted to stick with (1) alone.

At the Potsdam Conference, in July/August 1945, only point (1) entered the formal agreement signed by Truman, Attlee, and Stalin. But Stalin insisted that Potsdam had confirmed Yalta, which led to constant frictions in the new military government of Germany, the Allied Control Council, and its ultimate demise in March 1948 when the Soviets decided to boycott it.

Helga looked up.

"Surely," she said, "given what Germany did to the USSR, comrade Stalin had a valid point. You are being tendentious."

"No, I'm not," I said. *Comrade Stalin?* I thought. I couldn't believe it.

"Look at the Preface!" I said, "this is what I say: 'The Communist press, with great vigor, skill, and consistency depicts the Soviet Union as East Germany's greatest benefactor. Quite the contrary is true. At least until 1953, the overriding Soviet goal in East Germany has been the taking of reparations in all forms and ways imaginable. *However, the enormous extent of Soviet exploitation is quite understandable if one looks upon it as, perhaps, a small payment for the appalling physical and human wreckage visited upon the Soviet Union by the German invaders.'* Surely, that's not tendentious. Unlike *Neues Deutschland*, I'm just telling the truth."

"Alright," Helga said and returned to my summary.

Chapter 2. The Trophy Campaign. From the moment of occupation to the end of 1946, special Red Army 'trophy units' were busily gathering war booty. Unit commanders were personally responsible for the success of these operations, which accounts, perhaps, for the waves of physical violence that accompanied them. An estimated 2–8 billion RM of goods were confiscated, including equipment and stores of the German military, agricultural and industrial inventories (stores of grain, potatoes, semi-finished and finished industrial products), animals, agricultural machinery, telephone lines, rolling stock and signaling equipment of railroads, lumber derived from cutting down entire forests, and all sorts of items taken from hospitals, university laboratories, museums, and the homes of the civilian population.

"Goods worth 2–8 billion Reichsmark?" Helga asked. "How could you possibly know?"

"It's an estimate," I said, "but not entirely off the wall. Both the Russians and their East German friends are keeping meticulous accounts of everything—the good old Teutonic compulsion we know so well—and sooner or later these pieces of paper make their way into West Berlin. There are thousands of classified documents at the Free University, and I've been studying them for over a year. It's fascinating stuff!"

"So, basically," Helga said. "you are working in a nest of spies."

Nest of spies? I thought, *where is this coming from?* There was a chill in the air and I wished I hadn't brought my manuscript.

"I wouldn't put it that dramatically," I said. "I am just trying my best to find and tell the truth. Keep reading."

Her balcony door kept rattling and gusts of wind were banging on the windows.

"Alright," Helga said.

Chapter 3. Official Dismantling. According to the Communist press, 'the greatest part of East Germany's industry had been destroyed by the end of the war; hence dismantling has had minimal impact.' Not true. In fact, much of housing and transportation facilities had been destroyed, but industrial facilities were in fairly good shape even by the end of the war. An estimated 17% of East Germany's 1936 industrial capacity was destroyed by bombing and ground fighting. However, massive new investments had been made between 1936 and 1944, leaving East Germany's 1945 industrial capacity at least equal to 1936, possibly 50% higher. Soviet reparations teams targeted this prize in waves:

1) A first wave dismantled coal mine installations, railway repair shops, power plants, highly developed technical plants, such as Zeiss optics at Jena, Ohrenstein and Koppel locomotives at Potsdam, and the electro-technical works of AEG and Siemens-Halske.

2) A second wave dismantled railroad tracks, sugar factories, breweries, and installations for the production of building materials, textiles, and paper.

3) A third wave dismantled chemical and shoe factories.

4) A fourth wave dismantled the synthetic rubber works Buna Werke Schkopau.

An estimated 5 billion RM of equipment was so removed, but the procedure was chaotic and it is unlikely that a comparative gain occurred in the USSR. Much of the material was destroyed during the dismantling process or later by the weather, inept transportation, and feeble attempts to reassemble it at a time when many parts were missing, along with blueprints and technical expertise.

This time, Helga said nothing. She had been there when we dismantled Ziesar's power plant and she had seen parts of it rusting by the railroad station for years. Perhaps, she remembered. I kept having the weirdest thoughts while she read, like what one would have to do to disable an unexploded incendiary bomb. "Bury it with a pail of sand," they had said in Berlin, "or douse it with water if it's already sparking." But that's not what Captain Werther, our werewolf teacher in Ziesar had said. "Adding water will make it explode." I didn't know what to say to Helga.

Chapter 4. Deliveries from Current Production. Military Order #167, *On the Transfer of 213 Enterprises in Germany into the Property of the USSR on the Basis of Reparations Demands of the USSR*, set up the so-called SAGs, Soviet Stock Companies, the entire output of which was delivered to the USSR or the Red Army stationed in East Germany. Officially, this policy improved upon dismantling by 'acquiring reparations, while preserving jobs for the German working class.' The companies involved produced gasoline, machinery, nonferrous metals, steel, and ships, as well as food, drink, tobacco, textiles, and, last but certainly not least, uranium ore (Wismut Co.). From 1945 to 1952, these reparations totaled over 39 billion RM/DM-E, an amount equal to somewhere between a quarter and a third of East Germany's GNP.

"What's GNP?" Helga interrupted my thoughts.

"The gross national product," I said, "the total value of all commodities and services produced during a period."

She kept reading and I kept thinking of the perils of unexploded bombs.

Chapter 5. The Use of German Labor. Thousands of civilian specialists were arrested and moved to work in the USSR; hundreds of thousands of German POWs were retained in the USSR for years, long after the release deadline agreed upon by the wartime Allies. Almost everybody in East Germany knew of someone in this category. In addition, of course, additional thousands of Germans performed services for the Red Army stationed on German soil.

Helga read silently, but the silence seemed to demand to be filled. That rattling balcony door was of no help. With each gust of wind, it kept opening just a tiny bit, filling the room with a momentary chill.

"You don't have to read all of this," I said, "certainly not right now."

"I want to," Helga said.

Chapter 6. Unfavorable Terms of Trade. Before the war, the area now called the German Democratic Republic traded almost exclusively with countries in the west. Since then, commercial foreign trade has been reoriented towards the Communist bloc, with the USSR becoming East Germany's major trading partner. According to the East German press, 'in this trade, the Soviet Union has to a high degree been the giving partner,' meaning that the USSR has favored East Germany in foreign trade pricing compared to how she would have fared in trading with the capitalist west. *But nothing could be further from the truth!* Even foreign trade has become a new form of Soviet exploitation.

Based on 110 import and 176 export commodities—all measured in physical units and then evaluated at world market prices—a calculation of East Germany's *gross barter terms of trade*, the ratio of import quantity index over export quantity index, shows this: East Germany could have gotten more imports if she had sent the same exports to the west rather than to the USSR.

I looked over Helga's shoulder. "Almost done," I said.

Chapter 7. The Consequences. The consequences of the Soviet occupation policies are best seen by comparing the economic performance of East and West Germany since the end of the war.

**The Post-War Development of Gross National Product
in the Two German Areas, Compared to 1936 = 100**

	East Germany	West Germany
1936	100.0	100.0
1950	73.4	117.2
1953	94.6	151.9

Even by 1953, East Germany's annual output had not regained the same area's output of 1936. West Germany's annual output was 50% higher than in 1936. The explanation is fairly obvious. East Germany's poverty, which any visitor can see and which these numbers reflect, is the result of two factors. First, the huge reparations exacted from East Germany took away precious capital and labor resources, the key ingredients needed to produce output, and, in addition, by also claiming a large percentage of the lower output, they reduced the country's ability to make new investments and restore its capital stock. Second, the replacement of the market economy with an awkward system of central planning, which, among other things, directed foreign trade into unfavorable channels, did its part to slow economic growth.

"Wow!" Helga said. "And you really trust all these numbers?"

"They're the best we have." I said.

"And if you walk through East Berlin and then West Berlin you surely see the difference?" I asked.

"All this makes me feel uncomfortable." Helga said. "You better don't let anybody catch you with all this stuff. You could get 20 years as a spy."

That's what my mother said as well when I got home. She was very upset.

******

My mother also said I should never go to East Berlin again. I promised, but I lied. I had my reasons. For one thing, I wanted to see Helga; for another, after Stalin died, East Berlin had become much more interesting. Despite the fact that East Germany's secret police or *Stasi* [*Staatssicherheitsdienst* = State Security Service] was said to be larger than the Nazis' Gestapo, people everywhere were grumbling openly and comparing their miserable lives with the glittering showcase that was West Berlin. There were acts of defiance. One day in early June, Helga and I went to a restaurant near her apartment and they were openly playing RIAS, the West Berlin radio station. Everyone listened to the crowning of Elizabeth II and to the story of the gift she had received from a New Zealand beekeeper, Edmund Hillary and his Sherpa guide, Tensing Norkay. They had conquered Mount Everest and planted the British flag. But that was nothing compared to things to come.

On June 17, 1953—no one in Germany can forget that date—all hell broke out. I was with Helga at the time and we woke up because of all the shouting in the street. When we looked out, we couldn't believe our eyes. The whole street was filled with people, and some of them were climbing up on

Verein des 17. Juni 1953, e. V., Berlin, Germany

Stalin's statue. They put a rope around his neck and pulled hard. It fell! A shout of great joy rose to the heavens, and then the steel workers came around the corner with their trucks. They had on yellow hard hats and carried steel pipes. By then we were in the street ourselves and saw the workers march up to the police station, mocking the officers with a sign they had torn from a border crossing.

"End of the Democratic Sector," it said. A nice pun.

The workers made a lot of noise, shouting slogans about the government leaders, like "Goatee [Ulbricht], Belly [Pieck], and Glasses [Grotewohl] Are Not the Will of the Masses!"

We heard windows being smashed and saw cars being overturned. The Party offices down the street were on fire. Someone hooked up a big loudspeaker to RIAS Berlin, and the voice said that the red flag had been torn from the Brandenburg Gate, workers were singing the West German national anthem outside the Soviet Embassy at Unter den Linden, and the whole country was up in arms!

******

Later that day, in another part of town, the tanks came, and they fired over our heads. They rolled over a man, crushed him and squeezed him out like a tube. A second tank drove over a large pool of blood. I felt dizzy, my pulse raced, and we ran.

Behind us, people screamed, and the workers took their steel pipes and stuck them into the chains of the tanks. The chains twisted a lot and the tanks stopped. The Russians came out and ran. Some people put black smoke into the tanks. Others threw cobblestones at the Russians.

I asked Helga to come with me to West Berlin, but she wouldn't. I asked her again; she refused.

"Be smart," I said. "Please."

She wouldn't and my life changed. At that very moment, my life changed. I decided to leave while I could. The buses and street cars weren't running—they had in any case long since stopped crossing the border—and I walked along streets filled with thousands of people, walked past the Columbus House on Potsdam Square; it was on fire. So was a newspaper kiosk across the street and workers were tearing up the border installations. At the corner, on the poster column, a policeman was posting a notice:

MEASURES TAKEN BY THE GOVERNMENT OF THE GERMAN DEMOCRATIC REPUBLIC WITH THE AIM OF IMPROVING THE LIFE OF THE PEOPLE HAVE BEEN ANSWERED BY FASCIST AND OTHER REACTIONARY ELEMENTS IN WEST BERLIN WITH PROVOCATIONS AND SEVERE DISTURBANCES OF LAW AND ORDER IN THE DEMOCRATIC SECTOR.

The riots which have now occurred are the work of provocateurs and fascist agents of foreign powers and their accomplices in German capitalist monopolies. The government asks the population:

- To support all measures aimed at restoring immediate order and to create the conditions for normal and peaceful work at all places of work.

- To arrest the provocateurs and hand them over to the organs of the state.

Those guilty of disorderly conduct will be held strictly accountable and will be punished severely.

The Government of the German Democratic Republic
Otto Grotewohl, Prime Minister
Berlin, June 17, 1953

I found another notice as well; this one from the Russians:

ORDER OF THE MILITARY COMMANDANT OF THE SOVIET SECTOR OF BERLIN

Re: Declaration of a State of Emergency in the Soviet Sector of Berlin

For the sake of maintaining public order in the Soviet sector of Berlin, I command:

1) As of 13:00 hours of June 17, 1953, the Soviet sector of Berlin is in a state of emergency.
2) All demonstrations, meetings, pronouncements, and other assemblies of more then 3 persons in the streets and squares and public buildings are forbidden.
3) Any traffic by pedestrians and vehicles is forbidden between 9:00 hours in the evening and 5:00 hours in the morning.
4) Those who violate this order will be punished in accordance with the laws of war.

Military Commandant of the Soviet Sector of Berlin
Major General Pavel Dibrova
Berlin, June 17, 1953

On the next day, the West Berlin evening papers carried copies of another poster yet. Knowing that I had been in the middle of it all, my mother was almost hysterical.

NOTICE OF THE MILITARY COMMANDANT OF THE SOVIET SECTOR OF BERLIN

Berlin, June 18, 1953

It is hereby noted that **Willy Göttling,** a resident of West Berlin, who acted on behalf of a foreign intelligence service and was one of the active organizers of the provocation and unrest in the Soviet sector of Berlin, and who has participated in the bandit-like excesses directed against the government and population, has been sentenced **to death by firing squad.**

The sentence has been carried out.

Dibrova,
Military Commandant of the Soviet Sector of Berlin

Luckily, neither my mother nor I knew at the time that 124 other people were executed within days as well, including 41 Soviet soldiers who had refused to open fire on civilians. Some 25,000 others were arrested and sentenced to long prison terms, typically 10 or 20 years of hard labor. What we did learn at the time was that Julius and Ethel Rosenberg, on the other side of the Atlantic, had been convicted of giving the atom bomb to the Russians and had been executed as spies. According to President Eisenhower, they received the ultimate punishment for "having immeasurably increased the chances of atomic war" and for "having condemned to death tens of millions of innocent people all over the world." That thought made it difficult to fall asleep. And when I did sleep, there were scary dreams, always.

******

I looked at the Christmas trees and the suspense was awful. My heart was beating in my throat; each breath felt like it might be my last. I heard the roar of machine guns. An airplane veered off to the right, just missed the trees at the edge of the meadow. I felt blood trickle down my cheek; glass splinters lay in my lap. When I dared open my eyes, I saw the lieutenant slumped in his seat across from me. He didn't move. Dark blood poured from his mouth, slowly spreading over his chest, flowing over his medals, soaking his pants, the upholstered bench, dripping to the floor. And I saw two fingers lying on the floor, still clutching a cigarette....

And the heavens turned a fiery red. I saw airplanes diving out of clouds, spitting flames from their wings, and I felt the heat from the sea of flames surrounding our house, and I saw images of blood, the lieutenant's blood and Dieter's blood and that of the man who had been crushed by the tank. My heart pounded in my chest....

And I saw Mr. Albrecht cutting the throat of the pig and the blood was pouring into the bucket underneath its head and onto the soldiers, lying on thick beds of hay and straw—soldiers without arms or legs, with bloody stumps of knee, with chests or heads encased in white turned red to match the crosses on the side. A soldier screamed....

******

That summer and fall, I wrote down my dreams and then I went to see Dr. Paulsen at the university. He was a psychiatrist, but he didn't look like Dr. Freud. He was much too tall for that, and with his long white hair down to his shoulders and an even longer white beard, he reminded me of Rübezahl, the giant ghost of the Silesian Mountains, and that's what I always called him in my mind.

I wanted him to read my dream notes, but he disappointed me. He wouldn't do it.

"I don't do dreams," he said. "Träume sind Schäume." [Dreams are but effervescent bubbles]

So the good old German proverb took care of my dreams. Still, even without the dreams, Dr. Rübezahl had me all figured out within the hour.

"I know what your problem is," he finally said. "You are a classic case. *Fear of exams*! That's what it is. Put your nose to the grindstone and it'll all go away."

"Could I get some Valerian drops?" I asked.

Dr. Rübezahl looked at me, puzzled.

"Sure," he said. "They'll calm you down."

"Just three drops on a spoonful of sugar whenever you're upset," he added as he wrote the prescription. "Don't take more than that; we don't want your heart to stop."

I had heard that one before.

44. TRAPPED

[December 1953 – October 1955]

Even on the day we got our Christmas tree, my mother was still reeling from the thought that I could have been killed by the tanks in the spring of 1953 or, at the very least, could have been arrested as a spy with that manuscript in my briefcase. She begged me not to publish the stuff, lest my name become known to the People's Police and be put on their Wanted List.

"You can *think* about these things all you want," she advised, "but keep the thoughts to yourself, don't broadcast them."

"Look what happened to Vati twenty years ago," she added, "just because he couldn't keep his mouth shut. How different things might have been if he had kept his thoughts a secret."

"No," my father said, "secrecy is not the way to go. A man must speak out. Truth-telling is important, but one has to be smart about it. I learned that much."

"You can publish all the books and articles you want—here in the West," my father explained, "*but then don't be a fool and visit East Berlin*. You've got to stay away from Helga."

I said I would, but I am not so sure I meant it even then. Helga took up so much room in my head, it was hard to let her go. But my last visit had scared me, too, and I hadn't been back since. I had written to Helga in the summer and in the fall, had begged her to come at least for a visit or spend Christmas with me, if she couldn't come before then. I had even sent her a Christmas present, a new book by Ernest Hemingway, called *The Old Man and the Sea*. But she hadn't answered me, and I had been thinking of her day and night. What I didn't know at the time was that she *had* answered, but my mother had been hiding her letters. That's how determined my mother had been to keep me from being shot as an enemy of the people!

I was still thinking of Helga when we all went to Christmas services at the Martha Church. It was an unusual thing for us to do, going to church together on a holiday morning, but that's where my parents had been married in 1931 and the church had just been rebuilt after its destruction during the war. They were eager to have a look.

Just as we had so many years ago, we walked along the canal, fed the gulls, and crossed the bridge to Glogauer Strasse. That's where my grandmother and Aunt Martel had lived and my mother had grown up with all her siblings and the new church had now risen from the ruins of the old. The church bells rang as we crossed the bridge and I heard that sudden roar inside my head, a roar of something, I didn't know what. I felt dizzy by the time we entered the church yard and I felt *panic* at the thought of being trapped inside the church. As I had so often before in my life, I insisted on sitting in the last row, right next to the open door. The organ started to play, interrupting the silence with a loud noise, which startled me and made my heart jump. Just then, the ushers closed the door behind us. I tried my best to ignore this fact and to occupy my mind. I looked at the ceiling, where all the carved angels had been, but they were gone. Just like the alcoves and walls, the ceiling was whitewashed now; there wasn't a decoration in sight. A black spiral staircase, made of metal no doubt, led to the pulpit now; there were no more wooden angels carved from mahogany wood and holding up the pulpit with their trumpets. Even the windows had been modernized; they were now made of ordinary glass. Gone were the gorgeous stained-glass Bible scenes of years ago. The organ stopped; I couldn't breathe; I went and stood in the courtyard outside the door. I counted three Valerian drops onto a sugar cube.

******

By the spring of 1954, my reparations book had taken on its final form, but my mind was somewhere else. The news was filled with stories about the Atomic Energy Commission of the USA and all the atom bomb tests it was conducting on the Marshall Islands. By April 1, we learned that the hydrogen bomb had been perfected, and it was not an April Fool's Day joke. I found it scary to think of a bomb that could destroy any city with a single blast in the megaton range, some 700 times stronger, they said, than the Hiroshima/Nagasaki bomb of 1945. Radio East Berlin broadcast a plea by Vyacheslav Molotov, the Soviet Foreign Minister, who suggested the Cold War be called off and the USSR join NATO.

"The world is now facing the peril of a war," he said, "in which atomic and hydrogen bombs threaten incalculable disaster, including the annihilation of peaceful peoples, the wiping out of whole cities; of contemporary industry, culture and science; of ancient centers of civilization as well as the great capitals of the states of the world."

The western powers rejected his plea as "just a Trojan horse." I thought of what it must have been like for the Greek soldiers to be trapped like that inside the horse. That was also the day on which I was trapped in the university elevator! I was alone in it at the time and I wasn't *really* trapped, but the short trip from the ground level to the third floor turned into a nightmare. I was suddenly gripped by an uncontrollable *fear of being trapped* and couldn't shake it off. My heart skipped a beat and then another and my pulse was racing and I knew I was about to faint when a wave of nausea came upon me and I had a taste of plaster dust in my mouth. But then, just as suddenly, the door opened and, on weak and wobbly legs, I made my way to class. There I sat, numb and unable to think.

******

This time, Dr. Rübezahl was a great deal more helpful. The taste of plaster dust—that's what interested him.

"Been buried in an air raid shelter, have you?" he asked.

"The experience of war never ends with the war," he said. "Once you have experienced or witnessed an event that threatened death or serious injury to yourself or others and, with overwhelming force, rendered you helpless and terrified, a drama begins to unfold within your subconscious. Two powerful forces feud with another. One is called *Secrecy*; the name of the other is *Truth-Telling*.

Secrecy urges you to banish the horrible event from your consciousness, to deny it, to forget it, to treat it as too terrible to utter aloud, to make it *unspeakable*. Consciously, you end up feeling numb; you can't feel anything, because if I do, you can't survive.

Truth-Telling refuses to let the event be buried. It urges you to proclaim it aloud—in verbal narrative, if you can. But if you can't or won't do that, *Truth-Telling* conjures up a host of symptoms that call attention to the existence of your unspeakable secret. These symptoms, of course, are disguised representations of the intensely distressing event that *Secrecy* banished from memory, but that *Truth-Telling* wants you to remember and acknowledge and, perhaps, even relive."

"So am I condemned to reliving these events for the rest of my life?" I asked. "It's already been nine years since the end of the war!"

"Who knows how long it will last," Dr. Rübezahl said. "Look at all the symptoms you have told me about: How long it takes you to fall asleep, how often you wake up, how easily you are startled, how compulsively you turn off the lights or pull down the shades, how you have nightmares, how you have difficulty concentrating in class, how you suffer from an endless list of psychosomatic complaints...."

"Listen to your own words," Dr. Rübezahl added after looking at his notes. "You say 'I came upon the street corner, I entered the subway, the church, the elevator, and *something was pecking at my mind.* I heard a little voice in me, which I couldn't quite grasp. Something had happened here; if I'm not careful, it might happen again.' What are you saying there?"

"You show a persistent expectation of danger. You are on permanent alert for self-preservation. You are convinced that danger may return at any moment. Take something as harmless as the door to a church or a subway train or an elevator, let it close behind you, and you feel *trapped*, just as in the cellar of many years ago!"

"There's a name we have," Dr. Rübezahl said. *"Hyperarousal!* That's what we call it. Give it some thought! Once you understand what is going on, once you make the subconscious conscious, you'll be better."

******

I thought about it, but things didn't get better. One day, in the middle of class, I felt that familiar lightning flash in my head again *and I saw myself standing outside the subway station, looking down at the charred body of a woman or a man, a gold ring glistening on what used to be a hand. My heart was pounding and my eyes were stinging from the smoke drifting across the street, but that didn't keep me from seeing those little blue flames springing back to life among the piles of corpses in the middle of the square. And I felt the hot air and smelled the burning flesh and heard Aunt Martel say: "Come on, Hansel, we'll go home and all will be well."*

"There are three concepts then to consider here," Professor Conrad said, "the direct price elasticity of demand, the cross price elasticity of demand, and the income elasticity of demand. Which of the three would help us solve our problem?"

I certainly didn't know. By then, my senses had returned, but my mind was elsewhere. I was thinking of Dr. Rübezahl and wondered whether he could be trusted. Perhaps, he was as fickle as the Silesian ghost, offering his services to unsuspecting travelers as a guide, promising calm wind and sunny skies, but all the while leading them astray into ever deeper forests and ever wilder mountains and then, suddenly, disappearing before their eyes, rising into the sky, and drenching them with a deluge of water and hail and scaring them to death with lightning bolts and a thundering laughter that echoes from the rocky walls of their mountain trap.

"Could he be trusted?" I wondered.

"So what we need," Professor Conrad said, "is the percentage change in the quantity demanded of good A, divided by the percentage change in the price of good B. If the ratio is positive, what kinds of goods are we talking about? What if it's negative or even zero?"

******

During my last year at the university, things got even worse. In the world at large, Georgi M. Malenkov, who had been the Soviet Premier since Stalin's death, had been blamed for the unproductiveness of Soviet collective farms and been forced to resign. Nikolai A. Bulganin was the new Premier, but real power was said to lie in the hands of Nikita S. Khrushchev, the Communist Party boss. Under his watch, on May 14, 1955, the Warsaw Pact was signed and the Soviet version of NATO quickly claimed to have an even more powerful H-bomb than the USA. All the talk about war and destruction worried me; so did the fact that I still hadn't heard from Helga. That's when it happened one day.

I was sitting in the barber chair, with the white linen cover over me and tied at the back of my neck, when the metal of the barber's clippers touched my forehead and I freaked as I never had before. For a fraction of a terrified second, I was somewhere else.

The Mongol soldier decided to rest the barrel of his rifle at the center of my forehead. I saw him grin, but I felt the cold metal and I froze. Time stood still. I closed my eyes to escape that dreadful grin. I felt a colony of ants meandering across my feet. I heard crows fretting and shrieking in the branches of pine trees above, complaining about us who had disturbed their lives.

And then I found myself standing on the sidewalk outside the barber shop, the white linen cover still tied to my neck, my heart pounding and my legs trembling and the barber standing in the door, saying:

"What's the matter with you? We are only half done. Are you crazy or something?"

******

Dr. Rübezahl was clearly interested. In fact, he could hardly contain himself, fidgeting in his big leather chair. He made me tell the story of the firemen and SS soldiers and Hitler Youths, how I had watched them haul corpses to the middle of the street, stacking them up, two, three, and four layers at a time, many of them charred beyond recognition, some reduced to half their normal size like some of the mummies I had seen in the Egypt exhibit near our school….And he made me tell the story of Jutta, how the Mongols had come on their motorcycles and pointed a pistol at her, had dragged her out of sight, but I had heard them yell and her cry, and how the soldier with the slit eyes had rested the cold barrel of his rifle at the center of my forehead, while I had counted the last seconds of my life….

"And now it all comes back, in the middle of class, in the middle of the barber shop!" Dr. Rübezahl said excitedly. "A classic case of *intrusion*! That's what it is."

He lost no time to elaborate.

"When it all happened years ago, indelible imprints of these traumatic events were made in your soul and most of the time they are safely stored away in your subconscious. But all sorts of small, insignificant things can remind you of an horrific event. Quite inadvertently, you can be exposed to cues that resemble aspects of the event, like the cold metal of the barber's clippers touching your forehead, just as the barrel of that rifle did long ago. And at that moment, you can re-experience the event, you can relive it as if it were occurring *now*. A *flashback* breaks into your consciousness and a flood of distressing recollections interrupts and intrudes upon your normal life. You feel that time stopped at the moment of trauma; its frozen imagery and sensations vividly come to life. In fact, you enter a *dissociative state* that can last from a few seconds, as in your case, to several hours, as in other cases I have seen, and during that state you are unable to distinguish now from then. You are *trapped* in a moment of the past."

That explanation made a great deal of sense to me. I was even ready to make a new assessment of Dr. Rübezahl and entertain the notion that he might turn out to be truly helpful. I thought of another story about his ghostly namesake. One day, Rübezahl watched a poor widow collect edible roots in the forest for her hungry children. He approached her and suggested she collect leaves instead. When she followed his advice, however reluctantly, the leaves in her basket turned into gold coins.

******

During my last semester at the Free University, I learned something about myself that was stranger by far than all the details about the past that Dr. Rübezahl and I had managed to dredge up. Stepping out of a bookstore on that October day, I became aware of the pattern of squares on the cement sidewalk and I noticed how the air was filling up with thousands of giant snow flakes—big round flakes of snow that looked like cherry blossoms, falling slowly, ever so slowly, onto the trees and the cars parked beyond them, briefly obliterating the sidewalk squares, then melting away, followed by thousands more trying once again, but trying in vain, to cover up the sidewalk squares. Their failure was no surprise; it was much too early for a serious winter storm. And then, suddenly, I found myself trapped in one of those squares! My feet refused to move; I felt paralyzed, yet my mind was clear. And I suddenly *saw* the snow!

As if in a flash, I realized that I had seen those squares on the bridge when Dieter was killed, had seen his blood wash away the thin layer of snow, and that I had *never, never since seen snow again*! Standing in that square, still paralyzed, I thought of the past winter and the winter before that, and all the winters for a dozen years, winters in Berlin, winters in Ziesar, winters in Burg, and winters in Berlin once again, and I could not remember a single day on which it had snowed! Hadn't I played in the snow, gone to school in the snow? Hadn't Helmut and I gone sledding on a hill, built snowmen in the yard? Hadn't they plowed the streets, shoveled the sidewalks? Hadn't I dug my way through the snow to bring in the firewood from my pyramid behind Mr. Albrecht's house?

There was not a single image in my head that contained SNOW, neither heavy snow nor light snow nor cherry blossom snow of the kind that fell on the day Dieter and I had fed the gulls on that bridge…

******

Dr. Rübezahl was so excited!

"A classic case of *constriction*," he said. "That's what it is."

"Sometimes," he said, "in the face of some traumatic event, people save themselves by consciously avoiding the stimuli associated with the trauma. They shun thoughts, feelings, and conversations about the event."

I thought of my mother. "Now, Hansel," she had said one day that spring, "we will never raise the subject again." And we hadn't, neither between us nor with any other member of the family….

"Traumatized people," Dr. Rübezahl continued, "do their best to stay away from activities, places, and people that arouse recollections of the event. Much more often, though, something happens outside their conscious control. Without their knowing it, their field of consciousness becomes *constricted*. Important aspects of the event fall prey to a kind of amnesia. As a result, people are unable to recall their trauma. They don't feel pain because painful memories are split off from ordinary awareness. *In all these years, you didn't see the snow because it would have reminded you of a pool of blood that was melting the cherry blossom snow falling onto the bridge!* To avoid the pain of remembering the entire event, you allowed your mind to become detached, numbed, and paralyzed with respect to the one trigger—the snow—that would have taken you back to the moment of horror and possibly driven you insane."

"Actually," Dr. Rübezahl continued, "this is nothing new. Way back in the third millennium B.C., the Sumerian epic *Gilgamesh* described the suffering of a character who had survived a violent encounter that killed his friend. It caused constriction as well, although nobody used that term. And people have written about this type of suffering and its associated symptoms ever since, giving it different names, of course. During the Civil War in America, it was all about *battle fatigue*, in World War I we called it *shell shock*, in World War II *combat neurosis*. And now, in Korea, the Americans have come up with another term yet, *gross stress reaction*."

It all made sense to me and if I could have foreseen the future, I could have added another term yet to Dr. Rübezahl's list: *post-traumatic stress disorder*, destined to be introduced by the American Psychiatric Association into the 1980 edition of its famous diagnostic manual, DSM-III. Such logical explanations, however, were of little help to me at the time because I couldn't *feel* anything. In fact, despite Dr. Rübezahl's enthusiasm, I thought there was no point in my seeing him any longer. His "talking cure" didn't cure a thing. Things kept happening to me, as regularly as clockwork, and no explanation—neither fear of exams nor hyperarousal, neither intrusion nor constriction—put a stop to any of it.

That night, I *dreamed* of snow.

I saw snow everywhere, large beautiful snow flakes blanketing houses, trees, and roads, covering cars, buses, and trolley cars, and our school yard and the footbridge across the canal. And suddenly, the white sky turned red and I got scared and ran inside to play with Dieter. We read his Struwwelpeter book, but the pictures appeared on a large white wall that was made of snow and we saw Konrad being warned never again to suck his thumbs. But when his my mother left, he did and there was pounding at the door and the tailor came in with giant scissors and he sharpened them and quickly cut off Konrad's thumbs! Konrad screamed and screamed and the snow melted off the wall and there was blood all over the floor. And when Konrad's mother returned, he stood in a pool of blood and both of his thumbs were gone....

******

At graduation time that fall, I couldn't listen to the speeches. My parents said I had a far-away look, and they were right. I was thinking of Helga and the time we weeded the sugar beets on Ziesar's collective farm. That thought, in turn, made me think of Rübezahl, the Silesian ghost, whose name means "sugar beet counter." I remembered the story. He, too, had wanted a girl he couldn't have. But, unlike me, he hadn't been a wimp; he had taken drastic action! He had kidnapped Emma, a Silesian princess, and had taken her to his subterranean realm. And to ameliorate her loneliness, he had brought her a basket filled with sugar beets and also a magic wand that could turn any beet into a person or an animal for companionship.

My mother kept sending me hints with her elbow to pay attention to the ceremonies, but I didn't care. I kept thinking of the day on which Rübezahl, the ghost that is, had asked Emma in marriage and she had said that she would give him her answer once he had counted all the sugar beets in yonder field. And while he was counting the endless number of beets in the field, Princess Emma used her magic wand, turned a sugar beet into horse, and rode off, never to be seen again. I thought I'd do the same thing and escape all the traps by emigrating to the United States!

Otto Moravec, Vienna, Austria

A scene from the *Struwwelpeter* book

45. THE WALL

[November 1955 – May 1961]

So much happened in the next six years! Looking back at it now, time must have been passing at the speed of light. One day I was leaving Berlin, the next day I was back it seemed, but the calendar said otherwise. It all started with an unforgettable interview at the American consulate where I sought to attain my immigration visa.

"Is there anything you *know*?" the lady moaned after reading my application.

"The last thing America needs is another economist," she explained rather exasperatedly. "What we need is carpenters, electricians, and plumbers—people with a useful skill. In Westchester County back home, I have to wait for weeks to get that sort of help."

"I probably would have become a carpenter in East Germany, if I hadn't managed to get into high school," I said rather lamely.

"Bakers are good, too," she said. "Can you bake at least?"

******

Still, before long, I was on my way, beginning with a scary airplane flight from West Berlin to Hanover. It was my first flight ever, on a British DC3. You will remember the type: two propellers on the wings, a tiny wheel in back, and a steeply sloping aisle inside that made you think you were climbing a mountain when looking for your seat. Little did I know that I would fly one of those birds myself one day and have fun doing so. No fun on that day! When the props started, the noise terrified me and, when the aisle tipped level on takeoff, my heart almost stopped with fear. My mind must have blocked out the flight, but I do remember writing to my mother that the landing was a disaster—"straight down like an elevator"—which, of course, can hardly have been true.

The next part of my trip involved the *Arosa Kulm*, a tiny Panamanian freighter, which took three weeks to cross the Atlantic and even then missed its destination. We were blown into the St. Lawrence River by a hurricane and they deposited me in Quebec rather than New York. Having traded the image of Fort Frontenac for that of the Statue of Liberty, I ended up in the Midwest. Graduate school came next—economics at the University of Michigan—where I was not very happy, being fed an interminable diet of boring subjects: the specie-flow mechanism, the Mercantilist dilemma and the quantity theory of money, the optimum theory of population and subsistence wages, Say's identity and the dichotomization of the pricing process, the falling rate of profit and the stationary state, the marginal propensity to consume and the multiplier, the marginal efficiency of capital and psychological incentives to liquidity, the term structure of interest rates, the *IS* curve and the *LM* curve, Wicksell's proof of product exhaustion, the Pareto optimum and the Scitovsky double criterion, the limitations of the falsifiability criterion in economics—the list went on.

If I could have baked at least!

Fortunately, in the middle of graduate school, right after Soviet artillery, infantry, and tanks had put down the Hungarian Revolution and seized its "reactionary" leader, premier Imre Nagy, something else happened that changed everything in my life and even took care of what doctors in later years were to call my *PTSD* or post-traumatic stress disorder, which they considered chronic (symptoms having lasted for over three months) and of the delayed onset variety (symptoms having appeared at least six months after the stressor).

It started with a December 1956 letter from the President of the United States, sending me greetings and ordering me to appear, at precisely 7:00 A.M. one day, at the Greyhound Bus Station, 116 W. Huron St., Ann Arbor, Michigan. Before I knew it, I had taken and passed a large number of intelligence tests and was learning to fly! And this is the amazing thing: Being a pilot inside a plane, rather than a tiny, defenseless creature on the ground below it, made all my symptoms disappear. The talking cure had never worked very well; the flying cure did. It was so obvious in retrospect; how often had we talked about the safest place to be during the war-time years: *inside* the planes that rained destruction on us all and that had little to fear once the *Luftwaffe* [German air force] had been destroyed.

******

Our first two lessons took place on the ground. We learned about aerodynamics and basic airplane controls. Just as I had experienced in German schools, we were asked to copy graphs from the board and summarize what they were about. My initial aerodynamics graph looked like this:

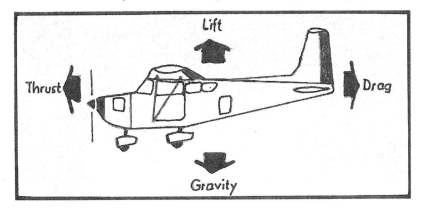

In this way, I illustrated the four forces affecting an airplane in flight: the natural forces of *gravity* and *drag*, which are opposed, respectively, by the man-made, artificial forces of *lift* and *thrust*. While upward lift is created by the movement of the air, known as *relative wind*, over a cambered wing, we learned, forward thrust is created by the engine spinning a propeller in front.

"In straight-and-level flight at a constant airspeed," our instructor said, "lift equals gravity and thrust equals drag."

My second graph was more complicated and illustrated three basic axes around which a plane can move under a pilot's control. First, a plane can move around a *lateral* or *pitch* axis that can be imagined to extend from wing tip to wing tip. By moving the "steering wheel" yoke forward or backward, a pilot can affect the position of horizontal tail surfaces, known as *elevators*, which makes the plane's nose go down or up. Second, a plane can move around a *vertical* or *yaw* axis that can be imagined to go vertically through the center of the plane. By moving foot-controlled rudder pedals right or left, a pilot can affect the position of the vertical tail surface or *rudder*, which makes the plane's nose go right or left. Third, a plane can move around a *longitudinal* or *roll* axis that can be imagined to go through the plane from back to front. By moving the "steering wheel" yoke right or left, a pilot can affect the position of trailing sections on the wings, known as *ailerons*, which makes the plane's right wing go down or up, while the left wing does the opposite.

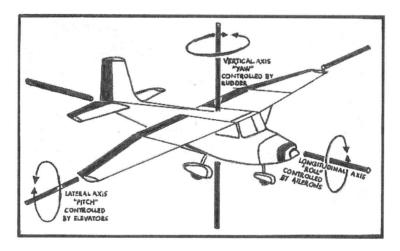

All this was interesting, but our lessons in the air were positively exciting. Looking at the world from above was such a beautiful experience! I loved the sunrises over Lake Huron and the morning fog snaking along the rivers. I loved the rainbow colors inside the clouds and the pink and purple skies after sunset. I loved climbing the plane at the precise moment of sunset and making the sun reappear on my horizon. By repeating the trick, I could look at several sunsets in a row. And I loved the day on which my macho instructor proudly showed me the "iron cross" he had allegedly taken from the chest of a dead German pilot whom he had downed. "Der Deutschen Mutter" the inscription said, "To the German Mother." I had seen that one before, on the day my grandmother had been given her Mother's Cross. My instructor was not happy with my translation.

******

By the summer of 1957, at just about the time Nikita S. Khrushchev was consolidating his power by ousting Vyacheslav M. Molotov, Georgi M. Malenkov, Lazar M. Kaganovich, and other Stalinists from important posts, I had mastered straight-and-level flight, level turns, climbs and descents at constant airspeeds, and even slow flight at constant altitudes. I was superb at ground reference maneuvers, deftly compensating for wind drift to fly a precise track over the ground, such as following a crooked road or a meandering stream, making S-turns across a road or steep turns about a *pylon*, such as the imagined point of intersection of two roads. After plenty of practice, my performance was second to none with respect to chandelles, gliding spirals, lazy eights, Dutch rolls. And I knew all there was to know about stalls—departure stalls, landing approach stalls, accelerated stalls—and also about spins, but I never managed to like accelerated stalls or spins.

"Keeping a constant altitude," my instructor would say, "roll the airplane into a 60 degree bank and keep it there. The total air load on the wings now corresponds to 2 Gs; likewise, your body weight is doubled, note how you are pressed into your seat, your cheeks sag, the blood begins to drain from your head…"

That kind of talk didn't make me happy at all. I tried to stay conscious by reciting in my head the latest stories I had read in *Pravda*, stories about Stalin's "excesses" and his collaborators' "persistent and deliberate actions to sabotage every effort to ease international tensions and improve the life of Soviet citizens at home." Somehow talking Russian to myself worked; I never passed out.

"Do the same thing at an 80 degree bank," my instructor continued, "and you have 5.75 Gs; you may grey out, even black out…now don't be a grandmother," said the man with the Mother's Cross, "stay with me, raise the pitch and you've got your accelerated stall…controlled flight becomes impossible, it's time to lower that nose, level the wings, give it full power to escape the stall. Do it *now!*"

And spins were even worse! There we are at 10,000 feet, wings level, power off to idle, pulling back the yoke to raise the nose…the airflow over the wings is interrupted, the airplane trembles and buffets, the stall warning light comes on, the horn blares, I give it full right rudder just then, and suddenly the nose points to the ground and the wings turn to the right, while I look north, then east, then south, then west and north again, and the altimeter reads 9,000 feet, 8,000 feet, 7,000 feet just as fast as you can read these words…and the instructor yells:

"You want to live? Opposite rudder, *now*! That slows the rotation…forward on the yoke, *ease* her out of the dive…add full power…" and there we are, flying straight-and level at 1,000 feet!

******

Take-offs and landings, on the other hand, were much more fun. I learned how altitude, temperature, and moisture affect the take-off run: the higher they are, the longer the run. Thus, on a high-elevation airport, on a hot and humid day, the runway may be too short to allow liftoff, and trying to take off can only lead to disaster. I liked knowing about things like that.

I equally liked the challenge of practicing take-offs and landings in different types of fields, such as short fields and soft fields and fields hampered by winds blowing across the runway rather than towards the plane. In a short field, I learned, the runway is surrounded by tall obstructions, such as trees and skyscrapers, and steep angles of climb and descent are needed, preferably without causing a stall. In a soft field, the runway itself is the problem, being covered with gravel, hay, mud, or snow and resisting all efforts to attain flying speed. And in a crosswind? One may have to land on a single wheel, while lowering one wing into the wind and pressing opposite rudder to keep the nose aligned with the runway!

******

By the time we started *night* flying, in October of 1957, the Soviets had just fired a 184 lb. satellite into space. We watched it through a telescope, a tiny speck of light circling the earth at 18,000 mph, some 560 miles up. We learned about all sorts of other lights, too: the blue lights along taxiways, the white runway lights, the red obstruction lights, the red light on the left wingtip, the green light on the right wingtip, and the brilliantly white strobe lights on the plane's belly and tail. And in the air, we learned about the night blind spot that could make an object seemingly disappear—it had something to do with those cones and rods—and our instructor did his best to get us lost in the invisible clouds of the night and experience the flicker vertigo caused by the strobe light reflecting on clouds and wings. It was easy to confuse stars and ground lights at first, but the experience of floating in the dark was amazing.

I was particularly fond of the VASI, the visual approach slope indicator, which was a set of lights on both sides of the runway's approach end. When a landing plane was on a perfect glide path to the runway threshold, the nearest set of lights appeared as white, a farther set appeared as red. When the plane was too high, assuring a disastrous landing near the end of the runway or beyond, all the lights appeared to be white. When the plane was too low, aiming for the ground before the runway was even reached, all the lights appeared as red. Moreover, and this was the most interesting part, a cockpit instrument known as the ADF, or automatic direction finder, contained an arrow pointing forward to a little broadcast station on the airport. If the plane flew over the station, the direction of the arrow reversed, pointing to the aircraft's tail. As I then learned, that little instrument was used during World War II to home in on regular broadcast stations, such as Radio Berlin or Radio Hamburg, which made it easy to find the cities in total darkness. While Dr. Goebbels shouted at us in the air raid shelters, he also guided Allied bombers to any target they wanted to reach! What irony! All they had to do was follow the ADF arrow to the station, watch the arrow reverse, and then fly any desired course for any desired length of time at any given speed to find any particular spot on the map. We practiced it: fly to the NDB [the nondirectional radio beacon] to which the ADF receiver is tuned, turn to a course of 095 degrees, adjusting for wind if necessary, hold the airspeed at 137 mph for 1 minute and 36 seconds, and we found ourselves over McDonald's red roof.

By then, I remember, it was November and we had something else to look for in the sky. The Soviets had fired a second satellite into orbit, this one weighing half a ton and carrying a dog, some 937 miles up. "Dedicated to the 40th anniversary of the Soviet revolution," *Pravda* said. It also reported on the fate of Marshal Georgi K. Zhukov, one of the conquerors of Berlin. Having been removed earlier as Minister of Defense, the paper said, he now also lost his Party posts. Marshal Ivan S. Konyev, whose troops had entered Ziesar so long ago and who was now commander of Warsaw Pact forces, condemned Marshal Zhukov for "errors in military science" (notably, his lack of preparedness for the June 1941 attack), for showing undue pride by twisting historical facts concerning the victories of Stalingrad and Berlin, and for promoting a cult of personality in the Red Army.

"With the help of sycophants and flatterers," said Marshal Konyev, "he was praised to the sky in lectures and reports, in articles, films, and pamphlets, and his person and role in the Great Patriotic War were overglorified."

******

As I said, flying seemed to be the perfect cure. My symptoms were gone by the time my military interlude was over and finishing graduate school became a breeze. By the time Eisenhower and Khrushchev had met and failed to end the Cold War in the fall of 1959, I had my Master of Arts degree in Economics. Before long, I was working on my Ph.D., writing a dissertation on *East Germany's Economic Integration into the Communist Bloc.*

Flying stories continued to dominate the news. I could not escape them, given my daily research into Soviet sources at the time. In the spring of 1960, it seemed, the Soviets downed a U.S. plane flying at 55,000 feet near Sverdlovsk. The U.S. claimed the unarmed U-2 was a weather observation plane chartered by NASA and flown by Francis G. Powers, 30, a civilian employee of the Lockheed Corporation. Allegedly, the civilian had innocently strayed across the Turkish/Soviet border, something even I wouldn't have done by mistake.

Khrushchev claimed the U.S plane had been on a mission of aggressive provocation aimed at wrecking the Paris summit conference scheduled for May. According to *Pravda*, Eisenhower wanted peace; the imperialists and militarists surrounding him did not. Then, when Khrushchev demanded and Eisenhower refused an apology for spying, the summit conference broke up. Prime Minister Macmillan, President de Gaulle, and President Eisenhower blamed Khrushchev, and the Cold War heated up. Before the next summer had passed, the Soviets shot down an RB-47 U.S. reconnaissance plane in the Barents Sea for violating Soviet territorial waters and a Soviet military tribunal sentenced Francis G. Powers to 10 years for spying.

By the time I received my Ph.D. in Economics, in the spring of 1961, the Soviets had orbited and recovered a man, Yuri Gagarin, in a 5-ton vehicle, called *Vostok* [East]. *Pravda* made fun of the U.S. mission that hurled Commander Alan B. Shepard, Jr., along a 115-mile suborbital path. By then, I had been in the U. S. for five and a half years and, suddenly, within the space of a month, it became unbearable. Something was unfinished; I simply had to visit Berlin.

******

Helga had a big apartment all to herself in East Berlin. It was located in one of the brand-new complexes that looked like the postcards from Moscow: a wide boulevard, flanked by 7-story buildings, lots of balconies, pillars, and statues, and white-slab blandness all around. Interestingly, her street name had just been changed; from Stalin Allee to Karl-Marx-Allee. Important people lived in her block: engineers and teachers, party officials, military men. Helga had become important, too. She taught at the Conservatory and was in charge of the concerts being broadcast over the radio in East Berlin. She was so important, in fact, she owned a *Trabant*, commonly known as *Trabi*, which was the new East German car made of "Duroplast," a fiber-reinforced plastic that could never rust.

It was easy to get to Helga. I took the city railway and waited for the Russian barracks. They were decorated with a big white sign. "Poslye Sputnika–Luna," it said. "After Sputnik–the Moon." That's where I got off. There was a big poster at her front door as well, although it was almost two years old. "German Democratic Republic," it said. "10 Years in Firm Alliance with the Soviet Union."

I brought Helga flowers from the West; I had been warned they only sold wilted ones in the East. It was awkward to meet again; what had I been thinking? We went to the opera; she got us in for nothing. I offered to reciprocate by taking her to a play or the ballet on the other side of town, but Helga complained about western decadence.

"People in the West only think of themselves," she said. "They only care about the latest clothes, TV sets, and cars. Who ever thinks of the public good?"

"That sounds like the Party line," I said. "Those Wednesday night political sessions haven't gotten to you, have they?" I asked.

That, of course, was the wrong thing to say. She lifted her left eyebrow in the way she had always done when she didn't agree with someone.

"I've read the pamphlet lying on your desk," I explained, "how did the author put it? 'The West condones the private pursuit of false material wants; we in the East prefer the public provision of true material needs.' Something like that."

I filled her coffee cup and took another piece of cake.

"You see what I mean?" I asked. "I'd rather let people decide for themselves what's good for them instead of having the Party decide on the grounds that it knows better."

"That leads to Coca Cola signs and neon lights," Helga said, picking up the plates.

"And indecent dress," she added.

"What about mental hospitals filled with dissidents?" I asked. "Isn't that indecent? And more so than ballet in the nude?"

She stood by the kitchen sink and said nothing.

"Never mind," I said.

I put my arms around her waist, from behind, but she freed herself. Nothing felt right.

"Well," I said, "I better go and do my work. May I see you on the weekend?"

******

On the weekend, my parents had a surprise. A letter arrived from Uncle Herbert who proved to us once and for all that he had gone mad. Had been flown out as a refugee by the Americans, he said, to Cologne, way back in '53. Had been to a birthday party in Kiel, he said, one for Grand Admiral Dönitz. Now we know for sure, he said, sabotage cost us the victory.

"Haven't seen him for ten years and haven't heard from him in eight," my father said. "I don't ever want to hear from that asshole again."

"You two certainly have fought each other long enough," I said, but I wasn't interested in Uncle Herbert. I was thinking of Helga and I didn't want to battle with her too.

I went to my old shelf of unread books to pick one for the ride to her apartment. I searched for an old one because I didn't care to be arrested for smuggling in subversive western thought. Frédéric Bastiat, Paris, 1845, looked safe enough.

At the station, I gave my last coins to the lady from the Salvation Army. Smuggling in western currency still was a crime as well. I opened Bastiat in the middle:

On coming to Paris for a visit, I said to myself: Here are a million human beings who would all die in a few days if supplies of all sorts did not flow into this great metropolis. It staggers the imagination to try to comprehend the vast multiplicity of objects that must pass through its gates tomorrow, if its inhabitants are to be preserved from the horrors of famine, insurrection, and pillage. And yet all are sleeping peacefully at this moment without being disturbed for a single instant by the idea of so frightful a prospect...

Yes. And I was frightened by the thought of losing my last chance of linking up with Helga. She was as beautiful as ever and she was still living by herself, I had noted. It was a sign, I thought. The sun was setting; the train crossed the Spree River. I returned to Bastiat:

We put our faith in that inner light which Providence has placed in the hearts of all men, and to which has been entrusted the preservation and the unlimited improvement of our species, a light we term self-interest, *which is so illuminating, so constant, and so penetrating, when it is left free of every hindrance. Where would you be, inhabitants of Paris, if some cabinet minister decided to substitute for that power contrivances of his own invention, however superior we might suppose them to be: if he proposed to subject this prodigious mechanism to his supreme direction to take control of all of it into his own hands, to determine by whom, where, how, and under what conditions everything should be produced, transported, exchanged, and consumed?*

"In East Berlin, that's where you'd be," I said to myself.

I thought of the wilted flowers in the East, of all shoes being the same size, of bathing suits finally arriving in the stores in winter, of everything breaking in no time and there being no spare parts for anything. I thought of the *Trabi* and its silly two-stroke engine that could accelerate from 0 to 60 in 21 seconds if you were lucky. And I thought of the barrels standing in East Berlin's food stores, filled with egg yolks and egg whites, labeled "Imported from the People's Republic of China," and destined to poison everybody with salmonella—just because nobody seemed able to get enough fresh eggs out of East Germany's collective farms.

"Government employees who get their pay no matter what they do," I thought, "will never be as enterprising and reliable as private owners in the West."

I also questioned my talent for picking a piece of literature that was safe enough for my trip to the East. Bastiat was getting more subversive by the minute:

Although there may be much suffering within your walls, although misery, despair, and perhaps starvation, cause more tears to flow than your warmhearted charity can wipe away, it is probable, I dare say it is certain, that the arbitrary intervention of the government would infinitely multiply this suffering and spread among all of you the ills that now affect only a small number of your fellow citizens.

"Spoken in 1845, like a true prophet," I thought. "West Berlin's prosperity versus East Berlin's drabness exactly proves his point."

******

I decided not to talk about ideology with Helga, not on that night. I felt anxious about us. I raced up the stairs to her apartment, taking two steps at a time. The elevator wasn't working, nothing unusual for East Berlin. But Helga saw the book when I took off my coat and asked about it. So I told her what I had read and thought. I shouldn't have; she would have none of it.

"Bastiat is outmoded," she said. "He may have been right in 1845. Modern central planners use science, as well as reason."

I decided to raise *my* left eyebrow.

"Planners have electric calculators now," she explained. "They are quite capable of managing the whole economy as if it were one single factory."

She handed me a mug with coffee.

"And central planners," she added, "can give people what is truly good for them and preserve them from the blind, selfish forces within themselves."

Where was the Helga I had known at Ziesar and Burg and even earlier in Berlin? What had they done with her? I heard nothing but the Party line, and I didn't like our conversation at all.

"My God," I said softly, "you are positively intoxicated by this cult of reason over here."

I wanted to hug her and shake her at the same time. So I hugged her and gave her a kiss.

"Why don't you come with me tonight and live with me?" I asked. "Forever!"

Her dark brown eyes turned soft and wet. A single tear flowed down her cheek.

"I'd be a traitor," she said, taking my hands. "They've educated me, they've offered me the position with the State Orchestra, they've given me this place. How can I leave now?"

"Easily," I said. "It takes one ticket for 30 pfennigs."

"I owe it to them," she said.

"And to my career," she added and stood up, raising a hand as if she wanted to ward off further discussion.

"Now there you are wrong," I said. "The very planners whom you now defend will ruin your career."

"And how is that?" she asked.

"Alright, I'll spell things out," I said, "but if it sounds like one of my lectures, I apologize ahead of time."

She smiled and sat down beside me on the couch.

"Central planners who want to get things done," I said, "done their own way, have to free themselves from constant criticism and griping. So they surround themselves with a loyal army and party. They create a secret police that forces others to submit to the planners' choices. Or they build a propaganda machine to induce everyone to accept a common creed and make these choices their own."

"So?" Helga asked.

"Before long," I continued, "the rule of fear and propaganda spreads to all areas of life, just as it does here, from purely economic matters of what is produced and who works where to questions of education and travel, of religion and family life, and certainly of art. And that'll be the end of your dream of a creative artistic career."

"Come with me," I said.

Helga said nothing.

I looked at her beautiful hair and the softness or her body, and I had thoughts I didn't like. Too much time had intervened, I thought, too many seasons, too many years had passed. Both of us remembered but dimly the flame of passion that had once brightened our lives. Something was forever lost; some door had closed forever.

"Let's talk more tomorrow," I said, but I felt the resistance of an alien spirit and the presence of an invisible wall that had grown up between us.

******

A few months later, they built another wall in Berlin, a 97-mile wall around the western sectors, 13 feet high, made of concrete and barbed wire. With watch towers, machine guns, and bright lights. With trip wires and land mines and roving packs of dogs. They called it the "antifascist protective barrier."

Helga was on the other side.

Thierry Noir, Wikimedia Commons

The Berlin Wall

46. A PERFECT FLIGHT

[May 1991]

Back to the beginning. Why did my plane crash? Was it the birds or was it me, perhaps, not paying attention and thinking about other things? You wanted details, all the details, about everything I did and thought. So let me try to reconstruct that fateful day.

Truth be told, it did start with a distraction. While picking up my morning mail on the way to the airport, I noticed the date on the big calendar at the Montague post office: May 23, 1991. And then I remembered. Precisely 30 years had passed since the day I had visited Helga in East Berlin! And I thought of Berlin because of the letter I was then holding in my hand. It had come from my Aunt Martel and proved that she was as alert as she had ever been, even at age 92. This time, she had sent me an article about mass graves they had discovered in Sachsenhausen after the fall of the Berlin Wall. Soon after the end of World War II, the article said, the place had become a concentration camp once again, first run by the Soviets, then the Stasi, the East German secret police. In fact, Sachsenhausen had been East Germany's biggest Stasi camp, holding 60,000 prisoners at one time or other. Some 12,000 of them had died from cold, hunger, disease, and cruelty.

But I didn't *want* to think about that or all the other terrible things that had happened a long time ago. This was the USA, not Germany. And it was a beautiful morning, made for flying—with cool crisp air and blue skies, they said, all along the East Coast from Maine to Florida.

"So you're going to Key West," Charlie said as he pumped the blue gasoline into my tanks. "That's a long trip, hope you won't fall asleep from boredom."

"Don't you worry, Charlie," I said, "I won't be bored. I'll keep myself busy by mentally reviewing my flight manuals. By the time I get there, I'll be the sharpest pilot on the East Coast."

"Good for you," Charlie said, "but you know what they say about flying: Hours of boredom, punctuated by moments of sheer terror."

"You seem to have had one of those moments yourself," I said, pointing to one of his airplanes sitting on its nose near the access road to the fire station, right next to the sign that stated "No Taxiway." The plane's tail was pointing straight up at the sky.

"Don't remind me," Charlie said. "Jeff was taking a woman for a scenic ride last weekend. Just as the plane lifted off, a wasp landed on the woman's nose. She went ballistic and screamed and kicked and tried to kill the thing and pushed forward on the yoke. You can guess the rest: The plane descended onto the runway, the propeller dug into the ground and got bent all out of shape, Jeff aborted the take-off, the left wing hit the hay wagon at the end of the runway, and the whole thing ended up in my celery field."

"No one was hurt, though," Charlie added, "unlike last year when the cows got out and Steven ran into one while trying to land at night. You know what the FAA report said? 'Pilot error: In-flight collision with a cow,' it said. Pretty funny, eh?"

He laughed uproariously, just like Mr. Albrecht always had way back in Ziesar.

******

By then I was busy with my preflight inspection. I removed the cowling from the engine, checked the oil quantity, the brake fluid, and the air intakes, found no leaks around the cylinders, fastened the cowling, and did my walk-around. The propeller was in good shape, no nicks and scratches or cracks as far as I could see. I took the tow bar off the front wheel and stashed it with the baggage, checking the battery through the baggage door at the same time. The newly waxed wings glistened in the sun, the flaps were okay, the ailerons moved freely and so did the elevator. The vertical stabilizer looked fine. So did the antennas and all the lights. The tanks were filled to the brim. A first lesson raced through my head: The fuel tank cap seals better be in perfect shape. If they are too tight, air can't enter the tank as the gasoline is used, a vacuum is created, and the wing can collapse. If they are too loose, fuel can be siphoned overboard. Neither one was a pleasant event, but there was no problem here; the seals were fine.

I crawled underneath the wings, drained some fuel from each tank into my fuel tester, and happily noted the absence of water, which, being heavier than gasoline, would settle at the bottom of the tank and appear as bubbles in my tube. Thus a second lesson came to mind: One doesn't want water mixed in with the gasoline, lest the engine sputter and stop; yet water can come from servicing the plane out of improperly filtered tanks (Charlie's were okay) or from parking the plane with partially filled tanks on a humid day when water condenses out of the moist air on the inside walls (I would never do that). Water isn't going to stop my engine on take-off, I thought, nor at any time during flight for that matter.

My eyes moved to the next two items on my checklist: Yes, my fuel sample was free of wasps and ants and other foreign materials. And, yes, the octane rating was 91/96, as evidenced by the color blue; one would be foolish to feed this engine with 80/87 red or 100/130 green or even the purple liquid that boasts a lean/rich anti-knock quality of 115/145.

I checked the tire pressure; I certainly didn't want a flat on take-off or landing, followed by cart wheeling across the ground at 80 mph. And I said hello to the all-important pitot tube underneath the left wing. Away from the propeller slipstream, I knew, it sampled the impact pressure of the relative wind and brought to life three crucial instruments, measuring airspeed, altitude, and vertical velocity. Nobody would want to fly without them working properly; yet a little gnat building a nest in that tube could force one to do just that!

******

Inside the cockpit, I checked the paper work. Everything was in its proper place: the airworthiness certificate, the radio station license, the manufacturer's flight manual, the maintenance logs for airframe, engine, and radios, and, last but not least, my pilot's license, medical certificate, and pilot's logbook. I clipped the aeronautical charts to my knees and took a last look at my weight and balance calculus: As required for safety, the plane's empty weight plus the day's useful load—the combined weight of pilot, oil, fuel, and baggage—fell short of the maximum weight authorized for take-off, known as the gross weight. I thought about the dangers of excessive gross weight: a shallow climb or none at all; increased fuel consumption and, therefore, decreased range; increased engine wear and, therefore, greater likelihood of stoppage; faster touchdown and, therefore, longer landing roll; weakened airframe structure and, therefore, possible break-up in turbulence; decreased stability and controllability in flight, and a dangerously higher stalling speed. I wanted none of these. Likewise, I rechecked my balance computations; on this day, the plane's center of gravity (CG), the point akin to the fulcrum of a balanced teeterboard at which the aircraft's weight was effectively concentrated, was well within the limits specified in the flight manual. I knew: An excessively forward CG would increase the speed at which the plane stalls; a CG too far behind would make it impossible to recover from a stall.

I locked the cabin door, tested the ELT [emergency locator transmitter], and thought how funny it was that newscasters always referred to it as a black box—mine was yellow! I glanced at the circuit breakers, set the elevator trim for take-off, and moved the fuel selector to L. To counteract the plane's annoying tendency to roll left because of my own weight in the left seat, I would burn off fuel from the left tank first. My checklist told me I was ready to start the engine. I set the hand brake and looked behind; no people or other planes about to be blown away by my prop. No one in front either; still, I opened the pilot's window and, just as the FAA demanded, yelled "Clear!" Master switch ON, fuel pump ON. I pumped the throttle three times, pressed the starter button and moved the magneto switch to BOTH. The propeller was purring. Quite automatically, my eyes moved to the oil pressure gauge, then the oil temperature gauge; both were in the green; no oil starvation here, no excess engine heat. Equally automatically, my hands had turned on all the radios; it was time to call for my instrument clearance and read it back:

"November Eight Eight One Two Juliet is cleared to the destination airport via Zero Bravo Five direct Gardner, Victor Two Two Niner Hartford, Victor One Norfolk International; climb to maintain Eight Thousand, squawk One Two Eight Zero; on departure contact Boston Center on One Two Three Point Seven Five."

"Read-back correct; clearance void if not off by Thirteen Thirty Zulu" was the response.

I had 15 minutes to get into the air.

******

I looked at the windsock. The surface wind was practically calm, favoring runway 16. I taxied to the run-up area, watching a Cessna on the downwind leg and a Mooney on final approach. I set the transponder to 1280, one of the radios to 123.75, and one of the navigation units to 110.6, the Gardner VOR [a navigational beacon, known as a Very high frequency Omni-directional Range] to which I would navigate right after take-off. I listened to its Morse code ID, a distinct GDM. Looking up, I noticed little clouds race across the sun, driven by northerly winds aloft. I was counting on those winds; they would speed up my trip. With my feet on the brakes, I advanced the throttle to gain 1,800 RPM, switched the magnetos to Right, then Left, and back to Both; turned on the carburetor heat and watched the RPM drop just as it should (carburetor heat would deal with icing in clouds or during power-off glides); checked the alternate static source (it would save me from instrument failure if the vacuum pump failed), noted the Mooney leaving the runway and the Cessna over the threshold about to touch down. No other traffic in sight.

"November Eight Eight One Two Juliet taking Runway One Six at Turners Falls," I said, while moving onto the threshold, setting the altimeter to 346 feet and the directional gyro to 160 degrees. Smoothly applying full power, I raced down the runway centerline, watched the speed build to 80 and lifted off at 13:23 Zulu [Greenwich Mean Time]. It would take about two hours and fifteen minutes to fly 420 nautical miles to Norfolk.

******

With a heavy foot on the right rudder pedal to compensate for the left-turning engine torque during take-off, I climbed over the hills to the east and nudged the plane towards the Gardner VOR on a course of 112 degrees. To my left, the Connecticut River came into view, stretching northwards towards mysterious places where it was born and I saw New Hampshire's Mount Monadnock, 3,165 feet high. Straight ahead, I noticed Orange Airport and, to my right, the giant Quabbin Reservoir, perfectly outlined with a white blanket of morning fog, but the green tops of some of the islands were beginning to peek through.

"Boston Center, November Eight Eight One Two Juliet airborne at Turners Falls, out of One Thousand, climbing to maintain Eight Thousand."

"November Eight Eight One Two Juliet, Boston Center, ident."

I pushed the small green button on my transponder and knew it would transmit a special position identification pulse (SPI) that would fill in the space between the two parallel lines representing my plane on the far-away radar scope and leave no doubt in the controller's mind that the fat green rectangle then forming on his scope was me, then climbing through 1,780 feet.

"One Two Juliet, Boston Center, radar contact," was the expected response.

"One Two Juliet," I said.

******

By the time I reached 8,000 feet and reduced the throttle to cruise power, I was on Victor Airway 229 steering 209 degrees towards the EAGRE intersection, which made me think of World War II when the current airway system was created and all the routes were called Victor in anticipation of Victory. The little green transponder light kept blinking at me and I should have been happy that Air Traffic Control was watching me, but my mind went elsewhere.

I thought of Mr. Eisler and how he had sent us out into the streets at night with green phosphorous buttons on our clothes to stamp out every last light that enemy pilots might see. The happy purr of my engine turned into something else as well. I heard the nerve-wracking hum of engines overhead my Spreewald train, droning like mosquitoes high up in the sky. And suddenly, dozens of lights flashed all around us. Parachutes, each sparkling with a thousand lights, it seemed, hung overhead, motionless. "Christmas trees, just Christmas trees," the lieutenant had said. "Nobody's going to get us." I heard the sound of machine guns, saw an airplane veer off to the right, just missing the trees at the edge of the meadow. I felt blood trickle down my cheek; glass splinters lay in my lap. I saw the lieutenant slumped in his seat across from me. Dark blood poured from his mouth, slowly spreading over his chest, flowing over his medals, soaking his pants, the upholstered bench, dripping to the floor...

"Stop it!" I said to myself. I had another look at the Quabbin Reservoir, again on my right, where some of the fog had disappeared and I could then see the oval racetrack that once stood beside the village now submerged. And there was Worcester airport and beyond it the city to the left, Westover Air Force Base and Springfield on the right, Bradley International in clear view. The sky was brilliant blue. It was a CAVU day: ceilings and visibility unlimited; a pilot's dream.

I slowly pulled the red knob of the mixture control and watched the EGT gauge. The exhaust gas temperature rose and rose; once it peaked, I slightly reversed the process and my fuel/air ratio was perfect for the trip. Mentally, I was in the midst of flight lesson #3: Ideally, for every pound of fuel entering the cylinder, there should be 15 pounds of air. At this chemically correct mixture, the cylinder temperature would be the hottest and all the fuel would be burned. But because air is less dense at higher altitudes, the 1:15 ratio can only be maintained by providing less fuel for a given volume of air at higher altitude, that is, by "leaning the mixture." I knew: If the mixture was too rich, with too much fuel per unit of air, the temperature in the spark plug center electrode (and the exhaust gas) would be too low, spark plugs would foul with carbon and lead deposits and the electric current would flow through the deposits instead of jumping the gap to ignite the fuel/air charge. And if the mixture was too lean, with too little fuel per unit of air, the engine would run rough, cut out, even detonate—provide spontaneous explosions of unburned charge in the cylinders rather than a slow burn. Eventually, that would cause dished piston heads, collapsed valve heads, broken rings, erosion of valves, pistons, and cylinder heads, and sudden, complete engine failure. Correct leaning at higher altitudes was a crucial procedure.

It was time for Lesson #4, my knowledge of the magnetic compass. I accelerated the plane and noticed the compass turn to the north—the acceleration error. I decelerated the plane and the compass turned to the south—the deceleration error. I remembered the memory aid: ANDS = accelerate, north; decelerate, south. Mentally, I also reviewed the turn error: While turning east or west from a northerly heading, the compass would lag and show a much lesser turn. While turning east or west from a southerly heading, the compass would lead and show a much greater turn. But I couldn't practice that; Boston Center would see me zigzagging across the sky; they wouldn't like it. And I thought of all the other things that could make the compass lie to an unsuspecting pilot—metal objects nearby, radios turned on, turbulence, and strobe lights on—but my review came to an end.

"One Two Juliet, traffic two o'clock, below you, United Twenty-Five Heavy, climbing to maintain Seven Thousand," Boston Center warned.

"Boston Center, One Two Juliet has the traffic," I said, as the giant plane slid below me.

At Eagre, I changed course and steered 248 degrees towards the Hartford VOR, confirmed the Morse code HFD on frequency 114.9, and had a clear view of Long Island Sound.

"One Two Juliet, contact Boston Center now on One Three Two Point Three," someone said.

"Boston Center, One Two Juliet maintaining Eight Thousand," I replied.

Soon I was on Victor Airway 1, flying 211 degrees to the Madison VOR (frequency 110.4 and

Morse code MAD), noting New Haven and Bridgeport on the right and then water underneath. I turned to 235 degrees and, thus, towards the Deer Park VOR (frequency 117.7 and code DPK).

"One Two Juliet, contact New York Center now on One Three Three Point Two," someone said.

"New York Center, One Two Juliet maintaining Eight Thousand," I replied.

"One Two Juliet, New York Center, radar contact."

I was flying 258 degrees towards the Kennedy VOR (frequency 115.9 and code JFK) when I spotted a Concorde landing 8,000 feet below and then I watched the skyscrapers of Manhattan and the Statue of Liberty, a majestic sight. Even at 8,000 feet I could see hundreds of seagulls flying around the statue, landing on its crown, its outstretched arm, the torch held high. I imagined tourists feeding them, as Dieter and I had done way back in Berlin. *That plane came out of nowhere! It flew low and fast along the canal and its wing tips almost touched the crowns of the linden trees. They had new green leaves, covered with a dusting of snow. I saw red-and-yellow tongues flickering along the wings, bullets stitching their way across the bridge. One plane, a burst of thunder, a single cry on Dieter's lips. I saw his head, half gone, half turned into a bloody mess. I saw the flutter of his hand, his body jerk, snow turning red. There was no solid ground beneath my feet, I could not breathe, my mind was numb, my body turned to stone. I couldn't move; my words, they wouldn't come. I heard seagulls cry in rage...*

"Stop it!" I said to myself. Continuing on Victor 1 and flying 221 degrees towards the DIXIE intersection, I crossed over the water from Long Island's south shore, over land again, with the Atlantic on the left and Lakehurst on the right. That was the very spot, I knew, where Germany's Zeppelin had burned during a thunderstorm in May of 1937, some 54 years ago. I remembered the book about the event that Mr. Barzel had given me—*Cabin Boy Werner Franz*—a reward for collecting all those newspapers during the war.

"One Two Juliet, traffic twelve o'clock, 500 feet above you, Boeing 747, opposite direction," New York Center warned, but I couldn't see anything for the life of me.

"New York Center, One Two Juliet negative on the traffic," I said.

I reviewed the story of wake turbulence: In the air, all aircraft produce wing-tip vortices, invisible horizontal tornadoes that stretch back from each wingtip while in flight. The vortices slowly settle down towards the ground, but in large aircraft these compact, fast-spinning air masses are particularly violent and extend behind the plane for miles. I didn't like the idea of flying underneath the path of one of these.

"One Two Juliet, clear of traffic," New York Center said and just then I ran into light turbulence similar to that encountered in and near small cumulus clouds or in lower altitudes when surface winds exceed 15 knots or cold air travels over warmer ground.

I was passing the Coyle VOR (frequency 113.4 and code CYN) when I spied Philadelphia on the right and Atlantic City ahead of me on the left, and soon reached the LEEAH intersection above the waters of Delaware Bay. Silently, I gave thanks to the fact that I had escaped *severe* turbulence in my encounter with the larger plane. Such turbulence, I knew, was usually found in and near growing and mature thunderstorms, put aircraft momentarily out of control, threw passengers violently against seat belts, and tossed unsecured objects about. Indeed, I had heard stories of smaller aircraft encountering the wake of giant military planes and experiencing *extreme* turbulence, a category usually found in growing, severe thunderstorms and squall lines that are accompanied by large hailstones and continuous lightning and toss aircraft violently about, making them impossible to control and inflicting upon them structural damage with fatal consequences. But this, clearly, was my lucky day.

"One Two Juliet, contact Washington Center now on One Three Two Point Zero Five," someone said.

"Washington Center, One Two Juliet maintaining Eight Thousand," I replied.

"One Two Juliet, Washington Center, radar contact."

Flying 213 degrees across the bay towards the Waterloo VOR (frequency 112.6 and code ATR), I noticed a thin, transparent, whitish cloud layer way above me. It looked like a veil, with pretty halos in spots; that was cirrostratus for sure. On the ground, to the right, I spotted Dover Air Force Base beyond the western coast and Cape May to the left, proceeded 216 degrees towards the Salisbury VOR (frequency 111.2 and code SBY), and surveyed the Atlantic on my left and Chesapeake Bay to the right. It was filled with sailboats. Via JAMIE intersection in the middle of the bay and 196 degrees to the Cape Charles VOR (frequency 112.2 and code CCV), I left the Delaware Peninsula for the short 29-mile trip across the water, flying 209 degrees towards the Norfolk VOR (frequency 116.9 and code ORF). That's when I abandoned my flight lessons, tuned a radio to 127.15, and listened to the ATIS.

"This is the Norfolk Automated Terminal Information Service. This advisory prepared at 15:00 Zulu. Current conditions 3,000 scattered, 18,000 overcast, visibility greater than 6, wind 240 degrees at 8. ILS/DME Runway 23 in use, altimeter setting 30.20. Caution: Flocks of birds in the vicinity of the airport."

The advisory, I noted, was fairly trustworthy, being a mere 20 minutes old. Given the weather, there was no need to fly the instrument approach to Runway 23. For all practical purposes, I was already lined up with the 9,000 foot runway. The instrument landing system (ILS), consisting of localizer (lining me up with the runway centerline), glideslope indicator (providing me with a perfect line of descent to the runway threshold), and distance measuring equipment (DME) or three-light marker beacons (providing precise distance information from the airport along a predetermined course)—all these were equally unnecessary. Once I was below the scattered clouds, I would see the entire airport from 25 miles out; I could fly a much more rapid, visual approach.

"One Two Juliet, contact Norfolk Approach on One One Eight Point Niner," Washington Center said.

"One Two Juliet," I replied and on another radio: "Norfolk Approach, November Eight Eight One Two Juliet, maintaining Eight Thousand, requesting visual approach."

"One Two Juliet, Norfolk Approach," came the reply, "cleared visual approach Runway Two Three, descend to maintain Two Thousand."

"One Two Juliet out of Eight for Two," I said, but for insurance and practice I still tuned in the Runway 23 localizer and glideslope (frequency 109.1 and code IJZQ).

By the time I reached 2,000 feet, my DME read 11.3 miles and I had the runway in sight.

"One Two Juliet, Norfolk Tower now on One Two Zero Point Eight," Approach Control said.

"Norfolk Tower, November Eight Eight One Two Juliet, Eleven mile final Runway Two Three, maintaining Two Thousand," I said.

"One Two Juliet, cleared to land Runway Two Three; altimeter setting Three Zero Point Two Zero; wind Two Hundred Forty degrees at six."

"One Two Juliet, out of Two Thousand," I said, reducing my speed to 80, flipping on carburetor heat, the fuel pump, and letting down the flaps, all at the same time.

Soon the blue outer marker light was blinking, 4.9 miles to go, then the yellow middle marker sounded, I was practically there, perfect alignment with the runway centerline, perfect altitude at 200 feet, perfect touchdown.

"One Two Juliet, contact Ground on One Two One Point Niner," someone said.

"One Two Juliet clear of active," I replied while leaving the runway.

"One Two Juliet cleared to Piedmont Hawthorne Aviation," the ground controller said and before I knew it, I had parked the plane, pulled out the mixture control, and starved the engine of gas. The propeller stopped.

A perfect flight? Not quite. While my hand reached out to turn off the Master Switch, I noticed something else. Strange. I had never even turned *on* the landing lights during my approach. Besides being a real help to binocular-wielding controllers on the ground, of course, those lights are supposed to scare away the birds and there are plenty of them at any airport near the shore.

47. THE CRASH

[May 1991]

At Norfolk, I gassed up the plane for the remainder of my trip, had lunch, got a new weather briefing, and then called Clearance Delivery on frequency 118.5.

"November Eight Eight One Two Juliet is cleared to the Key West International Airport via Victor One Craig, Victor Two Six Seven Miami, Victor One Five Seven; climb to maintain Eight Thousand, squawk Zero Seven Two Five; maintain runway heading on take-off, contact Departure on One Two Five Point Two."

I started the plane and contacted Ground Control.

"Norfolk Ground, November Eight Eight One Two Juliet, at Piedmont, with clearance, I-F-R to Key West, ready to taxi."

"November Eight Eight One Two Juliet, cleared to Runway Two Three via taxiways Charlie and Delta, follow the Piper Seneca passing in front of you."

"One Two Juliet," I said and, speaking those numbers, I thought of the days when my name had been Five.

By the time I got near the runway, I was Number 6 in line. I saw the Seneca in front of me, then a Beech Baron, a Comanche, an Aero Commander, and a Gates Learjet. A Mitsubishi MU-2B was touching down just then and a Grumman American was on short final. I did my run-up, set the altimeter to Norfolk's elevation of 26 feet, and contacted the Tower on 118.9.

"Norfolk Tower, November Eight Eight One Two Juliet ready for take-off in sequence."

By the time the Seneca was rolling down the runway, a Boeing 747 was on final approach. I knew what was coming next and carefully noted the Boeing's touchdown point, an unusual 1,000 feet from the threshold.

"One Two Juliet, position and hold," the Tower said after the Boeing had passed my nose.

I taxied onto the runway threshold, right on top of the big numbers, reading 23.

"One Two Juliet, position and hold," I said, watching the Boeing vacate the runway at the far end.

"One Two Juliet, cleared for immediate take-off," the Tower said, "wind 240 degrees at 15; caution wake turbulence."

He didn't have to remind me of that; I had been thinking of nothing else. I knew: The effects of vortices were strongest when larger aircraft took off at maximum gross weight; a smaller and lighter aircraft like mine that penetrated those little tornadoes could easily incur structural failure or flip over and be slammed into the ground. But a Boeing that was *landing* could wreak havoc on me as well, even long after it had left the runway! Except for one thing: The invisible vortices traveled between the plane's flight path and the ground; they stopped the moment the aircraft touched the ground. Thus, if I took off from somewhere *beyond* its touchdown point, I would be just fine. In fact, even in flight, regardless of any take-off or landing situation, a smaller craft would incur no harm as long as it stayed *above* the flight path of any offending plane; vortices were always settling towards the ground.

"One Two Juliet," I said and rapidly taxied 1,000 feet down the runway to the Boeing's touchdown point; only then did I push the throttle to FULL. About four and a half hours and 863 nautical miles to Key West; I should get there by sunset.

"Norfolk Departure, November Eight Eight One Two Juliet, out of Five Hundred, climbing to maintain Eight Thousand."

"One Two Juliet, Norfolk Departure, radar contact, proceed on course, contact Washington Center on One Two Three Point Eight Five."

"Washington Center, November Eight Eight One Two Juliet, level at Eight Thousand."

By then I was established on Victor Airway 1, steering 233 degrees towards the Cofield VOR (frequency 114.6 and code CVI). On my left, the Atlantic coastline was receding, but way in the distance I could see the spot where Kitty Hawk must be and the Wright Monument stood, next to the airport called *First Flight*. Way ahead and above, I spotted cirrocumulus, thin sheets of cloud with lots of small white puffs like patches of cotton balls, and to the right, altocumulus, white layers of solid clouds that gave the appearance of a wavy tin roof.

All was well; I decided to review my instruments, one at a time. My two best friends, both driven by a vacuum pump, were right in front of my eyes. I loved the *Attitude Indicator* with its horizon bar and miniature airplane, always providing an immediate indication of the aircraft's pitch and bank attitude in relation to the natural horizon. It was working perfectly: The wings sat on the horizon bar, as did the plane's nose; I was in straight and level flight. And the instrument was working because the suction gauge read between 3.75 and 5.1 inches of mercury, as it should.

I was equally enamored with the *Directional Gyro*, showing the number 25 just then under the hairline and confirming my magnetic course of 233 degrees, adjusted for the winds aloft. Unlike the magnetic compass, this one, when it was working, never lied.

Before long, I was steering 218 degrees towards the Kinston VOR (frequency 109.6 and code ISO). I watched the Chowan River pass under my left wing and then Phelps Lake and Lake

Mattamuskeet and the Pamlico River, but Cape Hatteras was hidden from view under dense, well defined domes of afternoon cumulus clouds. I could see their cauliflower heads developing below me and mentally pictured supercooled large drops fall from their bases, creating virga, those lovely trails of evaporating rain that never reach the ground.

"One Two Juliet, contact Washington Center now on One Three Five Point Three," someone said and I did.

"Washington Center, November Eight Eight One Two Juliet, maintaining Eight Thousand."

I turned to my pitot-static system instruments; there were three. The *Vertical Velocity Indicator* was the simplest one. It showed neither climb nor descent and, thus, a vertical speed of zero. The *Airspeed Indicator* was more complex; I reviewed its markings. The white arc was the flap operating range; something to remember during a landing approach. Its lower limit was the power-off stalling speed with flaps down; extending the flaps at higher airspeed would cause severe structural damage and was not advisable. The green arc was the normal operating range, that's were I was now. Its lower limit was the power-off stalling speed with flaps retracted. And the yellow arc was the caution range, containing a menu of speeds one would only use in the smoothest of air. The red line, of course, was the never-exceed speed; going there meant structural break-up and certain death.

The *Altimeter* was another friend; I had the three pointer sensitive type. I should set it, I remembered, to a current altimeter setting of some airport along my route. Otherwise, the instrument might lie: When flying into colder air or lower pressure, the altimeter readout would be higher than the truth! A simple test was in order. I tuned to the Wilmington ATIS; the altimeter setting was 30.00 inches of mercury, lower than Norfolk's 30.20. I entered the new setting into the altimeter; instantly the indicated altitude dropped from 8,000 to 7,800 feet! I climbed 200 feet and reviewed another lesson of long ago.

It was the story of atmospheric pressure, the force exerted by the weight of the atmosphere on a given area. Take an open dish of mercury and place into it the open end of an evacuated tube. At sea level and average temperature, the atmosphere's pressure causes the mercury to rise into the vacuum tube till it reaches a height of 29.92 inches. Thus the air at sea level weighs the same as a 29.92 inch-high column of mercury! At higher altitudes, however, the air balanced against the mercury column would weigh less. As a result, its pressure would create a shorter mercury column. Indeed, as experience has shown, the column of mercury tends to decrease by 1 inch per 1,000 feet of altitude. I knew: This little fact made it possible to create my *Altimeter*, a neat little scale to weigh the atmosphere, but a scale that happened to be calibrated to indicate altitude instead of the pressure created by the weight of the air.

I was so pleased with myself. How lucky I was that I could entertain myself with such lofty thoughts! Indeed, I recalled another thing my flying teacher had claimed: If one used water instead of mercury in the aforementioned experiment, one would create a column of water that was 32 feet high! That would hardly be useful for creating an instrument of manageable size. Somehow, thinking about water took me somewhere else. *"It is a matter we cannot bury and ignore,"* Mr. Barzel had said. *"You may well come into contact with phosphorus one of these nights and the only thing that will save you from terrible burns is having a sponge ready and a pail full of water nearby. Or you might drape your heads in wet towels as you sit in your shelters. Always remember: Phosphorus Hates Water."*

"One Two Juliet, Washington Center, traffic twelve o'clock, opposite direction 500 feet below you," someone said.

I couldn't possibly see any traffic; a gray uniform layer of stratus clouds had formed just below me, reaching in all directions as far as I could see.

"One Two Juliet, no joy," I said.

By then I was flying 219 degrees towards the Grand Strand VOR (frequency 117.6 and code CRE), located just north of Myrtle Beach, which soon emerged from the clouds, sitting there in the bright sun. *"Those bombs sprayed some people with phosphorus and they couldn't get it off: Gerda says they jumped into the canal or rolled in the sand to kill the flames, but the moment they stopped, the fire came back."*

"One Two Juliet, contact Jacksonville Center now on One Two Eight Point Seven," someone said and I did.

I turned to 234 degrees towards the Charleston VOR (frequency 113.5 and code CHS) and all the clouds disappeared. I watched the coastline on my left, passed Lake Moultrie on my right and, as newly instructed, switched to Jacksonville Center on frequency 127.95. There was ample time to talk to myself. As Charleston passed under me, I was in the midst of reviewing my *Turn-and-Bank Indicator*, commonly known as the *Needle and Ball*. This lovely instrument, I said to myself, shows an aircraft's rate of turn about its vertical axis. The turn needle always deflects in the direction of the plane's bank; right then, I noted, there was no deflection at all, confirming the fact that I was in straight flight. I also reviewed the turn indices, looking like little doghouses and so referred to by pilots. If the needle were to be pegged to a doghouse, right or left, the plane would be in a 3-degrees-per-second turn. One could hit the stopwatch and wait 1 minute to make a 180 degree turn and, thus, reverse course. And then there was the ball, sitting in its glass cage underneath the needle. When centered during a bank, the plane was in a *well coordinated* turn; passengers wouldn't feel as if they were being pushed to the right or left by some scary invisible hand. But they would feel just that if a pilot used too little rudder or excessive rudder in the direction of a turn. The former case, known as a "slipping turn," would move the ball in the direction of the turn; the latter case, known as a "skidding turn," would move the ball in the opposite direction from the turn. Either indication could be cured by pressing on the rudder pedal on the side of the non-centered ball. "Step on the ball!" flight instructors would yell. And then passengers would stop feeling as if they were being pushed out of the plane!

"Don't step on the glass," my mother had said. Mrs. Nussbaum's grocery store had been smashed to bits! The door was dangling from broken hinges. The giant store window lay in a thousand pieces on the sidewalk. Mrs. Nussbaum was sweeping up her window. She was sobbing. We stepped over huge slivers of glass, each one like a sword...

"Stop it!" I said to myself. I was flying over the ocean by then, steering 219 degrees towards TYBEE intersection and then 203 degrees to the Craig VOR (frequency 114.5 and code CRG). Savannah passed under my right wing and Jacksonville appeared straight ahead.

"November Eight Eight One Two Juliet, contact Jacksonville Center now on One Two Zero Point Eight Five, descend to maintain Four Thousand," someone said as I passed Craig.

I didn't like the altitude change; I had counted on the stronger tailwinds up high to push me along and save me from another refueling stop. And I certainly didn't like the prospect of later flying over the Gulf of Mexico at such a low altitude.

"Jacksonville Center, One Two Juliet requesting Eight Thousand for over-water flight," I said.

"One Two Juliet, Jacksonville Center, roger... maintain Eight Thousand, contact Jacksonville Center on One Two Six Point Seven Five."

"Jacksonville Center, One Two Juliet, thank you, maintaining Eight Thousand."

Proceeding along Victor 267 on a course of 178 degrees towards the Orlando VOR (frequency 112.2 and code ORL), I passed in rapid succession St. Augustine on the left, St. John's River and then Lake George on the right and Daytona Beach on the left. Farther to the south, the NASA Shuttle landing facility was hidden under lower clouds. Turning to 162 degrees, I passed over Orlando International and listened to the Southern Florida weather report. I didn't like it at all.

"This is the Miami Flight Service Station. This recording prepared at 20:55 Zulu; a briefing summary for Miami and the Keys. Weather advisory: An Airmet has been issued for IFR conditions, occasional ceilings less than 1,000, visibility less than 6 miles in precipitation and mist, occasional moderate turbulence below 10,000.

Current conditions at Key West: Marginal VFR, 1,300 overcast, surface winds 300 degrees at

8 knots, gusting to 12, temperature 60 degrees, altimeter setting 29.92. Forecast valid until 24:00 Zulu: 1,000 overcast, visibility greater than 3, surface winds 300 degrees at 15, gusting to 22.

After 24:00 Zulu: Ceilings and visibility lowering, with warm front passage after midnight local. Current position of front in the Gulf of Mexico, 90 miles to the west northwest, containing heavy rain showers and thundershowers, severe turbulence, and continuous lightning. The Coast Guard reports overcast cumulonimbus clouds with bases at 300-400 feet and excellent visibility underneath; a pilot report indicates cloud tops at flight level 450. Additional pilot weather reports are requested and appreciated.

Notices to Airmen: Restricted Area 2916 is active; unlighted balloon with ground cable at 14,000 feet 17 miles northeast of Key West International. Military training activity: Intensive jet fighter traffic at Naval Air Station Key West 3 miles east."

There was a lot to digest. The Airmet was not a problem. It indicated danger to inexperienced pilots and ill-equipped aircraft; neither one applied to me. I could forgo the VFR [visual flight rules] approach and land on instruments; that was the whole point of my IFR [instrument flight rules] flight plan. Clearly, the air pressure had continued to fall; I reset my altimeter to 29.92 and climbed another 80 feet to regain 8,000.

I glanced at my *Outside Air Temperature* gauge; it read 32 degrees Fahrenheit, which made perfect sense. As one gains altitude, the air temperature usually becomes lower. In the troposphere, which extends from the ground to somewhere between 25,000 and 65,000 feet (lower over the poles, higher over the equator), the temperature lapse rate averages 3.5 degrees Fahrenheit per 1,000 feet. Given 60 degrees on the ground, it should be freezing at 8,000 feet.

And yes, I remembered, on occasion, the usual decrease of temperature with altitude is inverted. Such inversions are most common near the ground on clear, still nights; then terrestrial radiation occurs and the ground loses heat rapidly, cooling the lowest layer of air and, simultaneously creating restrictions to vision, such as fog, haze, and low clouds. And then there are frontal inversions as well, as when cooler air moves under warm air, which thought brought me back to the big story, the warm front in the Gulf.

Wow! Cumulonimbus clouds reaching to 45,000 feet! While flying, I had often seen those heavy, dense clouds from afar, shaped like mountains or massive towers, with tops in the shape of anvils and with bases of dark, ragged clouds, producing torrential rain and severe turbulence, along with lightning and thunder, as well as hail, ice, sleet, and snow aloft and possibly tornados or waterspouts on the ground. Pilots knew all too well that these cbs—pronounced sea bees— constituted a great danger to *all* types of aircraft. Thus, I could foresee the Sigmet being issued a few hours later, scaring everyone to death, as these "significant meteorological development reports" were meant to do.

But I wasn't *overly* worried. If all went as planned, I would reach Key West at sunset time, four hours before the front arrived. Above me right then, way up high, I only saw cirrus—patches of thin, white featherlike clouds moving in narrow bands and composed, no doubt, of ice crystals, some of which trailed down a great vertical extent in pretty wisps, called "mare's tails."

By then I was established on Victor 267, passing Melbourne to my left and then Vero Beach and looking at Lake Okeechobee right in front. Crossing the center of the giant lake, I reached the Pahokee VOR (frequency 115.4 and code PHK) on its southern coast. Steering 157 degrees towards Miami, I looked in vain for West Palm Beach to my left—it was hidden under coastal clouds—but I could soon see the airports of Fort Lauderdale and then Opa Locka and, finally, Miami International. A right turn to 248 degrees put me on Victor 157, the final leg to Key West.

Crossing Everglades National Park, I could see the Florida Bay and Key Largo to my left, but by the time I had intercepted the 037 degree radial of the Key West VOR (frequency 113.5 and code EYW) and had steered the inbound course of 217 degrees for a while, I could see nothing but clouds underneath and more clouds way above. Rainbow colors shimmered all around me as I flew in a cavernous hall in-between two layers of clouds; it was a beautiful scene to behold. All was calm; the front was still far away. Below me, I knew, was the Gulf of Mexico and I would soon be on the ground. Someone must have been reading my mind.

"November Eight Eight One Two Juliet, Miami Center, descend to maintain Four Thousand, contact Navy Key West Approach Control on One Two Four Point Four Five," someone said.

"One Two Juliet out of Eight for Four Thousand," I replied and was soon enveloped in clouds.

According to my stopwatch, I was about 25 miles northeast of Key West; it was time to make my way through the landing checklist. Just then I got the news I had been waiting for.

"November Eight Eight One Two Juliet, Navy Key West Approach Control, radar contact. Key West International altimeter setting Two Niner Point Niner Two; Runway Two Seven in use, weather estimated Five Hundred scattered, One Thousand Five Hundred broken, Three Thousand overcast, visibility greater than Six, surface wind Three Hundred degrees at One Five, gusting to Two Zero; cleared NDB approach."

"One Two Juliet, cleared NDB approach," I replied and tuned my Automatic Direction Finder to 332 kilohertz, the frequency of Fish Hook, Key West's Non-Directional Beacon. I listened to the code:

Dit dit dah dit   dit dit   dit dit dit.

I was receiving FIS and changed my course towards the radio beacon. It occurred to me that I was then using the same technique that American bombers had used to find Berlin during the war.

Dit dit dah dit   dit dit   dit dit dit.

Stray thoughts came to me as I was scanning my instrument panel: The non-directional radio beacon would give erroneous bearing information if there was lightning or precipitation nearby, but that wasn't the case yet. And it was subject to annoying interference from distant radio stations at night, but the sun was still above the horizon, somewhere down there below the clouds. The carbon monoxide detector looked fine; I wasn't being poisoned by an invisible gas. And the tachometer held steady in the green at 23.5, indicating 2,350 engine revolutions per minute, well below the do-not-exceed red line, and the little tachometer window told me that the airplane had flown a total of 3,041.7 hours since its birth at the Piper plant in Vero Beach. It was almost like a homecoming....

Dit dit dah dit   dit dit   dit dit dit.

And then the ADF needle reversed itself! I was over the beacon at 4,000 feet. As the approach chart indicated, I turned outbound to 251 degrees and started my descent.

"Navy Key West Approach Control," I said," November Eight Eight One Two Juliet outbound at Fish Hook, descending to maintain One Thousand Five Hundred."

"One Two Juliet, roger," someone replied.

I broke out of the clouds at 3,000 feet, just as predicted, and saw the broken layer below me, even glimpses of water sparkling in the evening sun. And then, suddenly, it happened: A large flock of giant birds surrounded the plane; they had come out of nowhere, it seemed, and disappeared just as fast, but I had seen who they were. I had encountered a group of pelicans at 1,800 feet!

Dit dit dah dit   dit dit   dit dit dit.

Following the chart, I made my procedure turn at 1,500 feet, flying outbound 296 degrees in the middle of the broken layer of clouds, made a left turn to 116 degrees, and made my call.

"Navy Key West Approach," I said," November Eight Eight One Two Juliet, procedure turn inbound, maintaining One Point Five."

"One Two Juliet, roger, Navy Key West Approach, contact Tower now on One One Eight Point Two."

By then I was established on the 071 degree course back to the Fish Hook beacon and, therefore, authorized to continue the descent. My heart was still pounding about those pelicans. They could have done me in.

Dit dit dah dit   dit dit   dit dit dit.

"Key West Tower, November Eight Eight One Two Juliet, inbound NDB approach, out of One Point Five, descending to maintain Niner Hundred," I said.

"One Two Juliet, roger, Key West Tower," came the reply, "enter left downwind Two Seven; wind Three Hundred degrees at Twenty-One, gusting to Three Zero. Caution: Birds in the vicinity of the airport."

"One Two Juliet," I said calmly, but I didn't like what I had heard. For one thing, the surface wind was steadily increasing, that Gulf of Mexico warm front was clearly coming my way. For another, what was I supposed to do about those birds? Besides flying with blazing lights to scare them away, there was *nothing* I could do.

Dit dit dah dit   dit dit   dit dit dit.

As scheduled, I reached the beacon at 900 feet, now clear of the broken clouds, and I had the airport in sight, only partially hidden by a few scattered clouds between me and the ground.

"Key West Tower," I said, "November Eight Eight One Two Juliet at Fish Hook entering left downwind Two Seven."

"One Two Juliet, Key West Tower, report abeam the tower."

I finished my checklist. Fuel selector on fullest tank; bring back the yoke to slow the plane to 80 mph, trim the elevator to hold that speed; full flaps extended; fuel pump ON; carburetor heat ON. The ADF was still talking to me, ready for the unlikely event of a missed approach.

Dit dit dah dit   dit dit   dit dit dit.

I stared at the chart. Runway length 4,801 feet, it said, field elevation 3 feet. I descended to 800 feet, the pattern altitude.

"Key West Tower," I said, "November Eight Eight One Two Juliet abeam the tower."

"One Two Juliet, Key West Tower, in sight, extend your downwind, three aircraft on final."

Flying east above the south shore, I watched the tower slip under my left wing, then the terminal building and the runway threshold with the big 27 painted on it, and I saw a first plane touch down. Ahead of me, once again, was the sea, now filled with white waves rolling before the wind, glittering in the final rays of the sun and, from my perspective, dotted with dozens of little cotton ball clouds at 500 feet. I saw the second plane slip under my wing, way down to the left, a mile out from the threshold, and then the third about a mile behind it.

"One Two Juliet, cleared to land," someone said.

Reducing power, I turned left (and north) and flew right through one of those cotton balls at 500 feet. I turned left again (and now west) to line up with the runway then almost 2 miles away, and emerged below the lowest cloud to be instantly blinded by the fiery disk of the sun sitting right in front of me on the horizon line. I closed my eyes to escape the sun and BANG!

The airplane shook and trembled; for a moment, the instruments became an unreadable blur and a hurricane filled the cabin with a deafening roar. I saw a gaping hole in the windshield to my right and I saw black feathers on my lap and long pieces of Plexiglas pointing towards me like swords. *"Be careful, Hansel," Aunt Martel had said. And we stumbled and tripped over soft yielding bodies with torn clothes, trying not to step on faces, blinking away a flood of tears…And around the corner, just next to the U-Bahn sign, there lay a figure, all doubled up, in a pool of liquid that was still feeding small bluish phosphorous flames. I saw a wedding ring glimmer on a charred hand.*

Dit dit dah dit   dit dit   dit dit dit.

And then I saw it: Once again, I *hadn't* been flying with blazing lights to scare off the birds. My landing light was *off;* so were my two strobes, on the belly and at the top of the tail, allegedly brighter than the sun and supposedly designed to scare birds into an instant dive. What was the matter with me? *"Keep the lights off!" my mother used to say. And the Street Warden told everyone in no uncertain terms to black out all windows at night, lest we give aid to the enemy. "We will have patrols in the street," he said to my father, "and I assure you: If we see the slightest bit of light coming from your window, we will shoot into that window without warning!"*

Dit dit dah dit   dit dit   dit dit dit.

Entire sections of the city turned into a sea of flames, over a kilometer high. "The fires blazed so intensely," Mrs. Wagner said, "those phosphorous flames suck all the oxygen from places nearby and you'd be stupid to go near them. And worse! About an hour after the all-clear, a huge wind came up, pushing 1,000 degree flames around like a hurricane."

Dit dit dah dit   dit dit   dit dit dit.

"Key West Tower, November Eight Eight One Two Juliet," I said in the calm voice we had been trained to use, "two mile final, at Four Hundred, bird strike in windshield area."

"One Two Juliet, roger, wind Three Hundred degrees at Twenty-One, gusting to Three Zero, the runway is yours," was the equally calm response.

That sun in my eyes was driving me crazy!

Someone pointed a bright light at my face. Then the front door slammed shut and I heard an army of heavy boots make their way down the stairs to the third floor, somewhat more quietly down to the second, and then I lost count.

Dit dit dah dit   dit dit   dit dit dit.

And the lace curtains in my bedroom had rows of evil faces grinning at me. My mother said I only imagined them, but I knew better. A stream of dark figures flowed along the center of the street, with hundreds of torches held high and an eerie sound of drums. I went to get my mother, but she was angry. She put me back to bed, locked the balcony door, closed the curtains, and told me to keep things that way no matter what. The grinning faces came back again. This time, they had red, fiery eyes.

Dit dit dah dit   dit dit   dit dit dit.

I was one mile out, still at 400 feet, turning left a bit to recapture the runway centerline, and I saw a flock of sea gulls ahead, perhaps ten of them, slightly below the aircraft, which climbed over them, and then another group silhouetted against the horizon, this time there were dozens at my altitude, and then there were hundreds. I couldn't help it: I kept looking at the birds; they were so beautiful, I felt as if I was one of them. But then the aircraft shuddered and something went BANG! BANG! BANG!

I saw houses in flames and helmeted firemen and soldiers in SS uniforms and Hitler Youths, all of them busily hauling corpses to the middle of the street, stacking them up, two, three, and four layers at a time, many of them charred beyond recognition, some reduced to half their normal size like some of the mummies I had seen in the Egypt exhibit near our school, others looking almost untouched, but overcome, perhaps, by carbon monoxide in some closed cellar nearby, but rapidly stiffening even then and beckoning us for help with claw-like hands....

Dit dit dah dit   dit dit   dit dit dit.

And suddenly my yoke was stuck, I could not roll the plane back to the right, I could not move the plane's nose up or down, but—lucky me—full right rudder did the trick. The airplane was again flying straight. It would be insane to make a go-around, I thought, no way will I go UP and circle the airport for another try when two of my flight controls are jammed. *And then the engine just quit!* There was silence; the propeller was wind-milling in front of my nose. I raced through the emergency checklist in three seconds flat, but to no avail. In a fraction of a second, I knew I would never make it to the airport. I opened the cabin door and stuck the fat pillow in it, so the door wouldn't jam and I wouldn't get trapped. And I heard a voice; it must have been mine:

"Key West Tower, Mayday, Mayday, Mayday, November Eight Eight One Two Juliet, negative aileron control, negative elevator control, engine failure, ditching short of runway Two Seven."

Then I turned off the Master Switch and killed the smallest chance for a spark. I don't remember much of what happened next.

Someone had a flashlight and we watched its little circle of light move to the ceiling, catching clouds of tiny particles in its beam, examining the iron plates, still holding, probing the columns of steel, still standing, their red paint turned white from all the dust. There was a loud crack of wood splintering, then the thunder of more walls collapsing, taking another part of our house down with a roar, and stacking another pile of masonry on top of us. The air seemed acrid, even smoky—I had forgotten the gas mask, I suddenly thought—I felt a gritty mess on my teeth, my nose turning raw. Panic rose within me, choking me at the throat. And a paralyzing thought flashed through my mind:

What if they use the flamethrower to kill the maggots and the rats and the flies, as they often did before digging out the dead, when we aren't dead yet?

My radios were dead and it made no sense, but I could still hear the beacon's voice:

Dit dit dah dit   dit dit   dit dit dit.

The ravens were cursing as the grave digger flung the dirt into the open graves. I thought of the promised resurrection of the flesh, but my mind gave me images of beetles and maggots doing their work, leaving nothing but belt buckles and bones and buttons of uniforms, carrying tiny inscriptions, "God With Us." Just then, right on schedule, the church bells pealed above us, sending a large flock of pigeons aloft into sky, their wings resonating like the voice of God.

Dit dit dah dit   dit dit   dit dit dit.

And they pointed a pistol at Jutta. Three of them dragged her out of sight, but I could hear them yell and her cry. One soldier decided to rest the barrel of his rifle at the center of my forehead. I felt the cold metal and I saw him grin and stare at me, without mercy, with those fiery eyes of hate. I felt my heart in the middle of my throat, beating away the last seconds of my life… Time stood still. I felt a colony of ants meandering across my feet. I heard crows fretting and shrieking in the branches of pine trees above, complaining about us who had disturbed their lives.

I crawled out of the plane and waded to the shore. The water felt so warm. And there were seagulls circling overhead. Despite of everything, they are my favorite birds.

APPENDIX: NTSB ACCIDENT REPORT

NATIONAL TRANSPORTATION SAFETY BOARD

14 CFR Part 91: General Aviation

Accident occurred May 23, 1991 at KEY WEST, FL

Probable Cause Approval Date: 7/17/1992

Aircraft: PA 28-180, registration: N8812J

Injuries: 1 Minor

Following an instrument flight from Norfolk, VA, the pilot-in-command executed an NDB approach to Key West International. While in a left descending turn from base to final, and while passing through 400 feet mean sea level at an indicated airspeed of 80 knots, the pilot reported a bird strike in the windshield area, followed by debris in the cockpit. A succession of loud noises shortly thereafter suggested additional bird strikes elsewhere and was followed by instant loss of elevator and aileron control and subsequent total engine failure. The pilot had to apply full right rudder to keep the airplane from turning left and to stay aligned with the runway centerline.

The pilot declared an emergency on a 1-mile final and, rather than risk putting an out-of-control aircraft onto the airport grounds, elected to ditch it in the ocean ¼ mile short, and slightly left, of the runway 27 threshold. The aircraft touched down in a flat attitude, nosed over, and came to rest in an inverted position near a rock island. The pilot sustained minor injuries, consistent with the windshield shattering, and walked to shore.

Aircraft: According to the FAA inspector at the scene, the aircraft sustained substantial damage. He found the aircraft inverted in shallow waters with the nose approximately 70 degrees below the horizon and buried in sand up to the accessory case which is located on the rear of the engine. The engine had separated from the firewall. The engine cowling was located 10 feet from the engine. A quarter of the windshield was recovered; a bird was found on the rear seat and retained for identification. The cabin door was found about 40 feet in front of the fuselage; neither the handle nor the lock plunger was in the "locked" position.

The nose and main landing gears were broken. The vertical stabilizer and bottom of the fuselage were found buckled, as was the firewall near the nose landing gear. Both propeller blades were twisted and bent in the opposite direction of rotation. There was spar damage to the right wing and a foot of the right aileron was missing. There was a dent in the left wing's leading edge and another in the left horizontal stabilizer. Sea gulls were found entangled between the left wing and the left aileron, locking it into the up position; additional sea gulls were jammed between the vertical stabilizer and the elevator. The wing flaps were undamaged and in the landing position. The fuel selector was positioned to the fullest tank and a post-crash examination of the tanks revealed adequate, uncontaminated fuel aboard.

Inspection of the engine after recovery revealed that a seagull had been drawn into the carburetor air box and was blocking the air intake to the carburetor. In addition, numerous feathers had become trapped between the needle and seat assembly in the carburetor, cutting off the flow of fuel to the cylinders. Finally, the butterfly valve in the carburetor heat box had broken off, slid back into the carburetor opening, and blocked the airflow. Any one of these events would explain the complete loss of power experienced by the pilot.

Weather: Radar photos taken at the time of the accident indicate a level 6 thunderstorm, 20 nautical miles in diameter, located about 41 nautical miles northwest of the accident location, but the local weather at that time was still marginal VFR, 500 scattered, ceiling 1,500 broken, 3,000 overcast, and visibility greater then 6, wind 300 degrees at 21, gusting to 30. The temperature was 61, the dew point 59. According to FAA icing probability charts, conditions were conducive for carburetor icing during glide power or reduced-power descent. The carburetor heat control was ON when examined after the accident. The aircraft also had the correct (Kollsman) altimeter setting of 29.92 inches Hg.

Aircraft history: The aircraft was built in 1976 and had flown approximately 3,050 hours. The engine had a major overhaul at 2,010 hours. The tachometer showed only 15 hours of flight time since a routine annual inspection that had been conducted 3 days before the accident. The maintenance history was normal, including 100 hour inspections. A review of aircraft radio, engine, and airframe maintenance logs revealed that the pilot/owner performed preventative maintenance beyond the scope and intent of the regulations.

Pilot: The commercial-rated pilot was highly experienced, having flown over 10,000 hours as pilot-in-command. He was the sole occupant and had no prior infractions. He held a current medical certificate and had met the recent-experience requirements concerning instrument flight, night flight, and the carrying of passengers. The pilot verified that he had performed the required weight-and-balance checks before the flight. Immediately following the accident, the pilot passed a physical agility sobriety test. Subsequent toxicological tests on the pilot's blood and urine were negative with respect to alcohol and carbon monoxide.

The National Transportation Safety Board determines the probable cause(s) of this accident as follows:

An inadvertent in-flight collision with birds while on final approach, resulting in the loss of aileron and elevator control as well as engine power. It was confirmed that sea gulls and other birds feed actively at dusk, flying in flocks low over water, between sea level and 500 feet. Dr. Carla Dunn of the Smithsonian National Museum of Natural History in Washington, DC, identified one bird retrieved from the cockpit as a Black Vulture (Coryagyps atratus), which weighed 75 ounces.

Other factors contributing to the accident include

• unsuitable terrain encountered during the forced landing

• the pilot being blinded by the setting sun

• pilot fatigue after a long flight from New England, with a fuel stop at Norfolk, VA

Note: A review of the pilot's medical history reveals psychiatric treatment several decades ago. The pilot would not allow a review of his more recent medical records.

ACKNOWLEDGMENTS

The images from Heinrich Hoffmann, *Der Struwwelpeter* and Wilhelm Busch, *Max & Moritz* that appear on pages 6, 75, 319, and 351 have been reproduced with kind permission of the publisher. Copyright © 2009 by Otto Moravec, Vienna, Austria. For colorful versions of these and other children's books, see www.moravec.at, where the aforementioned books are listed as Artikel Nr. 6001 and 6004, respectively.

The political posters (or excerpts thereof) that appear on pages 9, 19, 25, 30, 38, 47, 57, 67, 81, 86, 101, 159, 178, 182/183, 203, 210, 260, 273, and 292 have been reproduced with kind permission of Kristof Wachinger, publisher of *Anschläge: 220 politische Plakate als Dokumente der deutschen Geschichte 1900-1980* (Ausgewählt und kommentiert von Friedrich Arnold.) Copyright © 1985 Langewiesche-Brandt, Ebenhausen bei München. For colorful versions of these and other posters, see www.langewiesche-brandt.de and click on Fundstücke>Anschläge.

The photographs appearing on pages 73, 107, 113, 124, 130, 168, 186, 193, 220, 242, 251, and 310 were supplied by www.akg-images.co.uk and reproduced with kind permission from the Archiv für Kunst und Geschichte in Berlin, Germany, and London, United Kingdom. Copyright © akg-images, London.

The photograph appearing on page 96 was supplied by www.defa-spektrum.de and reproduced with kind permission of defa-spektrum gmbH, Berlin. Copyright © DEFA-Stiftung/Klagemann, Eberhard.

The Spitfire photograph appearing on page 119 as well as on the front cover has been reproduced with kind permission of Ronnie Olsthoorn whose aviation art can be admired at www.skyraider3d.com. Copyright © Ronnie Olsthoorn.

The photograph appearing on page 331 (Honoré-Victorin Daumier, The Hypochondriac, 1841) was supplied by the Harvard Art Museum, Fogg Art Museum (M16718, Gift of Carl Pickhardt, Class of 1931) and reproduced with permission of their Imaging Department. Copyright © President and Fellows of Harvard College.

The photograph appearing on page 338 was supplied by the Verein des 17. Juni 1953, e. V., Berlin, Germany, and reproduced with kind permission of the Archiv Vereinigung 17. Juni 1953. Additional interesting materials about the 1953 uprising appear at www.17juni1953.de.

The photograph appearing on page 363 was acquired from the Wikimedia Commons. Permission is granted to copy, distribute and/or modify this document under the terms of the GNU Free Documentation License, Version 1.3 or any later version published by the Free Software Foundation. The image was taken in 1986 by Thierry Noir at Bethaniendamm in Berlin-Kreuzberg.

The remaining images come from the author's collection.

Last but not least, I want to thank my brother, Professor Günter Köhler of Berlin, Germany, who rendered invaluable help in getting many of these materials together and acquiring many of the permissions just noted.

AFTERWORD

This is a work of fiction. Yet it is also true that all of the events portrayed in it have actually occurred. Many of them were witnessed by the author within his immediate family. Others were observed by him indirectly as they affected friends, neighbors, or more distant relatives. The associated images—political posters, photographs, and more—are genuine, too. Still, this is a work of fiction because the author decided that his own personal experiences and that of many others could be woven together most effectively with the help of relatively few composite characters, while a dozen or so localities are similarly fused into a smaller number. The result is a *historical novel* that focuses on the life of one German family just before, during, and following the Second World War and thereby conveys a vivid picture of a time when the Nazis ruled Germany and, later, the Communists ruled a part of it. But the work is also a *story of suspense.* By searching for the causes of a plane crash in the 1990s, it shows how the psychological consequences of war—any war—may well emerge decades later and in faraway places.

This book was written because issues of war and peace, sadly, continue to be timely. It is of great importance, therefore, to give voice to the last witnesses of the Second World War before their memories are gone forever. These witnesses to human depravity have crucial lessons to teach—not only to the current generation but also to others not yet born—and, despite so much evidence to the contrary, this author harbors the hope that one day people will manage to learn from history. Czeslaw Milosz, winner of the 1980 Nobel Prize in Literature, put it succinctly: "Those who are alive receive a mandate from those who are silent forever. They can fulfill their duty only by trying to reconstruct precisely things as they were." The voices of the characters depicted in this book do just that.

Except for well-known historical figures, such as military or political leaders, the family names used herein are fictitious. No similarity to actual persons, living or dead, is intended or should be inferred. On the other hand, actual geographical names have been freely used, but except for well-known events and locales, such as the 1940 occupation of Paris or the 1945 battle for Berlin, many of the linkages of described incidents with particular geographic names are entirely coincidental.

Breinigsville, PA USA
23 February 2010
233080BV00003B/8/P